# ETERNAL

Craig Russell was born in 1956, in Fife, Scotland. He served as a police officer and worked in the advertising industry as a copywriter and creative director. Russell has a long-standing interest in the German language and in post-war German history. He has been a freelance writer for fifteen years. In 2007, Russell was presented with a *Polizeistern* (Police Star) award by the Polizei Hamburg for raising public awareness of the work of the Hamburg police.

For more information about Craig Russell and his books, please visit www.craigrussell.com

*Also available by Craig Russell*

Blood Eagle
Brother Grimm

# CRAIG
# RUSSELL

# ETERNAL

arrow books

Published by Arrow in 2008

2 4 6 8 10 9 7 5 3

First published in Great Britain in 2007 by Hutchinson
Random House,
20 Vauxhall Bridge Road, London SW1V 2SA

www.rbooks.co.uk

Addresses for companies within The Random House Group Limited
can be found at: www.randomhouse.co.uk/offices.htm

The Random House Group Limited Reg. No. 954009

A CIP catalogue record for this book is available
from the British Library

ISBN 9780099484233

The Random House Group Limited supports The Forest
Stewardship Council (FSC), the leading international forest
certification organisation. All our titles that are printed on
Greenpeace approved FSC certified paper carry the FSC logo.
Our paper procurement policy can be found at:
www.rbooks.co.uk/environment

Mixed Sources

Product group from well-managed
forests and other controlled sources
www.fsc.org Cert no. TT-COC-2139
© 1996 Forest Stewardship Council

Typeset in Sabon by Palimpsest Book Production Limited,
Grangemouth, Stirlingshire
Printed in the UK by CPI Bookmarque, Croydon, CR0 4TD

Dedicated to the memory of Gabriel Brown

# Acknowledgements

I would like to thank my wife Wendy for her comments and edits on the first draft of *Eternal*; my agent Carole Blake and all at Blake Friedmann Literary Agency; my friend and German translator Bernd Rullkötter; my accountants Larry Sellyn and Elaine Dyer; from Hutchinson, Paul Sidey, Nick Austin, Penny Isaac and Tess Callaway.

In writing this series, I have enjoyed the unrestricted and enthusiastic support of one of the world's finest police services: the Polizei Hamburg. I cannot state strongly enough how much the Polizei Hamburg have helped with information and advice. I owe special thanks to Erste Hauptkommissarin Ulrike Sweden who gave up much of her free time to read and correct my manuscript; Polizeipräsident Werner Jantosch, Chief of Police for Hamburg; Leitender Polizeidirecktor Bernd Spöntjes, Chief of Police for Hamburg's Waterways Police; and to all of the other Polizei Hamburg officers who have offered support, advice and help.

Special thanks also to Marco Schneiders, Barbara Fischer, Vibeke Wagner, Udo Röbel, Katrin Frahm, Anja Sieg, and Anne von Bestenbostel.

And to the people of Hamburg, one of the world's most captivating cities, *nochmal, bedanke ich mich herzlich*.

'We are eternal.

'The Buddhists believe that each life, each consciousness, is like a single candle flame, but that there is a continuity between each flame. Imagine lighting one candle with the flame of another, then using that flame to light the next, and that to light the next, and on and on for ever. A thousand flames, all passed from one to another across the generations. Each is a different light, each burns in a totally different way. But it is, nevertheless, the same flame.

'Now, I'm afraid, it is time for me to extinguish your flame. But don't worry . . . the pain I give you will mean that you will burn brightest at the end.'

# Prologue

# 1.

# Twenty-Eight Days After the First Murder: Thursday, 15 September 2005.

## Nordenham Railway Station, Nordenham, 145 Kilometres West of Hamburg

Fabel could not help but reflect on the irony that Nordenham railway station was a terminus. In so many ways, this was where their journey ended. From here, there was nowhere else left to go.

The headlights of the police cars ranged on the other side of the tracks illuminated the platform as if it were a stage. It was a crystal moment: diamond-sharp and clear and hard. Even the painted plaster façade of the turn-of-the-century station seemed bleached of colour: its edges etched with artificial clarity, like an architectural drawing, or a theatre set against which were cast the giant shadows of the two figures on the platform, one standing, the other forced to its knees.

And nothing was sharper or clearer than the bright, eager gleam on the blade in the hand that hung at the side of the figure who stood, illuminated, behind the kneeling man.

Fabel's mind raced through the thousand possible ways this could all end. Whatever his next words were, whatever action he now took, would have consequences; would set in train a sequence of events.

And an all too conceivable consequence would be the death of more than one person.

His head ached with the weight of it. Despite the time of year, the night air felt meagre and sterile in his mouth and made grey ghosts of his breath, as if in coming together to this moment, to this low-lying landscape, they had actually reached a great altitude. It seemed as if the air was too thin to carry any sound other than the desperate half-sobbed breathing of the kneeling man. Fabel glanced across at his officers, who stood, taking aim in the hard, locked-muscle stance of those who stand on the edge of the decision to kill. It was Maria he paid most attention to: her face bloodless, her eyes glittering ice-blue, the bone and sinew of her hands straining against the taut skin as she gripped her SIG-Sauer automatic.

Fabel made an almost imperceptible movement of his head, hoping that his team would interpret his signal to hold back.

He stared hard at the man who stood in the centre of the harsh cast light. Fabel and his team had struggled for months to put a name, an identity, to the killer they had hunted. He had turned out to be a man of many names: the name he had given himself in his perverted sense of crusade was 'Red Franz'; while the media, in their enthusiastic determination to spread fear and anxiety as far as possible, had christened him the 'Hamburg Hairdresser'. But now Fabel knew his real name.

In front of Red Franz, facing in the same direction, was the middle-aged man whom he had forced to his knees. Red Franz held the kneeling man by a fistful of grey hair, angling his head back so that the throat lay exposed and white. Above the throat, above the terror-contorted face, the flesh of his fore-head had been sliced across in a straight line the full width of his brow, just below the hairline, and the wound gaped slightly as Red Franz yanked his head back by the hair. A pulse of blood cascaded down the kneeling man's face and he let out a high-pitched animal yelp.

And all the time the blade by Red Franz's side sparkled and gleamed with malevolent intent in the night.

'For Christ's sake, Fabel.' The kneeling man's voice was tight and shrill with terror. 'Help me . . . Please . . . Help me, Fabel . . .'

Fabel ignored the pleading and kept his gaze locked like a searchlight on Red Franz. He held his hand out into empty air, as if halting traffic. 'Easy . . . take it easy. I'm not playing along with any of this. No one here is. We're not going to act out the parts you want us to play. Tonight, history is not going to repeat itself.'

Red Franz gave a bitter laugh. The hand that held the knife twitched and again the blade flashed bright and stark.

'Do you honestly think that I am going to walk away? This bastard . . .' He yanked again on the hair and the kneeling man yelped again through a curtain of his own blood. 'This bastard betrayed me and all that we stood for. He thought that my death would buy him a new life. Just like the others did.'

'This is pure fantasy . . .' said Fabel. 'That was not your death.'

'Oh no? Then how is it that you started to doubt what you believe while you searched for me? There is no such thing as death; there's only remembrance. The only difference between me and anyone else is that I have been allowed to remember, like looking through a hall of windows. I remember *everything*.' He paused, the small silence broken only by the distant sound of a late-night car passing through the town of Nordenham, behind the station and a universe away. 'Of course history will repeat itself. That's what history does. It repeated *me* . . . You're so proud that you studied history in your youth. But did you ever truly understand it? We're all just variations on the same theme – all of us. What was before will be again. He who was before shall be again. Over and over. History is all about beginnings. History is made, not unmade.'

'Then make it your own history,' said Fabel. 'Change things. Give it up, man. Tonight history *won't* repeat itself. Tonight no one dies.'

Red Franz smiled. A smile that was as scalpel-bright and hard and cold as the knife in his hand. 'Really? Then we must see, Herr Chief Commissar.' The blade flashed upwards to the kneeling man's throat.

There was a scream. And the sound of gunfire.

# 2.

## Vernal Equinox, AD 324.

### One Thousand, Six Hundred and Eighty-One Years Before the First Murder: Bourtanger Moor, East Frisia

The sky was pale and blank and gazed down on the flat, featureless moor with a cloudless eye.

He walked with pride and dignity. His nakedness did not embarrass him nor demean him: he wore the air and the sun on his skin as if they were royal robes. His thick newly washed and scented hair shone gold in the bright day. Faces he had known for a lifetime lined the route he took, ranged along the edges of the wooden walkway that led over and across the marshy ground, and they cheered to salute his naked procession.

He walked with his attendants beside and behind him: the priest, the chieftain, the priestess and the honour guard. And all along the way, voices were raised in adulation. Among the faces and the voices were those of the women who had been wives to him in the preceding days, some of whom were of noble rank. As, now, was he: his low-born status forgotten, meaningless. This day, this act, elevated him above the stature of a chief or a king. He was, himself, almost a god.

And as he passed, they started to sing. They sang of beginnings and ends; of rebirths; of suns and moons and of seasons renewed. Of the great, wondrous, mysterious cycle. And the rebirth of which they sang most was that which was to be his. A glorious rebirth. He would be renewed. He would be brought again to a better, purer life.

He and his attendants neared the end of the wooden causeway and he saw where they had gathered to one side the hazel branches that would be laid over him and weighted with rocks, so that he would not rise again until his true time had come. They reached the causeway's end and the sleek obsidian surface of the pool opened out before them and offered up a dark reflection of the bright sky.

Now was the time.

He felt his heart begin to pound in his chest. He stepped from the wooden causeway and perceived the world around him with a vivid keenness: the damp, yielding mulch and hard marsh grass beneath his naked feet; the air and the sun on his skin; the strong hands of his honour guards as they grasped his upper arms tightly. Together, the three men stepped forward and into the pool. They sank to their waists and he felt the cold of the water tingle on his naked legs and on his genitals.

He started to breathe hard and the rhythm of his heart increased even more, as if aware that it would soon be still and was trying to squeeze as many beats as possible into these few, final seconds. He had to believe. He forced himself to believe. It was the only way to keep a step beyond the panic that seemed to be running screaming towards him, racing along the wooden causeway, unheard by and invisible to the onlookers.

The priestess slipped the gown from her body and stepped naked into the pool. She held the sacrificial knife tight in her fist, which in turn she held pressed to her breast. The blade glittered in the bright day. Such a small knife: he had been a warrior and could not equate this ornament with the ending of his life. The priestess stood before him, the water around the tight circle of her waist; dark against her pale skin. She reached up and laid the palm of her hand on his forehead, incanting the words of the ritual. He succumbed, as he knew he must, to the gentle pressure of her hand and he lay back into the water. His head sank slowly and the water pulled a murky, peat-coloured curtain across the light of the day.

The two attendants still held his upper arms firm, and he now felt other hands on his body, on his legs. His eyes were open. All around him the bog swirled dark and thick, as if undecided as to which element it truly belonged: earth or water. His golden hair billowed and writhed around his head, its lustre dimmed by the peaty water.

He held his breath. He knew he should not do so, but instinct told him to hold onto the air in his lungs, the life in his body. His lungs started to scream for more air and, for the first time, he pushed against the priestess's hand. She pushed back only slightly, but the grips on his arms and legs tightened and he felt himself pushed deeper, until the sunken bracken and stones at the bottom of the pool scraped at his back.

The panic that he had sensed hurtling towards him now caught up with him and screamed that there would be no rebirth, no new beginning. Only death. It was his turn to scream, and his cry exploded into a huge cluster of bubbles that frothed through the murk and up to the day that he would never again see. The cold brackish water flooded his mouth and throat. It tasted of soil and worms, of roots and decaying vegetation. Of death. It surged into the protesting lungs. He convulsed and writhed but now more hands were upon him, pressing down on him and binding him to his death.

It was then that he felt the kiss of the priestess's blade on his throat and the swirl of water around him clouded even darker. Redder.

But he had been wrong: there would, after all, be rebirth. However, before he would again come out into the light of day, more than sixteen centuries would pass, and his golden hair would become changed to a burning red.

Only then would he be reborn. As Red Franz.

# 3.

## October 1985:
## Twenty Years Before the First Murder.

### Nordenham Railway Station, Nordenham,
### 145 Kilometres West of Hamburg

Nordenham's main railway station stood elevated on a dyke above the river Weser. It was an October afternoon and a family stood waiting for a train. The large station building, the platform and the latticed ironwork were sharply etched by a late-autumn sun that was bright but lacked any warmth.

They stood – the father, the mother and the child – at the far end of the platform. The father was tall and lean, in his mid-thirties. His longish, thick, almost too-dark hair was brushed severely back from a broad pale brow but rebelled in a fringe of curls that frothed on his coat collar. The black frame of long sideburns, moustache and goatee beard emphasised the paleness of his complexion and the vermilion of his mouth. The mother, too, was tall: only a few centimetres shorter than the man, with grey-blue eyes and long bone-coloured blonde hair that hung straight from under a knitted woollen hat. She wore a tan ankle-length coat and a vast colourful macramé bag hung on long straps from her shoulder. The boy was about ten, but tall for his age, obviously having inherited his parents' height. Like his father, he had a pale, sad face under a mop of curling, discordantly black hair.

'Wait here with the boy,' the father said firmly but kindly. He pushed back a stray strand of ash-blonde hair that had fallen across the mother's brow. 'I'll approach Piet alone when he arrives. If there's any sign of trouble, take the boy and get clear of the station.'

The woman nodded determinedly, but a cold bright fear sparkled in her eyes. The man smiled at her and gave her arm a squeeze before moving away from her and the boy. He took up his place in the middle of the platform. A Deutsche Bahn railway worker came out of the maintenance office, dropped down onto the track from the platform, and sauntered diagonally and with complacent arrogance across the rails. A woman in early middle-age, dressed with the expensive tastelessness of the West German bourgeoisie, exited the ticket office and stood about ten metres to the man's right. The tall, pale man seemed to pay no attention to any of this activity; in reality his eyes followed every move of every individual in the provincial station.

Another figure stepped out of the ticket office and onto the platform. He, too, was a tall, lean man, this time with long blond hair scraped back into a ponytail. His thin, angular face was pock-marked with the ancient scars of a childhood illness. Again, his movements and expression were intended to be casual and disinterested; but, unlike the dark-haired man, there was an intensity, a nervousness, in his eyes and an electric tension in every step he took.

They were now only a metre apart. A broad smile dissolved the dark-haired man's severe expression like sunshine through clouds.

12

'Piet!' he said enthusiastically but quietly. The blond man did not smile.

'I told you this was inadvisable,' said the blond man. His German was tainted with a sibilant Dutch accent. 'I told you not to come. This was not a good idea at all.'

The dark-haired man did not let the smile fade and shrugged, philosophically. 'Our whole way of life is inadvisable, Piet, my friend, but it is absolutely necessary. And so is this meeting. God, Piet . . . it's great to see you again. Did you bring the money?'

'There's been a problem,' said the Dutchman. The dark-haired man glanced down the platform to the woman and the boy. When he turned back to the Dutchman, the smile had gone.

'What kind of problem? We need that money to travel. To find and set up a new safe house.'

'It's over, Franz,' said the Dutchman. 'It's been over for a long time and we should have accepted that. The others . . . they feel the same.'

'The others?' The dark-haired man snorted. 'I expect nothing from them. They're just a bunch of middle-class wankers pretending to be activists. Half-involved and half-afraid. The weak playing at being strong. But you, Piet . . . I expect more of you.' He allowed a smile again. 'Come on, Piet. You can't give up now. I . . . *we* need you.'

'It's *over*. Can't you see that, Franz? It's time to put that life behind us. I just can't do this any more, Franz. I've lost my faith.' The Dutchman took a few steps back. 'We've lost, Franz. We've lost.' He took another few steps back, opening up the space between them. The Dutchman looked anxiously from right to left and the dark-haired man mirrored his glances, but could see nothing. Nonetheless, he felt a tightening in his chest. His hand closed around the Makarov nine-millimetre automatic in his coat pocket. The Dutchman spoke again. His eyes were now wild.

'I'm sorry, Franz . . . I'm so sorry . . .' He turned and began to run.

It all happened within a matter of seconds, yet time itself seemed impossibly stretched.

The Dutchman was shouting something to someone unseen as he ran. The railwayman leaped towards the mother and son, a glittering black automatic in his outstretched hands. The bourgeois housewife dropped down onto one knee with astonishing agility and produced a handgun from inside her coat. She aimed at the tall dark-haired man and screamed at him to place his hands on his head.

He snapped his head around to check the woman and the boy. The woman's hand was rammed deep in her shoulder bag and the front of the bag burst open and burned as she pulled the trigger of the Heckler Koch MP5 machine pistol that she had hidden inside. Simultaneously, she pushed the boy sideways and down with a violent shove. The burst from the Heckler & Koch ripped angrily at the chest of the fake railway worker's overalls and tore open his face.

The blonde woman spun round, swinging the machine pistol, still in its ripped and smoking macramé bag, to bear down on the GSG9 cop dressed as a housewife. The policewoman snapped her aim from the man to the woman and fired twice, then twice more. Her shots hit the boy's mother in the chest, face and forehead and she was dead before her falling body crashed onto the platform.

The man saw the woman die, but there was no

time for grief. He heard the screaming of a dozen GSG9 officers, in helmets and body armour, as they flooded out onto the platform from inside and around the sides of the station building. A group of them were gesturing furiously for the Dutchman to stop running and get out of their line of fire. The policewoman now swung her pistol to bear on the dark-haired man again. He struggled to free his Russian Makarov from his coat pocket and, when he did, he did not aim it at the policewoman or any of the GSG9 troops.

The policewoman's first bullet ripped into his chest at exactly the same moment that his round smacked into the back of the Dutchman's head.

Franz Mühlhaus – Red Franz, the notorious anarchist terrorist whose pale face had stared out at frightened West Germans from wanted posters from Kiel to Munich – fell to his knees, his arms hanging at his sides, the Makarov automatic lying limply in his half-open hand and his chin resting on his bloodstained chest.

As he died, he could just see, on the fringes of his failing vision, the pale face, wide-eyed and wide-mouthed in a silent scream, of his son. Somehow, the dying Red Franz Mühlhaus found the breath to utter a single word, thrown out into the world with his final, explosive exhalation.

'Verräter . . .'

Traitors.

# Part One

# I.

## Three Days Before the First Murder: Monday, 15 August 2005.

### List, Island of Sylt, 200 Kilometres North-West of Hamburg

It was a moment he wanted to hang on to.

His senses reached out into every corner of the land, the sea and the sky around him. He stood on naked feet and felt the texture of the dry sand that abraded his soles and squeezed between his toes. He felt as if this place, this time, was all he could remember of himself. Here, he thought, there was no past, no future, only this perfect moment. Sylt lay long and thin and low in the North Sea, offering no profile to hinder the hastening wind that pushed at the vast sky above, seeking out the more substantial flank of Denmark beyond. As he stood there, the wind protested at his presence by tugging angrily at the fabric of his chinos, snapping the loose tails and collar of his shirt and flapping the broken wing of blond hair that hung over his forehead. It scoured his face and pushed into the creases of his skin as he stood watching the scurry of the clouds across the impossibly huge pale-blue shield of the sky.

Jan Fabel was a man of a little over medium height and in his early forties, but a certain boyishness lingered indistinctly, like a reluctant evictee, in his appearance, in his lean, angular frame and in the flapping blond hair. His eyes were a pale blue and shone with intelligence and wit, but at that moment were reduced to narrow slits in the folds of the creased face that he presented to the angry wind. His face was tanned and unshaven and, just as the lingering boyishness in his posture hinted at the youth who had preceded him, the silver that sparkled in the gold of his three-day-old stubble prefigured the older man to come.

A woman approached from the dunes behind him: she was as tall as him and was dressed in a shirt and trousers of white linen. She also was barefoot, but carried a pair of low-heeled black sandals in one hand. The wind wrapped itself around her too, pressing and smoothing the white linen sleek against the curves of her body and making wild cables of her long dark hair. Fabel did not see Susanne approach and she stood behind him, dropping the sandals onto the sand and snaking her arms through his arms and around his body. He turned round and kissed her for a long time, before they both turned back to face the sea.

'I was just thinking,' he said at last, 'that you could almost forget who you are, just standing here.' He looked down at his naked feet and pushed at the sand with his toe. 'It's been wonderful. I'm so glad you came with me. I just wish we didn't have to leave tomorrow.'

'It has been wonderful. It really has. But, unfortunately, we have our lives to get back to . . .' Susanne smiled consolingly, and when she spoke her voice was spun through with a light Bavarian accent. 'Unless, that is,' she continued, 'you want to ask your brother if he needs another waiter.'

Fabel drew a deep breath and held it for a moment. 'You know, would that be so bad? Not to have to deal with all the crap and the stress.'

She laughed. 'You've obviously never worked as a waiter.'

'I could always do something else. Anything else.'

'No, you couldn't,' she said. 'I know you. You would start missing it within a month.'

He shrugged. 'Maybe you're right. But I feel like a different person here. Someone I prefer being.'

'That's just being on holiday . . .' The wind blew a webbed veil of hair across Susanne's face and she tugged it out of the way.

'No, it's not. It's being here. It's not the same thing. Sylt has always been special for me. I remember the first time I came here – I felt I'd known it all my life. This is where I came after I was shot,' Fabel said, and his hand brushed, involuntarily, against his left flank, as if he were unconsciously checking that the two-decades-old wound had really healed after all. 'I guess I always associate this place with getting better. With feeling safe and at peace, I suppose.' He laughed. 'Sometimes when I think of the world out there . . .' He nodded vaguely over the sea to where the mass of Europe lay unseen. 'The world we have to deal with, I get scared. Don't you?'

Susanne nodded. 'Sometimes. Yes, I do.' She circled him with her arm and placed her hand over his, over where his wound had been. She kissed him on the cheek. 'I'm getting chilly. Come on, let's go and eat . . .'

Fabel did not follow right away. Instead he let the North Sea wind scour his face for a few moments more, watching the waves froth against the wide shore and the few wind-driven clouds scud across the huge shield of sky. He listened to the cry of the seabirds and the fuzzy roaring of the ocean and wished, desperately, that he could think of some alternative to becoming a waiter. Or any alternative to becoming, once more, an investigator of death.

Fabel turned and followed Susanne towards the dunes and his brother's hotel and restaurant that lay beyond.

The North Frisian island of Sylt lies almost parallel to the coastline where the neck of Germany becomes Denmark. Sylt is now connected to the mainland by a thread of man-made causeway, the Hindenburgdamm, upon which a rail line conveys Germany's wealthy and famous to their favoured domestic holiday location. The island also has a regional airport and a regular ferry service running to and from the mainland, and in summer the narrow roads and traditional villages of Sylt clog with shining Mercedes and Porsches.

Partly in reference to his hotel's origins as a farmhouse, Fabel's elder brother Lex habitually described these affluent seasonal immigrants as his 'summer herd'. Lex had run this small hotel and restaurant in List, at the northern tip of Sylt, for twenty-five years. The combination of Lex's indisputable talent as a chef and the restaurant's unbroken view over a scythe of golden sand and the sea beyond had guaranteed a steady stream of guests and diners throughout the season. The hotel had originally been a traditional Frisian farmhouse and had retained its façade of *Fachwerk* oak beams and sat solidly, turning its wide-roofed, resolute shoulder to the North Sea winds. Lex had added the modern restaurant extension, which wrapped itself around two sides of the original building. The hotel offered only seven guest rooms, all of which were booked up months in advance. But Lex also had a separate small suite of rooms tucked into the low ceilings and wide beams under the rafters of the old farmhouse, which he never let out. He kept these rooms for use by family and friends. Most of all, he kept them for when his brother came to stay.

Fabel and Susanne came down to dine about eight. The restaurant was already filled with smart, well-heeled-looking customers, but, as he had done throughout their stay, Lex had reserved one of the best tables for Fabel and Susanne, over by the picture window. Susanne had changed her linen shirt and trousers for a black sleeveless dress. She had dressed her long raven hair up onto her head and her elegant slender neck was exposed. The dress hugged her figure and stopped high enough above the knee to display her shapely legs but low enough to look restrained and tasteful.

Fabel was very much aware of Susanne's beauty, as he was of the male heads that turned in their direction as they entered the restaurant. Their relationship had lasted more than a year and they had passed through the awkward stages of mutual discovery. They were now an established couple, and Fabel drew a feeling of security and comfort from it. And when Gabi, his daughter, spent time with him and Susanne he had, for the first time since his marriage to Renate broke up, a sense of being part of a family.

Boris, Lex's Czech head waiter, led them to their table. The low sun had repainted in more golden hues the bands of sand, sea and sky that filled the panoramic window. Once they were seated, Boris asked them in pleasantly accented German if they wanted anything to drink before their meal. They ordered white wine and Susanne went through the restaurant nesting ritual of settling into her chair and checking out the other diners. Someone over Fabel's shoulder seemed to catch her attention.

'Isn't that Bertholdt Müller-Voigt, the politician?'

Fabel started to turn. Susanne placed her hand on his forearm and squeezed.

'For God's sake, Jan, don't be so obvious. For a policeman, your surveillance skills stink.'

He smiled. 'That could explain my lousy conviction rate . . .' He turned again, this time making a deliberately clumsy show of taking in all of the restaurant. To his left and behind him sat a fit-looking man in his early fifties, wearing a dark jacket and roll-neck sweater, both of which had the contrived casualness of a seriously expensive designer label. The man's receding hair was swept severely back and some grey flecked his neatly trimmed beard. He had the studied arty look of a successful film director, musician, writer or sculptor. Fabel recognised him, however, as someone whose art was controversial politics. The slim blonde woman who sat with him was easily twenty years his junior. She sat poised and radiated a sleek, insolent sexuality. Her gaze caught Fabel's for a moment. He turned back to Susanne.

'You're right. It's Müller-Voigt. I'm sure Lex will be delighted to know that his restaurant is cool enough to attract the darlings of the environmental Left.'

'Who's that with him?'

Fabel grinned gleefully. 'I don't know, but she's certainly environmentally friendly.'

Susanne tilted her head slightly to one side: a pose of concentration that, for Fabel, was uniquely Susanne's. 'Seriously, I think I've seen her before. It's hard to keep up with his sexual exploits. He seems to relish the headlines they generate in the tabloid press.'

'He's not so keen on the headlines Fischmann has been generating about him.' Fabel referred to Ingrid Fischmann, the journalist who made it her business to 'out' people in public life who had flirted with left-wing extremism or terrorism in the 1970s and 1980s.

'Do you think it's true, Jan?' Susanne leaned forward, almost conspiratorially. 'I mean, about him being connected to the Wiedler case?'

'I don't know . . . There's a lot of speculation and circumstantial stuff. But nothing that would remotely add up to a case as far as the Polizei Hamburg are concerned.'

'But?'

Fabel screwed his face up as if trying to weigh the imponderable. 'But who knows what the BKA Federal Crime Office have on him.' Fabel had read Fischmann's article on Müller-Voigt. In it she had written about the abduction and later assassination in 1977 of the wealthy Hamburg industrialist Thorsten Wiedler. Wiedler had ordered his chauffeur to stop at the scene of what appeared to be a serious road accident. The accident had been faked by members of Franz Mühlhaus's notorious terrorist gang. Mühlhaus was infamously known as 'Red Franz'. The terror group he had headed had been as nebulous as the politics behind it and Mühlhaus had been the only one to have been tracked down.

The Red Franz group had shot Wiedler's chauffeur, bundled the industrialist into the back of a van and had driven off. The chauffeur had only just survived his injuries. Wiedler, however, was not to survive his captivity. Exactly what had happened to him remained a mystery. The last known image of Wiedler was his bruised and camera-flash-bleached face, above a held-up newspaper showing the date, staring bleakly out of a photograph sent to his family and the media by his captors.

An announcement had been made that the industrialist had been 'executed' but the body, unlike those of other terrorist victims, had not been dumped somewhere it could be found. This successfully fudged the date of Wiedler's death and removed any opportunity to examine his body for forensic evidence. Despite hundreds of arrests, and the fact that everyone knew it was Mühlhaus's group behind the abduction, no one had ever been convicted of the murder.

In her article, the journalist Ingrid Fischmann had made much of the fact that Bertholdt Müller-Voigt, at that time a much more radical political figure, had been picked up and questioned by the police for forty-eight hours. The truth was that almost every political activist had been turned over in the desperate search for Wiedler. Ingrid Fischmann had, however, highlighted the fact that while nothing was known about the other members of the terrorist group involved there was evidence to suggest that the driver of the van in which Wiedler was abducted had gone on to achieve public prominence. She had left her readers to infer that the driver had been Müller-Voigt without making a direct accusation that would allow him to sue.

Fabel turned again to look at the small, arty-looking man with the sexy blonde companion. They were having a conversation without looking at each other, their expressions empty, as if merely filling silence between each forkful with their words. Müller-Voigt made an unlikely terrorist suspect, but his politics had been radical. In the 1970s and 1980s he had hung out with Daniel Cohn-Bendit, Joschka Fischer and other left-wing and green notables. Now he promoted politics that were difficult to define. Despite his mixed political directions, he had managed to be elected to the Hamburg Senate and was Environment Senator in the Hamburg State Government of First Mayor Hans Schreiber.

'Anyway,' concluded Fabel, 'we will probably never know how deeply he was involved. If at all.'

Boris returned and took their orders. For the rest of the meal they indulged in the idle, mildly melancholic talk of a couple at the end of a much-enjoyed holiday. As they ate and chatted, the sun slowly melted into the sea, bleeding its colour out into the water. They took their time over their food and the other diners thinned out to a handful of tables and the buzz of conversation lessened. As their coffee arrived, Lex, Fabel's brother, emerged from the kitchen and came over to their table. He was significantly shorter than Fabel and his hair was thick and dark. His face had the well-creased look of someone who had spent a lifetime smiling. Fabel's mother was Scottish, but any Celtic genes seemed to have concentrated themselves in his brother. Lex was older than Fabel, but had always seemed the younger in spirit. It had always been the more sensible Fabel who had pulled his older brother out of scrapes when they had been kids in Norddeich. Back then, Lex's immaturity had irritated Fabel. Now he envied it. Lex still wore his chef's tunic and checked trousers, and although his good-natured features broke into their habitual smile there was a weariness about his movements.

'Long night?' asked Fabel.

'Every night's a long night,' said Lex, pulling up a chair. 'And we're only really at the start of the season.'

'Well, that was a truly beautiful meal, Lex,' said Susanne. 'As always.'

Lex leaned over, lifted Susanne's hand and kissed it. 'You're a very intelligent and discerning lady, Susanne. Which is what makes it all the more difficult to understand why you've ended up with the wrong brother.'

Susanne smiled broadly and was about to say something when the sound of raised voices drew their attention to the table in the corner. Müller-Voigt's companion stood up suddenly, scraping her chair back, and threw down her napkin onto her dessert plate. She hissed something they could not make out at the still-sitting Müller-Voigt and marched out of the restaurant. Müller-Voigt simply stared at his plate, as if trying to read from it what he should do next. He beckoned Boris over with his credit card, paid without checking the bill and walked from the restaurant without looking at any of his fellow diners.

'Maybe it was something to do with his policy on greenhouse gases,' said Fabel, with a smile.

'He's been in here a few times over the last month,' said Lex. 'Apparently he has a house on the island. I don't know who the girl is, but she's not always with him. And it doesn't look like she'll be back.'

Susanne stared at the doorway through which the woman and then Müller-Voigt had left, then shook her head as if trying to shake off the thought that buzzed around it. 'I'm sure I've seen her somewhere before.' She took a sip of her coffee. 'I just can't, for the life of me, think where it was.'

# 2.

# The Night of the First Murder:
# Thursday, 18 August 2005.

10.15 p.m.: Schanzenviertel, Hamburg

The secret was to remain unnoticed.

He knew how these things worked: how a meaning-less glance into the car from a passer-by, seemingly forgotten in an instant, could be resurrected by an investigator in a week's or a month's time and pieced together with a dozen other tiny inconsequences that would lead the police straight to him. He had to diminish his presence at the scene of his crime, in the immediate location, in the area.

So he sat, unmoving, in the dark and the silence. Waiting for the moment of convergence.

Hamburg's Schanzenviertel is an area known for its energy and even this late on a Thursday evening there was a fair amount of activity. But this narrow side street was quiet and lined with cars. It was a risk to use his own car, but a calculated risk: it was a dark VW Polo and anonymous enough to sit incon-spicuously among all the other parked cars. No one would notice the car; but the danger was that they might notice him sitting in it. Waiting.

Earlier, he had switched the car radio on low and had let the chatter wash over him. He had been too preoccupied to listen; his mind too full with the raw energy of anticipation for the reports of the campaigns of the various contenders for the Chancellorship to stimulate the contempt that they normally provoked in him. Then, as the time approached and his mouth grew dry and his pulse grew faster, he had switched the radio off.

Now he sat in the dark and silence and fought back the emotions that surged up in great waves from deep within. He had to be in the moment itself. He had to shut everything else out and focus. Be disciplined. The Japanese had a word for it: *zanshin*. He had to achieve *zanshin*: that state of peace and relaxation, of total fearlessness while facing danger or challenge, that allowed the mind and body to perform with deadly accuracy and efficiency. Yet there was no denying the feeling of a monumental destiny about to be fulfilled. Not only had his entire life been a preparation for this moment, more than one lifetime had been dedicated to bringing him to this place and to this time. The point of convergence was close. Seconds away.

He carefully laid the velvet roll-pouch on the passenger seat. He cast a glance up and down the street before untying the ribbon fastener and unrolling the pouch flat. The blade gleamed bright and hard, sharp and beautiful in the street light. He imagined its keen edge parting flesh. Paring it from the bone. With this instrument he would still their treacherous voices; he would use its blade to shape a shining silence.

There was a movement.

He flipped the dark blue velvet over to conceal the beautiful blade. He placed his hands on the steering wheel and stared straight ahead as the bicycle passed the car. He watched the rider swing one leg over, the bicycle still in motion, before dismounting. The cyclist removed his chain and padlock from the bike's pannier and wheeled the bike into the passage at the side of the building.

He laughed quietly as he watched the cyclist's small ritual of security. There's no need, he thought. Leave it for someone to steal. You won't need it again in this lifetime.

The cyclist reappeared from the passage, slipped his keys from his pocket and let himself into the apartment.

In the dark of the car, he sheathed his hands in the latex of a pair of surgical gloves. He reached into the back, picked up the toiletry bag from the back seat and placed it next to the velvet roll-pouch.

Convergence.

He felt a great calm descend on him. *Zanshin*. Now justice would be fulfilled. Now the killing would begin.

# 3.

# The Day After the First Murder:
# Friday, 19 August 2005.

## 8.57 a.m.: Schanzenviertel, Hamburg

She stood for a moment and looked up at the sky, screwing up her eyes against the morning sun that shone so optimistically on the Schanzenviertel. It was her first appointment of the day. She checked her watch and allowed herself a small, tight smile of satisfaction. 8.57 a.m. Three minutes early.

Above all else, Kristina Dreyer prided herself on never being late. In fact, as she was about many things in her life, Kristina was obsessive about her punctuality. It was part of her reinvention of herself: of how she defined the person she had become. Kristina Dreyer was someone who had known Chaos: she had known it in a way that most people could never begin to imagine. It had engulfed her. It had stripped her of her dignity, of her youth and, most of all, it had ripped away from her any sense of control over her life.

But now Kristina was back in charge. Where her life had previously been anarchy and tumult beyond her understanding, far less her control, it was now characterised by her absolute regulation of every day. Kristina Dreyer led her life with an uncompromising exactitude. Everything about her life was simple, clean and neat: her clothes, including her working clothes, her small, pristine apartment, her VW Golf, with the lettering *Dreyer Cleaning* on the door panels; and her life, which, like her apartment, she had chosen to share with no one.

Kristina's uncompromising exactitude really came into its own in her work. She was supremely good at her job. She had built up a client list across Eimsbüttel that meant her week was full, and each customer trusted her for her thoroughness and honesty. And most of all, they trusted her for her total reliability.

Kristina cleaned well. She cleaned apartments, she cleaned villas. She cleaned homes large and small, for young and old, for German and foreigner. Every home, every task, was approached with the same scrupulously methodical approach. No detail was missed. No corner cut.

Kristina was thirty-six but looked considerably older. She was a short, thinnish woman. At one time in her life, less than a dozen years before but a life-time away, her features had been fine; delicate. Now it merely seemed as if her skin was pulled too tight over the angular framework of her skull. Her high, sharp cheekbones jutted aggressively from her face and the skin that stretched across them was slightly reddened and rough. Her nose was small, but again, just below the ridge, bone and cartilage seemed to protest against being confined and hinted at an ancient break.

Three minutes early. She let the smile fade. Being too early was almost as bad as being too late. Not that her customer would be any the wiser: Herr Hauser would already be at work. But Kristina's punctuality meant that the order of *her* universe was maintained; that no randomness would enter into it and spread, like cancer, to become sanity- and life-threatening Chaos. The way it had been before.

She turned the key and opened the door, pushing against the spring with her back as she swung her vacuum cleaner into the hallway.

The way Kristina thought of it was that she had given birth to herself. She had no children – and no man to father children – but she had created herself anew: given herself a new life and put aside all that had gone before. 'Don't let your history define who you are or who you can become,' someone had once said to her when she had been at her lowest. It had been a turning point. Everything had changed. Everything that had been part of that old life, that dark life, had been abandoned. Dumped. Forgotten.

But now, as Kristina Dreyer stood, halfway across the threshold of the apartment that she was due to clean that bright Friday morning, history reached out from her old life and seized her by the throat in an unyielding grip.

That smell. The rich, nauseous, coppery odour of stale blood hanging in the air. She recognised it instantly and started to shake.

Death was here.

### 9.00 a.m.: Eppendorf, Hamburg

The anxiety was hidden deep. To the casual observer, there was nothing in her composure that hinted at anything other than confidence and absolute self-certainty. But Dr Minks was no casual observer.

His first patient of the day was Maria Klee, an elegant young woman in her thirties. She was very attractive, with blonde hair combed back from the broad, pale brow; her face was a little long and seemed to have stretched the nose a fraction of a centimetre too low and made it slightly too narrow and therefore robbed her of true beauty.

Maria sat opposite Dr Minks, her slender, expensively trousered legs crossed with her manicured fingers resting on her knee. She sat upright: perfectly composed, alert but relaxed. Her grey-blue eyes held the psychologist in a steady, assured, yet not defiant gaze. A look that seemed to say that she was expecting a question to be posed, or a proposition to be expounded, but that she was perfectly content to wait, patiently and politely, for the doctor to speak.

For the moment, he didn't. Dr Friedrich Minks took his time as he examined the patient's notes. Minks was of indeterminate middle age: a short, dumpy man with dull skin and thinning black hair; his eyes were dark and soft behind the panes of his spectacles. In contrast to his poised patient, Minks looked as if he had been dropped into his chair and that the impact had crumpled him further into his already crumpled suit. He looked up from his notes and took in the carefully constructed edifice of confidence that Maria Klee presented with her body language. Nearly thirty years of experience as a psychologist allowed him to see through the sham instantly.

'You are very hard on yourself.' Minks's long-gone Swabian childhood still tugged on his vowels as he spoke. 'And I have to say that is part of your problem. You know that, don't you?'

Maria Klee's cool grey eyes didn't flicker, but she gave a small shrug. 'What do you mean, Herr Doktor?'

'You know exactly what I mean. You refuse to allow yourself to be afraid. It's all part of these defences you've built around yourself.' He leaned forward. 'Fear is natural. After what happened to you, to feel fear is more than natural . . . it's an essential part of the healing process. Just as you felt pain as your body healed, you have to feel fear to allow your mind to heal.'

'I just want to get on with my life, Dr Minks. Without all this nonsense getting in the way.'

'It's not nonsense. It's a stage of post-trauma recovery that you have to go through. But because you see fear as a failure and you fight against your natural reactions, you are stretching out this stage of recovery . . . and I'm worried it's going to be stretched out indefinitely. And that is exactly why you are having these panic attacks. You have sublimated and repressed your natural fear and horror at what happened to you until it has burst through the surface in this distorted form.'

'You're wrong,' Maria said. 'I have never tried to deny what happened to me. What he . . . what he *did* to me.'

'That's not what I said. It's not the event that you're denying. You're denying your right to experience fear, horror, or even outrage at what this man did to you. Or that he has yet to be held to account for his actions.'

'I don't have time for self-pity.'

Minks shook his head. 'This has nothing to do with self-pity. This has everything to do with post-trauma stress and with the natural process of healing.

Of resolution. Until you resolve this conflict within, you will never be able to connect properly with the world around you. With people.'

'I deal with people every day.' The patient's grey-blue eyes now glinted with defiance. 'Are you saying I'm compromising my effectiveness?'

'Perhaps not now . . . but if we do not start laying ghosts to rest, it will, ultimately, manifest itself in how you conduct yourself professionally.' Minks paused. 'From what you've told me, you are increasingly showing signs of aphenphosmphobia. Considering the type of work you're involved with, I would have thought it would present significant difficulties. Have you discussed this with your superiors?'

'As you know, they arranged physical and psychological therapy.' Maria angled her head back slightly and there was a defensive edge to her voice. 'But no. I haven't discussed these current . . . *problems* with them.'

'Well,' said Dr Minks, 'you know my feelings on this matter. I feel that your employers should be aware of the difficulties you're having.' He paused. 'You mentioned this man with whom you began a relationship. How is that going?'

'Okay . . .' There was no longer a defiant tone in Maria's voice and some of the tense energy seemed to have seeped from her shoulders. 'I am very fond of him. And he of me. But we haven't . . . we haven't been able to be *intimate* yet.'

'Do you mean you have no physical contact . . . no embracing or kissing? Or do you mean sex?'

'I mean sex. Or anything approaching it. We do touch. We do kiss . . . but then I start to feel . . .' She drew her shoulders up, as if her body were being squeezed into a small space. 'Then I get the panic attacks.'

'Does he understand why you withdraw from him?'

'A little. It's not easy for a man – for anyone – to feel that their touch, their close proximity, is repellent. I've explained some of it to him and he's promised to keep it to himself. I knew he would anyway. But he understands. He knows I'm seeing you . . . well, not you specifically . . . He knows I'm seeing *someone* about my problem.'

'Good . . .' Minks smiled again. 'What about the dreams? Have you had any more?'

Maria nodded. Her defences were beginning to crumble and her posture sagged a little more. Her hands still rested on her knee but the manicured fingernails now gathered up a small clutch of expensive tailoring.

'The same thing?' asked Minks.

'Yes.'

Dr Minks leaned forward in his chair. 'We need to go back there. I need to visit your dream with you. You understand that, don't you?'

'Again?'

'Yes,' said Minks. 'Again.' He gestured for her to relax into her seat.

'We're going back to your dream. Back to where you see your attacker again. I'm going to start counting, now. We're going back, Maria . . . one . . . two . . . three . . .'

### 9.00 a.m.: Schanzenviertel, Hamburg

Kristina left the door open, leaning the vacuum cleaner and her cleaning tray as checks against the door spring; leaving her escape route clear. Old instincts started to rouse themselves from somewhere deep within her, awoken by the scent of fresh death in the air. She became aware of a rhythmic rushing noise and realised that it was the sound of her pulse in her ears. She reached down and picked up a spray bottle of cleaning fluid from her tray, gripping it tight in her trembling hand, like a gun.

'Herr Hauser?' She called into the hall, into the quiet rooms beyond. She strained to hear any sound, any movement. Any sign of something living within the apartment. She gave a jump as a car drove past on the street outside, the thudding bass of raucous American dance music synchronising with the pulsating rush of blood in her ears. The apartment remained silent.

Kristina edged down the hall towards the lounge, the hand with the cleaning-fluid bottle held out hesitantly before her, the other offering uncertain support, tracing its way along the bookshelves that lined the hallway wall. As she did so, Kristina couldn't help her trembling fingers registering a hint of dust on a shelf needing special attention.

She felt her anxiety ease as she stepped into the bright lounge and found nothing untoward, other than that Herr Hauser had left it particularly untidy: a whisky bottle and half-drained glass sat on the table beside the armchair; some books and magazines lay scattered on the sofa. Kristina had always marvelled that someone who was always so concerned about the environment in general could be so careless of his personal surroundings. Kristina Dreyer, the assiduous cleaner of other people's homes, swept the room with her gaze, registering and mentally timetabling the work that needed doing. But a former Kristina, a past-tense Kristina, screamed at her from deep within that there was death here: its wraith smell hanging in the stuffy air of the apartment.

She stepped back out into the hall. She stopped in her tracks, as if the energy from even the slightest movement had to be diverted to her hearing. A sound. From the bedroom. Something tapping. Someone tapping. She moved towards the bedroom door. She called out 'Herr Hauser' once more and paused. No answer, except the ominous sound from within the bedroom. Her grip tightened on the cleaning-fluid bottle and she threw open the door so hard that it banged against the wall and swung back, slamming shut again in her face. Again she pushed it open, more carefully this time. The bedroom was large and bright, with off-white walls and a polished wooden floor. The window was open slightly and a breeze stirred the vertical blinds, which tapped rhythmically against the window. Kristina let go the breath she did not know she had been holding with a half-laugh, half-sigh of relief. But still the anxiety didn't fully leave her, and pulled her back out into the hall.

The apartment's hall was L-shaped. Kristina moved with slightly more confidence now and made her way down to where the hall took a right turn and led to a second bedroom and the bathroom. As she turned the corner, she noticed that the second bedroom's door was open, casting the bright sunlight from the windows onto the bathroom door, which was closed. Kristina froze.

There was something nailed to the bathroom door. She felt a nauseous surge of terror. It was some kind of animal pelt. A small animal, but Kristina couldn't guess what kind. The fur was wet and matted and bright red. Unnaturally red. It was as if the pelt had been freshly skinned and blood ran down the white painted surface of the door.

She edged her way towards the door, her breaths coming short and fast, the searchlight of her gaze locked on the oozing rawhide.

She stopped half a metre from the door and stared at the pelt, trying to make sense of it. Her hand reached out, as if to touch it, her fingers stopping just short of the glossy red fur.

It took a time too brief to be measured for her brain to analyse what her eyes were seeing and to make sense of it. The thought was a simple one. A simple statement of fact. But it ripped into Kristina and in that instant shredded her ordered world. She heard an inhuman shriek of terror reverberate along the hall and tumble out through the still-open front door. Somehow, as the fragile fabric of Kristina Dreyer's world was rent asunder, she realised that the shriek was hers.

So much terror. So many long-forbidden memories flooding back. All from a single realisation.

What she was looking at was not fur.

### 9.10 a.m.: Eppendorf, Hamburg

Maria stood in the heart of the dreamscape field. As it always was in her dream, reality was exaggerated. The moon that hung in the sky was over-large and over-bright, like a stage light. The grasses caressing her naked legs and swirling silently to the command of an unheard breeze moved too sinuously. There was no sound. There were no odours. For the moment, Maria's world was stripped down to two senses: sight and sensation. She looked out across the field. The silence was broken by a soft voice with a hint of a Swabian accent. A voice that belonged somewhere other than the world she now stood in.

'Where are you now, Maria?'

'I'm there. I'm in the field.'

'Is it the same field and the same night?' the spirit voice of the psychologist asked.

'No . . . no, it's not. I mean it is . . . but everything is different. It's larger. Wider. It's like the same place but a different universe. A different time.' Far in the distance she could see a galleon – its great white sails rippled insubstantially in a weak wind as it sailed towards Hamburg. It seemed to drift through the swirling grass instead of the water. 'I see a ship. An old-fashioned sailing ship. It's going away from me.'

'What else?'

She turned and looked in another direction. A broken building, like a ruined castle, sat small and dark at the edge of the field, as if at the edge of the world. A cold, harsh light seemed to shine from one of the windows.

'I see a castle, where the disused barn should be. But I am so far away from it. Too far away from it.'

'Are you afraid?'

'No. No, I am not afraid.'

'What else do you see?'

Maria turned around and gave a small jump. He had been there, behind her, all the time. And because she had dreamed the same dream so many times before she had known he was going to be

43

there, yet she had still given a start when she found herself face to face with him again. But, as in all her dreams before, she felt none of the raw, stark fear that his face stimulated in her waking hours: whenever she saw it in a photograph, or whenever it appeared suddenly and unbidden from within the dark hall of memory where she tried to keep it locked up.

He was tall and his heavy shoulders were encased in an exotic armour and draped in a black cloak. He removed his ornate helmet. His face was built of sharp Slavic angles and possessed a callous handsomeness. His eyes were a piercing, bright and dreadfully cold emerald-green and they burned into hers. He smiled at her: a lover's smile, but the eyes stayed cold. He stood close to her. So close that she could feel his chill breath on her.

'He is here,' she said, looking into the green eyes but speaking to a doctor in another dimension.

'I am here,' said the cruelly handsome Slav.

'Are you afraid?' Minks's voice, the voice from another dimension, suddenly became fainter. Further away.

'Yes,' she answered. 'Now I am afraid. But I like this fear.'

'Do you feel anything other than fear?' asked Minks, but his voice had faded almost beyond hearing. Maria felt her fear change. Sharpen.

'Your voice is becoming faint,' she said. 'I can hardly hear you. Why is your voice fainter?'

Minks replied, but his voice had now drifted so far away and she couldn't make out his answer.

'Why can't I hear you?' Now there was a new magnitude to her fear. It burned furnace raw and deep. 'Why can't I hear you?' She screamed into the dark sky with its too-big moon.

Vasyl Vitrenko leaned forward, tilting down to kiss her on the forehead. His lips were dry, cold. 'Because you've got it wrong, Maria.' His voice was heavy with an Eastern European accent. 'Dr Minks isn't there. This isn't one of your hypnotherapy sessions. This is real.' He reached beneath his billowing black cloak. 'This is no dream. And there's no one here except you and me. Alone.'

Maria wanted to scream but couldn't. Instead she stared as if hypnotised at the evil moonlight gleam on Vasyl Vitrenko's long, broad-bladed knife.

### 9.10 a.m.: Schanzenviertel, Hamburg

Kristina had never seen a human scalp before, but she knew with absolute certainty that that was exactly what she was looking at. To start with, it had been the colour of the hair that had prevented her identifying it as something human. Red. Unnaturally red.

But there was now no doubt in her mind that this was human hair. Glistening wet hair. And skin. A large ragged disc of it. It had been nailed to the bathroom door with three panel pins. The top of it had folded over, revealing a little of the puckered bloody underside where the skin had been sliced and pulled away from the skull beneath. A long 'Y' shape of glistening red streamed from it and down the wooden bathroom door.

Blood.

Kristina shook her head. No. Not again. She had seen too much blood in her life. No more. Not now.

45

Not when she had just got her life back. This was so unfair.

She leaned forward again and felt her legs shudder, as if they were struggling to support the weight of her body. Yes, there was blood, but there was too much of it to be blood alone. And too vivid a red. The same vivid red as the sodden, matted hair.

Her pulse thudded in her ears, a tempo that increased as a simple but obvious thought hit her. Whose hair?

Kristina reached out with trembling fingers and pressed them against an area of the door's wooden surface that was not streaked with glistering red.

'Herr Hauser . . . ?' Her voice was high and tremulous.

She pushed and the door of the bathroom swung open.

### 9.12 a.m.: Eppendorf, Hamburg

Vitrenko smiled at Maria. He looped his arm around her back and pressed her close to him, as if they were about to dance. She could feel the unyielding solidity of his body tight against hers.

'Do you love me?' he asked her.

'Yes,' she said, and meant it. Her terror subsided. He eased his body from hers but still held her firm. He lifted the knife and ran its keen edge over her shoulders, her breast and let it rest just below her chest, its cold sharp tip pressing lightly into the soft space just below her sternum.

'Do you want me to do it?' he asked. 'Again?'

'Yes. I want you to do it again.' She looked into the green eyes that still shone cold and cruel.

There was a crash of thunder. Then another. She

felt the knife-point pressure on her abdomen increase, and the keen pain as the tip pierced her skin. There were another two loud claps of thunder and the world around her dissolved into darkness.

Maria opened her eyes and found herself looking across at Dr Minks. He held his hands together before him as if he had been clapping. The thunder that had brought her back. She straightened herself up and looked around his office, as if reassuring herself that she was back in reality.

'You closed me out, Maria,' he said. 'You didn't want me there.'

'He took control,' she said, and coughed when she realised that her voice was shaking.

'No, he didn't,' said Dr Minks. 'You took control. He doesn't exist in your dreams. *You* recreate him. You control his words and actions. It was your will that sought to exclude me.' He paused and crumpled back into his chair, again examining his notes, but the frown did not fade from his brow. 'You saw the same landmarks and motifs again?'

'Yes. The galleon where the harbour-police patrol boat was that night and the castle where the old barn was. What I don't understand is why it is all so elaborate in the dream. Why is he dressed in armour? And why is everything changed into some kind of historical counterpart?'

'I don't know. It could be that you are trying, in your mind, to place what happened that night into the past . . . A distant past: like a previous life, almost. Do you *feel* like it's the same night as you were stabbed?'

'Yes and no. It's like the same night, but in another dimension or universe or something. Like

47

you said, as if it were a completely different time, as well.'

'And, in this scenario, you let your attacker come close to you? You permit him to have close personal contact?'

'That's the thing I can never understand,' said Maria. 'Why do I allow *him* to touch me, when I can't let anyone else touch me?'

'Because he is the origin of your trauma. The source of your fear. Without this man, you would have no post-traumatic stress, no aphenphosmphobia, no panic attacks.' Minks took out a thick leather-bound pad and started to scribble on it. He ripped a page out and handed it to Maria. 'I want you to take these. I feel we have too big a mountain to climb with therapy alone.'

'Drugs?' Maria did not reach to take the prescription. 'What is it?'

'Propanolol. A beta blocker. The same sort of thing that I'd prescribe if you had high blood pressure. It's a very mild dose and I only want you to take one eighty-milligram tablet on, well, difficult days. You can make it a hundred and sixty milligrams if it's really bad. You don't suffer from asthma or any respiratory problems, do you?'

Maria shook her head. 'What does it do?'

'It is a noradrenalin inhibitor. It restricts the chemicals that your body generates when you're afraid. Or angry.' Dr Minks thrust the prescription in Maria's direction and she took it from him.

'Will it affect my performance at work?'

Minks smiled and shook his head. 'No, it shouldn't do. Some people feel tired or lethargic with it, but not in the same way it would if I were to give you Valium. This might slow you down a little, but otherwise you should feel no ill effects. And, as I said, I only want you to take it when you really feel you need to.'

Dr Minks stood up and shook Maria's hand. She noticed that the psychologist's palm was cool and fleshy. And rather moist. She pulled her hand away a little too quickly.

After confirming the following week's appointment with Minks's secretary, Maria made her way to the elevator. As she did so she paused to take two things from her shoulder bag. The first was a handkerchief with which she wiped vigorously at the hand that Minks had shaken. The second was her police service-issue SIG-Sauer nine-millimetre automatic, sheathed in its clip-on holster, which she attached to the belt of her trousers before pressing the button to summon the lift.

### 9.12 a.m.: Schanzenviertel, Hamburg

Kristina Dreyer stood framed in the bathroom doorway. She opened her mouth to scream, but her fear strangled the sound in her throat. For four years, twice a week, Kristina had cleaned Herr Hauser's bathroom until it shone scalpel-bright. She had wiped every surface, swept every corner, polished every tap and fitting. It was a space so familiar to her that she could have navigated it with her eyes closed.

But not today. Today it was an unknown hell.

The bathroom was large and bright. A tall curtain-less window, its lower half frosted glass, looked out onto the small square courtyard behind the apartment. At this time of morning when the sun was angled right, it flooded the bathroom with light. For some, the decor would have been too clinical. But not for Kristina, for whom nothing could be too clean; too sterile. The entire room was lined with ceramic tiles: large and pale sky-blue on the floor; smaller and bright white on the walls. Herr Hauser's bathroom had always been a delight to clean because the light sought out each corner and the tiles always responded to Kristina's abstergent touch with a keen gleam.

There was a great rainbow-shaped smear of blood that arced across the pale blue floor tiles. At its end, Herr Hauser sat slumped where he had been dragged, between the toilet and the side of the bath. Bright blood glistened against the gleaming white porcelain of the toilet bowl. Hauser glowered across the bathroom at Kristina, his mouth gaped wide, with an expression that could have been almost surprise were it not for the way his brow hooded his eyes in a disapproving frown. There was silence, broken only by a dripping tap beating a slow tattoo on the bath's enamel. Again something gurgled and struggled to free itself from Kristina's constricted throat: something between a cry and a retch.

Hauser's face was streaked with gouts of bright viscous blood. Someone had sliced a line, mostly straight but in places ragged, across his forehead about five or six centimetres above his eyebrows. The cut had been deep. To the bone. And it swept around the temples and above the ears. The skin, flesh and hair above the slash had been ripped from Hauser's head and the blood-mottled dome of his skull was exposed. Hauser's gore-smeared face and the exposed skull above looked to Kristina like some horrific parody of a boiled egg rammed into an eggcup. Even more blood had soaked into Hauser's shirt and trousers, and Kristina saw that a second cut ran across his throat and neck. She dropped the cleaning-fluid spray onto the floor and leaned her shoulder against the wall. Suddenly she felt all the strength ebb from her legs and she slid down the wall, her cheek sliding against the chill kiss of the porcelain tiles. She was now slumped in the corner by the door, mirroring the posture of her dead client. She started to sob.

There was so much to clean. So much to clean.

### 9.15 a.m. Polizei Hamburg Police Headquarters, Alsterdorf, Hamburg

The new headquarters of the Hamburg police – the Police Presidium – lay to the north of Winterhuder Stadtpark city park. It never took Jan Fabel long to drive to Alsterdorf from his Pöseldorf apartment, but today was his first day back from four days' leave. Just a couple of days before he had stood with Susanne on the wide, curving beach at List, on the North Sea island of Sylt. A couple of days and a lifetime away.

Driving through the dapples of sunlight that danced between trees of the Stadtpark, Fabel felt in no hurry to step back into the reality of his life as head of a murder squad. But as he listened to his car radio, each news report seemed to sink into him like lead, anchoring him further into his accustomed world, while the memory of a long scythe of golden sand under a vast, bright sky drifted further from him.

Fabel caught the end of a report about the forth-coming general election: the conservative CDU/CSU coalition led by Angela Merkel had increased its already dramatic lead in the polls. It looked like Chancellor Gerhard Schröder's gamble of calling an early election was not going to pay off. A commentator discussed Frau Merkel's change of style and appearance: apparently she had taken Hillary Clinton as a model for her hairstyle. Fabel sighed as he listened to how the various party leaders 'positioned' themselves with the electorate: it seemed to him that German politics were no longer about firm convictions or political ideals, but about individuals. Like the British and Americans before them, Germans were beginning to value style over substance; personalities over policies.

While he drove through the sunlit park, Fabel's attention perked up as he listened while two of those personalities clashed. Hans Schreiber, the Social Democrat First Mayor of Hamburg, was engaged in an ill-tempered debate with Bertholdt Müller-Voigt, the city's Environment Minister – who was a member of the *Bündnis 90/Die Grünen* political party. The same Müller-Voigt that Fabel and Susanne had seen in Lex's restaurant on Sylt. The SPD and the Greens were part of Germany's ruling coalition, and the political complexion of Hamburg's city government was also red-green, but there was little evidence in the recorded exchange that Müller-Voigt was, indeed, a Schreiber-appointed minister. The pre-general election cracks in Germany's political structures were beginning to show. The animosity between the two men over the past month or so had been well documented: Müller-Voigt had referred to Schreiber's wife, Karin, as 'Lady Macbeth' in reference to her ruthless ambitions for her husband; specifically an ambition that he become Federal Chancellor of Germany. Fabel knew Schreiber – knew him better than Schreiber would have liked – and did not find it difficult to believe that he fully shared his wife's ambitions.

Fabel stopped for a red signal at the traffic lights in Winterhuder Stadtpark. He watched idly as a Lycra-clad cyclist crossed in front of him, then turned to see that the car that had pulled up next to him was being driven by a woman in her thirties. She berated the two children in the rear seat for some misbehaviour or other, conducting her wrath through the rear-view mirror, her mouth moving animatedly, her anger mute behind the closed car windows. Beyond the annoyed mother's car, a city parks employee brushed litter from the path that ran between towering trees up to the vast dome-capped tower of the Winterhuder Wasserturm.

The everyday routine of a city. Small lives with small worries about small things. People who did not deal with death as their day-to-day business.

The news switched to the latest from London, which had recently been rocked by suicide bombings. A second campaign of attacks had failed, most likely because of faulty detonators. Fabel tried to reassure himself that Hamburg was far away from such troubles. That it was another land. The terrorism that had rocked Germany in the 1970s and 1980s had passed into history, roughly at the same time as the Wall had come down. But there was a saying in Germany about Hamburg: *If it rains in London, they put up their umbrellas in Hamburg*. It was a sentiment that the half-British Fabel had always liked, that had given him a sense of place, of belonging; but today it gave him no cheer. Today, nowhere was safe.

Even in Hamburg, terrorism and its consequences

were insidiously encroaching on people's daily lives. Just driving into Hamburg city centre from his flat in Pöseldorf had been changed for Fabel since the atrocities of 11 September in the USA. The American Consulate in Hamburg sat on the shore of the Alster and the shore-front road had been permanently sealed off after the attacks, meaning that Fabel had had to change the route to work he had taken every day since moving to Pöseldorf.

The lights changed and the driver behind him tooted his horn, snapping Fabel out of his reverie. He turned up towards the Presidium.

The next item on the radio news was, ironically, about the protests over the closure of the British General Consulate in Hamburg. Germany's most Anglophile city was stung by the suggestion. Hamburg also prided itself on being, after New York, the city with the most consulates in the world. But the 'War on Terror' was changing how states connected with each other. As Fabel pulled up in the secure car park of the Presidium, the future took a shadowy and vague form in his mind and darkened his post-leave mood even more.

Hamburg's police headquarters – the Police Presidium – was less than five years old and still had the look and feel of a new building, like a newly tailored coat yet to yield to the shape of its wearer. The architectural concept behind the Presidium was to recreate the 'Polizei Stern', the police star, in building form, with the five-storey Presidium radiating outward towards each compass point from an unroofed circular atrium.

The Murder Commission – the Polizei Hamburg's homicide squad – was on the third floor. As he emerged from the lift, Fabel was greeted by a bristle-scalped, middle-aged man with a tree-stump build. He had a file tucked under one arm and was carrying a coffee in his free hand. His heavy features broke into a smile as he saw Fabel.

'Hi, *Chef*, how was your break?'

'Too short, Werner,' said Fabel and he shook hands with Senior Criminal Commissar Werner Meyer. Werner had worked with Fabel longer, and more closely, than anyone else in the Murder Commission. His intimidating physical presence was actually totally at odds with his approach to police work. Werner was an almost obsessively methodical processor of evidence whose attention to detail had been the key factor in solving more than a few difficult cases. He was also Fabel's close friend.

'You should have taken another day,' said Werner. 'Stretched it over another weekend.'

Fabel shrugged. 'I only have a few days' leave left and I want to take another long weekend on Sylt in a couple of months. My brother's birthday.' The two men made their way along the curving corridor that followed, like all the main corridors of the Presidium, the circle of the central atrium. 'Anyway, it's been pretty quiet recently. Makes me nervous. I feel we're overdue a big case. What's been happening?'

'Certainly nothing we had to bother you with,' said Werner. 'Maria got the Olga X case tied up, and there's been a brawl killing in St Pauli, but other than that not much. I've set up a team meeting to brief you.'

The team assembled in the Murder Commission's main meeting room just before noon. Fabel and

Werner were joined by Senior Criminal Commissar Maria Klee: a tall, elegant woman in her thirties. She had a look that one would not automatically associate with a police officer. Her blonde hair was expensively cut and her restrained, tasteful grey suit and cream blouse gave her more the look of a corporate lawyer. Maria shared the second line of command under Fabel with Werner Meyer. Over the last year and a half, Werner and Maria had begun to jell as colleagues, but only after the team had nearly lost her in the same operation that had left another of the Murder Commission's team dead.

There were two younger officers already at the table when Fabel arrived. Criminal Commissars Anna Wolff and Henk Hermann were both protégés of Fabel's. He had picked each for their very different styles and attitudes. It was Fabel's management style to team up opposites: where others would see the potential for strife, Fabel would see the opportunity for a balance of complementary qualities. Anna and Henk were still finding that balance: it had been Anna's former partner, Paul Lindemann, who had been killed. And he had died trying to save her life.

Anna Wolff looked even less like a police officer than Maria Klee, but in a completely different way. She was more youthful-looking than her twenty-eight years, and she habitually dressed in jeans and an oversized leather jacket. Her pretty face was topped by black hair cut short and spiky, and her large dark eyes and full-lipped mouth were always emphasised by dark mascara and fire-truck-red lipstick. It would have been much easier to imagine Anna working in a hair salon rather than as a Murder Commission detective. But

Anna Wolff was tough. She came from a family of Holocaust survivors and had served in the Israeli army before returning to her native Hamburg. In fact, Anna was probably the toughest member of Fabel's team: intelligent, fiercely determined but impulsive.

Henk Hermann, Anna's partner, could not have contrasted more with her. He was a tall, lanky man with a pale complexion and a perpetually earnest expression. Just as Anna could not have looked less like a police officer, Henk could not have looked more like one. The same could also have been said about Paul Lindemann, and Fabel knew that, initially, the physical similarity between Henk and his dead predecessor had taken the other members of the team aback.

Fabel looked around the table. It always struck him as odd just how different this disparate group of people were. An unlikely family. Very different individuals who had somehow stumbled into a very peculiar profession and into an unspoken dependence on each other.

Werner led Fabel through the current caseload. While he had been on leave, there had only been one murder: a drunken Saturday-night fight outside a nightclub in St Pauli had ended with a twenty-one-year-old haemorrhaging to death in the street. Werner handed over to Anna Wolff and Henk Hermann, who summarised the case and the progress to date. It was the type of murder that made up ninety per cent of the Murder Commission's workload. Depressingly simple and straightforward: a moment of senseless rage, usually fuelled by drink, leaving one life lost and another in ruins.

'Do we have anything else on the books?' Fabel asked.

'Just tying up the loose ends on the Olga X case.' Maria flipped back through a few pages in her notebook. Olga X not only had no surname, her first name was unlikely to have been Olga. But the team had felt the need to give her some kind of identity. No one knew for sure where Olga had come from, but it was certainly somewhere in Eastern Europe. She had been working as a prostitute and had been beaten and strangled to death by a customer: a fat, balding thirty-nine-year-old insurance clerk called Thomas Wiesehan from Heimfeld with a wife and three children and no criminal record of any kind.

Dr Möller, the pathologist, had estimated Olga's age to have been between eighteen and twenty.

Fabel looked puzzled. 'But Werner told me that the Olga X case is all done and dusted, Maria. We have a full admission of guilt and unshakeable forensics to back it up. What "loose ends" do you have to tie up?'

'Well, none really on the murder itself. It's just I get the feeling there's a people-trafficking connection to this. Some poor kid from Russia or God knows where being trapped into a prostitution career with promises of a proper job and a place in the West. Olga was a victim of slavery before she became a victim of murder. Wiesehan killed her all right . . . but some gang boss put her there for him to kill.'

Fabel examined Maria closely. She reflected his gaze with her frank, unreadable blue-grey eyes. It was not like Maria to invest herself so deeply in a case: Anna, yes; even Fabel himself. But not Maria. Maria's efficiency as a detective had always been typified by her cool, professional, detached approach.

'I understand how you feel,' Fabel sighed. 'I really do. But that's not our concern. We had a murder to solve and we've solved it. I'm not saying that we just leave it there. Pass everything you've got on to Vice. And a copy to LKA Six.' Fabel referred to the Polizei Hamburg's newly re-formed, ninety-officer-strong State Crime Bureau 6 unit, the so-called Super LKA, that had been set up specifically to take on organised crime.

Maria shrugged. There was nothing to read in her pale blue-grey eyes. 'Okay, *Chef.*'

'Anything else?' asked Fabel.

The phone rang before anyone had a chance to answer. Werner picked up the receiver and made confirming noises as he scribbled notes on a pad.

'Right on cue,' said Werner as he hung up. 'A body's been uncovered at an archaeological dig, down by the Speicherstadt.'

'Ancient?'

'That's what they're trying to establish, but Holger Brauner and his team are on their way.' Werner referred to the forensics-squad leader. 'Whom shall I pass this to, *Chef*?'

Fabel held out an open hand across the table. 'Give it to me. You guys have enough on, tidying up this brawl killing.' Fabel took the pad and wrote the details down in his notebook. He stood up and took his jacket from the back of his chair. 'And I could do with some fresh air.'

## Noon: Schanzenviertel, Hamburg

Kristina knew that she was face to face again with Chaos. She had lived with it for years. It had taken her to the brink of madness once before and she had cut it out of her life: an excision that had been as traumatic and as painful as if she had carved it out in flesh from her own body.

Now Chaos stormed and raged around her. Some distant sea wall had been breached and a tidal wave of turmoil had been silently hurtling towards her, waiting to collide with her the moment she opened the door to Herr Hauser's apartment. In that moment she knew that she faced the greatest struggle of her life: that she must defeat Chaos anew.

It was midday now. She had worked at the bathroom all morning. Once more the porcelain shone sterile and cold; the gleam had been restored to the floor. Herr Hauser now lay in the bath. Kristina had fought Chaos with Method. She had refused to let her terror blind her and she had shaped a strategy for restoring the bathroom to order.

She had begun by hoisting Herr Hauser into the bath, to contain the mess in one area. As she had struggled with him, his exposed skull, cold and clammy with blood and ribbons of remaining tissue, had pressed against her cheek. Kristina had had to run to the toilet bowl to vomit, had taken a few moments to recompose herself, and then had returned to her task. She had stripped Herr Hauser and placed his blood-soaked garments into a plastic bin bag. Then she had taken the shower head down from its cradle and rinsed the blood from him by hand. She had placed a second black plastic bin bag over his head and neck, binding it tight with some parcel tape which she'd found in one of Herr Hauser's drawers, and had sealed the bag around his shoulders. Then she had carefully removed the shower curtain from its rail and wrapped Herr

Hauser's body in it, again taking some parcel tape and binding the improvised shroud tight.

Kristina had once more been faced with lifting Hauser's dead weight. She had lugged the body out of the bath and had laid it on the clean floor, and had then set about sanitising the bath. Herr Hauser had always insisted that Kristina use environmentally friendly cleaning materials: vinegar to clean the toilet, that kind of thing. It had made Kristina's job that much harder, but she hadn't minded. She loved scrubbing, scouring and polishing. But this task was too much. She had used bleach on the bath, toilet and sink and had washed the floor and wall tiles with a bleach solution. Then she had gone over every surface with an antibacterial spray.

Now she was done. She had not defeated Chaos. She knew this. She had merely deflected it. She had been here the whole morning: it meant that she had let down the other customer who was scheduled in her diary for before lunch on Fridays. It would not even have been so bad if she had only been late for them: she simply hadn't turned up. It would have a domino effect on an entire day's clients – then tomorrow's, and then a whole week's. A reputation for punctuality and reliability that it had taken four years to build up was gone in four hours. Her cellphone had started to ring just after her next appointment was due and Kristina had been forced to switch it off so that she could concentrate on her task.

Kristina surveyed the bathroom. At least here order had been restored. With the exception of the carefully polythene-shrouded Herr Hauser, who lay untidily on the floor by the tub, the bathroom looked cleaner and shone brighter than ever.

She leaned back against the wall, a cleaning cloth hanging in her rubber-gloved hand, and allowed herself a small smile of satisfaction. It was then that she became aware of someone standing behind her in the bathroom doorway. She turned suddenly and they both gave a start. A tall, slim, dark-haired young man with delicate features and large bewildered blue eyes stared at Kristina, then saw the shower-curtain mummy by the bath. His face blanched grey-white and he made a startled noise before turning and running down the hall towards the door.

Kristina gazed blankly at the now empty doorway for a moment before turning back to the bathroom. There was a corner she had perhaps missed.

## Noon: HafenCity site, by the Speicherstadt, Hamburg

If there was any landscape that defined the city of Hamburg for Fabel, it was this one.

As he drove down Mattenwiete and across the Holzbrücke bridge towards the Elbe, the horizon opened up ahead of him and the elaborate spires and gables of the Speicherstadt pierced a stretched silk sky of unbroken blue.

Speicherstadt means 'Warehouse City' and that was exactly what it was: towering ornate red-brick warehouses, row after row, interlaced with cobbled streets and canals, dominating the city's waterfront. These beautiful nineteenth-century buildings had been the lungs that had breathed life into Hamburg commerce.

For Fabel, there was something about the architecture of the Speicherstadt that summed up his adopted city for him. The architecture was ornate and confident, but always practical and restrained. It was how Germany's richest city and its people displayed wealth and success: clearly, but with decorum. The Speicherstadt was also a symbol of Hamburg's independence and its special status as a city-state within Germany. An independence that had, at various times in Hamburg's history, been more than a little precarious. The statues of Hammonia and Europa, the personifications of Hamburg and Europe as goddesses, stood guard on the stanchions of Brooksbrücke bridge and looked down on Fabel as he crossed into the Speicherstadt.

Until recently the Speicherstadt had been the world's biggest bonded area, with customs posts at every point of entry. Fabel passed the old customs office to his right, which had found a new life as a trendy coffee shop. Across from the coffee shop, on the other side of the cobbled Kehrwieder Brook, the first warehouse in the Speicherstadt had also found a new role: a snaking queue of tourists and locals were waiting to be admitted to the 'Hamburg Dungeon', an idea that Hamburg, along with many other ideas, had imported from Britain. Fabel could never understand the need that others felt to be made afraid, to experience ersatz horrors, when he felt he had had a bellyful of the real thing.

Fabel turned left into Kehrwieder Brook before taking Kibbelsteg, which dissected the Speicherstadt in a straight, unbroken line, and the vast brick warehouses on either side, trimmed and capped with ornate verdigris-tinged bronze, glowed red in the midday sun. Here all kinds of real trades were still carried out. Cradles, suspended from the jutting winches at the tops of the warehouses, hoisted up deep stacks of oriental carpets and, as he passed the Kaffeerösterei, the warm air filled with the Speicherstadt's trade-mark smell, the rich odour from the coffee roasters preparing the beans for storage.

Fabel drove on and eventually the nineteenth century surrendered to the twenty-first, as he passed under an arching forest of perpetually moving cranes that marked Germany's biggest building site. Hamburg's HafenCity.

Hamburg had always been a city of opportunists: of traders and entrepreneurs. The city's fiercely independent character was founded on its ability to look beyond its own horizons and connect with the wider world. In the Middle Ages, Hamburg's politicians had always been merchants, businessmen. And, invariably, they would put trade before politics. Nothing had changed.

The HafenCity was a big idea, just as the Speicherstadt had been before it. A bold vision. It would take up to twenty years to complete. One row at a time, the new cathedrals of commerce, all steel and glass and youthful energy, were taking their serried places behind the old: the stately red-brick warehouses of the Speicherstadt. Two visions, born in separate centuries, fused by the heat of the same ambition: to make Hamburg Europe's leading trading port. The HafenCity was being completed in planned stages. A row of buildings would be built all at the one time, combining luxury apartments with sleek, electronic-age office blocks; once complete, the next row would be started. Yet as high-speed internet connections were plumbed into each shining new building, the smell of the roasting coffee beans would drift in, reminding the brave new twenty-first century world that the old Speicherstadt was still very much part of the city's life.

Hamburg liked to share its vision of the future, and a thirteen-metre-high observation platform, in the shape of an elevated ship's bridge, and with the name, in English, *HafenCity VIEWPOINT* emblazoned against its terracotta-coloured flank, had been erected down by the edge of the Elbe. The viewing platform allowed visitors a 360-degree vista of the future. In one direction they could see where the new Opera House was to be built, its high-tech roof billowing like waves or sails, on top of the old Kaispeicher A storage quay. In the other, their view would arc around and past the new luxury-liner terminal to where the Elbe took a sweep and was spanned by the arched ironwork bridges that connected Hamburg to Harburg. All around the viewing tower the land had been cleared and levelled and lay naked, awaiting its shining new vestments.

Fabel parked on the uneven improvised car park, two hundred metres or so from the viewing platform. Two members of the Polizei Hamburg's uniformed branch were already at the site and had done their usual thing of cordoning off the scene. In this case, their efforts seemed redundant: archaeology is forensic in its methodology, and the dig site had already been ringed off and divided into quadrants. As Fabel made his way across to the site he saw the familiar figure of Holger Brauner, the forensics chief. Brauner was dressed in his white coveralls and blue shoe-covers, but had his hood down and was not wearing his mask. He was engaged in conversation with a younger, taller man with long dark hair, swept back from his face and tied in a ponytail. The younger man's dull green T-shirt and his slightly darker green cargo pants hung loosely on his angular frame. They both turned in Fabel's direction as he approached.

'Jan . . .' Holger Brauner beamed at Fabel. 'This is Herr Dr Severts, from the Universität Hamburg's archaeology department. He's in charge of the dig. Dr Severts, this is Principal Chief Commissar Fabel from the Murder Commission.'

Fabel shook Severts's hand. It felt callused and rough, as if the sand and earth in which Severts worked had become ingrained in the skin of his palm. It fitted with the colouring of his clothing; it was as if Severts was himself something of the earth.

'Dr Severts and I were just discussing how close our disciplines are. In fact, I was explaining that my deputy, Frank Grueber, would have been even better suited to this case. He trained as an archaeologist himself before turning to forensics.'

'Grueber?' said Fabel. 'I had no idea he'd been an archaeologist.' Frank Grueber had only been a member of Brauner's team for a little over a year, but Fabel could already see why Brauner had picked him as his deputy: Grueber had shown the same ability as Brauner at a crime scene to read both detail and context. It made sense to Fabel that Grueber had trained as an archaeologist: reading the story of a landscape and that of a crime scene took the same type of intellect. Fabel recalled how he had once asked Grueber why he had become a forensic specialist. 'Truth is the debt that we owe to the dead' had been his reply. It was a reply that had impressed Fabel: it was also a reply that fitted just as well with a career as an archaeologist.

'Archaeology's loss is forensics' gain,' said Brauner. 'I'm lucky to have him on the team. Actually, Frank has an interesting sideline going. He reconstructs faces from skeletonised archaeological remains. Universities from all over the place send him skulls to rebuild. It's something I've always thought could come in handy in identifying unknown remains . . . who knows, maybe today's the day . . .'

'Fraid not,' said Severts. 'This victim's got a face . . . This way, Herr Chief Commissar.' The archaeologist paused while Fabel put on the blue forensic overshoes that Brauner handed him and then led the way across the archaeological site. In one corner the soil had been dug away deeper, in wide stepped tiers. 'We have been taking the opportunity that all this land clearance offers to check out the area for early medieval settlement. This would have been largely marshland, and at one point completely inundated, but this has always been a natural harbour and crossing point . . .'

Brauner interrupted Severts. 'Chief Commissar Fabel studied medieval European history himself.'

The concept of a Murder Commission policeman having an academic background obviously fazed Severts somewhat, because he stopped and looked at Fabel in blank appraisal for a moment. Severts had a long, lean face. After a moment his wide mouth broke into a smile.

'Really? Cool.' He recommenced leading Fabel and Brauner to the corner of the site. They had to step down two levels and stood on an area about five metres square. Each level was smooth and even and Fabel noticed that he could still, just, see out across ground level around them. He couldn't imagine the patience that would be needed for such work – then he gave a small laugh as the image of Werner came to mind.

The excavated ground beneath them was banded,

like rock strata laid on their side: a strange mix of pale sand, dry, black earth and some kind of bright, coarse silicate that glittered in the sunlight. The surface was punctuated with fragments of what looked like rough sacking and then broke into more irregular rubble and stone towards the edges of the area. In one corner of the excavation the upper half of a man's body had been exposed. He was recumbent, on his side with his back to them, but lying at a slight angle so that he remained buried from the waist down. It gave him the appearance of lying in bed.

'We found him early this morning,' Severts explained. 'The team like to get started early . . . get down here before rush hour.'

'Who found him?' asked Fabel.

'Franz Brandt. He's a postgrad student of mine. After we exposed enough of the body to establish that it wasn't ancient, we stopped and contacted the Polizei Hamburg. We photographed and documented every stage of the exposure.'

Fabel and Brauner moved closer to the body. It certainly wasn't ancient. The dead man was wearing a suit jacket of coarse blue serge. They moved around the body until they could see the face. It was thin, pale and pinched, topped with frazzled wisps of blond hair. The closed eyes were sunken into the skull and the neck seemed too thin and scrawny for the still-white shirt collar. The dead man's skin had the look of old, yellowing paper and his wide, sharp jaw was patchily stubbled with two or three days' pale growth. The emaciation made fixing the dead man's age difficult, but there was something about the face and the patchy stubble that suggested youth. His lips were slightly parted, as if he were about to speak, and one hand seemed to grasp at something in the air. Something invisible to the living.

'He can't have been here long,' said Fabel, squatting down. 'As far as I can see, decomposition is limited. But it's the weirdest corpse I've come across in a while. He looks like he has starved to death.' He stood up and looked around the site, his expression puzzled. 'It took a lot of effort for someone to bury him this deep. A lot of effort and a lot of time. I don't see how they could have done it without being noticed, even at night.'

'They didn't,' said Severts. 'There was no sign of the ground around him having been disturbed.'

Brauner bent closer to the body. He touched the face with his latex-sheathed fingers, then, sighing in frustration, he snapped off one of his forensic gloves and touched the papery skin with his naked hand. He smiled grimly and turned to Severts, who nodded knowingly.

'He didn't starve to death, Jan,' said Brauner. 'It's lack of moisture and air that's done this to him. He's desiccated. Completely dried out. A mummy.'

'What?' Fabel crouched down again. 'But he looks like a normal corpse. I thought mummified bodies were all brown and leathery.'

'Only the ones you find in bogs.' A tall, lean young man with red hair tied back in a ponytail had joined them.

'This is Franz Brandt,' said Severts. 'As I told you, it was Franz who uncovered the body.'

Fabel stood up and shook hands with the young red-haired man.

'When I first saw him I suspected right away that he had been mummified.' Brandt continued his explanation. 'Dr Severts here is a leading expert on the subject and I have a great interest in mummies myself. The bog bodies you're thinking about go through a different process entirely: the acids and the tannin in peat bogs tan the skin of the bodies within them. They literally turn into leather bags: sometimes all that's left is their hide, while the internal organs and even the bones can dissolve to nothing.' He nodded towards the body. 'This fellow has the appearance of a desert mummy. The emaciated appearance and the parchment texture of the skin . . . he's been dried out almost immediately in an oxygen-deprived environment.'

'And, despite his appearance, he didn't die recently. But, as you can see from his clothing, he is no relic of the Middle Ages.' Severts indicated the area of the excavation they were in with a sweep of his hand. 'The evidence around the body gives me an idea how it happened. Our geophysics and the records we have for this site suggest that where we are standing was a loading wharf during the Second World War.'

Brauner moved across to the band of glittering dirt. He picked some up and rolled it between his fingers. 'Glass?'

Severts nodded. 'It was sand. Everything here is basically the same pale sand. It's just that some has been mixed with black ash while this outer ring has been subjected to such intense heat that it has turned into crude glass crystals.'

Fabel nodded grimly. 'The British firebombing of nineteen forty-three?'

'That would be my guess,' said Severts. 'It would fit with what we know of this location. And with this form of mummification, which was a common result of the intense temperatures created by the firestorm. It looks to me as if he took cover in some kind of quayside air-raid shelter, improvised with sandbags. There must have been an incendiary burst very close which, basically, baked and buried him.'

Fabel's gaze remained locked on the mummified body. Operation Gomorrah. Eight thousand, three hundred and forty-four tons of incendiaries and high explosives had been dropped on Hamburg by the British by night, the Americans by day. In parts of the city the temperature of the air, out in the open, had reached more than a thousand degrees. Some forty-five thousand Hamburg citizens had burned in the flames or been roasted to death by the intense heat. He gazed at the thin features, made too fine by having the moisture sucked from the flesh beneath the skin. He had been wrong. Of course he had seen bodies like this before: old black-and-white photographs from Hamburg and from Dresden. Many had been baked into mummies without being buried: dried out within moments, exposed to blast-furnace temperatures in the airless open streets or in the air-raid shelters that had been turned into bake ovens. But Fabel had never seen one in the flesh, albeit desiccated flesh.

'It's difficult to believe this man has been dead for more than sixty years,' he said eventually.

Brauner grinned and slapped his broad hand on Fabel's shoulder. 'It's simple biology, Jan. Decomposition requires bacteria; bacteria require oxygen. No oxygen, no bacteria, no decomposition. When we dig him out, we'll probably find some limited putrefaction in his thorax. We all carry bacteria in our gut, and when we die they're the first things to start work on us. Anyway, I'll do a full forensics on the body and then I'll pass it on to the Institute for Legal Medicine in Eppendorf for a full autopsy. We might still be able to confirm a cause of death, which I would gamble a year's salary on being asphyxiation. And we'll be able to work out the rough biological age of the corpse.'

'Okay,' said Fabel. He turned to Severts and his student, Brandt. 'I don't see that we need to hold up the rest of your excavation. But if you find anything in your dig that relates or you think relates to the body, please let me know.' He handed Severts his Polizei Hamburg contact card.

'I will do,' said Severts. He nodded in the direction of the corpse, who still shunned them with his turned shoulder, as if trying to return to a rudely disturbed sleep. 'Looks like he wasn't a murder victim after all.'

Fabel shrugged. 'That all depends on your point of view.'

## 1.50 p.m.: Schanzenviertel, Hamburg

The call had come in as Fabel was making his way back to the Presidium. Werner had phoned to say that he and Maria were in the Schanzenviertel. A killer had been caught, almost literally red-handed, cleaning up the murder scene and about to dispose of the body.

It was clear that Werner had everything in hand, but Fabel felt the need to get involved in a 'live' inquiry after a morning with a cold case that was almost certainly sixty years old and not a homicide. He told Werner that he would head straight over to the address he had given.

'By the way, Jan,' Werner said, 'I think you ought

to know we've got a bit of a celebrity victim . . . Hans-Joachim Hauser.'

Fabel recognised the name immediately. Hauser had been a reasonably prominent member of the radical Left in the 1970s: he was now a vocal environmental campaigner who had a taste for the media limelight. 'God . . . that's weird . . .' Fabel spoke as much to himself as to Werner.

'What is?'

'Synchronicity, I suppose. You know, when something that you would not expect to encounter that often crops up several times in a short space of time. On the way into the Presidium today I heard Bertholdt Müller-Voigt on the radio. You know, the Environment Senator. He was giving his boss Schreiber a really rough time. And two or three nights ago he was in my brother's restaurant at the same time as me and Susanne. If I remember rightly, Müller-Voigt and Hauser used to be very much of a double act back in the nineteen seventies and nineteen eighties.' Fabel paused, then added gloomily: 'That's all we need. A public-figure murder. Any sign of the press yet?'

'Nope,' said Werner. 'Mind you, despite his best efforts, and unlike his chum Müller-Voigt, Hauser really was yesterday's news.'

Fabel sighed. 'Not any more . . .'

There was an untidy exuberance to the Schanzenviertel. It was a part of Hamburg that, like so many others in the city, was undergoing a great many changes. The Schanzenviertel lay just to the north of St Pauli and had not always enjoyed the most salubrious of reputations. The quarter still had its problems, but it had recently become the focus for more affluent incomers.

And, of course, it was the ideal city quarter in which to live if you were a left-wing environmental campaigner. The Schanzenviertel had the credentials of Cool in exactly the right mix: it was one of the most multicultural of Hamburg's districts and its vast range of fashionable restaurants meant that most of the world's cuisines were represented. Its arthouse cinemas, the open-air theatre in the Sternschanzen Park and the requisite number of pavement cafés made it trendy enough to be up and coming; but it also had enough social problems, principally drug-related, not to be seen as too 'yuppie'. It was the kind of place in which you cycled and you recycled, where you wore second-hand chic, but where, while you sat sipping your fair-trade mocha at a pavement table, you tapped away at your ultra-cool, ultra-slim, ultra-expensive titanium laptop computer.

Hans-Joachim Hauser's residence was on the ground floor of a solidly built 1920s apartment block in the heart of the quarter, near where Stresemannstrasse and Schanzenstrasse crossed each other. There was a clutch of police vehicles, in the Polizei Hamburg's new silver and blue livery, parked outside and the pavement in front of the block's entrance was ringed with red-and-white-striped crime scene tape. Fabel parked his BMW untidily behind one of the patrol cars and a uniformed officer headed determinedly over from the perimeter tape to tackle him; Fabel got out of the car and held up his oval *Kriminalpolizei* disc as he strode towards the building and the uniform backed off.

Werner Meyer was waiting at the doorway of Hauser's apartment. 'We can't go in yet, Jan,' he said, gesturing to where, a little way down the hall,

Maria was talking to a young, boyish-looking man in white forensics coveralls. His surgical mask hung loose around his neck and he had the hood pulled down from a thick mop of black hair above a pale bespectacled face. Fabel recognised him as Holger Brauner's deputy, Frank Grueber, whose archae-ology background he had discussed with Brauner and Severts. Grueber and Maria were clearly talking about the crime scene, but there was a relaxed informality about Grueber's posture as they talked. Fabel noticed that Maria, in contrast, leaned back against the wall with her arms folded in front of her.

'*Harry Potter and the Ice Maiden* . . .' Werner said dryly. 'Is it true those two are an item?'

'No idea.' Fabel lied. Maria kept almost all of her personal life locked up tight, along with her emotions, whenever she was at work. But Fabel had been there – the only one there – as she had lain, close to death, after she had been stabbed by one of the most dangerous killers the team had ever hunted. Fabel had shared Maria's terror in those stretched, tense minutes until the Medicopter had arrived. Their shared fear had been a forced intimacy that had created an unspoken bond between them and, during the two years since, Maria had imparted to her boss small confidences about her personal life – but only those things that could possibly have had some bearing on her work. One of these confidences had been that she had become involved with Frank Grueber.

Down the hall, Grueber concluded his briefing to Maria. He touched her elbow in a gesture of farewell and headed back down the apartment hallway. There was something about that gesture that bothered

Fabel. Not the informality of it: rather the almost imperceptible tensing of Maria's posture in response. As if a very faint electric current had been passed to her.

Maria came back down the hall to the doorway. 'We still can't go in,' she explained. 'Grueber has his work really cut out for him. The killer – a woman – was disturbed cleaning up the scene. Apparently she made too good a job of it and forensics are finding it hard to pick up anything worthwhile.' She shrugged. 'But it's academic, I suppose. If you catch the killer at the scene then there's no better forensic trace than that.'

Fabel turned to Maria. 'The suspect was disturbed cleaning up the scene . . . by whom?'

'A friend of Hauser's . . .' said Maria. 'A very young, pretty male friend of Hauser's called Sebastian Lang, who found the door unlocked . . . although apparently he did have a key himself.'

Fabel nodded. Hans-Joachim Hauser had never made any secret of his homosexuality.

'Lang had come back to pick something up from the apartment before going into town for lunch,' continued Maria. 'He heard noises from the bathroom and, assuming it was Hauser, went through and disturbed the killer as she cleaned up the scene.'

'Where is the suspect?' asked Fabel.

'Uniform have taken her back to the Presidium for us,' Werner answered. 'She seems a pretty disturbed individual . . . no one could get much sense out of her, other than she wasn't finished cleaning.'

'Okay. If we can't get into the crime scene, then we should maybe head back to the Murder

Commission and interview the suspect. But I'd like Frau Doctor Eckhardt to do a psychological assessment of her first.' Fabel snapped open his cellphone and hit a pre-set button.

'Institute for Legal Medicine . . . Doctor Eckhardt speaking . . .' The voice that answered was female: deep and warm and tinged with a soft Bavarian accent.

'Hi, Susanne . . . it's me. How's it going?'

She sighed. 'Wishing we were back on Sylt . . . What's up?'

Fabel explained about the arrest of the woman in Schanzenviertel and that he wanted Susanne to do an assessment before they interrogated her.

'I'm tied up until late afternoon. Is four p.m. okay?'

Fabel looked at his watch. It was one-thirty. If they waited for the assessment it would mean they would not get to interview the suspect until the early evening.

'Okay. But I think we'll have to have a preliminary with her beforehand.'

'Fine. I'll see you at four at the Presidium,' said Susanne. 'What's the suspect's name?'

'Just a second . . .' Fabel turned to Maria. 'What name do we have for the woman in custody?'

Maria flipped open her notebook and scanned her notes for a moment.

'Dreyer . . .' she said eventually.

'Kristina Dreyer?'

Maria looked at Fabel in surprise. 'Yes. You know her?'

Fabel didn't answer Maria but spoke again to Susanne. 'I'll call you back,' he said, and snapped his cellphone shut. Then he turned to Maria. 'Get

Grueber. Tell him I don't care what stage forensics are at – I want to see the murder scene and the victim. Now.'

## 2.10 p.m.: Schanzenviertel, Hamburg

It was clear that Grueber recognised the futility of trying to deny the Murder Commission team access to the murder scene. But with a determined authority that did not sit well with his youthful looks he had insisted that, instead of the usual requirement of blue forensic overshoes and latex gloves, the team should all wear the full forensic coverall suits and face masks.

'She has left us practically nothing,' explained Grueber. 'It's the most thorough clean-up of a scene that I've ever come across. She's gone over almost every surface with a bleach-based cleaner or solution. It destroys practically all forensic traces and degrades any surviving DNA.'

After they were suited up, Grueber led Fabel, Werner and Maria through the hall. Fabel took in each of the rooms as he passed. There was at least one forensic technician working in each. Fabel noticed how tidy and clean the apartment was. It was large and spacious, but had an almost cramped feeling to it that came from the way nearly every free square metre of wall space was devoted to bookshelves. There were magazines carefully stacked on a unit and the hall's shelves had obviously been used to cope with the overflow of books, vinyl LPs and CDs from the living room. Fabel paused and examined some of the music. There were several Reinhard Mey albums, but they were mostly older stuff that had been reissued on CD.

Hauser had obviously felt the need to hear the protest songs of one generation on the technology of the next. Fabel gave a small laugh of recognition as he noticed a CD of *Ewigkeit* by Cornelius Tamm. Tamm had styled himself as Germany's Bob Dylan and had enjoyed fair success in the 1960s before taking a spectacular dive into obscurity. Fabel removed a large, glossy-sleeved book from the shelves: it was a collection of Don McCullin's Vietnam photographs; next to it was a travel book in English and various textbooks on ecology. All was just as you would have expected. Where there was a break in the shelving, any clear wall space had been filled with framed posters. Fabel stopped in front of one: it was a framed black-and-white photograph of a young man with flowing shoulder-length hair and a moustache. He was stripped to the waist and was sitting on a rustic bench, an apple in his hand.

'Who's the hippie?' Werner was now at Fabel's shoulder.

'Take a look at the date on the picture: eighteen ninety-nine. This guy was a hippie seventy years before anyone even thought of the concept. This' – Fabel tapped the glass with his latex-sheathed finger – 'is Gustav Nagel, patron saint of all German eco-warriors. A century ago he was trying to get Germany to reject industrialisation and militarism, embrace pacifism, become vegetarian and to get back to nature. Mind you, he also wanted us to stop using capital letters with nouns. I don't know how that fits into a green agenda. Maybe less ink.'

Fabel returned Nagel's clear-eyed, defiant stare for a moment, and then followed Grueber and the others to the corner of the hall.

The main focus of the forensic team's attention was at the far end of the hall and in the bathroom itself.

'We found a couple of plastic bin bags here,' explained Grueber as they approached the bathroom door. 'We've removed a couple of items separately but the bags are back at Butenfeld.' Grueber used the shorthand for the forensics unit at the Institute for Legal Medicine, the same facility in which Susanne worked as a criminal psychologist. The Institute was part of the University Clinic at Butenfeld, to the north of the city. 'One of our finds was this . . .' Grueber beckoned to one of the technicians who handed him a large square transparent plastic forensics bag. The plastic was thick and semi-rigid: inside, spread flat, was a disc of thick skin and hair. A human scalp. Viscous puddles of blood had gathered in pockets between the bag's plastic walls and in its corners.

Fabel examined the contents without taking the bag from Grueber. He ignored the nausea that churned in his gut and the disgusted muttering of Werner behind him. The hair was red. Too red. Grueber read Fabel's mind.

'The hair has been treated with dye. And there's evidence of the dye fresh on the scalp and contiguous skin areas. I can't tell yet whether the killer used hair dye or some other type of pigment. Whatever was used, my guess is that it was done immediately before the scalp was removed from the body.'

'Speaking of which . . . where is it?' Fabel snapped his attention away from the magnetic horror of the scalp. After all these years in the Murder Commission, after so many cases, he still often found himself left shocked and uncomprehending by the cruelty that human beings are capable of inflicting upon one another.

Grueber nodded. 'This way – you can guess this isn't going to be too pleasant to look at . . .'

Fabel could tell as soon as they set foot in the bathroom that Grueber really had not exaggerated the difficulty they faced forensically. There was absolutely nothing, other than the body-shaped package next to the bath, that would have given any hint that this was a murder scene. Even the air smelled bleach-rinsed and slightly lemony. Every surface gleamed.

'Kristina Dreyer may be our murder suspect,' said Werner grimly, 'but I think I'll find out what her hourly rate is . . . we could do with her over at my place.'

'It's funny you should say that,' said Maria, without the slightest hint that she had picked up on Werner's humour. 'She really is a professional cleaner. She works for herself and had a carload of cleaning materials parked outside . . . Hence the efficiency with which she tidied this lot up.'

'Okay,' said Fabel. 'Let's have a look at what we've got.'

It was as if the forensic specialists had added another layer of bandages to a mummy. The killer had already wrapped the body in the shower curtain and bound it up with parcel tape. Now the forensic technicians had added individually numbered strips of Taser tape to every square centimetre of the outer shower curtain and parcel tape. The body had been photographed from every angle, and would now be moved back to the forensics lab at Butenfeld. Once there, the Taser would be removed strip by strip, and transferred to clear perspex sheets and any forensic traces would therefore be secured for analysis. If the body underneath the shower curtain was discovered to be wearing clothes, the process would be repeated to gather any fibre or other traces from the clothing.

Fabel gazed down at the man-shaped package. 'Open up the face. I want to make sure this is Hauser.'

Grueber eased away the shower curtain. Underneath, the head and shoulders were encased in black plastic. Fabel gave an impatient nod and Grueber delicately cut through the parcel tape and exposed the face and head. Hans-Joachim Hauser gazed out at them with clouded-glass eyes beneath his frowning brow. Fabel had expected to feel another lurch in his gut, but instead he felt nothing as he looked down at the thing before him. And that was what it was: a thing. An effigy. There was something about the disfigurement of the head, about the exposed bone of the dead man's cranium, about the blood-drained waxiness of the flesh on Hauser's face, that robbed the corpse of its humanity.

Fabel had also expected to experience some form of recognition: Hans-Joachim Hauser had been very much involved in the radical movement of the 1970s and 1980s. Hauser had been photographed with the appropriate luminaries of the radical Left over the years – Daniel Cohn-Bendit, Petra Kelly, Joschka Fischer, Bertholdt Müller-Voigt – but, despite his best efforts, he had lingered somewhere between the centre and the fringes of the media spotlight. Fabel thought how people seemed trapped in a time: how some found it impossible to move on. The image of Hauser filed in Fabel's memory was that of a slim, almost girlish young man with long, thick hair, berating the Hamburg Senate in the 1980s. Nothing in the grey, waxy and slightly puffy flesh of the dead face gave Fabel a point of reference from which to retrieve the earlier Hans-Joachim Hauser. Fabel even tried to imagine the corpse with hair. It didn't help.

'Nice,' said Werner, as if there was a bad taste in his mouth. 'Very nice. A cleaning lady who takes scalps. I don't suppose she's a Red Indian, by any chance.'

'Scalping is an ancient European tradition,' said Fabel. 'We were at it millennia before the Native Americans. They probably learned it from European settlers.'

Grueber eased more of the shower-curtain wrapping from the body, exposing Hauser's neck. 'Take a look at this . . .'

There was a wide sweeping gash across the throat. The edge was clean and unbroken, almost surgical, and Fabel could see a stratum of marbled grey and white flesh beneath the skin. The cut was also bloodless: Kristina Dreyer had washed the body and what Fabel could see of it had the look of rinsed death that he associated with mortuary bodies.

Fabel turned to Maria and Werner. He was about to say something when he noticed that Maria was gazing fixedly at Hauser's mutilated head and neck. It was not a horror-struck stare, nor was it her usual look of cool appraisal: it was more a blank, expressionless gaze, as if what was left of Hans-Joachim Hauser held her hypnotised.

'Maria?' Fabel frowned questioningly. Maria seemed to snap back from some distant place.

'It must have been very sharp . . .' she said, dully. 'The blade, I mean. To cut so cleanly, it must have been razor sharp.'

'Yes, it was,' answered Grueber, still crouched at the body. Fabel noticed that although Grueber delivered a professional answer, there was a hint of personal concern in his expression as he looked up at Maria. 'It might have been a surgical blade, or even an open razor.'

Fabel straightened up. He thought about the woman who had been taken into custody. About a face he vaguely remembered from more than a decade ago.

'This is all so methodical,' he said at last. He turned to Werner. 'You sure the suspect, Kristina Dreyer, was actually caught cleaning this up? I mean, we know for sure that she did all this?'

'No doubt about it,' said Werner. 'In fact, the uniform unit had to restrain her. She wouldn't stop cleaning, even after they arrived.'

Fabel scanned the bathroom once more. It shone as sterile and as cold as an operating theatre. 'It doesn't make any sense,' he said at last.

'What doesn't?' asked Maria.

'Why all of the mutilation? The scalping, the over-done cut to the throat. It all seems significant . . . as if there's a message in it.'

'There usually is,' said Grueber, who had now straightened his gangly frame and was standing beside the three detectives. They all gazed down, gathered in a semicircle, at the flesh-and-bone effigy of what had once been a human being. When they spoke, it was as if they addressed the corpse: a silent moderator through whom they could better transmit their thoughts. 'And the whole point of scalping is that you *take* scalps. I don't understand why your killer would scalp her victim and then put the scalp in a bin liner with the intention of dumping it.'

'That's my point,' said Fabel. 'This all points to some kind of message. Some kind of sick symbolism. But it's almost always done so that others may bear witness to it. It's hardly ever done especially for the victim, who's usually dead before the mutilation.'

Maria nodded. 'So why screw it all up? Why do all of that and then go to so much trouble to clean up the crime scene and hide the body? And why just dump your trophy?'

'Exactly. I want us to get back to the Presidium. I need to talk to Kristina Dreyer. This just isn't fitting together for me.'

Just then, one of the forensic technicians called over to Grueber. Fabel, Maria and Werner gathered behind Grueber as he crouched down to examine the area indicated by the forensic technician, on the seam between the tiled bath side and the floor. Whatever it was, Fabel couldn't see it.

'What are we looking at?'

The technician took out a pair of surgical tweezers, eased something free and held it up. It was a hair.

'I don't get it . . .' said the technician. 'I checked here before and completely missed this.'

'Don't worry about it. It's easy to do,' said Grueber. 'I was over here earlier myself and didn't see it either. The important thing is that you found it.'

Fabel strained to see the hair. 'I'm surprised you discovered it at all.'

Grueber took the tweezers from the technician and held up the hair to the light. He flipped open a magnifying lens from its case and peered at the hair like a jeweller appraising a valuable diamond.

'Funny . . .'

'What is?' asked Fabel.

'This hair is red. Naturally red, not dyed like the scalp. Anyway, it's too long to have been the victim's. Does the suspect have red hair?'

'No,' answered Fabel, and Maria and Werner exchanged looks. Kristina Dreyer had been taken from the scene before Fabel had arrived.

### 3.15 p.m.: Police Presidium, Alsterdorf, Hamburg

When Fabel entered the interview room, Kristina Dreyer's expression was almost one of relief. She sat, small and forlorn, dressed in the too-big white forensic coverall they had given her when they took her own clothes for analysis.

'Hello, Kristina,' said Fabel, and drew up a chair next to Werner and Maria. As he did so, he handed Werner a file.

'Hello, Herr Fabel.' Tears welled up in Kristina's dull blue eyes and one escaped across the roughened terrain of her cheekbone. There was a stretched vibrato in her voice. 'I hoped it would be you. I've got all messed up again, Herr Fabel. It's all gone . . . crazy . . . again.'

'Why did you do it, Kristina?' asked Fabel.

'I had to. I had to clear it all up. I couldn't let it win again.'

'Let what win?' asked Maria.

'The madness. The mess . . . all that blood.'

Werner, who had been flicking through the file, closed it and leaned back in his chair with an expression that suggested everything had suddenly fallen into place for him.

'I'm sorry, Kristina,' said Werner. 'I didn't recognise

your name to start with. We've been here before, haven't we?'

Kristina looked to Fabel with a beseeching terror in her eyes. Fabel noticed that, at the same time, she began to tremble, and her breathing became laboured and fast. Fabel had seen frightened suspects before, but there was something body-racking about the terror that seemed suddenly to seize Kristina, and an alarm sounded somewhere in Fabel's mind.

'Are you feeling all right, Kristina?' he asked. She nodded.

'This isn't the same. This isn't the same at all . . .' she said to Werner. 'The last time . . .' Her voice trailed off and Fabel noticed that the trembling had become a pronounced shake.

'Are you sure you're feeling all right?' he asked again.

It all happened so fast that Fabel didn't have time to react. Kristina's breathing took on an emphatic, urgent stridor; her face first flushed a bright, feverish red and then drained of all colour. She half-rose from her chair and grasped the edges of the table with a grip that turned her detergent-reddened knuckles yellow-white. Each inhalation became a long spasm that convulsed her body, yet her exhalations seemed short and insubstantial. She looked like someone trapped in a vacuum: desperately sucking at the void to fill her screaming lungs. Kristina lurched forward, jackknifing at the waist, her head coming down fast and hard towards the table top. Then, as if tugged at by an invisible rope, she lurched to the right and keeled over sideways. Fabel rushed forward to catch her.

Maria moved so fast that Fabel did not notice her send her chair crashing to the floor. Suddenly she had shouldered him out of the way and had grabbed Kristina firmly by the upper arms and eased her to the floor. She loosened the zip of Kristina's coveralls at the neck.

'A bag . . .' Maria barked at Fabel and Werner, who stared down at her uncomprehendingly. 'Get me a bag. A paper bag, a carrier bag – anything.'

Werner dashed from the room. Fabel kneeled down next to Maria. She took hold of Kristina's face between her hands and locked stares with her.

'Listen to me, Kristina, you're going to be all right. You're just having a panic attack. Try to control your breathing.' Maria turned to Fabel. 'She's in a state of extreme panic. She's over-oxygenating her bloodstream . . . Get a doctor.'

Werner burst back in the room, clutching a brown paper bag. Maria placed it over Kristina's nose and mouth, clamping it tight. Each gasping breath crumpled the bag in on itself. Eventually something approaching a regular rhythm returned to Kristina's breathing. Two paramedics came into the interview room and Maria stood up and moved back to let them work.

'She'll be all right now,' she said. 'But I think you'd better let Frau Doctor Eckhardt carry out her assessment before we re-interview her.

'That was very impressive,' said Werner. 'How did you know what to do?'

Maria shrugged, unsmiling. 'Basic first aid.'

But, for the second time in a day, there was something about Maria's body language that gave Fabel a vague feeling of uneasiness.

Fabel, Maria and Werner sat in the Police Presidium canteen, drinking coffee at a table near the wide window that looked over and down to the Riot Squad barracks across the car park below.

'So it was your case?' asked Werner.

'One of my first in the Murder Commission,' said Fabel. 'The Ernst Rauhe case. He was a serious sexual sadist – a serial rapist and murderer who chalked up six victims in the 1980s before he was nailed. He was judged to be criminally insane and they put him in the Krankenhaus Ochsenzoll high-security hospital wing. He'd already been there for several years before I came to the Murder Commission.'

'He escaped?' asked Maria.

'He certainly did . . .' It was Werner who answered. 'I was in uniform at the time and got involved in the manhunt . . . a lowly grunt traipsing across the moors in search of a lunatic. But he had had help.'

'Kristina?'

'Yes.' Fabel stared at his coffee, swirling its surface with a spoon, as if stirring his memories in the cup. 'She was a nurse at the hospital. Ernst Rauhe was not particularly intelligent, but he was a consummate manipulator of people. And, as you can see, Kristina doesn't have the most resilient of personalities. Rauhe persuaded Kristina that she was the love of his life, his salvation. She was absolutely won over by him and became totally convinced that he was innocent of all the charges against him. But, of course, because he had been committed to a mental hospital he would never be believed if he tried to prove it. Or so he claimed.' Fabel paused and took a sip of his coffee. 'It came out later that Kristina had wanted to campaign for his freedom. But he had convinced her it would be futile and that she needed to hide her support for him from the world, until they were ready to use it to its best advantage.'

'And that was by helping him escape . . .' said Werner. 'If I remember correctly, she didn't just help him escape, she hid him in her apartment.'

'Oh God . . .' said Maria. 'I remember!'

Fabel nodded. 'As Werner said, almost every uniform and detective unit in Greater Hamburg, Niedersachsen and Schleswig-Holstein searched for him. No one considered that he might have had inside help nor that he had been driven away in comfort from the secure wing. For nearly two weeks every barn, outbuilding and doss-house was turned over. It was over a month later that the hospital got in touch. They had been increasingly concerned about the well-being of one of their nurses. She had been losing weight and had turned up for work with bruises. Then she had failed to come into work at all for several days and hadn't made any kind of contact. It was then that the hospital worked out that, although it had been limited, she had had some contact with Rauhe. In addition to the weight loss and bruises, colleagues had reported that this nurse's behaviour had become increasingly strange and furtive in the weeks before her disappearance.'

'And that nurse was Kristina Dreyer.' Maria concluded the thought.

Fabel nodded. 'Our first thought was that Rauhe had stalked her after his escape, having targeted her while a patient; and that he had subsequently abducted and probably murdered her. So the Murder Commission became involved. I took a unit up to Kristina's flat in Harburg. We heard sounds from inside . . . whining . . . so we broke down the door.

And, just as we'd expected, there was a murder scene waiting for us. But it wasn't Kristina who'd been murdered. She was standing, naked, in the middle of the apartment. She was covered from head to toe with blood. In fact, the whole room was covered in blood. She was holding an axe in her hand and there, on the floor, was what was left of Ernst Rauhe.'

'Now we've got history repeating itself?' said Maria.

Fabel sighed. 'I don't know. It just doesn't fit. It came out during the investigation that Ernst Rauhe had amused himself during the latter part of his liberty by repeatedly raping and torturing Kristina. She had been a pretty little thing, apparently, but in the last few days he beat her face to a pulp. But it was maybe the psychological torment he inflicted more than the physical abuse that drove her to kill him. He had made her crawl around naked, like a dog. He wouldn't let her wash. It was awful. Then, repeatedly, he strangled her, always almost to the point of death. She realised that it was only a matter of time before he tired of her. And when he tired of her, she knew that he would murder her, as he had all the others.'

'So she struck first?'

'Yes. She hit him in the back of the head with the axe. But she was too small and light and the blow didn't kill him. When he came at her, she just kept hacking and hacking at him with the axe. Ernst Rauhe eventually bled to death, but the evidence showed that Kristina went on hacking at him long after he was dead. There was blood, flesh and bone all over the place. She had really mashed up his face. At that time it was by far the worst murder scene I had ever attended.'

Maria and Werner sat quiet for a moment, as if transported to the small rented apartment in Harburg, where a younger Fabel had stood, stunned and horrified in a scene from hell.

'Kristina was never convicted of Rauhe's murder,' Fabel continued. 'It was acknowledged that she had been driven temporarily insane by Rauhe's sadistic treatment of her and, in any case, had a pretty good reason to believe that he was going to kill her. But she did get six years in Fuhlsbüttel for aiding his escape. If he had actually killed someone else while he'd been at liberty, I doubt if Kristina would have got less than fifteen.'

'You're right,' said Maria eventually. 'It doesn't make any sense. As far as we know, Kristina had no involvement with Hauser other than as his weekly cleaner. And we saw the mutilation of the corpse. That took time. It was deliberate and it would have taken premeditation . . . planning. And it was meant to have some kind of significance. From what you've said, when Kristina killed Rauhe it was a frenzy, brought on by a build-up of sustained terror that tipped over into sudden panic or fury. It was all hot blood. Hauser's killing was clearly planned. Cold-blooded.'

Fabel nodded. 'That's what I think. Just look at the attack she just had. She's clearly highly strung. It doesn't fit with what we saw at the murder scene.'

'Hold on,' said Werner. 'Aren't we forgetting the fact that she was caught trying to hide her handi-work . . . if you're innocent, why try to conceal evidence? Plus, it's a hell of a coincidence that the person we catch there just happens to have been convicted of killing someone before.'

'I know,' said Fabel. 'I'm not saying that it isn't

Kristina. All I'm saying is that the pieces don't yet fit and we have to keep an open mind.'

Werner shrugged. 'You're the boss . . .'

## 5.30 p.m.: Police Presidium, Alsterdorf, Hamburg

By the time that Susanne had given Fabel the okay to re-interview Kristina Dreyer, the accumulated dragging weight of his first day back at work was slowing him down. He and Susanne sat in his office, drinking coffee, and discussed Kristina's state of mind. The dull, resigned tiredness in Susanne's dark eyes reflected Fabel's own. What had started out as a quiet first day back for them both had turned into something complex and taxing.

'You are going to have to take it very easy with her,' said Susanne. 'She's in a very fragile state. And I really feel that I'd like to sit in on the interview.'

'Okay . . .' Fabel rubbed his eyes, as if trying to banish the tiredness from them. 'What's your assessment of her?'

'It's clear that she suffers from severe neurosis rather than any kind of psychosis. I have to say that, despite the evidence against her, I feel she is a highly unlikely candidate for this murder. My take on Kristina Dreyer is that she is more victim than perpetrator.'

'All right . . .' Fabel held open the door for Susanne. 'Let's go and find out.'

Kristina Dreyer looked small and vulnerable in the white forensic coverall that she was still wearing from earlier in the day. Fabel sat over by the wall and allowed Maria and Werner to lead the interview.

Susanne sat beside Kristina, who had declined the right to legal representation.

'You feel up to talking, Kristina?' Maria asked, although there was not much solicitude in her voice and she switched on the black tape recorder before waiting for an answer. Kristina nodded.

'I just want to get this whole thing cleared up,' she said. 'I didn't kill him. I didn't kill Herr Hauser. I hardly ever saw him.'

'But, Kristina,' said Werner, 'you've killed before. And we found you cleaning up the scene of this murder. If you want to get this "all cleared up", why don't you just tell us the truth? We know you killed Herr Hauser and you tried to cover it up. If you hadn't been disturbed, you would have got away with it.'

Kristina stared at Werner but didn't answer. Fabel thought he could see her tremble slightly.

'Ease up a little, Chief Commissar,' said Susanne to Werner. She turned to Kristina and softened her tone. 'Kristina, Herr Hauser has been murdered. What you did by cleaning up the mess has made it very difficult for the police to find out exactly what happened. And the longer it takes them to get to the bottom of it all, the more difficult it will be to find the killer, if it wasn't you. You need to tell the officers everything you can about exactly what happened.'

Kristina Dreyer nodded again, then shot a look across Maria's shoulder at Fabel, as if seeking support from the officer who had arrested her over ten years before. 'You know what happened before, Herr Fabel. You know what Ernst Rauhe did to me . . .'

'Yes, I do, Kristina. And I want to understand

what happened this time. Did Herr Hauser do something to you?'

'No . . . God, no. Like I said, I hardly ever saw Herr Hauser. He was always out at work when I cleaned his place. He would leave me my money in an envelope on the hallstand. He didn't do anything to me. Ever.'

'So what happened, Kristina? If you didn't kill Herr Hauser, why were you found cleaning up the murder scene?'

'There was so much blood. So much blood. Everywhere. It drove me mad.' Kristina paused; then, although it still quivered, her voice hardened, as if she had drawn a steel line taut through her nerves. 'I arrived to clean Herr Hauser's place this morning, just as usual. I have a key and I let myself in. I knew there was something wrong as soon as I went into the apartment. Then I found . . . Then I found that *thing* . . .'

'The scalp?' asked Fabel.

Kristina nodded.

'Where was it?' asked Maria.

'It was pinned out on the bathroom door. It took an age to clean.'

'Just a moment,' said Werner. 'What time did you arrive at Herr Hauser's apartment?'

'Eight fifty-seven. Exactly eight fifty-seven a.m.' As she answered, Kristina rubbed at a point on the surface of the interview table with her fingertip. 'I'm never, ever late. You can check my appointment book.'

'So after you found the scalp, you put it in the bin bag and started to clean up the door?' asked Werner.

'No. First I went into the bathroom and found Herr Hauser.'

'Where was he?'

'Between the toilet and the bath. Half-sitting, sort of . . .'

'And you say he was already dead at this point?' asked Maria.

'Yes.' Kristina's eyes glossed with tears. 'He was sitting there with the top of his head ripped off . . . it was horrible.'

'Okay,' said Susanne. 'Just take a moment to calm yourself.'

Kristina sniffed hard and nodded. She absent-mindedly moistened her fingertip with her tongue and rubbed again at the same spot on the table top, as if trying to wipe off some blemish that was totally invisible to the others in the room.

'It was horrible,' she continued eventually. 'Horrible. How could anyone do that to a person? And Herr Hauser seemed so nice. Like I told you, he was almost always at work when I was in to clean, but whenever I did meet him he seemed very friendly and polite. I just don't know why anyone would do such a thing to him . . .'

'What we don't know or understand,' said Maria, 'is why anyone, if they found a murder scene, would choose not to contact the police but instead set about cleaning it up . . . and in the process destroy essential evidence. If you're innocent, Kristina, why did you try to hide all traces of the crime?'

Kristina continued to rub at the invisible stain on the veneer surface of the interview table. Then she spoke without looking up.

'They said I was mentally unsound when I killed Rauhe. That the balance of my mind was disturbed. I don't know about that. But I do know that in prison, for a while, I was crazy. I nearly lost my mind completely. It was because of what Rauhe did to me. Because of what I did to him.' She looked up, her face hard, her eyes red-rimmed and moist with tears. 'I would have panic attacks. Really bad ones. Much worse than the one I had today. I would feel as if I were suffocating, being smothered by the air I was breathing. It was like everything I was afraid of, everything I'd ever been afraid of, and all that terror Rauhe had put me through . . . all coming together at the one moment. The first time I thought it was a heart attack . . . and I was glad. I thought I was getting out of this hell. The prison put me on suicide watch and sent me for sessions with the prison psychiatrist. They said I was suffering from extreme post-traumatic stress and obsessive-compulsive disorder.'

'What form did the OCD take?' asked Susanne.

'I developed a severe phobia about contamination . . . dirt, germs. Especially anything to do with blood. It became so strong that I stopped menstruating. I spent most of my time in prison in and out of the hospital wing. Anything could spark me off. The panic attacks became more and more severe until eventually they put me in the prison hospital wing permanently.'

'What did they treat you with?' asked Susanne.

'Chlordiazepoxide and amitriptyline. They took me off the amitriptyline because it zonked me too much. I also got plenty of therapy and that helped a lot. If you've been through my record, you'll know I was released early.'

'So the therapy worked?' asked Werner.

'Yes and no . . . I got much better and was able to cope. But it was after I was released that I really started to get better. I was referred to a special clinic here in

Hamburg. One that only deals with phobias, anxiety disorders and obsessive-compulsive disorders.'

'The Fear Clinic run by Dr Minks?' asked Maria.

'Yes . . . that's the one.' Kristina sounded surprised.

There was a brief silence as everyone waited for Maria to follow up her question. But she did not, instead holding Kristina in her steady blue-grey gaze.

'Dr Minks worked wonders,' Kristina continued. 'He helped me get my life back. To get myself together again.'

'It must have been effective.' Werner leaned back in his chair and smiled. 'For you to become a cleaner. I mean, does that not mean you face your worst fear each and every day?'

'But that's exactly it!' Kristina suddenly became animated. 'Dr Minks got me to confront my demons. My fears. It started in small steps, with Dr Minks there to support me. I was exposed more and more to the things that would trigger my panic attacks.'

'Flooding . . .' Susanne nodded. 'The object of terror becomes an object of familiarity.'

'That's right – that's exactly what Dr Minks called it. He said I could learn to control and channel my phobia, ultimately diminishing and conquering it.' It was clear from the manner in which Kristina delivered the words that she was using an unaccustomed vocabulary learned from her psychologist. 'He showed me that I could control chaos and get my life in order. So much so that it ended up that I became a cleaner.' She paused and the zeal disappeared from her expression. 'When I walked into Herr Hauser's apartment . . . when I saw Herr Hauser and what had been done to him, I thought my world was falling apart. It was like I was right back in my old apartment, when I . . .' She let the thought die. 'But Dr Minks taught me that I have to stay in control. He told me that I shouldn't allow my past or my fear to define me, to define what I was capable of becoming. Dr Minks explained that I have to contain what I fear and by doing so contain the fear itself. There was blood. So much blood. It was like I was standing on the edge of a cliff or something. I really felt I was one step away from going mad. I had to take control. I had to get hold of the fear before it got hold of me.'

'So you started to clean? Is that what you're saying?' Werner asked.

'Yes. The blood first. It took so long. Then everything else. I didn't let it win.' Kristina rubbed again at the invisible spot on the table top. One last time. Decisively. 'Don't you see? The Chaos didn't win. I stayed in control.'

### 7.10 p.m.: Police Presidium, Alsterdorf, Hamburg

The team had a brief meeting after the Kristina Dreyer interview. She remained the prime suspect and she was to be held in custody overnight, but it was clear that none of the team was convinced of her guilt.

After Fabel had wound the meeting up, he asked Maria to stay behind.

'Is everything okay, Maria?' he asked her when they were alone. Maria's expression eloquently transmitted impatience and confusion. 'It's just that you didn't say much in there.'

'I tend to think there wasn't much to say, to be honest, *Chef*. I think we'll have to see what the forensic and pathology exams tell us about exactly what happened. Not that Kristina Dreyer left us much to go on.'

Fabel nodded thoughtfully, then asked: 'How do you know about this Fear Clinic she was attending?'

'It got quite a bit of publicity when it opened. There was an article about it in the *Abendblatt*. It's unique, and when Kristina Dreyer said she was attending a special clinic it was the only one that would fit.' If Maria was hiding something, then Fabel could not read it in her face. Fabel found himself, not for the first time, becoming deeply irritated by her closed-off countenance. After what they had been through together, he felt that he deserved her confidence. He felt the urge to confront her; to ask just what the hell her problem was. But, if there was anything Fabel knew about himself, it was that he was a typical male of his age and background: he habitually repressed spontaneous expression of his feelings. It meant that he approached things in a more measured way; it also meant that he often churned deep inside with the turmoil of his feelings. He dropped the subject. He did not mention that he was concerned about Maria's behaviour. He did not ask her if her life remained shredded by the horror of what had happened to her. Most of all, he did not give name to the monster whose spectre would, at times like these, stand between them: Vasyl Vitrenko.

Vitrenko had entered their lives as a shadowy suspect in a murder inquiry and had made a very tangible mark on every member of the team. Vitrenko, a Ukrainian, had been a former Spetsnaz officer and was as skilled with the instruments of death as a surgeon was with those of life. He had used Maria as a delaying tactic while he made his escape: callously leaving her life hanging in the balance and forcing Fabel to give up his pursuit.

'What do you think, Maria?' he said eventually. 'About Dreyer, I mean . . . Do you think she did it?'

'It's entirely possible that she took that step into madness again. Maybe she doesn't remember killing Hauser. Maybe cleaning up the murder scene has wiped the memory of the murder from her mind. Or maybe she is telling the truth.' Maria paused. 'Fear can make us all behave in a strange way.'

## 8.00 p.m.: Marienthal, Hamburg

It was, after all, what Dr Gunter Griebel had devoted much of his life to. As soon as he had seen the pale, dark-haired young man, there had been that instant of recognition; the instinctive knowledge that he was looking at a face that was familiar to him. Someone he knew.

But the young man was not someone whom Griebel knew. As they talked, it became clear that they had not met before. Yet the sense of familiarity remained, and with it the unshakeable, tantalising feeling that complete recognition was only a moment away; that if only he could place the face in a context then all would fall into place. And the gaze of the young man was disconcerting: a laser beam fixed on the older man.

They moved into the study and Griebel offered his guest a drink, which he declined. There was something strange about the way the young man moved around the house, as if each movement was measured, calculated. After a moment's awkwardness Griebel indicated that his guest should sit.

'Thanks for agreeing to meet with me,' said the

younger man. 'I apologise for the unorthodox manner in which I introduced myself to you. I had no intention of disturbing you while you paid your respects to your late wife, but it was pure chance that we were at the same place at the same time, just when I was going to phone you to try to arrange a meeting.'

'You said you are a scientist yourself?' Griebel asked, more to prevent an awkward silence than out of genuine interest. 'What's your field?'

'It's not unrelated to yours, Dr Griebel. I am fascinated by your research, particularly how a trauma suffered in one generation may have consequences for the generations that follow. Or that we pile one memory on another, generation after generation.' The younger man stretched his hands out on the leather of the armchair. He looked at his hands, at the leather, as if contemplating them. 'In my own way I am a seeker after the truth. The truth I seek perhaps isn't as universal as yours, but the answer lies in the same area.' He brought his laser-beam gaze back to bear on Griebel. 'But the reason I am here is not professional. It's personal.'

'In what way personal?' Griebel again sought to remember if and where they had met before, or of whom it was that the young man reminded him.

'As I explained to you when we met in the graveyard, I am looking for answers for some of the mysteries in my own life. All my life I have been haunted by memories that are not mine . . . by a *life* that is not mine. And that is why you, your research, interests me so much.'

'With the greatest respect.' Griebel's voice was edged with irritation. 'I've heard all this kind of thing before. I'm not a philosopher. I'm not a psychologist and I'm certainly not some kind of quasi-New Age guru. I am a scientist investigating scientific realities. I didn't agree to meet you to explore the enigmas of your existence. I only agreed to meet you because of what you said about . . . well, about the past . . . the names you mentioned. Where did you get those names? What made you think the people you mentioned have anything to do with me?'

The young man smiled a broad, cold, joyless smile. 'It seems so very long ago, doesn't it, Gunter? A lifetime ago. You, me and the others? You've tried to move on . . . make a new life. If you can call the bourgeois banality you've been hiding behind a life. And all the time trying to pretend that the past didn't happen.'

Griebel's brow creased into a frown. He concentrated hard. Even the voice was familiar: tones he had heard – somewhere, sometime – before. 'Who are you?' he asked at last. 'What do you want?'

'It's been so very long, Gunter. You all felt safe in your new lives, didn't you? You all thought that you had put everything behind you. Put me behind you. But you all built your new lives on treachery.' The younger man indicated Griebel's study, the equipment, the books, with a dismissive sweep of his hand. 'You have devoted so much time, so much of your life, to your studies. Your search for answers. You told me that you are a scientist looking for scientific realities; but I know you, Gunter. You are desperately seeking the same truths as I am. You want to see into the past, into what makes us what we are. And for all of your work, you are no further forward. But I am, Gunter. I have seen the answers you seek. I *am* the answer you seek.'

'Who the hell are you?' Griebel asked again.

'But Gunter . . . you know already who I am . . .' The younger man's bright, frigid smile stayed fixed in place. 'Don't tell me you can't see?' He stood up, and removed a large velvet roll-pouch from the briefcase that he had set on the floor beside him.

### 8.50 p.m.: Pöseldorf, Hamburg

Fabel felt bone weary. What he had anticipated as an easy first day back had unexpectedly taken a massive, dense form and had lain immovable and unavoidable in his path. He felt as if negotiating round it had sucked all the light from his day and all the energy from his body.

Susanne had arranged to meet a girlfriend in town for dinner and Fabel found himself at a loose end on his first evening back from his vacation. Before leaving the Presidium he phoned his daughter, Gabi, who lived with her mother, to see if she was free to meet up for something to eat, but she had already made plans. Gabi asked how his vacation had been and they chatted for a while before arranging to meet up later in the week. Chatting to his daughter usually brightened Fabel's mood – she had something of the careless cheerfulness that typified Fabel's brother Lex – but tonight her unavailability only served to unsettle him further.

Fabel did not feel like cooking for himself. He felt the need to be surrounded by people, so he decided to go back to his apartment to freshen up before going out to eat.

Fabel had lived in the same place for the past seven years. It was a block back from Milchstrasse, in what had become arguably Hamburg's hippest locations: Pöseldorf, in the Rotherbaum district of the city. Fabel's apartment was an attic conversion in a large turn-of-the-century building. The former grand villa had been ambitiously converted into three separate stylish apartments. Unfortunately, Germany's economic performance at the time had not been able to match the ambition of the developers and property prices in Hamburg had plummeted. Fabel had seen the opportunity to own rather than rent and had bought the attic studio. He had often thought of the irony of the situation: that he had ended up in this cool, perfectly located apartment because his marriage and the German economy had hit the skids at almost exactly the same time.

Even with the drop in property prices, all Fabel had been able to afford to buy in Pöseldorf had been this studio flat. It was small, but Fabel had always felt that the sacrifice of space for location had been worth it. When the developers had converted the building, they had recognised the potential of its view and had installed huge picture windows, almost floor-to-ceiling, along the side of the building that looked over Magdalenen Strasse and the green Alsterpark out onto the park-fringed Aussenalster lake. From his windows, Fabel could watch the red and white ferries crossing the Alster and, on a clear day, he could see all the way across to the stately white villas and the glittering turquoise dome of the Iranian mosque of the Schöne Aussicht on the far shore of the Alster.

It had been the perfect place for him. His unshared space. But now, as his relationship with Susanne developed, all that was changing. A new phase in his life was beginning; maybe even a new life. He had asked Susanne to move in with him and it was clear that Fabel's Pöseldorf apartment would be too cramped for two of them. Susanne's apartment was large enough, but it was rented and Fabel, having made the tricky leap into German home ownership, did not want to go back to renting. They had decided, therefore, to pool their resources and buy an apartment. The economy was pulling out of its eight-year-long dip and Fabel's current flat would attract a good price, or it could be rented out, and their combined incomes would mean that they would be able to afford somewhere half-decent and not too far away from the city centre.

It all sounded good and sensible, and it had been Fabel himself who had suggested moving in together. But every time he contemplated the move from Pöseldorf and his small, independent space with its great views, his heart sank a little. To start with, Susanne had been the reluctant one. Fabel knew she had had a bad relationship before, with a domineering partner. This guy had done a real number on her self-esteem and the relationship had been a disaster for Susanne. The result had been that she was very protective of her independence. That was about all Fabel knew: Susanne was a normally open and frank person but that was all she had been prepared to tell him about it. That part of her past lay sealed and locked from Fabel and anyone else. Nevertheless, she had gradually warmed to the idea of them moving in together and was now, if anything, the driving force behind finding a new place to share.

Fabel parked in the dedicated space for his apartment building and let himself into his flat. He took a quick shower and changed into a black shirt and trousers and a lightweight English jacket before heading out again and walking down to the Milchstrasse.

Pöseldorf had started off as the *Armeleutegegend* – Hamburg's poor people's quarter – and it still had the slightly dissonant feel of a village in the heart of a great city. Since the 1960s, however, Pöseldorf had become increasingly trendy and, consequently, the financial status of its residents had swung from one extreme to the other. Pöseldorf's image of impeccably chic affluence had been underlined by the success of names like the designer Jill Sander, whose fashion empire had started out as a Pöseldorf studio and boutique. The Milchstrasse was at the heart of Pöseldorf: a narrow street crowded with wine bars, jazz clubs, boutiques and restaurants.

It took Fabel less than five minutes to walk from his apartment to his favourite café-bar. It was already busy when he arrived and he had to squeeze through the throng of customers that had gathered in the bottleneck at the bar. He made his way to the elevated seating area at the rear and sat at a free table in the corner, with the exposed brick of the wall at his back. As he sat down he suddenly felt tired. And old. His first day back at work had taken a great deal out of him and he was finding it harder to get back into the swing of things.

Trying to summon an appetite, he sought to push the image of the scalped head of Hans-Joachim Hauser from his mind. But he found that another strangely took its place: the mortuary photograph of a young, pretty girl with high Slavic cheekbones who had been robbed of her name and her dignity by people traffickers and robbed of her life by a fat, balding nobody. Fabel had agreed with Maria more than he could admit: he would have loved to allow her to follow up the Olga X case, to track down the organised criminals who had dragged the girl down into a life of prostitution by offering the pretence of a new life. But that was not their job.

Fabel's thoughts were interrupted by the arrival at his table of a waiter. He had served Fabel before on several previous occasions and chatted with him unhurriedly before taking his order. It was a small ritual that marked Fabel as a regular; but it also underlined for Fabel himself a sense of place, a sense of belonging. Fabel knew he was a creature of habit: a predictable man who liked routines with which to measure and maintain the order of his universe. As he sat in the café that he invariably chose to dine in, he found that he became annoyed with himself: with the fact that the intuitive gambles he was prepared to take in his work did not seem to extend into how he managed his private life. But that was exactly how his private life was: managed. For a moment he thought about making an excuse and leaving; going a few paces down Milchstrasse to dine somewhere different. But he didn't; instead he ordered a Jever beer and a herring salad. His usual.

The waiter had just brought over his beer when Fabel became aware of someone standing beside him. He looked up to see a tall woman in her mid-twenties, with long dark brown hair and large hazel eyes. She was dressed in a smart skirt and top which were plain and tasteful, but which could not conceal the deadly curves of her figure. She smiled, and her teeth shone in the full, lipsticked mouth.

'Hello, Herr Fabel . . . I hope I'm not disturbing you.'

Fabel half-rose. For a second he recognised the

face but could not quite put a name to it. Then he remembered.

'Sonja . . . Sonja Brun . . . How are you? Please . . .' He indicated the seat opposite. 'Please sit down . . .'

'No . . . no, thank you.' She gestured vaguely with her hand towards a group of women sitting at another table, nearer the window. 'I'm here with friends from work. It was just that I saw you here and wanted to say hello.'

'Please, do sit down for a moment. I haven't seen you in over a year. How are you?' he asked again.

'I'm fine. I'm more than fine. The job is working out really well. I've been promoted. That was the other thing . . .' Sonja paused. 'I really wanted to thank you again for all that you did for me.'

Fabel smiled. 'There's no need. You already did that. Many times. I'm just glad things are working out for you.'

Sonja's expression became serious. 'It was much more than things working out for me, Herr Fabel. I have a new life now. A good life. No one knows about . . . well, about the past. I owe that to you.'

'No, Sonja. You owe that to yourself. You've worked very hard to achieve everything that you have.'

There was an awkward pause and then they chatted briefly and pointlessly for a while about Sonja's work.

'I must get back to my friends. It's Birgit's birthday and we're out celebrating. It was really nice to see you again.' Sonja smiled and extended her hand.

'It was good to see you again, Sonja. And I really am pleased that things are working out for you.' They shook hands but Sonja lingered for a moment. She held her smile but looked uncertain about what she was going to do next. Then she took a small notebook from her purse and scribbled on it before tearing the sheet out and handing it to Fabel.

'Here's my number. Just in case you're ever in the area . . .'

Fabel looked down at the piece of paper. 'Sonja . . . I . . .'

'It's okay . . .' She smiled. 'I understand. But keep it – just in case.'

They said goodbye and Fabel watched her as she walked back to her friends. She moved on her long shapely legs with the catlike elegance he remembered. Sonja rejoined her friends and they shared a joke and laughed, but she turned her head and looked back at Fabel, holding his gaze for a moment before re-immersing herself in the predictable jollity of an office night out.

He looked again at the scrap of paper and at the telephone number written in large figures.

Sonja Brun.

Fabel had come across her during a case in which a very brave undercover policeman called Hans Klugmann had lost his life. As part of his cover, Klugmann had become the boyfriend of Sonja Brun, a vivacious young girl who had somehow become drawn into porn shoots and part-time prostitution. Klugmann had clearly genuinely felt something for Sonja and had sought to free her from a degrading and self-destructive life. After Klugmann had been killed, Fabel had made a silent promise to a dead colleague: to finish the job and help Sonja escape from Hamburg's notorious half-world of vice and corruption.

Fabel had used his contacts to find Sonja a small

rented apartment on the other side of town, along with a job in a clothes shop. He had obtained details of courses she could take and before long Sonja had moved on to working in a shipping office.

Simple steps, but they had transformed her life at a time when she could have sunk even deeper by giving in to the grief of losing her lover and the anger of discovering that he had been living a lie. Fabel was pleased to see her so settled, and was relieved that she had succeeded in putting so much distance between herself and her past life.

Fabel had known the instant she had handed him her number that he was going to tear it up and drop it into the ashtray as soon as she left. But he found himself staring at the piece of paper and considering for a moment what he should do with it. Then he folded it in half and placed it in his wallet.

Fabel had just finished his coffee when his cellphone rang. He was annoyed that he had forgotten to switch it off. He often found himself out of step, out of time, with the modern world: cellphones in restaurants and bars were one of the many intrusions of twenty-first-century life that he found intolerable. All through the meal, as he had eaten alone, there had been a hollow feeling within him. He knew it was something to do with having encountered Sonja and her new life. It made him think of Kristina Dreyer. Maybe she really had cleaned up the murder scene simply to keep whole the universe of order and punctuality that she had built around herself.

Fabel answered his cellphone.

'Hi, Jan, it's me.' Fabel recognised Werner's voice.

'You should have taken my advice about extending your holiday over the weekend . . .'

## 10.00 p.m.: Speicherstadt, Hamburg

Most of the lights were now out, but a central spotlight beamed down like a full moon onto the architectural model that stretched across the table top. Paul Scheibe gazed at it. There was still a butterfly flutter of pride in his chest each time that he saw this three-dimensional representation of his vision. His thoughts, his imagination, given solid form, even if that form was in miniature. But soon, very soon, his concepts would be written large on the face of the city. His proposal for *KulturZentrumEins* – Culture Centre One – overlooking the Magdeburger Hafen would be the centrepiece of the HafenCity's Überseequartier. His monument, right at the very heart of the new HafenCity. It would more than match the visual impact of the new concert hall and opera house on Kaispeicher A and it would rival the elegance of the Strandkai Marina.

Building would start in 2007, if his proposal got approval from the Senate and the design jury selected it. There were, of course, other proposals contending, but Scheibe knew with absolute certainty that none of them stood a chance against the boldness and innovation of his vision. At press conferences he had taken to wittily describing the competing proposals as pedestrian-area concepts. His reference was, of course, not to the function of the area but to the pedestrian abilities of his competitors.

The pre-launch party could not have gone better. The press had turned out in force and the presence of Hamburg's First Mayor, Hans Schreiber, as well as that of the city's Environment Senator Müller-Voigt and several other key members of the city's Senate, had underlined the importance of the project. And the full public launch would not take place for another two days.

Now Scheibe stood alone, all his guests gone, and contemplated his vision spread out before him. So close. The sequence of events that was already in train would see his ideas turn into a concrete reality. He would stand in a few short years on a riverfront boardwalk and look up at art galleries, a theatre, performance spaces and a concert hall. And all who viewed it would be stunned by its audacity, its vision, its sheer beauty. Not one building; yet not separate structures. Each space, each form, would link organically, in terms of its architecture and in terms of its function. Like separate but equally vital organs, each element would combine with the others to give life and energy to the whole. And all engineered to have practically zero environmental impact.

It would be a triumph of ecological architecture and engineering. But, most of all, it would be a testament to Scheibe's radicalism. He took a long thick pull on his glass of Barolo.

'I thought I'd find you still here.' The voice was that of a man. He spoke from the shadows over by the doorway.

Scheibe did not turn, but sighed. 'And I thought you'd gone. What is it? Can't it wait until tomorrow?'

There was a fluttering sound and a folded copy of the *Hamburger Morgenpost* flew into the pool of light, crashing down onto the miniature landscape.

Scheibe snatched up the newspaper, leaning forward and checking the model for damage.

'For God's sake, man, be careful . . .'

'Look at the front page . . .' The voice spoke with an even, steady tone. Still the man made no move out of the shadows.

Scheibe opened out the newspaper. The cover photograph showed the giant Airbus 800 making its maiden flight, captured as it swept over der Michel – the spire of the St Michaelis church. A headline proclaimed that a hundred and fifty thousand proud Hamburg citizens had turned out to watch the fly past. Scheibe turned to the shadows and shrugged.

'No . . . smaller article, near the bottom . . .'

Scheibe found it. Hans-Joachim Hauser's death had only made it to a headline in a smaller font: *1970s Radical and Eco-warrior found murdered in Schanzenviertel apartment*. The article gave what scant details the press had on the death and went on to highlight Hauser's career. The *Morgenpost* had found it necessary to use Hauser's relationships with other, more memorable figures of the radical left to identify him. It was as if he had only existed in reflections. There was very little to report after the mid-1980s.

'Hans is dead?' Scheibe asked.

'More than that – Hans has been killed. He was found earlier today.'

Scheibe turned. 'You think it's significant?'

'Of course it's significant, you idiot.' There was little anger in the voice of the man in the shadows: more irritation, as if his low expectations of his partner in the conversation had been confirmed. 'The fact that one of us has died a violent death could be a coincidence, but we have to make sure there's no connection to . . . well, to our former lives, is probably the best way of putting it.'

'Do they know who did it? It says here that they have someone in custody.'

'My official contacts at the Police Presidium wouldn't give me details. Other than to say that it's early days in the investigation.'

'You worried?' Scheibe reconsidered his question. 'Should *I* be worried?'

'It could be nothing. Hans was a pretty promiscuous gay, as you know. It can be a pretty dark world, out there among our mattress-munching chums.'

'I never took you to be a reactionary homophobic . . . You keep that side of your personality well hidden from the press.'

'Spare me the political correctness. Let's just hope that it was related to his lifestyle – some kind of random thing.' The man in the doorway paused. For the first time he sounded less than sure of himself. 'I've been in touch with the others.'

'You've spoken to the others?' Scheibe's tone was somewhere between astonishment and anger. 'But we all *agreed* . . . You and I – our paths have had to cross – but I haven't seen any of the others in over twenty years. We all agreed that we should never instigate contact between each other.' Scheibe's eyes ranged wildly over the delicate, fragile topography of the *KulturZentrumEins* model, as if reassuring himself that it was not dissolving, evaporating as they spoke. 'I don't want anything to do with them. Or with you. Anything at all. Especially not now . . .'

'Listen to me, you self-important little prick . . . Your precious project counts for nothing. It is an inconsequence . . . nothing more than a dull expression of your middlebrow egotism and bourgeois conceit. Do you think anyone will be interested in this crap if everything comes out about you? About us? And remember where your priorities lie. You are still *involved*. You still take orders from me.'

Scheibe threw the newspaper to the floor and took a long and too-fast draught of his Barolo. He snorted with contempt. 'You're not telling me that you still believe in all that crap?'

'This is not about beliefs any more, Paul. This is about survival. Our survival. We didn't do much for the "revolution", did we? But we did enough – enough for it still to destroy all our careers if it were to come out now.'

Scheibe gazed into his glass and swirled what was left of his wine contemplatively. 'The "revolution" . . . my God, did we really think *that* was the way forward? I mean, you saw what the East was like when the wall came down – was that really what we were struggling for?'

'We were young. We were different people.'

'We were stupid.'

'We were idealistic. I don't know about you, but the rest of us were fighting against fascism. Against bourgeois complacency and the same kind of rampant, unfeeling capitalism that we now see turning the whole of Europe, the whole world, into an American-inspired theme park.'

'Do you ever listen to yourself? You're a self-parody – and it strikes me that you've embraced capitalism pretty enthusiastically yourself. And I do my bit . . .' Scheibe let his gaze range over the model again. 'In my own way. Anyway, I'm not interested in having a political debate with you. The point is that it's madness for us to be in touch with each other after all these years.'

'Until we know what's behind Hans-Joachim's death, we all have to be vigilant. Maybe the others have noticed something . . . *unusual* recently.'

Scheibe turned round. 'You really think we could be in danger?'

'Don't you see?' The other man became irritated again. 'Even if Hans's death is nothing to do with the past, it's still a murder. And murder means police sniffing about. Raking around in Hans-Joachim's history. A history we shared with him. And that places us all at risk.'

Scheibe was silent for a moment. When he spoke, it was hesitantly, as if he was afraid of stirring something from a long sleep. 'Do you think . . . Could this have anything to do with what happened all those years ago? The thing with Franz?'

'Just report to me if you notice anything unusual.' The man in the shadows left Scheibe's question unanswered. 'I'll be back in touch. In the meantime, enjoy your toy.'

Scheibe heard the door of the conference room slam shut. He drained his glass and again examined the model on the round table top: but instead of a radical vision of the future, all he saw was a clutter of white card and balsa.

### 10.00 p.m.: Marienthal, Hamburg

Dr Gunter Griebel regarded Fabel without interest over the reading glasses that sat almost on the tip of his long, thin nose. He watched Fabel from his leather armchair, one hand resting on the textbook on his lap, the other on the chair's armrest. Dr Griebel was a man in his late fifties whose tall frame had retained the angular gangliness of his youth but had lately gained a paunchiness around the middle, as though two incompatible physiques had melded together. He was dressed in a check shirt, grey woollen cardigan and grey casual trousers. All of which, like the chair and the textbook on his lap, were liberally spattered with splashes of blood.

Dr Griebel looked for all the world as if he had been so lost in contemplating the content of the textbook on his lap that he had not noticed when someone had slashed open his throat with a razor-sharp blade. Nor did he seem to have been distracted by his assailant then slicing across his forehead and around his head before ripping the scalp from his skull. Beneath the glistening dome of his exposed cranium, Griebel's long, thin face was expressionless, the eyes blank. Some blood had splashed onto the right lens of his spectacles, like a sample collected on a microscope slide. Fabel watched as it gathered in one corner of the lens as a thick, viscous globule before dripping onto his already gore-stained cardigan.

'Widower.' Werner pronounced the lifetime status of the corpse from where he stood behind Fabel. 'Lived here alone since the death of his wife six years ago. Some kind of scientist, apparently.'

Fabel took in the room. Apart from Fabel, Werner and the departed Dr Griebel, there was a team of four forensic technicians, led by Holger Brauner. Griebel's house was one of those substantial but not ostentatious villas found in the Nöpps part of Marienthal: solid Hamburg prosperity combined with an austere streak of North German Lutheran modesty. This room was more than a study. It had the practical, organised feel of a regular workplace: in addition to the computer on the desk and the books that lined the walls, there were two expensive-looking microscopes, which were clearly for professional use, in the far corner. Next to the microscopes was some other equipment which, although Fabel had no idea of its purpose, again looked like serious scientific kit.

But the centrepiece of the room had been added very recently. There was practically no wall space free of books, so the killer had nailed Griebel's scalp to the shelves of a bookcase, from where it dripped onto the wooden floor. Griebel had obviously been thinning on top and the scalp was as much skin as hair. It had been stained the same vivid red as Hans-Joachim Hauser's scalp, but the paucity of hair made it even more nauseating to behold.

'When was he killed?' Fabel asked Holger Brauner, still focused on the scalp.

'Again, you'll have to get a definitive answer from Möller, but I'd say this one's very fresh. A matter of a couple of hours, at the most. There's the beginning of rigor in the eyelids and lower jaw, but his finger joints, which will be the next to go, are still fully mobile. So a couple of hours or less. And the similarities with the Schanzenviertel murder are obvious . . . I had a quick look at Frank Grueber's notes.'

'Who raised the alarm?' Fabel turned to Werner.

'A friend. Another widower, apparently. They get together on Friday evenings. Take turns to go to each other's house. But when he arrived, he found the door ajar.'

'It sounds like he maybe disturbed our guy. Did he see anyone when he arrived?'

'Not that he can remember, but he's in a hell of a state. A fellow in his sixties. A retired civil engineer with a history of heart problems. Finding this' – Werner indicated Griebel's mutilated body with a nod of his head – 'has put him in a state of shock. There's a doctor giving him the once-over, but it's my guess that it will be a while before we get much sense out of him.'

For a moment Fabel was distracted by the thought that someone could go through sixty years of life without encountering the kind of horror that was Fabel's everyday stock-in-trade. The concept filled him with a kind of dull wonder and more than a little envy.

Maria Klee entered the study. The way her eyes were drawn to the scalped body reminded Fabel of how she had seemed almost hypnotised by the disfigurement of Hauser. Maria had always been pretty detached emotionally when examining murder victims, but Fabel had noticed a subtle change in her behaviour at crime scenes, particularly those involving knife wounds. And the change had only been apparent since her return to duty after recovering from her attack. Maria snapped her gaze away from the corpse and turned to Fabel.

'The uniform units have been doing a door-to-door,' she said. 'No one saw anything or anyone unusual today or this evening. But given the size of these properties and the fact that they're reasonably far apart, it's not particularly surprising.'

'Great . . .' Fabel muttered. It was frustrating to be so close to the time of commission, only to see a hot trail turn cold.

'If it's any consolation, one thing is now certain,' said Werner. 'Kristina Dreyer was telling us the truth. She's still in custody – so this can't be her.'

Fabel watched as the forensic team started the

slow, methodical processing of the body for trace evidence. 'It's not much consolation,' he said dully. 'The fact is that we have a scalp-taker out there on the loose . . .'

# 4.

## Two Days After the First Murder: Saturday, 20 August 2005.

### 10.00 a.m.: Pöseldorf, Hamburg

Fabel knew it was something big as soon as he heard his boss, Criminal Director Horst van Heiden, on the phone. The fact that he was calling Fabel at home was enough on its own to start alarm bells ringing: that van Heiden had broken into his Saturday to make the call made it really serious. Fabel had not got back to his apartment until three a.m. and he had lain awake in the dark for another hour trying to banish from his exhausted brain the images of two mutilated heads. Van Heiden's call had woken him from a deep sleep. It therefore took Fabel a few seconds to rally his sleep-scattered mental resources and make sense of what van Heiden was telling him.

It seemed that the murdered man from the previous night, Dr Gunter Griebel, had been one of those obscure members of the scientific community who tend not to dominate public imagination, or even attention, but whose work in some recondite scientific realm could totally change the way we live our lives.

'He was a geneticist,' explained van Heiden. 'I'm afraid science is not my thing, Fabel, so I can't really enlighten you about what exactly it was that Griebel did. But apparently he was working in an area of genetics that could have monumental benefits. Griebel documented all his research, of course. But according to experts, even with that the result of Griebel's demise will be that an entire area of research – very important research – will be put back ten years.'

'And you don't know what that area was?' asked Fabel. He understood when van Heiden said that 'science was not his thing'. Nothing was Criminal Director van Heiden's thing other than straightforward police work: and the more bureaucratic side of police work at that.

'They did tell me, but it was all in one ear and out the other. Something to do with genetic inheritance, whatever that means. All I *do* know is that the press are already getting very steamed up about it. Apparently the details of the method of killing have been leaked to the media – this whole scalping thing.'

'It didn't come from one of my team,' said Fabel. 'I can guarantee that.'

'Well, *someone* leaked it.' Van Heiden's tone suggested he was not entirely convinced by Fabel's assurance. 'In any case, I need you to move fast on this one. Griebel was clearly a major loss to the scientific community, and that means there will be political flak to contend with. Added to that is the minor political celebrity of the first victim.'

'Obviously, I'm dealing with this case as a priority,' said Fabel, not disguising his irritation that van Heiden obviously felt the need to give him a nudge. 'And that has nothing to do with the status of the victims. If they had been down-and-outs I would be treating the case with the same urgency. The focus of my concern is that we clearly have two murders close together in commission where the disfigurement of the corpses indicates a psychotic agenda.'

'Just keep me updated on progress, Fabel.' Van Heiden hung up.

Fabel had told Susanne he would be working half the night so she hadn't come round to his place. They met for lunch in the *Friesenkeller* near the Rathausmarkt, Hamburg's main city square. Despite Susanne being the psychologist who would work with Fabel on profiling the killer, they didn't discuss the case: they had an unspoken rule of keeping their professional and personal relationships very separate. Instead they chatted idly about their holiday on Sylt, about going back for Lex's birthday, and about the forthcoming election.

After lunch, Fabel headed into the Presidium. He had scheduled a meeting with his team, calling everyone in from their weekend. Holger Brauner and Frank Grueber came into the conference room shortly after Fabel had arrived: Fabel was pleased to see that the two most senior forensics officers had both taken the time to attend. Brauner had two forensic-trace collection bags with him, making Fabel hopeful that something of value had been retrieved from the second murder locus.

The inquiry board was quickly set up, with photographs of the two victims: photographs taken in life and those taken in death at the scenes. Maria had written a brief biography of each victim. Despite them being roughly the same age, there was no evidence that their paths had ever crossed.

'Obviously, Hans-Joachim Hauser had enjoyed an element of public recognition in his time.' Maria indicated one of the photographs on the board. It had been taken in the late 1960s: a young, girlish Hauser was stripped to the waist and his long wavy hair hung down to his naked shoulders. The photograph had been intended to look natural but was contrived; posed. Fabel realised that the young and arrogant Hauser had been making a statement, a reference, with this photograph: it was deliberately redolent of the image that Fabel had seen in Hauser's apartment, the one of Gustav Nagel, the nineteenth-century environmental guru. There was a cruel irony in the contrast between the cascade of dark hair in the photograph of the youth and the image beside it, of the dead, scalped, middle-aged Hauser.

'Gunter Griebel, on the other hand,' continued Maria, moving across to his side of the board, 'seemed to have actively sought to avoid the limelight. The acquaintances we have spoken to, including his boss whom I got on the phone, all say that he even hated having his photograph taken for periodicals or at university events. So it would appear that the killer was not motivated by envy of Hauser's fame.'

'Is there any suggestion that Griebel might have been gay?' asked Henk Hermann. 'I know that he had been widowed recently but, with the first victim being openly homosexual, I wondered if we may have a sexual or homophobic motive here.'

'There's absolutely nothing that we've found so far to suggest anything like that,' said Maria. 'But we're still checking into the victims' respective backgrounds. And if Griebel was a closet gay then he will of course have been secretive about it and we may never find out for sure.'

'But you're right, Henk . . . it is a line of inquiry that we should follow up.' Fabel was keen to encourage the positive contribution from his newest

125

team member. He joined Maria over by the board and studied the details of the two men; the photographs of them in life and in death. The only live picture of Griebel was a blow-up from some kind of staff group shot. He stood stiffly between two white-coated colleagues, his awkward stance and tense expression clearly communicating his discomfort at being photographed. Fabel focused on the grainy detail of the same long, narrow face with the precariously balanced spectacles that had stared at him from beneath an exposed dome of skull. Why was Griebel so ill at ease in front of a camera? Fabel's train of thought was broken when Holger Brauner spoke.

'I think we should talk about the forensic evidence recovered,' said Brauner. 'Or rather the lack of it. That's why Herr Grueber and I came along. I think this will interest you.'

'When you say lack of forensic evidence, I take it you're referring to the first killing – where Kristina Dreyer destroyed anything evidential?'

'Well, that's the thing, Jan,' said Brauner. 'It's true of both crime scenes. The killer seems to know how to eliminate his forensic presence . . . except for what he wants us to find.'

'Which is?'

Brauner placed the two evidence collection bags on the conference table. 'As you say, Kristina Dreyer destroyed any traces at the first scene, except for this single red hair.' He pushed one bag forward across the table. 'But I suspect that there was nothing for her to destroy. We have been able to recover nothing from the second scene either, and we know that was fresh and untouched. It is practically impossible for someone to occupy a space without leaving retrievable forensic evidence. Unless, that is, he or she goes to considerable lengths to conceal their presence. Even then, they would have to know what they were doing.'

'And our guy does?'

'It would appear so. We only found one piece of trace evidence that we cannot allocate to the scene or the victim.' Brauner pushed the second bag across the table. 'And it is this . . . a second hair.'

'But that's good,' said Maria. 'If these hairs match, then surely that means that we have evidence to link the two murders. And a DNA fingerprint. Obviously the killer has slipped up.'

'Oh, the two hairs match, all right,' Brauner said. 'The thing is, Maria, that this hair is *exactly* the same length as the first hair. And there is no follicle at the end of either. Not only are they from the same head, they were cut from it at exactly the same time.'

'Great . . .' said Fabel. 'We've got a signature . . .'

'There's more . . .' said Frank Grueber, Brauner's deputy. 'The two hairs were indeed cut from the same head at the same time – but that time was somewhere between twenty and forty years ago.'

# 5.

## Four Days After the First Murder: Monday, 22 August 2005.

### 11.15 a.m.: Marienthal, Hamburg

Fabel stood alone in the garden at the rear of the late Dr Griebel's villa, screwing up his pale blue eyes against the bright sun. The house was white-walled and laid out over three storeys under a vast red-tiled roof that swept down on either side to ground-floor level. It was flanked by neighbours that differed only nominally in design. Another row of equally impressive villas stood behind Fabel, presenting their backs and gardens to him.

Griebel's garden was laid out to lawn with some heavy shrubs and a cluster of trees offering a partial screen. But it was overlooked. The killer had not come in this way. But there was even less opportunity to break in from the front or the sides, unless the killer was as skilled at burglary as he was at forensic-free murder. And Brauner and his team had yet to find any evidence of a forced entry here or at Hans-Joachim Hauser's apartment.

'They let you in,' Fabel said to the empty garden; to the phantom of a killer long gone from the scene. He walked purposefully around to the front of the house and stopped at the main door, which was banded by strips of red-and-white police tape and bore a police notice forbidding entry. 'No one saw you here. That means Griebel admitted you quickly. Was he expecting you? Had you arranged to meet him here?'

Fabel took out his cellphone, hit the pre-set button for the Murder Commission and got Anna Wolff.

'I need Griebel's phone records for the last month. Everything we can get. Home, office, cellphone. I need names and addresses of anyone he spoke to. Start with the last week. And I want Henk to do the same thing with Hauser's phone records.'

'Okay, *Chef*, we'll get onto it,' said Anna. 'Are you coming back to the Presidium?'

'No. I've arranged to meet with Griebel's colleagues this afternoon. How are Maria and Werner getting on with the Hauser follow-up?'

'Haven't heard, *Chef*. They're still out in the Schanzenviertel. The reason I was asking if you're coming back in is we've had a Dr Severts phoning for you.'

'Severts?' Fabel puzzled for a moment, then remembered the tall young archaeologist whose skin, hair and clothing all seemed toned in with the earth in which he worked. It had been only three days ago that Fabel had stood looking at the mummified body of a man frozen in a moment that had passed more than sixty years ago. And it had been only four days since Fabel had sat in his brother's restaurant on Sylt, chatting carelessly with Susanne about the most inconsequential things.

'He's asked if you could arrange to meet him at the university.' Anna gave Fabel a cellphone number for Severts.

'Okay, I'll give him a ring. In the meantime get onto those phone records.'

'By the way,' said Anna, 'have you seen the papers this morning?'

Fabel felt his heart sink in dull anticipation. 'No – why?'

'They seem to have a lot of information about the scenes of crime. They know all about the hair dye as well as that the victims were scalped.' Anna paused, then added reluctantly: 'And they've given our scalp-taker a name. *Der Hamburger Haarschneider*.'

'Brilliant. Absolutely bloody brilliant . . .' said Fabel and hung up.

'The Hamburg Hairdresser' – the perfect name with which to terrify the entire population of Hamburg.

## 1.45 p.m.: Blankenese, Hamburg

Scheibe replaced the receiver. The committee member who had been charged with breaking the good news to him had clearly been surprised at Scheibe's response. Or lack of it. Scheibe had been polite, restrained; modest, almost. Anyone who knew the egotistical Paul Scheibe to any degree would have been amazed at his muted reaction to the news that his concept for *KulturZentrumEins* had won the architectural competition for the Überseequartier site.

But for Paul Scheibe this triumph, which only a few days ago would have seemed the crowning glory to his career, was absorbed as a vague, dull impact somewhere deep in his gut. A bitter victory: almost a taunt, given his current situation. Scheibe was too consumed with a more immediate, more elemental emotion – fear – to even feign enthusiasm.

He had been driving back to his Blankenese villa when he heard the news on NDR radio. Gunter. Gunter was dead. Scheibe had braked so hard when he pulled his Mercedes over to the kerb that the cars behind had had to swerve to avoid him, the drivers blasting their horns and gesticulating wildly. But Scheibe had been oblivious to all that went on around him. Instead, his universe was filled by one sentence that consumed everything else like an exploding sun: Dr Gunter Griebel, a geneticist working in Hamburg, had been found murdered in his Marienthal home. The rest of the report washed over Scheibe: police sources refused to confirm that Griebel had been murdered in a manner similar to Hans-Joachim Hauser, the environmental campaigner, whose body had been found on the previous Friday.

They had been six. Now they were four.

Paul Scheibe stood in the kitchen of his home, his hand still resting on the wall-mounted phone, gazing blankly out of the window towards his garden and seeing nothing. He watched as a light breeze teased and the sun danced on the branches and blood-red leaves of the acer that he had so carefully cultivated and tended. But he could see nothing other than his own impending death. Then, as if a high-voltage jolt had passed through him, he snatched up the telephone and stabbed in a number. A woman answered and he gave the name of the person he wanted to be put through to. A man's voice started to say something but Scheibe cut him off.

'Gunter's dead. First Hans, now Gunter . . . this is no coincidence . . .' Scheibe's voice shook with emotion. 'This cannot be a coincidence – someone is after us. They are killing us one by one—'

'Shut up!' The voice on the other end hissed. 'You bloody fool – keep your mouth *shut*. I'll contact you later this afternoon. Or tonight. Stay where you are . . . and don't do anything, don't speak to anyone. Now get off this line.'

The dialling tone burred loud and harsh in Scheibe's ear. He slowly replaced the receiver. He stared at his hand as it hovered, trembling violently, above the phone. Scheibe leaned forward against the marble kitchen worktop and his head slumped forward. For the first time in twenty years, Paul Scheibe wept.

### 2.30 p.m.: University Clinical Complex, Hamburg-Eppendorf, Hamburg

Fabel had no difficulty in finding the genetics facility in which Griebel had worked. It lay within the same complex of buildings that housed both the Institute for Legal Medicine and the Psychiatry and Psychotherapy Clinic where Susanne was based. The University Clinical Complex was the centre for all major clinical and biomedical research in Hamburg as well as many of the city's main medical functions. Fabel's main involvement had been through its world-leading forensics facility. It had grown over the years and now stretched back on the north side of Martinistrasse like a small town in its own right.

Professor von Halen, who headed up the facility, was waiting for Fabel in reception. Von Halen was much younger than Fabel had expected and did not fit with Fabel's idea of a scientist. Perhaps because of the stereotype imprinted in Fabel's mind, and perhaps because of the photograph for which Griebel had so unwillingly posed, Fabel had expected von Halen to be wearing a white scientific dust coat. Instead he was dressed in an expensive-looking dark business suit and a slightly too-bright tie. As Fabel was guided through the reception doors, he half expected von Halen to lead him into a showroom filled with top-of-the-range Mercedes cars for sale. Instead his preconceptions were restored as he was led through a laboratory and a suite of offices, all the occupants of which were suitably attired in white coats. Fabel also noticed that most of them stopped what they were doing and watched as he passed by. Word had obviously already spread about Griebel's death, or von Halen must have made some kind of official announcement.

'It's been a massive shock to us all.' Von Halen seemed to read Fabel's thoughts. 'Herr Dr Griebel was a very quiet man who largely kept his own counsel, but he was well liked by the staff who worked directly with him.'

Fabel scanned the laboratory as they passed. There were fewer test tubes than he would have imagined in a science lab, and many more computers. 'Was there ever any gossip about Dr Griebel?' asked Fabel. 'Sometimes we gain more leads through *Kaffeeklatsch* than through known facts about a victim.'

Von Halen shook his head. 'Gunter Griebel was not someone you would associate with gossip of any kind – either as source or subject. Like I said, he kept his personal life very distinct from his working life. I don't know of anyone here who socialised with him or who knew any of his friends or acquaintances outside work. No one had any personal knowledge of him to gossip about.'

They passed through some double doors and out of the laboratory. At the end of a wide corridor, von Halen showed Fabel into an office. It was large and bright and expensively furnished in a contemporary style. Von Halen sat down behind a vast expanse of beech and indicated that Fabel should take a seat. Again, Fabel was struck by how 'corporate' von Halen's office was. Fabel put this together with von Halen's sharp-suitedness and decided that the facility chief was very much in the business of science.

'Are there any commercial aspects to the work you do here?' Fabel asked.

'In today's world, Herr Fabel, all research activity with any potential biotechnical or medical applications has a commercial aspect to it. Our genetics unit here straddles the academic and the business worlds . . . we are part of the university but we are also a registered company. A business.'

'Did Dr Griebel work in a commercial area of research?'

'As I said, all research ultimately has a commercial application. And a price. But to give you a simple answer: no. Dr Griebel was working in a field that will ultimately offer enormous advantages in the field of diagnosing and preventing a vast range of diseases and conditions. The fruits of Dr Griebel's research will be of great commercial value. But we are talking about years into the future. Dr Griebel was a *pure* scientist. He was in it for the challenge and the potential breakthrough – the leap forward in human science and all of the benefits that come from such advances.' Von Halen leaned back in his executive leather chair. 'And, to be honest, I indulged Gunter more than a little. He would occasionally go "off brief", as our English friends would say. He had a few windmills to tilt at along the way, but I knew that he never lost sight of the aims of his research.'

'So you would say there's no possible link between Dr Griebel's work and his murder?'

Von Halen gave a mirthless half-laugh. 'No, Herr Chief Commissar – I can see no motives there. Nor anywhere else. Gunter Griebel was an inoffensive, hard-working, dedicated scientist and why anyone would do . . . well, what was done to him . . . is totally beyond my understanding. Is it true? What the papers said?'

Fabel ignored the question. 'What, exactly, was Dr Griebel's field of research?'

'Epigenetics. It studies how genes are switched on and off, and how this prevents or promotes the development of certain diseases and conditions. It is a field still very much in its infancy, but it will become one of the most important life sciences.'

'Whom did he work with?'

'He was the head of a team of three. The other two were Alois Kahlberg and Elisabeth Marksen. I can introduce you if you wish.'

'I would like to talk to them, but perhaps another day. I can ring to make an appointment.' Fabel rose. 'Thank you for your time, Herr Professor.'

'You're welcome.'

As Fabel rose to leave, he examined a picture on the wall next to the door. It was a group shot of the entire research team: the same staff he had passed through on his way to von Halen's office.

'Is this a recent photograph?' he asked the sharp-suited scientist.

'Yes. Why?'

'It's just that Herr Dr Griebel seems to be absent from it.'

'No – he's there, all right.' Von Halen indicated a tall figure at the back. The person in the picture had moved partly behind another colleague and his head was slightly lowered, depriving the camera of a clear image of his face. 'That's Gunter . . . messing up the photograph as usual.' Von Halen sighed. 'Not a problem we'll have any more, I suppose . . .'

## 4.10 p.m.: Police Presidium, Hamburg

As soon as Fabel returned to the Presidium he phoned Severts, the archaeologist, and arranged to meet him the following morning at his office at the Universität Hamburg. Severts told Fabel that they had uncovered some personal items at the HafenCity site that clearly belonged to the mummified man.

But Fabel had the more freshly dead at the front of his mind and as soon as he hung up he called Anna Wolff and Henk Hermann into his office.

'We've got most of the phone records for both victims,' said Anna in response to Fabel's asking. 'We're trying to match numbers to names or institutions now. I have to say that Griebel was not the most social of animals – there's not much to go through in his phone accounts. Hauser, on the other hand, seemed to be permanently attached to a phone. We're starting with the numbers that Hauser called or was called from most.'

'That makes sense, of course,' said Fabel. 'But the number I am looking for may not have connected often. Perhaps only once. It may even have been a payphone.'

'What is it that you're looking for, *Chef*?' asked Henk.

'It looks like both victims admitted their murderer

136

to their homes,' said Fabel. 'That would suggest either that Hauser and Griebel knew their killer or killers, or that the killer had pre-arranged a meeting with them.'

'But we are dealing with someone who is clearly most careful to avoid leaving forensic traces,' said Anna. 'Isn't it a bit much to hope that they would leave their phone numbers on record?'

'It is . . .' Fabel sighed at the futility of the exercise. 'But my thinking is that contact had to be established somehow. Like I say, I would expect it to be a payphone or a disposable cellphone number – something we cannot trace to anyone in particular. There is always the chance that the contact was made some other way. Maybe even approaching the victims on the street with some plausible story. But the telephone is a more likely form of initial contact. I just want to know if my theory is justified before we go off looking in the wrong direction.'

'And anyway,' said Henk, 'there's always the outside chance that our guy got sloppy – maybe thinking that we wouldn't look for a phone contact.'

Fabel smiled grimly. 'I wish I could believe that . . . but "sloppy" does not seem to fit with this killer.'

'There is one thing that's interesting . . .' Henk laid out some pages from a file side by side on Fabel's desk. They consisted of press cuttings and photographs of Hans-Joachim Hauser. The most recent was a still from an NDR news report. 'Do you see the common denominator?'

Fabel shrugged.

Henk pointed to each image in turn. 'Hans-Joachim Hauser was always keen to be seen to practise what he preached. He didn't have a car and never travelled in other people's cars.'

Fabel looked at the photographs again. In a couple of them Hauser was pictured cycling through Hamburg's crowded streets. In the others, Fabel could see the bike either deliberately positioned in the background, or accidentally caught half in shot.

'It's missing . . .' Henk said.

'The bike?'

Henk nodded. 'We've checked everywhere and it's nowhere to be seen. It was very distinctive, covered in hundreds of small stickers with environmental messages on them. He never went anywhere without it. I asked Sebastian Lang, Hauser's friend, about it . . .' Henk emphasised the word 'friend'. 'He said that Hauser always kept his bike chained up in the small courtyard behind his apartment. Obviously forensics did a fingertip search in the yard and checked the windows at the back. They found nothing. According to Lang, Hauser had had the same bike since he was a student. It was his pride and joy, apparently.'

Fabel looked at the photographs again. It was a very ordinary, very old-fashioned bicycle; not a particularly obvious choice for a psychotic killer to take as a trophy. Unless, of course, the killer knew of Hauser's attachment to it. But why would you leave the scalp and take the bike?

'Do we know if there is anything else missing from Dr Griebel's home?'

'Not that we can ascertain . . .' It was Anna who answered. 'Dr Griebel also had a housekeeper – probably not as thorough as Kristina Dreyer, but she says she can't see anything obviously missing.'

'Okay . . .' Fabel handed the photographs back to Henk. 'Get on to uniform branch – I want this to be the most hunted missing bicycle in German police history.'

After Henk and Anna had left his office, Fabel phoned Susanne at the Institute for Legal Medicine. Susanne was doing a fuller assessment of Kristina Dreyer before it was decided if charges should be brought against her for wilfully destroying evidence. Officially, she was still a suspect for the first murder, but the single red hair left at each of the murder scenes, as well as the scalping of the victims in exactly the same manner, indicated that they were dealing with the same killer in each case.

'I'll have my report ready tomorrow, Jan,' Susanne explained. 'To be honest, I am recommending that she has a clinical assessment by a hospital psychologist and we involve social services. My opinion is that she cannot be held responsible for her actions in cleaning up the murder scene.'

'I tend to agree with you, just from talking to her and knowing her history. But I'm going to talk to this Dr Minks, the Fear Clinic psychologist, about her.' Fabel paused. 'It almost wasn't worth going away, was it? Being hit by all this crap as soon as we got back.'

'Never mind . . .' Susanne's voice was warm and sounded almost sleepy. 'Come over to my place tonight and I'll cook us something nice. We can go through the property pages in the *Abendblatt* and see what's available in our price range.'

'I know two properties that are about to come on the market,' said Fabel glumly. 'Their owners have no need for them now.'

### 5.30 p.m.: Blankenese, Hamburg

By the time the phone rang, Paul Scheibe had managed a good three hours' drinking. The warmth of the French grape had not, however, managed to thaw the chill of fear that bound his gut tight. His face was pasty and sleeked with a greasy cold sweat.

'Find a payphone and call me back on this number. Do not use your cellphone.' The voice on the other end gave the number and the line went dead. Scheibe reached clumsily for a pencil and paper and scribbled down the number.

The late-afternoon light seemed to dazzle Scheibe as he walked from his villa down towards the Elbe shore. Blankenese was built on a steep bank and is famed for its pathways made up of thousands of steps. Scheibe, his feet heavy after his afternoon's drinking, shambled his way to the payphone that he knew was down by the beach.

His call was answered after one ring. He thought he could hear the sound of heavy equipment in the background. 'It's me,' said Scheibe. The three bottles of Merlot had made his voice thick and slurred.

'You prick,' the voice at the other end of the phone hissed. 'You never, *ever* use my office or cellphone number for anything other than official calls. After all these years, and particularly with everything that's going on, I would have thought that you would have had enough sense not to risk exposure.'

'I'm sorry—'

'Don't say my name, you fool . . .' The voice at the other end cut him off.

'I'm sorry,' Scheibe repeated lamely. Something more than the wine thickened his voice. 'I panicked. Christ . . . first Hans-Joachim, now Gunter. This is

140

no coincidence. Someone is taking us out one by one . . .'

There was a small silence on the other side of the line. 'I know. It certainly looks like that.'

'It *looks* like that?' Scheibe snorted. 'For God's sake, man – did you read what they did to them both? Did you read about the thing with the hair?'

'I read it.'

'It's a message. That's what it is – a message. Don't you get it? The killer dyed their hair *red*. Someone is going after every member of the group. I'm getting out. I'm going to drop out of sight. Maybe go abroad or something . . .' There was a note of desperation in Scheibe's voice: the desperation of a man without a plan, pretending he had a strategy for dealing with something there was no dealing with.

'You'll stay where you are,' the voice on the other end of the phone snapped. 'If you make a run for it, you'll draw attention to yourself – and to the rest of us. For the moment the police think they're looking for a random killer.'

'So I just sit here and wait to be scalped?'

'You sit there and wait for instructions. I'll make contact with the others . . .'

The phone went dead. Scheibe continued to hold the receiver to his ear and stared blankly out over the grass-fringed sand of the Blankenese shore, across the Elbe and watched as a vast container ship slipped silently by. He felt his eyes sting and a great, leaden sadness seemed to coalesce in his chest as he thought of another Paul Scheibe: the Paul Scheibe he had once been, swaggering with the arrogant certainties of youth. A past-tense Paul

Scheibe whose decisions and actions had now come back to haunt him.

The past was tearing his present asunder. His past was catching up with him . . . and it would cost him his life.

# 6.

## Five Days After the First Murder: Tuesday, 23 August 2005.

### 10.00 a.m.: Archaeology Department, Universität Hamburg

Severts's smile was as wide as his long narrow face would permit. He was not dressed in the same way as he had been on site in the HafenCity: he wore corded trousers, a rough tweed jacket with unfashionably narrow lapels and a checked shirt, open at the neck and with a dark T-shirt underneath. But while the style of his clothing was nominally more formal than it had been on the site, the earth-toned colour scheme remained the same. Severts's office was bright and spacious but cluttered with books, files and archaeological objects. A vast picture window flooded the room with light, but only afforded a view of another wing of the university.

The archaeologist asked Fabel to take a seat. As he did so, Fabel was surprised that there was something about Severts's dress, his office, the accoutrements of his trade that stimulated a small, sad envy in him. For a moment Fabel considered how he had so very nearly followed a similar path; how his passion had been European history and how as a student he had already rolled out the map of his future and plotted out the route of his career. Then there had been a single, senseless act of intense violence, the shock of the death of someone close to him at the hands of a stranger, and all the expected landmarks had been erased from his landscape.

Instead of becoming an investigator of the past, he became an investigator of death.

On the wall behind Severts's desk a large map of Germany detailed all the major archaeological sites in the Federal Republic, the Netherlands and Denmark. Next to it was a huge poster. The image was striking: it was of a dead woman, lying on her back. She was wearing a hooded woollen cloak bound tight around her long, slim body. The hood was capped with a tall feather and the woman's long red-brown hair was centre-parted. The skin of her face and that of her legs, which could be seen between the fringe of her cloak and her fur moccasins, had the same papery look as the HafenCity corpse, but had stained darker.

'Ah . . .' Severts noticed that the poster had caught Fabel's attention. 'I see you are captivated by her too . . . The love of my life. She possesses a unique ability to capture men's hearts. And to bewilder us – she has done more than her fair share of setting everything we believed about Europe on its head. Herr Fabel, allow me to introduce a true woman of mystery . . . the Beauty of Loulan.'

'The Beauty of Loulan,' repeated Fabel. 'Loulan . . . where is that, exactly?'

'That is the thing!' Severts said animatedly. 'Tell me, where do you think she is from? Her ethnicity, I mean?'

Fabel shrugged. 'I'm assuming that she's European, from her hair colour and features. Although I suppose the feather gives her a native North American look.'

'And how old do you think my girlfriend is?'

Fabel looked closer. The woman had clearly been mummified, but she was much better preserved than any of the bog bodies he had seen. 'I don't know . . . a thousand years . . . fifteen hundred at most.'

Severts shook his head slowly, his beaming smile still in place. 'I told you she was a woman of mystery. This mummified body, Herr Fabel, is over four thousand years old. She is nearly two metres tall, her hair colour in life was either red or blonde. And as for where she was discovered . . . there's the mystery and the intrigue.' He walked over to a filing cabinet and pulled out a thick box file.

'My family scrapbook,' explained Severts. 'Mummies are a passion of mine.' He sat down at his desk and flicked through the file's contents, all of which seemed to be large photographs with yellow notes attached to each with a paper clip. Then he handed Fabel a large glossy print. 'This gentleman is from the same part of the world. He is known as Cherchen Man. I was going to show you him anyway, because he is rather pertinent to the case of the mummified body down by the Elbe in HafenCity. Take a look. This man has been dead for three thousand years.'

Fabel looked at the photograph. It was astonishing. For a moment the policeman became once more the student of history and he felt the old butterflies-in-the-stomach excitement that he experienced when a window into the past opened. The man in the picture was perfectly preserved. The similarity with the HafenCity corpse was astounding, except that the man in the picture, dead for three millennia, had even preserved his skin tone. He was fair-skinned and his hair was a dark blond. He had a neatly trimmed beard and his full lips were slightly parted, twisted up in one corner to expose perfect teeth.

'Cherchen Man was preserved because he lay undisturbed for three thousand years in an anaerobic environment. The process of mummification is exactly the same as the body in the HafenCity. Both represent a moment in time seized and kept perfect for us to look into.'

'It is amazing . . .' said Fabel. He studied the man again. It was a face he could have encountered that same day, in modern Hamburg.

'We talk about the distant past.' Severts seemed to have read Fabel's thoughts. 'But although he lived three thousand years ago, that only represents one hundred-odd generations. Think about it: such a small number of people, father and son, mother and daughter, separate this man from you and me. Herr Brauner told me that you studied history, so you'll understand what I mean when I say that we are not as separated from our histories, from our pasts, as we like to think. But there's more to this gentleman. Like the Beauty of Loulan, Cherchen Man was tall, over two metres in height. He would have been about fifty-five when he died. As you can see, he was fair-haired and fair-skinned.'

Severts leaned forward. 'You see, Herr Fabel, none of us are who we think we are. Both the Beauty of Loulan and Cherchen Man are among a number of incredibly well-preserved bodies found in the same area with the same cultural indicators. They wore multicoloured plaid, similar to Scottish tartans, they were all tall and fair. And they all lived, between four thousand and three thousand years ago, in the same part of the world. You see, Herr Fabel, Cherchen and Loulan are both in modern China.

These bodies are known as the mummies of Ürümchi. They're from the Tamir Basin in the Uyghur Autonomous Region of Western China. It is an arid area and these bodies were buried in extremely dry, extremely fine sand. It is said that the Chinese archaeologist who uncovered the Loulan woman wept when he looked upon her beauty. Their discovery caused quite a stir, and the Chinese authorities and archaeological establishment are very much opposed to the premise that Europeans migrated to and occupied the region four millennia ago. Uyghur lies where the Turkic and Chinese ethnicities collide and Turkic nationalists have claimed the Beauty of Loulan as a symbol of their hereditary right to occupy the region. However, these mummies are no more Turkic than they are Chinese. These people were culturally Celts. Perhaps even Proto-Celts. DNA tests on the mummies carried out in 1995 proved once and for all that they were Europeans. They had genetic markers that linked them to modern-day Finns and Swedes, as well as some to people living in Corsica, Sardinia and Tuscany.'

'Of course,' said Fabel. 'I recall reading something about the discoveries. If I remember correctly, the Chinese government did all they could to play down the finds. It challenged their sense of ethnic singularity as a nation.'

'And we all know the dangers of that kind of mentality,' said Severts. 'As I said, none of us are who we think we are.' He swivelled his chair around and again looked up at the picture of the mummified woman. 'Whatever the debate that surrounds them, the Beauty of Loulan and Cherchen Man are part of our world now. Our time. And they are here to talk to us about their previous lives. Just as your mummy in the HafenCity has something to say about his much nearer time.' Severts pointed to the photograph in Fabel's hands of the three-thousand-year-old man. 'Despite the vast difference between the times they lived in, there is very little difference in the state of preservation of your mummy and Cherchen Man. If we hadn't uncovered him, "HafenCity Man" could also have lain undisturbed for three thousand years. And he would have emerged unchanged from his rest. He would have looked exactly the same . . . obviously we can use dating technology to establish rough timescales but, generally speaking, we often depend more on the artefacts and the immediate excavated environment to establish the exact time to which a body belongs. Which brings me back to our twentieth-century mummy.' Severts reached into his desk drawer and took out a sealed plastic bag. It contained a small black wallet and a pocket-sized piece of what looked like dark brown card.

Fabel took the bag and opened it. The card was folded into a small booklet form. On the front was the eagle and swastika emblem of the Nazi regime.

'His identity card,' said Severts. 'Now you have a name for your body.'

The identity card felt dry and brittle in Fabel's hands. Everything seemed to be different shades of the same brown, including the photograph. He could, however, make out the unsmiling face of a young blond man. Adolescence lingered in the face, but the harder angles of manhood were becoming apparent. Fabel was surprised that he recognised him instantly as the body by the river.

Karl. The face Fabel was looking at now, the face he had looked down on in the HafenCity site was that of Karl Heymann, born February 1927, resident in Hammerbrook, Hamburg. Fabel read the details again. He would have been seventy-eight. Fabel found the fact difficult to comprehend. Time had simply stopped for Karl Heymann, sixteen years old, in 1943. He had been condemned to an eternal youth.

Fabel examined the leather wallet. It too had lost any suppleness and its surface was like coarse parchment under the detective's fingertips. Inside were the remains of some Reichsmark notes and a photograph of a young blonde girl. Fabel's first thought was that it was Heymann's sweetheart, but he could just discern a common look. A sister, perhaps.

Fabel thanked Severts and, as he rose to his feet, handed him back the photograph of Cherchen Man. As Severts opened the box file to replace the picture, another image caught Fabel's eye.

'Now there's someone I know . . .' Fabel smiled. 'An East Frisian, like myself. May I?'

Fabel removed the photograph. Unlike the other mummies, the face was almost completely skeletonised, with only intermittent patches of brown leathery skin stretched across the fleshless bone. What made this mummy remarkable was the fact that his full, thick mane of hair, along with his beard, had remained completely intact. And it had been his hair that had given him his name. Because, although this mummy was officially known by the name of the Frisian village near to which he had been uncovered in 1900, it had been his mane of vibrant, strikingly red hair that had captured the imagination of archaeologists and public alike.

'Yes indeed,' said Severts. 'The famous "Red Franz". Or more correctly, Neu Versen Man. Magnificent, isn't he? And from your neck of the woods, you say?'

'More or less. I'm from further north in Ostfriesland. Norddeich. Neu Versen is on the Bourtanger Moor. But I've known about Red Franz since I was a kid.'

'Now he's a perfect example of what I was saying about these people having a second life – a life in our time. He's currently touring the world as part of the "Mysterious People of the Bog" exhibition. He's in Canada at the moment, if I'm right. But he highlights what Franz Brandt said to you down at the HafenCity about the different types of mummification. He is a bog body and totally different from the Ürümchi bodies. All his flesh has rotted away and only his skin remains, toughened and tanned by the bog's acids into what is basically a leather sack containing his skeleton. But it's his hair that's amazing. Obviously it wasn't that colour originally. It has been dyed by the tannins in the bog.'

Fabel stared at the image in his hands as he listened to Severts. Red Franz, the corona of his red hair flamebursting from his skull, his jaw gaping wide, seemed to scream out at Fabel. The hair. The dyed red hair.

Fabel felt a chill run down his spine.

### 11.00 a.m.: Altona Nord, Hamburg

Maria asked Werner if he could cover for an hour or so. However, while she asked she was already standing up and taking her jacket from the back of her chair, making it more of a statement than a request. Werner pushed his chair back from his desk, which faced Maria's, and leaned back, looking at her appraisingly.

'He's not going to be happy if he finds out . . .' Werner rubbed his bristly scalp with both hands.

'Who?' Maria said. 'Find out what?'

'You know what I'm talking about. You're off to sniff around this Olga X case, aren't you? The *Chef* has made it clear that you're to drop it.'

'I'm just doing what he asked me. I'm going over to Organised Crime to brief them on the background. Will you cover for me or not?'

Werner responded to the aggressive edge in Maria's voice by shrugging his heavy shoulders. 'I can handle anything that comes in.'


It depressed Maria each time she saw it.

This structure had once contained a purpose. At one time people had spent their working days here, had eaten their lunches in the canteen, had chatted with each other or had discussed productivity, profits, wage rises. This wide single-storey building in Altona-Nord had been a factory once: a small one, probably engaged in light engineering or something similar, but now it was a bleak, empty shell. Hardly any of the windows remained intact; the walls were scarred by patches of missing plaster or punctuated by graffiti; the floors were thick with powdery plaster dust and piles of rubble or litter.

It was an unlikely venue for love.

But this building provided somewhere for the 'lower end' of Hamburg's prostitution business to conduct its trade: mostly heroin- or other drug-dependent girls who undercut the prices of the more appealing Herbertstrasse and other *Kiez* hookers. The girls who worked down here were volume traders: turning over as many tricks as fast as possible to feed their habits or their pimps' wallets. The evidence was there, starkly presented in the bleak daylight: used condoms lay scattered across the filthy factory floor.

Olga X had not been a drug user. The post-mortem had established that. Olga had been driven to sell her body in this sordid, squalid place by some other compulsion.

Maria walked across the large void of the main part of the factory, stopping a few metres short of the corner. Ironically, it was clean and empty: the forensic team who had attended the scene had removed every piece of rubble for examination. That had been three months ago, and it seemed that this particular corner had been avoided by the girls who brought their clients here. Perhaps they felt it was jinxed. Or haunted. Only one item had been added: a small posy of wilted flowers sat forlornly in the corner. Someone had left it as a pathetic remembrance of the life that had been snuffed out there.

Maria remembered the corner the way it had been when she had first seen it. As if her mind had photographed and filed the scene, it always came perfect and complete to her recollection. Olga had not been a big girl. She had been slightly built and light-boned and had lain in a tangle of legs and arms in this corner, her blood and the dust of the floor mixed in a dull, gritty paste. Maria had never let murder scenes get to her the way her male colleagues did. But this killing had got to her. She had not really understood why seeing the fragile remains of an anonymous prostitute had caused her sleepless nights, but the thought had come to her more than once that it might have had something to do with the fact that she herself had so very nearly become a murder victim. The other thing that had stung her about this girl's death was the way Olga had been cheated. Most of the murders that the Polizei Hamburg Murder Commission investigated belonged to a certain milieu: the hard-core drinkers and drug users, the thieves and the dealers, and, of course, the prostitutes. But this girl had been forced into this world. What had seemed the promise of a new life in the West with a proper job and a brighter future had been a sham. Instead Olga, or whatever her real name had been, had handed over her own cash, probably all the money she had or could scrape together, to sell herself unknowingly into slavery and a sordid, anonymous death.

Maria knelt down and examined the wilted posy. It wasn't much, but at least someone had recognised that a person, a human being with a past, with hopes and dreams, had lost her life here. Someone had cared enough to lay the flowers here; and now, after a lot of discreet asking around, Maria knew who that someone was.

She straightened up when she heard the echoing slam of the door at the far side of the factory, followed by the sound of footsteps.

### 11.10 a.m.: Eppendorf, Hamburg

'This is highly irregular, you know.' Dr Minks led Fabel into his consulting room and gestured towards the leather chair in a vague invitation for Fabel to be seated. 'I mean, I will not compromise patient confidentiality, as you will already understand.' Minks crumpled into the seat opposite Fabel and regarded the Chief Commissar over the top of his glasses. 'Normally I would not discuss a patient without a warrant being issued, but Frau Dreyer has assured me personally that she is happy for me to discuss any aspect of her condition or treatment with you. I have to say that I am not as comfortable with the situation as she seems to be.'

'I understand that,' said Fabel. He felt strangely vulnerable sitting in the chair facing this odd little man in a creased suit. Fabel realised that he was seated where he would be were he a patient of Dr Minks; he felt more than a little ill at ease. 'But I have to tell you that I do not believe that Kristina Dreyer is guilty of anything other than destroying valuable forensic evidence. Even that is not something that we are likely to pursue. It was clearly a product of her mental state.'

'But you have my patient in custody,' said Dr Minks.

'She will be released today. I can assure you of that. However, she will be subject to further assessments of her psychological health.'

Minks shook his head. 'Kristina Dreyer is my patient and I say she is perfectly fit to be released into the community. Your criminal psychologist made a request for my assessment, too. I sent it off to her this morning. By the way, I was surprised to hear that your criminal psychologist was Frau Dr Eckhardt.'

'You know Susanne?' Fabel asked, surprised.

'Obviously not as well as you do, Chief Commissar.'

'Dr Eckhardt and I are . . .' Fabel struggled for the right words. He was annoyed to feel a flush of heat in his face. '. . . Involved with each other personally as well as professionally.'

154

'I see. I knew Susanne Eckhardt in Munich. I was her lecturer. She was an uncommonly bright and insightful student. I'm sure she's a great asset to the Polizei Hamburg.'

'She is . . .' said Fabel. He had mentioned to Susanne that he was going to meet Minks, and he puzzled for a moment over why she had not mentioned that she knew him.

'Actually, she doesn't work directly for the Polizei Hamburg. She's based at the Institute for Legal Medicine here in Eppendorf . . . she is a special consultant to the Murder Commission.'

There was a pause, during which Minks continued to study Fabel as if he himself were a patient needing assessment. Fabel broke the silence.

'You were treating Kristina Dreyer for her phobias, is that correct?'

'Strictly speaking, no. I was treating Frau Dreyer for a constellation of psychological problems. Her irrational fears were merely the manifestation, the symptoms of these conditions. A key element of her treatment was to develop strategies to help her lead a relatively normal life.'

'You know the circumstances in which Kristina Dreyer was found – and about her claim that she felt compelled to clean up the murder scene. I have to ask you directly: do you think that Kristina Dreyer would have been capable of committing the murder of Hans-Joachim Hauser?'

'No. I am not normally in the business of conjecture about where my patients' mental states may lead them, but no. I can categorically state that, like you, I believe Kristina's account and that she did not murder Hauser. Kristina is a frightened woman. That's why I'm treating her here at my Fear Clinic.

When she killed before, it was because her fear became amplified to an extent that you or I cannot fully comprehend. It gave her a strength beyond anything one would expect from a woman of her stature. She responded to a direct and immediate threat to her life after a period of sustained abuse. But, there again, you know this already, don't you, Herr Fabel?'

'Thank you for your opinion, Herr Doctor . . .' Fabel rose to go and waited for Minks to uncrumple himself from his chair. Instead the psychologist remained seated and held Fabel in his soft but steady gaze. There was nothing to read in Minks's expression, but Fabel sensed that he was weighing up his next words carefully. Fabel sat down again.

'I knew Hans-Joachim Hauser, you know,' Minks continued. 'Your murder victim.'

'Oh,' Fabel said, surprised. 'You were friends?'

'No . . . God, no. It would perhaps be more correct to say that I used to know him. Years ago. I've met him a couple of times since, but we didn't really have much to say to each other. I never really cared for the man.' Minks paused. 'As you know, I treat the causes and effects of fear here. Phobias and the conditions that cause them. One of the main things I teach my patients is that they must never let their phobias shape their personalities. They must not allow their fears to define who they are. But, of course, that is not true. It *is* our fears that define us. As we grow up we learn to fear rejection, failure, isolation or even love and success. I've become an expert in analysing people's backgrounds from the fears they manifest. You, for example, Herr Fabel . . . I would guess that you come from a typical provincial North German background and you've lived in the North all your life. You have the typical North German approach: you stand back from things, think them over thoroughly before you speak or act. Then you need the reassurance of having your observations or actions confirmed by someone else. You fear the false step. The error. And the consequences of that false step. That is why you needed the comfort of me confirming your view of Frau Dreyer.'

'I don't need you to approve my theories, Herr Doctor.' Fabel failed to keep the edge out of his voice. 'All I need are your views on your patient. And, actually, you're wrong. I haven't lived in North Germany all my life. My mother is Scottish and I lived in the UK for a while as a child.'

'Then the mind-set must be similar.' Minks shrugged somewhere in the crumpled fabric of his jacket. 'Anyway, we all have fears and those fears tend to shape how we react to the world.'

'What's this got to do with Herr Hauser?'

'One of the most common fears we all have is that of exposure. We all have sides to our personalities that we dread being revealed to the world. Some people fear, for example, their past. The different person they used to be.'

'Are you saying that Hauser was such a person?'

'It is probably hard for you to believe, Herr Fabel, but I was once something of a radical. I was a student in 1968 and was very much part of all that went on at that time. But I am happy with everything I did and who I was back then. We all did things then that were perhaps . . . ill-advised . . . but it had a lot to do with the ardour of youth and the excitement of the time. But what's most important is that we *changed* things. Germany is a different country because of our generation and I'm proud of the part I played. Others, however, are perhaps not so proud of their actions. It was back in sixty-eight that I first encountered Hauser. He was a pompous, self-important and incredibly vain youth. He was particularly fond of holding court and passing off all kinds of borrowed ideas and bons mots as his own.'

'I don't see how that is relevant. Why does that give a man reason to fear his own past?'

'It does seem harmless, doesn't it? Stealing the thoughts of others . . .' Minks was now so sunken into the chair that it was as if he had studied the art of repose all his life, but some distant brilliance burned behind the soft eyes that remained focused on Fabel. 'But the point is *whose* thoughts did he borrow . . . *whose* clothes did he take as his own? The thing about an exciting and dangerous time is that the excitement can make one blind to the danger. One is seldom aware that among the people one knows at such times are those who are themselves dangerous.'

'Dr Minks, do you have something specific to tell me about Herr Hauser's past?'

'Specific? No. There's nothing *specific* I can point to . . . but I can indicate the direction. My advice to you is that I think you should engage in a little archaeology, Herr Chief Commissar. Do some digging in the past. I'm not sure what you'll find . . . but I'm sure you'll find something.'

Fabel regarded the small man in the armchair, with his wrinkled suit and wrinkled face. No matter how hard he tried, Fabel could not imagine Minks as a revolutionary. He thought about pushing the psychologist further, but it would be a useless effort. Minks had given as much away as he ever would.

Cryptic though he was, Minks had clearly been doing his best to give Fabel a lead.

'Did you also know Dr Gunter Griebel?' asked Fabel. 'He was murdered in the same way as Hauser.'

'No . . . I can't say I did. I read about his death in the papers, but I didn't know him.'

'So you know of no connection between Hauser and Griebel?'

Minks shook his head. 'I believe Griebel and Hauser were contemporaries. Maybe your archaeology will reveal that they shared a past. Anyway, Herr Chief Commissar, you have my opinion about Kristina. She is quite incapable of the kind of murder that you're investigating.'

Fabel rose and waited for Minks to stand up. They shook hands and Fabel thanked the psychologist for his help.

'Oh, by the way,' said Fabel as he reached the door, 'I believe you know one of my officers. Maria Klee.'

Minks gave a laugh and shook his head. 'Now, Herr Fabel, I may have allowed you some latitude because I had Kristina Dreyer's permission, but I'm not going to compromise patient confidentiality by confirming or denying knowledge of your colleague.'

'I didn't say she was a patient,' said Fabel as he stepped through the door. 'Just that I believed that you knew her. Goodbye, Herr Doctor.'

## 11.10 a.m.: Altona Nord, Hamburg

As the footsteps grew louder Maria drew back into the corner where a young woman had been beaten and strangled to death. Despite most of the disused factory's windows being broken, the air in the corner hung still and warm and heavy around Maria. A woman appeared at the doorway and looked around anxiously before entering. Maria stepped out of the shadows and the woman spotted her, then, re-assured, made her way across the factory with renewed confidence.

'Is not possible for me to stay long . . .' she said in greeting as she approached Maria. Her voice was thick with an Eastern European accent and she spoke with the grammar of someone who has learned German on the street. Maria guessed she was no more than twenty-three or twenty-four, but from a distance she had looked older. She was dressed in a cheap, brightly coloured dress that had been taken up so that the hem just covered the tops of her thighs and no more. Her legs were naked and her shoes were high-heeled sandals that fastened around the ankle. The dress was of a thin material that clung to her breasts and clearly outlined her nipples. It was held up by thin straps, and her neck and shoulders were exposed. The whole outfit was intended to convey some kind of brash, available sexiness. Instead its colour compared discordantly with the girl's pale, bad skin and combined with her bony shoulders and thin arms to make her look sickly and somewhat pathetic.

'I don't need you to stay long, Nadja,' answered Maria. 'I just need a name.'

Nadja looked past Maria towards the corner of the disused factory. The corner in which she had placed the flowers.

'I told you before, I don't know what her real name was.'

160

'It's not *her* name I'm after, Nadja,' said Maria in an even tone. 'I want to know who put her on the street.'

'She didn't have a pimp. Not a single one, anyway. She was new to the group.'

'The group?'

'We all work for the same people. But I'm not going to tell you who. As it is, they would kill me if they knew I was talking to you at all.'

Maria took hold of Nadja's hand and held it palm up. With her other hand she stuffed some fifty-Euro notes into it and closed Nadja's fingers around the cash.

'This is important to me.' Maria held Nadja's gaze with her pale blue-grey eyes. '*I'm* paying you for this information. Not the police.'

Nadja opened her fist and looked at the crumpled notes. She pushed them back towards Maria. 'Save your money. I didn't agree to meet you to get money from you. Anyway, I can make more than this in a couple of hours tonight.'

'But you won't get to keep it, will you?' Maria made no move to take the money back. 'How did you come to know Olga?'

Nadja laughed emptily and shook her head. Every movement seemed electrified by fear. She paused to light a cigarette and Maria saw that her hands trembled. She tilted her head back and forced a jet of smoke into the thick, warm air. 'You think that your money means anything? I used to think that money was answer to all evils. And I thought that Germany was where I could make money. And this is how I ended up. But I take your money. And I take it because I have to prove that every second I out of their sight I earning for them.'

Nadja took three fifty-Euro notes and handed the rest back to Maria. 'The girl you call Olga. She not Russian, she from Ukraine. She brought here by the same people who brought me.'

Maria felt the thrill of a suspicion being confirmed. 'People traffickers?'

There was a noise from somewhere outside the building, near the main doors. Both women turned and watched the door for a moment before continuing their conversation.

'You should know this,' said Nadja. 'Things have changed in Hamburg. Before there used to be only two types of whore: the girls that work the Kiez in St Pauli – you even get university students up there making extra cash – and the junkies who do it to get drugs. These girls very bottom of the business. Now you got something new. Us. The other girls, they call us the Farmers' Market . . . we brought in from East like cattle and sold off. Most girls from Russia, Belarus or Ukraine. Many also from Albania and a few from Poland and Lithuania.'

'Who runs the Farmers' Market?'

'If I tell you, you go looking for them. Then they work out who tell you about them and they kill me. But they torture me first. Then they kill my family. You no idea what these people like. When they bring girls in they start by raping them. Then they beat them and say that they kill our families back home if we not earn good for them.'

'And this is what happened to you?'

Nadja didn't answer, but a tear began to trace the outline of her nose before she swept it away with a brisk movement of her hand.

'And they did it to the girl you call Olga. She

trusted them. They told her they had a good job for her in West. She trusted them because they were Ukrainian like her.'

'Ukrainians?' Maria felt a tightness in her chest: as if her body were clenching around her old wound. 'Did you say the people behind the Farmers' Market are Ukrainians?'

Nadja looked nervously out towards the factory door. 'I must go now . . .'

Maria stared hard at the skinny young prostitute. 'Does the name Vasyl Vitrenko mean anything to you?'

Nadja shook her head. Maria suddenly scrabbled in her bag. She produced a head-and-shoulders colour photograph of a man wearing a Soviet military uniform.

'Vasyl Vitrenko. Maybe you've heard it in connection with the people who are farming these Eastern European girls? Could this man be the person in charge?'

'I would not know. I don't recognise him. I give my money to different man.'

'Are you sure you've never seen him?' Maria held the photograph closer to Nadja's face and her voice became infused with urgency. 'Look at his face. *Look* at it.'

Nadja examined the picture more closely. 'No . . . I've never seen him before. It is not a face to forget.'

The tension seemed to evaporate from Maria's posture. She looked down at the photograph in her hands. Vasyl Vitrenko stared back at her with emerald eyes that were as cruel and cold and bright as the centre of hell.

'No . . .' she said. 'I don't suppose it is.'

Dirk Stellamanns had been a uniformed officer when Fabel had first joined the Polizei Hamburg. Dirk was a large, amiable bear of a man with a ready smile. It had been from Dirk that Fabel had learned all the things about being a policeman that you did not learn in the State Police School: the subtleties and the nuances, the way to walk into a room and read the situation and assess the dangers with your first scan.

Dirk Stellamanns had been on the beat in St Pauli, based in the famous Davidwache station. With two hundred thousand people passing every weekend through the two square kilometres of bars, theatres, dance clubs, strip joints and, of course, the notorious Reeperbahn, it was a beat where the policeman's most effective weapon was his ability to talk to people. Dirk had shown Fabel how you could defuse an explosive situation with a few well-placed words; how someone who seemed destined for arrest could be sent on their way with a smile on their face. It all depended on how you dealt with things. Fabel had been in awe and more than a little envious of Dirk's verbal skills. He was well aware of his own strengths as a policeman, but also of his weaknesses: sometimes Fabel knew that he could have got more out of a suspect or a witness if he had only handled them a bit better.

Dirk had been there when Fabel and his partner had been shot. A botched robbery by members of a terrorist group had left Fabel seriously wounded. Fabel's partner had not survived. Franz Webern, twenty-five years old, married for less than three years, father of an eighteen-month-old son, had lain in the street outside the Commerzbank and had shuddered with cold as the warmth of his blood slipped from him and bloomed dark on the pale asphalt.

It had been the darkest day of Fabel's career. It had ended with him standing wounded on a pier down by the Elbe, facing a seventeen-year-old girl armed with political clichés and an automatic handgun which she refused to lower.

She refused to lower the gun . . . Fabel had repeated the phrase like a mantra over the years in an attempt to somehow ease the intolerable burden of the knowledge that he had taken her life; that he had shot her in the face and head and she had tumbled like a broken doll into the dark, cold water. Dirk had been there for Fabel. Every day, whenever he had been off duty. As soon as Fabel regained even the vaguest, most tenuous grasp of consciousness, he had been aware of Dirk's quiet, solid bulk sitting by his hospital bed.

There were some bonds, Fabel had learned, that, once forged, cannot be broken.

Now Dirk was retired from the police. He had been running this snack cabin down by the harbour for three years. And Fabel came here at least once a fortnight; not because he particularly appreciated Dirk's variation on the *Currywurst* but because both men felt the need for the aimless, meaningless, trivial banter that rippled on the surface of their friendship.

But sometimes Fabel needed to go deeper. Whenever there was a case that got under his skin, a murder with the power to shock him even after all his years of dealing with death – it was not to

Otto Jensen, his best friend with whom he had much more in common, that Fabel would go. It would be to Dirk Stellamanns.

Dirk's snack stall was an extension of the man's already huge personality. It was bright and scrupulously clean and surrounded by a scattering of chest-high tables capped with white parasols. Dirk, his large frame protesting at the tight wrapping of his immaculately white chef's tunic and apron, beamed a smile when he saw Fabel approach.

'Well, well . . . I see you have had your fill of the overpriced eateries of Pöseldorf . . .' Dirk spoke to Fabel in Frysk. Both men were East Frisian and had always communicated with each other in the distinctive language of the region: an ancient mix of German, Dutch and Old English. 'Can I get you some real food?'

'A Jever and a cheese roll will do fine,' said Fabel, smiling desolately. He always ordered the same thing when he came down here at lunchtimes. Again he found himself irritated by his own predictability. He took a sip of the crisp, herby East Frisian beer.

'You look your usual cheery self.' Dirk leaned forward, his elbows on the counter. 'What's up?'

'Did you read about the Hans-Joachim Hauser killing?'

'The Hamburg Hairdresser thing?' Dirk pursed his lips. 'Hauser and some scientist fellah. You on that?'

Fabel nodded and took another sip of beer. 'It's a doozy. God knows how the press got the details, but they're pretty much accurate. This guy really has been taking scalps.'

'Is it true he dyes them red?'

Fabel nodded again.

'What's all that about?' Dirk made an incredulous face. 'God knows I've seen a lot of things in my time, but there's always some sicko who'll come up with something new to surprise you. This guy must be a complete psycho.'

'So it would appear.' Fabel examined his beer glass before taking another sip. 'Thing is, he doesn't take his trophies away with him. He pins them up for everyone to find.'

'A message?'

'That's what I've begun to wonder.' Fabel shrugged. Despite the sunshine, he felt a chill deep inside. Maybe it was the beer. Or maybe it was the unthawed splinter of unease that had remained with him ever since he'd seen the photograph of Neu Versen Man: Red Franz, whose hair had been dyed vivid red by a thousand years of sleep in a cold, dark moor.

'But why does he do it?' Fabel posed the question more to himself than to Dirk. 'What is the significance of the colour red?'

'Red? It's the colour of warning, isn't it? Or political. Red is the colour of revolution, the old East Germany, communism, that kind of crap.' Dirk paused to serve a female customer. He waited until she was out of earshot before continuing. 'Wasn't Hauser on the fringes of all of that stuff back in the nineteen sixties and nineteen seventies? Maybe your killer has something against Reds.'

'Could be . . .' Fabel sighed. 'Who knows what goes on in a mind like that? I was talking to someone this morning who suggested that I should be looking at Hauser's past. Specifically his political past. Maybe even more than I would normally with a case like this. But I don't remember any suggestion that Hauser was involved in anything approaching "direct action".'

'You never know, Jan. There's a lot of people in top political jobs now who have skeletons in their cupboards.'

Fabel sipped his beer. 'I'll look into it, anyway . . . God knows I need a straw to clutch at.'

## 9.30 p.m.: Osdorf, Hamburg

Maria sat on the sofa and held her empty wine glass above her head, waggling it as if ringing a bell. Frank Grueber came through from the kitchen and took it from her.

'Another refill?'

'Another refill.' Maria's voice was flat and joyless.

'Are you okay?' Grueber had been in the kitchen, placing the dishes from the meal he had cooked into the dishwasher. Despite being thirty-two, Grueber retained the look of a schoolboy. He had his shirt sleeves rolled up to the elbows, exposing his slender forearms, and his thick dark hair flopped over his brow, which was furrowed in a concerned frown. 'You've had quite a bit already . . .'

'Tough day.' Maria looked up at him and smiled. 'I've been looking into the background of that young Russian girl who was murdered three months ago.' She corrected herself. 'Ukrainian girl.'

'But I thought you got someone for that?' Grueber called through from the kitchen. He re-emerged with a glass of red wine, which he placed on the table in front of Maria before sitting down on the sofa next to her.

'I did . . . we did. It's just that she hasn't got a name. Her own name, I mean. I want to give it back to her. All she wanted was a new life. To be some-where and someone else. God knows, at times I can sympathise with that.' Maria took a long draw on her Barolo. Grueber rested his arm on the back of the sofa and gently stroked Maria's blonde hair. She gave a weak smile.

'I'm worried about you, Maria. Have you seen that doctor again?'

Maria shrugged. 'I've an appointment this week. I hate it. And I've no idea if he's doing any good. I don't know if *anything* would do any good. Anyway, let's change the subject . . .' She gestured towards the large antique sideboard that sat against the living-room wall. 'New?' she asked.

Grueber sighed while still stroking her hair. 'Yes . . . I bought it at the weekend.' His tone made it clear that he was reluctant to change the subject. 'I needed something for that wall.'

'Looks expensive,' said Maria. 'Like every-thing . . .' She swung her wine glass to indicate the room and the house generally.

'I'm sorry,' said Grueber.

'What for?'

'For being rich. You can't choose the life you're born into, you know. I didn't ask to have wealthy parents any more than other people ask to be born into poverty.'

'Doesn't bother me . . .' Maria said.

'Doesn't it? I make my own way, you know. I always have.'

Maria shrugged again. 'Like I said, doesn't bother me. It must be nice to have money.' She took in the room. The decor was tasteful and clearly very expen-sive. Maria knew that Grueber owned this large two-floor apartment outright. It was the lower part of a massive villa in the Hochkamp area of Osdorf. She suspected that he also owned the other part of the house, which was rented out. On its own, the apartment represented a seriously valuable piece of real estate: Maria could only guess at the value of the villa as a whole. Hamburg was Germany's richest city and Grueber's parents, Maria knew, were rich even by Hamburg standards. What was more, Frank Grueber was their only child. He had once explained to Maria that his parents had all but given up hope of having a child. As a consequence, Grueber had grown up in a world where all he wanted was lavished on him. And now he stood to inherit a fortune and obviously already had considerable financial resources at his disposal. Why, Maria had often wondered, would you pick the career of a forensic scientist when you could choose to do anything you wanted?

'Having money doesn't guarantee you happiness,' said Grueber.

'That's funny.' Maria gave a small, bitter laugh. 'Not having it guarantees *un*happiness . . .' She found herself thinking again of Olga X, and Nadja, and the dreams they must have had of a new life in the West. For Olga, Grueber's apartment would probably have been the embodiment of her dream; a little piece of which, in her naivety, she would have thought achievable through hard work in a German hotel or restaurant. Maria always imagined Olga's background in the same way: a stereotype of a small village on a vast steppe, with hefty babushkas in black headscarves carrying huge, heavily laden baskets. And always she imagined a fresh-faced, smiling Olga gazing expectantly westwards. Maria knew that it was more likely that Olga had come from some grey, depressed post-communist metropolis, but still she couldn't shake the cliché from her head.

'You're a good man, Frank,' said Maria, smiling. 'Do you know that? You're kind, you're gentle. A decent person. I don't know why you bother with me with all of my hang-ups. Life would be so much simpler for you if you weren't involved with me.'

'Would it?' said Grueber. 'It's my choice. And I'm happy with it.'

Maria looked at Grueber. She had known him for a year now. They had been involved for six months, yet they still had not had sex. She looked at his large blue eyes, his boyish face and the thick mop of black hair. She did want him. She put down her glass and leaned forward, cupping her hand behind his head and pulling him towards her. They kissed and she pushed her tongue into his mouth. He slipped his arm around her and she could feel the heat of his body on hers.

'Let's go to the bedroom,' she said, standing up and leading him by the hand.

Maria undressed so quickly that she lost a button on her blouse. She didn't want the moment to pass; she didn't want this window of normality suddenly to slam shut. She lay on the bed and pulled him onto her. She hungered for him so much. Then she felt Grueber on top of her, pressing against her. She felt his body on hers and suddenly felt stifled, choking. A wave of nausea came over her and she wanted to scream at him to get off her, to stop touching her. She looked up at the gentle, boyishly handsome face of Frank Grueber and felt a deep, violent revulsion. Grueber saw that something was wrong and eased back. But Maria closed her eyes and pulled him towards her. Through her closed lids she imagined that another face looked down at her and the revulsion was gone.

Maria kept her eyes closed and, as Frank Grueber penetrated her, she kept her disgust at bay by bringing another face to mind: an angular and cruel face. A face that looked at her with loveless, cold, green eyes.

# 7.

## Nine Days After the First Murder: Saturday, 27 August 2005.

### 8.30 p.m.: Neumühlen, Hamburg

Susanne had not said anything directly, but Fabel could tell that she was not happy that he had not responded more enthusiastically to any of the apartments she had circled in red highlighter pen. He knew that it was partly because instead of seeing each advertised property as an opportunity to gain, to advance their relationship, he saw it in terms of loss. Loss of his independence. Loss of his own space. He had been so convinced that it was what he had wanted, but now that it had moved closer to happening Fabel felt a vague ache of uncertainty.

The other reason why he had failed to be more decisive about the apartments was that all his mental resources were devoted to trying to pry an opening into the Hamburg Hairdresser case; choosing a new apartment was simply falling off his radar.

Fabel's uncertainty had deepened after spending the afternoon with his daughter Gabi. They had met in the city centre and Fabel had felt a suppressed panic as he watched his sixteen-year-old daughter approach. Gabi was growing up too fast and Fabel felt as if he had lost control of time; that there had been so much of his daughter's life that he had missed out on.

They had spent their afternoon together shopping for fashions on Neuer Wall; something that only a year before would have been anathema to the tomboy Gabi. It also pained Fabel a little to see how much Gabi was beginning to look like her mother, Fabel's ex-wife Renate. Lately she had taken to wearing her hair longer and the ghost of Renate's red hair burned in its auburn. As he had watched her make her purchases, Fabel had found himself observing Gabi's gestures, her mannerisms. Just as her hair held the ghost of Renate, Gabi's movements carried echoes of Fabel's mother and her smile and easy manner echoes of his brother. It made Fabel think of what Severts had said about how we are all much closer to our histories than we think.

After shopping, Fabel and Gabi had a coffee in the Alsterarkaden. The Rathausmarkt and all along the Alster was thronging with tourists. The Hamburg tourist office had recently announced that it had been the most successful year ever for tourism in the city, and Fabel and Gabi experienced the truth of the statement by having to wait ten minutes for a table. It took the waiter some time to clear the debris left by a family of Americans, then Fabel and Gabi were seated looking out at the Alsterfleet and the Rathausmarkt beyond. Fabel confided in Gabi about his dilemma.

'If you don't feel comfortable about moving in together, then you shouldn't,' she said.

'But I suggested it. I pushed for it to start with.'

'You're clearly having doubts, *Dad*,' Gabi habitually used the English word. 'It's too big a step to make unless you are absolutely sure. Maybe Susanne is not the one for you after all.'

Suddenly, Fabel felt awkward about discussing his love life with his daughter. He had, after all, once thought that Gabi's mother was the 'one for him'. 'I thought you liked Susanne,' he said.

'I do. I really do. She's perfect.' Gabi paused and looked out over the Alsterfleet. 'That's the thing, Dad . . . she is perfect. She is beautiful, intelligent, she's easy to get on with . . . she's got a super-cool job . . . Like I said, perfect.'

'Why do I get the feeling you're saying that as if it were a bad thing?'

'I'm not – it's just that sometimes Susanne can be *too* perfect.'

'I don't know what you mean,' Fabel lied.

'I dunno . . . she's really easygoing, but just sometimes she seems more buttoned up than . . .' Gabi let the sentence die.

'. . . Than me?' Fabel smiled.

'Well, yes. It's like she's keeping something bottled up all the time. Maybe she's totally different with you, but I get the feeling that we only get to see the Susanne that Susanne chooses to show us – the *perfect* Susanne.' Gabi gave a frustrated shrug. 'Oh, you know what I mean . . . anyway, there's absolutely nothing wrong with her. The problem is with you. Whether you're ready or not to make this kind of commitment.'

Fabel grinned at his daughter. She was only sixteen, yet she sometimes seemed infinitely wiser than Fabel. And, as they sat there among the tourists and the shoppers, watching the swans glide across the surface of the Alsterfleet, Fabel thought about just how right Gabi had been about Susanne.

Whatever the final decision, Fabel knew that Susanne was becoming irritated by his lack of focus. He decided to book a table at an expensive restaurant in Neumühlen. It was only a matter of minutes from Susanne's Övelgönne apartment, so they met there first before taking a cab to the restaurant. The restaurant had huge picture windows that looked out across the Elbe to a forest of cranes on the far side. The vast hulks of illuminated container freighters slid silently by. It was an industrial landscape, yet one with a strange and hypnotic beauty and Fabel noticed how many of the diners seemed mesmerised by it. Susanne and Fabel arrived at eight-thirty when the soft warm evening light was pressing against the vast sheets of the windows and for the first time in days Fabel felt relaxed. His mood lightened even more when he and Susanne were guided to a table over by the window.

Tonight, thought Fabel, I am not going to screw things up by talking shop. He smiled at Susanne and admired the perfect sculpting of her head and neck. She was a beautiful, intelligent, generous woman. She was perfect. Just as Gabi had said. They ordered their meals and sat chatting until the first course arrived. Fabel suddenly became aware of someone standing beside them and looked up, expecting to see the waiter. The man by their table was tall and expensively dressed. As soon as Fabel saw him he realised that he knew the well-groomed man from somewhere, but he could not place him.

'*Jannick?*' The tall man used the diminutive form of Fabel's first name. It was what his parents and his brother used to call him; what he'd been known as at school; but the only person in Hamburg who ever called Fabel *Jannick* was Fabel's fellow Frisian, Dirk Stellamanns. 'Jannick Fabel . . . is that you?' The man turned to Susanne and made a half bow. 'I'm sorry to disturb you . . . but I am an old school friend of your husband's.'

Susanne laughed but did not correct the stranger. 'That's quite all right . . .' She turned to Fabel and grinned mischievously. 'Won't you introduce us . . . *Jannick?*'

'Of course.' Fabel stood up and shook the man's hand. At that point, everything fell into place and he returned Susanne's grin superciliously. 'Susanne, allow me to introduce Roland Bartz. Roland was one of my best friends at school.'

Susanne shook hands with Bartz, who again apologised for the interruption.

'Listen, Jan,' said Bartz. 'I don't want to disturb you, but we really should catch up. I'm here with my wife . . .'

'Why don't you join us?' suggested Susanne.

'No, really, we don't want to impose.'

'Not at all,' said Fabel and beckoned for a waiter. 'It'll be good to catch up . . .'

Bartz returned briefly to his table and came back with an attractive woman who was clearly much younger than him. Fabel had heard – through his mother, probably – that Bartz had divorced his first wife a couple of years previously. The new Frau Bartz, who introduced herself as Helena, shook hands with Susanne and Fabel and sat down at their table.

Fabel and Bartz quickly became deeply engrossed in a conversation about what had happened to their respective school friends. Names that Fabel had forgotten were resurrected and he often struggled to put a face to a name. When he could, it was normally the face of a teenager whom he could not imagine now in middle age. Even Bartz looked wrong to Fabel. He had been an awkward, gangly youth who had been the first in their class to smoke, which had not helped the acne that had mottled his pale skin. Now he was an elegant middle-aged man with flecks of grey throughout his hair, and skin that was no longer pale and blemished but had been tanned by a sun that did not shine on Hamburg. He had clearly done well for himself and the topic turned to what the two men had done since they'd last met. Bartz was taken aback by the news that Fabel was a murder detective.

'God, Jannick . . . no offence, but that is so weird. I would never have put you in that profession. I thought you went on to study history . . .'

'I did,' said Fabel. 'I kind of got sidetracked.'

'My goodness . . . a policeman. And a Principal Chief Commissar, at that. Who would have guessed?'

'Who indeed,' said Fabel. He was beginning to become annoyed with Bartz's difficulty in seeing him as a policeman. Bartz seemed to pick up on it.

'Sorry . . . I don't mean to offend. It's just that you were always so clear that you wanted to be a historian. I mean, it's great what you do . . . God knows I couldn't do it.'

'Sometimes I don't think I can, either. It's a job that gets to you after a while. What about you?'

'Me? Oh, I've been in the computer software business for years. My own company. We specialise in software for research and academic purposes. We employ over four hundred people and export all over the world. There's hardly a university in the western hemisphere that doesn't have one of our systems in one department or another.'

The two couples then fell into general chat. Helena, Bartz's wife, was a friendly and cheerful woman, but was a less than engaging conversational partner. It was clear to Fabel that Bartz had not married her for her intellect. Fabel found that he enjoyed talking with his old school friend and grew to like again the man whom he had befriended as a boy. Susanne, as usual, won the couple over with her easygoing nature. Now and again, however, Fabel caught Bartz looking at him in a strange way. Almost as if he were appraising him.

They ate and talked until the restaurant emptied of its other guests. Bartz insisted on picking up the bill and ordered a taxi to take him and his wife back to Blankenese, where they had 'a nice place', as Bartz put it.

The night air was still warm and pleasant when Fabel and Susanne accompanied Roland and Helena Bartz out to their taxi. The sky was clear and the stars sparkled above the twinkling lights of dockyards on the far shore of the Elbe.

'Can we drop you anywhere?' asked Bartz.

'No, thanks, we're fine. It was great seeing you again, Roland. We must make an effort to keep in touch.'

The two women kissed and said goodbye and Helena Bartz climbed into the back of the taxi. But Roland lingered a moment.

'Listen, Jan. I hope you don't mind me saying, but you didn't sound very contented when you were talking about your work.' Bartz handed Fabel a business card. 'As it happens, I am looking for an overseas sales director. Someone to deal with the Yanks and the Brits. I know that you speak English like a native and you were always the brightest guy in school.'

Fabel was taken aback. 'Gosh . . . thanks, Roland. But I don't know the first thing about computers . . .'

'That's not what's important. I've got four hundred people working for me who know about computers. I need someone who knows about people. God knows, in your line of work you have to know what makes people tick. And what you don't know about computers I know that you can learn within a couple of months. Like I said, you were always the brightest guy in school.'

'Roland, I just don't know . . .'

'Listen, Jan, what you could earn with me would make your police pay look like peanuts. And the hours would be a hell of a lot better. And much less stress. Susanne said tonight that you're looking for a new place together. Trust me, this job would make the world of difference to what you could afford. I always liked you, Jannick. I know we're different people now. Grown up. But I don't know if we really change that much inside. All I'm asking is that you think about it.'

'I will, Roland.' Fabel shook his old school friend's hand warmly. 'I promise.'

'Give me a call and the job is yours. But don't wait too long. I need to get fixed up with someone soon.'

After they had gone, Susanne linked her arm through Fabel's.

'What was that all about?'

'Nothing.' Fabel turned to her and kissed her. 'Nice couple, weren't they?' he said, and slipped Bartz's business card into his pocket.

# 8.

## Eleven Days After the First Murder: Monday, 29 August 2005.

### 9.30 a.m.: Neustadt, Hamburg

Cornelius Tamm sat and considered just what the generational gap between him and the youth opposite him would be: he was certainly young enough to have been his son; without too much of a stretch of imagination or chronology even his grandson. Cornelius's seniority in age, however, had not seemed sufficient to deter the young man, who had introduced himself as 'Ronni', and who had gelled hair, ugly ears and a ridiculous little goatee beard, from using the informal *du* form of address when he spoke to Cornelius. He obviously felt that they were colleagues; or that his position as head of production entitled him to be informal.

'Cornelius Tamm . . . Cornelius Tamm . . .' Ronni had spent the last ten minutes talking about Cornelius's career, and his use of the past tense had been conspicuous. Now he sat repeating Cornelius's name and looking at him across the vast desk as if he were regarding some item of memorabilia that aroused nostalgia while not having the value of a true antique. 'Tell me, Cornelius . . .' The boy with the big ideas and bigger ears stretched his lips above the goatee in an insincere grin. 'If you don't mind me asking, if you want to do a "greatest hits" CD, why aren't you doing it with your existing label? It would be much simpler with the rights, et cetera.'

'I wouldn't call them my *existing* label. I haven't recorded with them for years. Most of my work nowadays is doing live concerts. It's much better . . . I get a real kick out of interacting with—'

'I notice you sell CDs on your website.' The young man cut Cornelius off. 'How are sales? Do you actually shift any stuff?'

'I do all right . . .' Cornelius had started off by disliking the look of the young man. As well as the irritating goatee beard, Ronni was short and, oddly enough, one of his prominent ears, the right one, projected at a much more dramatic angle from his head than the other. In a remarkably short time, Ronni had succeeded in cultivating Cornelius's initial vague dislike into a blossoming, fire-red hatred.

'I guess it's mostly oldies who buy your stuff . . . not that there's anything wrong in that. My dad was a big fan of yours. All that nineteen sixties protest stuff.' Cornelius had spent hours working on his presentation document, setting out why he felt that a CD of his greatest hits would sell not only to his traditional fan base but to a new generation of disaffected youth. The document lay on the desk in front of Ronni. Unopened.

'There's a lot of your *generation* of singer-songwriters out there. I'm afraid that they just don't sell any more. Those who do make a mark are the ones that have tried to come up with new material that's relevant today – like Reinhard Mey. But, to be honest, people don't want politics in their music these days.' Ronni shrugged his shoulders.

'I'm sorry, Cornelius, I just don't think that we belong together . . . I mean our label and your style.'

Cornelius watched Ronni smile and felt his hate bloom even more. It was not just that Ronni's smile was perfunctory and insincere, it was that he had meant Cornelius to *notice* that it was perfunctory and insincere. He picked up his proposal document and smiled back.

'Well, *Ronni*, I'm disappointed.' He walked to the door without shaking hands. 'After all, it's clear you have a good ear for music. The right one, that is . . .'

### 10.30 a.m.: University Clinical Complex, Hamburg-Eppendorf, Hamburg

It was clear that Professor von Halen considered he should be present throughout the interview, like a responsible adult being present while two children were questioned by police. It was only after Fabel asked if he could talk alone to Alois Kahlberg and Elisabeth Marksen, the two scientists who had worked with Gunter Griebel, that he reluctantly surrendered his office to Fabel.

Both scientists were younger than Griebel had been and it became evident during Fabel's questioning that they held their deceased colleague in great esteem. Awe, almost. Alois Kahlberg was in his mid-forties: a small birdlike man who habitually tilted his head back to adjust the angle of his vision, rather than pushing his unfashionably large and thick-lensed spectacles back up to the bridge of his nose. Elisabeth Marksen was a good ten years younger and was an unattractive, exceptionally tall woman with a perpetually flushed complexion.

Fabel questioned them about their dead colleague's

habits, his personality, his personal life: all that was revealed was Griebel's two-dimensionality. No matter how much light was focused on him, no shadows formed, no sense of depth or texture emerged. Griebel simply had never had a conversation with Marksen or Kahlberg that was not either work-related or the smallest of small talk.

'What about his wife?' Fabel asked.

'She died about six years ago. Cancer,' answered Elisabeth Marksen. 'She was a teacher, I think. He never talked about her. I met her once, about a year before she died, at a function. She was quiet, like him . . . didn't seem very comfortable in a social context. It was one of these company functions that we are all more or less compelled to attend, and Griebel and his wife spent most of the time in a corner talking to each other.'

'Did her death have a big impact on him? Was there anything about his behaviour that changed significantly? Or was he particularly depressed?'

'It was always difficult to tell with Dr Griebel. Nothing showed much on the surface. I do know that he visited her grave every week. She's buried somewhere over near Lurup, where her family came from. Either in the Altonaer Volkspark Hauptfriedhof or in Flottbeker Friedhof.'

'There were no kids?'

'None that he ever mentioned.'

Fabel looked around von Halen's expensive office. In one of the glass-fronted cabinets he could see a pile of glossy brochures, which he guessed were used to sell the facility to investors and commercial partners.

'What exactly was the type of research Dr Griebel was engaged in?' he asked. 'Professor von Halen mentioned it but I didn't really understand.'

'Epigenetics.' Kahlberg answered from behind his thick lenses. 'It is a new and highly specialised field of genetics. It deals with how genes turn themselves on and off, and how that affects health and longevity.'

'Someone said something about genetic memory. What is that?'

'Ah . . .' Kahlberg became what Fabel guessed was the closest he could ever get to being animated. 'That is the very newest area of epigenetic research. It's quite simple, really. There is increasing evidence that we can fall victim to diseases and conditions that we shouldn't . . . that really belong to our ancestors.'

'I'm afraid it doesn't sound quite simple to me.'

'Okay, let me put it this way . . . There are basically two causes of illness: there are those conditions we are genetically predisposed to – that we have a congenital tendency towards. Then there are environmental causes of illness: smoking, pollution, diet, et cetera . . . These were always seen as quite different, but recent research has proved that we can actually inherit environmentally caused conditions.'

Fabel still did not look enlightened, so Elisabeth Marksen picked up the thread.

'We all think we are detached from our history, but it has been discovered that we aren't. There is a small town in northern Sweden called Överkalix. It is a very prosperous community and the quality of life and the standard of living are very high. Yet local doctors noticed that the population tended to develop health problems that were normally only ever associated with malnutrition. There were two other factors that also made Överkalix distinctive. Firstly, it lies north of the Arctic Circle and has been relatively isolated for all of its history, meaning that the population today tends to be descended from the same families that were there one hundred or two hundred years ago. Secondly, Överkalix is unusual in the detail of its church and civic records. They record not just births and deaths, but the causes of death as well as good and bad harvests. The town became the focus of a major research project and the results showed that a century to a century and a half ago the town, which relied on agriculture, suffered several famines. Many died as a result, but among the survivors an even greater number suffered malnutrition-related medical conditions. By using contemporary medical records and comparing them to the historical ones, it became clear that the descendants of famine victims were exhibiting exactly the same health problems, although they and their parents had never gone hungry in their lives. It was proof that we were wrong to think that we pass on only those chromosomes and genes that we are born with, complete and unaltered, to our children. The fact is that what we experience, the environmental factors that surround us, can have a direct effect on our descendants.'

'Incredible. And this theory is based exclusively on this one Swedish town?'

'Only to start with. The research net was cast wider and a range of other examples have been found. The descendants of Holocaust survivors have proved to be susceptible to stress- and trauma-related conditions. One, two, three generations on, they are suffering the post-trauma stress symptoms of an event they did not themselves experience. To begin with this was dismissed as the result of their parents or grandparents relating details of their experiences, but it was found that the same stress indicators, including elevated cortisol in the saliva, were to be found in descendants who had not been exposed to first-hand accounts from Holocaust survivors.'

'I still don't understand how it works,' said Fabel. 'How is this passed from one generation to the next?'

'It depends on gender. In males the transgenerational response is sperm-mediated, in females it lies in foetal programming.'

Again, Fabel looked bemused.

'These environmental and experiential factors that pass on are specifically those experienced by pre-pubescent and pubescent boys and by female foetuses in the womb. Basically the "data", for want of a better word, is stored in the sperm that is formed in puberty. Girls are born with all their ova, so the crucial time for them is while the female is in the womb. What the expectant mother experiences during pregnancy or before is passed to the foetus which then stores the genetic memory in the forming ova.'

'Amazing. And this is what Herr Dr Griebel was researching?' asked Fabel.

'There are a great many researchers working in this field worldwide. Epigenetics has become a major and growing field of exploration. You probably remember the great hopes that we all had for the Human Genome Project. It was believed that we could track down the gene for every disease and condition, but we were disappointed. An unimaginable amount of money, resources and computer time has been devoted to mapping the human genome only to find that it was not, after all, that complicated. The complexity lies in all the combinations and permutations within the genome. Epigenetics may provide the key we've been looking for. Herr Dr Griebel was one of only a handful of scientists worldwide leading the way in understanding the mechanisms of genetic transference.'

Fabel sat for a moment considering what the two scientists had told him. They waited patiently, birdlike Kahlberg behind the thick screens of his spectacles, Marksen with her flushed face empty of expression, as if understanding that it took time for a layman to process the information. Fabel found the information fascinating, but it seemed useless to his inquiry. What motive could Griebel's killer have found in the man's work?

'Professor von Halen said something about Dr Griebel having pet projects that he indulged him with,' he said eventually.

Kahlberg and Marksen exchanged a knowing look.

'If the commercial application is not immediately apparent,' said Kahlberg, 'then Herr Professor von Halen sees it as a diversion. The truth is that Dr Griebel was looking into the wider field of genetic inheritance. Specifically the possibility of inherited memory. Not just on the chromosomatic level, but actual memory passed from one generation to the next.'

'Surely that's not possible?'

'There is evidence for it in other species. We know that in rats, for example, a danger learned by one generation is avoided by the next . . . we just don't understand the mechanism behind that inherited awareness. Dr Griebel used to say that "instinct" was the most unscientific of scientific concepts. He claimed that we do things "instinctively" because we have inherited the memory of a required survival behaviour. Like the way a human baby makes a walking movement within minutes of birth, yet has to relearn the ability to walk nearly a year later – an instinct we learned somewhere in our distant genetic past, when we lived out on the savannah and immobility was potentially fatal. Dr Griebel was fascinated by the subject. Obsessed, almost.'

'Do you believe in inherited memory yourself?'

Kahlberg nodded. 'I believe it is perfectly possible. Probable, even. But, as I said, it's just that we don't understand the mechanics of it yet. The full science is yet to be done.'

Elisabeth Marksen smiled bleakly. 'And, without Dr Griebel, it will have to wait longer to be done.'

'You get anything?' Werner asked when Fabel phoned him on his cellphone from the car park of the Institute.

'Nothing. Griebel's work has no bearing on his death, as far as I can see. Anything there?'

'As a matter of fact, Anna has something. She'll explain when you get back. And Kriminaldirektor van Heiden wants you and Maria to report to him this afternoon, at three.'

Fabel frowned. 'He asked specifically for Maria too?'

'Very specifically.'

## 11.45 a.m.: Police Presidium, Hamburg

Anna Wolff knocked on Fabel's office door and entered without being asked. Fabel always made a conscious effort not to notice how attractive Anna was, but her skin shone in the morning light from his office window and the red lipstick emphasised the fullness of her mouth. She looked young and fresh and energetic and Fabel found himself resenting her youth and her insolent sexuality.

'What have you got?'

'I reinterviewed Sebastian Lang, Hauser's *friend* . . . the one who found Kristina Dreyer cleaning up the murder scene. It would appear that he and Hauser were far from setting up house together. According to Lang the relationship faltered because of Hauser's predatory promiscuousness. Apparently he was fond of casual encounters, whether he was in a relationship or not. And he liked them young. Lang really didn't want to talk about it. I think he was afraid that his jealousy would be seen as a potential motive, but his alibi for the time of Hauser's death seems tight.'

Fabel processed the information for a moment. 'So it could be that it *does* have something to do with Hauser being gay. In which case, we should be looking more closely at Griebel's sexuality. Where did Hauser pick up his casual encounters?'

'Where he met Lang, apparently. A gay club in St Pauli . . . it has an English name . . .' Anna frowned and flicked through her notebook. 'Yes . . . a place called The Firehouse.'

Fabel nodded. 'Get onto it. You and Paul get down there and ask around.'

Anna stared at Fabel in blank confusion for a moment. 'You mean me and Henk?'

For a few seconds Fabel had no idea what to say. Paul Lindemann had been Anna's partner. Lindemann's death had hit Anna harder than anyone else in the team: and it had hit the team hard. Why had he said that? Had Fabel picked Henk Hermann to replace Paul simply because he reminded him of his dead junior officer? Confusing two names was an easy thing to do; particularly the names of two people who occupied the same space, as it were. But Fabel never confused names.

'God, Anna, I'm sorry . . .'

'It's okay, *Chef* . . .' Anna said. 'I keep forgetting Paul's not here any more too. Henk and I will
get on to checking out this gay club and anything
else we can find on Hauser's background.'

Fabel followed Anna out of his office and made his
way over to Maria's desk, which was directly opposite Werner's. Fabel noticed that both desks were
perfectly ordered and tidy. He had teamed Maria
and Werner together because he had felt they
combined very different skills and approaches: a
teaming of complementary opposites. The irony was
that they were identical in their meticulousness.
Again Fabel thought of how he had confused Paul
and Henk when he had been talking to Anna. He
had always allowed himself the conceit of thinking
that he was innovative and creative in his choice of
team members. Maybe he was not so innovative
after all; maybe, without thinking, he merely picked
variations on a theme.

'It's time we headed up to Criminal Director van
Heiden's office,' he said to Maria. 'You any idea
what this is all about?' Fabel was frequently
summoned to his boss's office, particularly during
the course of a high-profile investigation, but it was
rare for van Heiden to specify a junior officer to
accompany Fabel.

Maria shrugged. 'No idea, *Chef.*'

For Fabel, his boss represented the perpetual
policeman: there had always been a policeman like
Horst van Heiden, in every police force, in every
land, for as long as the concept of a policeman had
existed. Before then, even – Fabel could imagine

someone like van Heiden as a medieval town watchman or village constable.

Criminal Director van Heiden was in his mid-fifties and not a particularly tall man, but his ramrod-back posture and broad shoulders gave him a presence disproportionate to his size. He always dressed well but unimaginatively and today he wore a well-cut blue suit and a crisp white shirt with a plum-red tie. The suit, the shirt and the tie all looked expensive, but van Heiden somehow always managed to make even the most expensive tailoring look like a police uniform.

As well as van Heiden, there were two other men waiting for Fabel and Maria. Fabel recognised a squat, powerfully built man in a business suit as Markus Ullrich, of the BKA. The BKA was the Federal Crime Bureau, which operated across the whole of Germany. Fabel and Ullrich had crossed paths before on a couple of major investigations and the BKA man had struck Fabel as someone who was easy to deal with, if a little protective of his own investigative territory. The other man was the same height as Ullrich but lacked his muscular build. He wore frameless spectacles behind which the small marbles of his pale blue eyes shone with a keen intelligence. His thick blond hair was meticulously brushed back from his wide forehead.

'You already know Herr Ullrich, of course,' said van Heiden. 'But allow me to introduce Herr Viktor Turchenko. Herr Turchenko is a senior investigator with the Ukrainian police.'

Fabel felt a chill somewhere deep inside, as if someone had left a door open to a forgotten winter. He turned to look at Maria: her face revealed nothing.

'It is my pleasure to meet you both,' said Turchenko as he extended a hand to each officer in turn. His face broke into a wide and engaging smile, but his heavily accented, stilted German brought back too many memories for Fabel and he felt the chill inside intensify.

'Herr Turchenko is here as part of an investigation he's been pursuing in the Ukraine,' continued van Heiden once everyone was seated. 'He asked if we could arrange this meeting. Herr Turchenko specifically wanted to speak to you, Frau Klee.'

'Oh?' Maria's tone was laced through with suspicion.

'Indeed, Frau Klee. I believe that you have been working on a case – two cases, in fact – that are directly related to my investigation.' Turchenko removed a photograph from his briefcase and handed it to Maria. As he did so, the warm smile was replaced by a sombre expression. 'I have a name for you – a name you have been looking for, I believe.'

Maria looked at the picture. A teenage girl, somewhere around seventeen years old. The image was slightly grainy and Maria guessed it was a blown-up detail from a larger image. The girl in the photograph smiled as if at someone or something far off-camera. In the distance. Perhaps, thought Maria, she was looking towards the West.

'What was her name?' Maria asked in a flat voice. 'Her real name, I mean.'

Turchenko sighed. 'Magda Savitska. Eighteen years old. From outside Lviv, in western Ukraine.'

'Magda Savitska . . .' Maria said the name out loud as she passed the photograph to Fabel. 'Olga X.'

'She is from the same part of the Ukraine as I

am,' Turchenko went on. 'Her family are good people. We believe Magda fell victim to a scam that was a front for sex trafficking. She brought home a letter that was given to her promising training at a hairdressing college in Poland, after which she was guaranteed employment in a salon here in Germany. We checked out the address of the hairdressing college in Warsaw. Of course, it doesn't exist. No college in Poland, no job in Germany.'

'You've come a long way to find this one girl,' said Fabel, handing the picture back to the Ukrainian. Turchenko took the photograph and looked at it for a while before answering.

'This one girl is one of many. Thousands of girls are lured or abducted and forced into slavery – every year. Magda Savitska is not special. But she is representative. And she is someone's daughter, someone's sister.' He looked up from the photograph. 'I believe you have her killer in custody.'

'That's correct. The case is closed,' said Maria and exchanged a look with Fabel. 'She was working as a prostitute here in Hamburg and one of her clients murdered her. We already have his confession. But thank you for providing us with her true identity.'

'Herr Turchenko is not here to find her murderer,' said Ullrich, the BKA man. 'As he said, his visit is also connected to another case.'

'I am after the organised criminals who trafficked Magda and coerced her into prostitution,' said Turchenko. 'Specifically, I want to cut off the head of the organisation. Which brings me to the other case you were involved with . . .' Turchenko took another photograph from his briefcase and handed it to Maria.

'Damn it,' said Maria with a sudden vehemence. She merely glanced at the photograph and handed it to Fabel. She did not need to examine the face. After all, it haunted her dreams and her waking hours. It was the same face, a copy of the same photograph, that she carried in her handbag. 'I knew it! I knew that bastard was involved in the "Farmers' Market". Bloody Ukrainians.'

Turchenko gave a small laugh and shrugged. 'I assure you, Frau Klee, we are not all the same.'

Fabel gazed at the photograph of Vasyl Vitrenko . . .

'I know this opens up old wounds—' said Ullrich.

Fabel cut across him. 'That is a rather tasteless choice of expression, Herr Ullrich.'

'I'm sorry . . . I didn't mean . . .'

Maria brushed aside Ullrich's apology. 'I knew there were Ukrainians involved in the trafficking of women to Hamburg. I suspected that Vitrenko was somewhere behind it all.'

'Way behind it,' continued Ullrich. 'We did a pretty good job . . . by "we" I mean the Polizei Hamburg organised-crime division and the BKA . . . we succeeded in dismantling the Vitrenko operation in Hamburg. And, of course, you and your team were central in flushing Vitrenko out. However, there were a couple of elements that we didn't get. We believe that Vitrenko is rebuilding his power base in Germany.'

'Vitrenko is still in Germany?' Maria's complexion bleached paler.

'Not necessarily,' said Turchenko. 'As you know, Vitrenko is a master at building complex command structures that separate him from the activity yet which maintain this powerful personal loyalty to him. It is possible that he is running things remotely. He certainly is not in Hamburg and may even be orchestrating things from abroad. Perhaps even from back home in Ukraine. But yes – my money is on him being somewhere in Germany. And I am here to find him.'

'We've also ascertained that his operations are no longer focused on Hamburg or any other single German city,' said Ullrich. 'Instead, Vitrenko is using a network of "niche" organised-crime activities to build a power base. Last time he sought to take over all organised crime in Hamburg. Now his aim seems to be to control key lucrative activities across the Federal Republic. Among these is people trafficking, specifically for the sex trade.'

Maria looked perplexed. 'But we took out most of his key men – the so-called "Top Team". Who is he using now to build his power base?'

'Just as before, he is using ex-Spetsnaz troops. The best he can source. And, as before, they are bound to him personally. But he has reinvented himself – and his operation. This latest incarnation of Vasyl Vitrenko is, if anything, even more shadowy than the last.' Ullrich pointed to the picture in Fabel's hands. 'For all we know, he may not even look like that now. It's perfectly possible that he has a new face. A new face and a new life somewhere completely different.'

'So how can we help?' Fabel asked with little enthusiasm. He felt surrounded by ghosts unwillingly summoned up with the mention of Paul Lindemann's name immediately before the meeting. For someone who had studied history, Fabel was beginning to hate the past and the way it kept returning to haunt him. It was van Heiden, who had so far contributed nothing to the conversation, who answered Fabel's question.

'Actually, it is Senior Commissar Klee who can help. Frau Klee, I believe you have been carrying out a . . . well, I suppose the best way to describe it is as a *background* investigation into this girl's death. We need to know everything you have found out so far.'

'I told you to leave that alone, Maria,' Fabel said sharply. 'Why did you go against my orders?'

'All I did was a little asking around . . .' She turned to van Heiden and told him about her meeting with Nadja and what she had been told about the 'Farmers' Market'. 'That's as much as I've been able to find out. It just seemed that no one was doing anything about these people traffickers.'

Markus Ullrich walked over to Maria and laid out a series of large photographs on the desk before her as if he were dealing cards. They showed Maria in the street talking to prostitutes, in clubs talking to barmen and hostesses. Ullrich laid the last photograph on top of all the others as if it were his trump card.

'You know this girl? Is this "Nadja"?'

Maria stood up. 'Have you been keeping me under surveillance?'

Ullrich laughed cynically. 'Trust me, Frau Klee, you're not important enough to warrant surveillance. But we *do* have a long-established, very complex and very expensive surveillance operation focused on the activities of this Ukrainian gang. And lately it's been difficult to carry it out without you barging your way into the picture. Literally. Now, Frau Klee, do you know this girl?'

Maria sat down again. She nodded without

looking at Ullrich. 'Nadja . . . I don't know her surname. She is helping me. As much as she can, anyway. She was close to Olga . . .' Maria corrected herself. 'I mean Magda.'

'As you can see, Frau Klee' – van Heiden picked up the thread – 'someone *was* doing something about these people traffickers. We had the entire operation, with the help of BKA surveillance experts and with the cooperation of our Ukrainian colleagues, under the closest scrutiny. It is a major operation aimed at locating and capturing the very man who injured you so severely. And you have compromised the whole operation.'

'What is more' – Ullrich stabbed a finger at the picture of Maria talking to Nadja – 'you have probably cost her her life. We have no way of knowing what has happened to her. She has disappeared from our radar – immediately after she spoke to you.'

'I have to point out,' said Maria, 'that I handed over all my notes on the so-called Olga X case to the organised-crime division. I also told them of my concerns that there was a major people-trafficking ring involved with the case, if not directly with Olga's – or should I say Magda's – death. I would have thought it prudent for you to have advised me at the time that you were actively investigating them. Then—'

'Senior Commissar Klee,' van Heiden interrupted her. 'You were instructed by your commanding officer to hand everything over to LKA Six and to have no further involvement with the case. Your interference may have cost a young woman her life and widened the gap between our investigation and its ultimate aim of locating and capturing Vitrenko.'

Maria's expression hardened, but she remained silent.

'With the greatest respect to our colleagues at LKA Six and the BKA,' said Fabel, 'I have to point out that the only people who ever came close to capturing Vitrenko were myself and Frau Klee. And Frau Klee nearly paid for it with her life. So, although I admit that it was irregular for her to pursue her investigation solo, I believe she is due a little more respect as a professional police officer than is being shown here.'

Van Heiden frowned but Turchenko spoke before he had a chance to respond.

'I have read the file on what happened on that night, and I am aware of the great courage displayed by Frau Klee, yourself and the two unfortunate officers who lost their lives. It is my duty to track down Colonel Vitrenko and I am grateful for all that you have already done. I am ashamed that my country produced such a monster and I promise you that I am totally committed to bringing Vasyl Vitrenko to justice. I am, so to speak, passing through Hamburg as I follow his trail. I would be most obliged if I could ask any further questions that come to mind during my stay here.'

Fabel examined the Ukrainian. He had the look of an intellectual rather than a police officer, and his quiet, determined manner and the perfect but stilted and accented German with which he spoke seemed to invite trust.

'If we can be of help, of course we shall,' said Fabel.

'In the meantime' – Ullrich spoke directly to Maria – 'I would be obliged if you could supply a full report on your dealings with the missing prostitute and anything else you have discovered.'

Fabel and Maria made to leave.

'Before you go, Herr Fabel . . .' Van Heiden leaned forward in his chair, resting his elbows on the desk. 'Where are we with these two scalping murders?'

'We know that the woman found at the first scene is not directly linked to the murder and forensics are trying to find out to whom the hairs left behind as signatures belong. There is a possibility – but at this stage it is only a possibility – that the victims might have been selected because they were gay. We're currently checking that out. Other than that, we are pretty much without any strong leads.'

Van Heiden's expression was one of expected disappointment. 'Keep me informed, Fabel.'

Fabel and Maria did not exchange a word until they exited from the lift.

'My office,' said Fabel. 'Now.'

As instructed by Fabel, Maria closed the door behind her after she entered his office.

'What the hell is going on, Maria?' Barely contained anger stretched Fabel's quiet tone taut. 'I expect this kind of behaviour from Anna occasionally, but not from you. Why do you insist on keeping things from me?'

'I'm sorry, *Chef*. I know you told me not to follow up the Olga X case . . .'

'I'm not just talking about that. I'm talking about you keeping things from me generally. Things I ought to know. For example, why the hell didn't you tell me that you are a patient at Dr Minks's Fear Clinic?'

There was a beat of silence and Maria stared blankly at Fabel. 'Because, frankly,' she said at last, 'it is a personal issue that I didn't think was your concern.'

'For God's sake, Maria, your psychological state

is such that you have to seek treatment in a phobia clinic and you're telling me that, as your commanding officer, it's none of my business? And don't try to tell me this isn't work-related. I saw your face when Turchenko told us who his target is.' Fabel sat back in his chair, letting the tension ease from his shoulders. 'Maria, I thought you trusted me.'

Again Maria did not answer right away. Instead she turned to the window and looked out over the tops of the thick, high swathe of trees in Winterhude Stadtpark. Then she spoke in a quiet, flat voice without looking at Fabel.

'I suffer from aphenphosmphobia. It's reasonably mild but it has been getting progressively worse and Dr Minks has been treating me for it. It means that I have a fear of being touched. That's what Dr Minks is treating me for. I cannot bear the close physical presence of others. And it is a direct result of Vitrenko stabbing me.'

Fabel sighed. 'I see. Is the treatment working?'

Maria shrugged. 'Sometimes I feel that it is. But then something sparks it off again.'

'And this obsession with the Olga X case . . . I take it that was because you thought Vitrenko was involved?'

'Not at first. It was just . . . well, you were there at the murder scene. It just got to me. Poor kid. I just felt it was wrong for her to die that way. Then, yes . . . I saw that there was possibly a Vitrenko connection.'

'Maria, the Vitrenko case was just that . . . a case. We can't turn it into some kind of personal crusade. Like Turchenko said, we all want to bring Vitrenko to justice.'

'But that's just it . . .' There was an urgency in

Maria's voice that Fabel had not heard before. 'I don't want to bring him to justice. I want to kill him . . .'

## 2.30 p.m.: Hamburg Altstadt, Hamburg

Paul Scheibe stood outside the Rathaus city chambers. The vast plain of Rathausmarkt, Hamburg's main city square, seemed to writhe with tourists and shoppers under the hot summer sun. Scheibe had worn a lightweight suit in black linen and a white, collarless shirt to the meeting with Hamburg's First Mayor Hans Schreiber and the city's Environment Senator Bertholdt Müller-Voigt. Yet despite the lightness of the fabric Scheibe felt clammy trickles of sweat gather on the nape of his neck and in the small of his back. The meeting had been arranged to congratulate him on the selection of his *KulturZentrumEins* design for the site on the HafenCity's Überseequartier and Scheibe had done his best to look pleased and interested. Perhaps that was why so many people had asked him if everything was all right: Scheibe's professional trade mark had always been his arrogance; his aloofness from the crude commercial aspect of architecture. But everyone had been happy and the champagne corks had popped. And there had been lots of champagne; now Scheibe's mouth tasted coppery and dry and the alcohol had had no effect on him other than to enervate him.

Life must go on, he had thought to himself. And maybe it will. Maybe it was just a coincidence that two members of the cast of his previous life had been murdered. The same way. By the same person. Or maybe it wasn't.

He watched the sightseers and the shoppers, the office workers and the business people scuttle across the Rathausmarkt. A street musician was playing Rimsky-Korsakov on an accordion somewhere over by the Schleusenbrücke bridge across the Alsterfleet. Paul Scheibe was surrounded by people, by noise; he stood at the very heart of a great city. He had never felt so isolated or exposed. Was this what it was like to be hunted?

He walked. He walked quickly and with a sense of purpose that he did not understand, as if the act of deliberate motion would stimulate some idea about what he should do next. He crossed the Rathausmarkt diagonally and headed up Mönckebergstrasse. The throng of people grew denser as he came into the main pedestrianised part of Mönckebergstrasse, lined with stores. Still he let his feet lead him. He felt hot and dirty, his hair was beginning to cling to his damp scalp and he wished that he could cast off the mantle of warm summer air that seemed to stifle his ability to think. He did not want to die. He did not want to go to prison. He had made a name for himself and he knew that the wrong step taken now would tarnish that name for ever.

He stopped outside an electrical store. A regional NDR news programme played mutely on a large-screen TV behind the glass. It was a pre-recorded interview with Bertholdt Müller-Voigt. Scheibe had found it hard enough to stomach Müller-Voigt's sneery, patronising presence at the lunch and now he watched as he smiled his politician smile at him through the glass. It was as if he were mocking Scheibe, just like he used to all those years ago.

Müller-Voigt had always possessed, naturally and without effort, the kind of self-confident poise and intellectual credibility that Scheibe worked so hard to project. Müller-Voigt had always been smarter, had always been cooler, had always been at the focus of things. Paul Scheibe found it impossible to forgive Bertholdt Müller-Voigt any of these things. But there was something else that fuelled Scheibe's loathing for his contemporary, something deeper and more fundamental that burned white-hot at the core of his hatred: Müller-Voigt had taken Beate from him.

Of course, back then they had all forsworn anything so bourgeois as monogamy, and Beate, the raven-haired, half-Italian mathematics student with whom Scheibe had been besotted, would never have allowed any man to think of her as belonging to him. But it was the closest that Paul Scheibe had ever been to love. It wasn't just that Müller-Voigt had slept with Beate; it was that he had done so with the same thoughtless arrogance with which he had slept with dozens of other women. It had meant nothing to him then and Scheibe was pretty certain that today Müller-Voigt probably wouldn't even remember it.

And now, two decades later, every time Paul Scheibe met Müller-Voigt – or even heard the politician's name mentioned – it provoked exactly the same feelings of envy and loathing in Scheibe that it had provoked back then, when they had been students. Afterwards, Scheibe had built a new life for himself, a different and successful life. But Müller-Voigt had somehow managed to build an even more successful new life. Most of all, Müller-Voigt had remained on the fringes of Scheibe's world: a constant and unwelcome reminder of the old days. But now Müller-Voigt was not the only reminder of that time.

Scheibe pressed his forehead against the electrical store's window, expecting it to be cool, but it reflected the damp warmth of his brow. A passing shopper bumped shoulders with him and nudged him out of his reverie. What was he doing here? What was he going to do next? He knew he had stridden out of the Rathausmarkt determined to find an answer.

He had to find somewhere to think. Somewhere to make sense of it all.

Scheibe tore his gaze from the TV screen and started to walk purposefully on up Mönckebergstrasse. Towards the Hamburg Hauptbahnhof railway station.

## 2.30 p.m.: Police Presidium, Hamburg

There is a bureaucracy of death: each murder case generates a mountain of forms to be filled and reports to be filed. After the meeting with the Ukrainian policeman and Markus Ullrich, Fabel had found it difficult to focus on the paperwork that had piled up. There were so many things circulating in his head that he lost track of time and he suddenly realised that he had not eaten since breakfast.

He took the lift down to the Police Presidium's canteen and placed a filled roll and a coffee on his tray. The canteen was all but empty and he headed over towards the window to take a seat. It was then that he noticed Maria sitting with Turchenko. The Ukrainian detective was leaning back in his chair, looking down at the coffee that sat on the table in front of him, and seemed to be in the middle of a detailed explanation of something. Maria was concentrating on the Ukrainian's words. There was something about the set-up that Fabel did not like.

'Do you mind if I join you?' he asked.

Turchenko looked up and smiled broadly. 'Not at all, Herr Chief Commissar. Be my guest.'

Maria also smiled, but her expression suggested that she was irritated by the interruption.

'You speak excellent German, Herr Turchenko,' said Fabel.

'I studied it at university. Along with law. I spent some time in the former East Germany as a student. I have always had a fascination for Germany. Which made me the obvious choice to send here to try to track down Vitrenko.'

'Do you have a special-forces background too?' asked Fabel.

Turchenko laughed. 'God, no . . . in fact, I have not been a police officer that long. I was a criminal and civil lawyer in Lviv. After the Orange Revolution, in which I had been active, I became a criminal prosecutor and was then approached by the new government. They asked me if I would oversee the setting up of a new organised-crime unit to deal with people-smuggling and forced prostitution. Basically, my job is to stop what has become the new slave trade. I was chosen because I am free from the taint of the old regime.'

'Things are changing in Ukraine, I believe.'

Turchenko smiled. 'Ukraine is a beautiful country, Herr Fabel. One of the most beautiful in Europe. People here have no idea. It is also a country laden with almost every type of natural bounty – an incredibly fertile land that was the bread basket of the former USSR. It is also rich in every kind of mineral and it has enormous potential for tourism. I love my country and I have a great belief in what it can become. And what I believe it will become is one of the richest and most successful nations in Europe. It will take more than a generation to achieve, of course, but it *will* happen. And the first steps have been taken

– democracy and liberalisation. But there are problems. Ukraine is divided. In western Ukraine, we look to the West for our future. But in eastern Ukraine, there are still those who believe we belong in some kind of unity with Russia.' Turchenko paused. 'You Germans should be able to understand this. Your country has been reborn many times, and sometimes the incarnation has not been a good one. This is our rebirth in Ukraine. Our country is beginning a new life. A life that we took to the streets to create. And people like Vasyl Vitrenko have no part in it.'

'Vitrenko is extremely dangerous game to hunt,' said Fabel. 'You will have to take a lot of care.'

'I am a naturally cautious man. And I have your police here to protect me.' Turchenko made an open-armed gesture, as if embracing the entire Presidium. 'I have a GSG9 bodyguard with me all the time.' He gave a small laugh and tapped his temple with his forefinger. 'I am no man of action. I am a man of thought. I believe that the way to find and capture this monster is to out-think him.'

Fabel smiled. He liked the small Ukrainian: he was a man who clearly believed in all that he had said. Who had an enthusiasm for what he did for a career. Fabel found himself envying him.

'I wish you luck,' he said.

### 3.40 p.m.: Hohenfelde, Hamburg

'How did it go?' Julia frowned as she spoke. Cornelius Tamm resented the fact that her frown created so few creases on her brow, as if her youth refused to yield to her concern. It seemed to Cornelius that he was surrounded by youth. It mocked him wherever he went.

'It didn't.' Cornelius threw his keys onto the table and took off his jacket.

Julia was thirty-two; Cornelius exactly thirty years her senior. He had left his wife for Julia three years before, on the eve of his fifty-ninth birthday. His marriage had been almost as old as the woman he had ended it for and Julia was nearer to his children's age than to his own. At the time, Cornelius had felt that he was regaining a sense of youth, of vigour. Now he just felt tired all the time: tired and old. He sat down at the table.

'What did he say?' Julia poured him a cup of coffee and sat down opposite him.

'He said my time is past. Basically.' Cornelius gazed at Julia as if trying to work out what she was doing in his kitchen, his apartment. His life. 'And he's right, you know. The world has moved on. And somewhere along the way it left me behind.' He pushed the coffee aside. He took out a tumbler and a bottle of Scotch from a kitchen cabinet and poured himself a large glass.

'That doesn't help, you know,' said Julia.

'It may not cure the disease.' He took a substantial sip and screwed up his face. 'But it sure as hell helps the symptoms. It anaesthetises.'

'Don't worry.' Julia's comforting smile only irritated Cornelius further. 'You'll get a deal soon. You'll see. By the way, someone phoned for you while you were out. About fifteen minutes ago.'

'Who?'

'They wouldn't leave a name at first. Then he said to tell you that it was Paul and that he would phone you later.'

'Paul?' Cornelius frowned as he tried to think which Paul it could be, then dismissed it with a

209

shrug. 'I'm going to my study. And I'm taking my anaesthetic with me.'

It was another name that caught his attention. As he stood up, he noticed the copy of the *Hamburger Morgenpost* on the table. Cornelius put his drink down and picked up the paper. He stared at it long and hard.

'What is it?' asked Julia. 'What's wrong?'

Cornelius didn't answer her and stayed focused on the article. It named someone who had died. Been murdered. But the name was one that had already been dead to Cornelius for twenty years. It was the report of the death of a ghost.

'Nothing,' he said and put the paper down. 'Nothing at all.'

It was then that he worked out who Paul was.

### 7.40 p.m.: Nordenham Railway Station, 145 Kilometres West of Hamburg

It was a beautiful evening. The embers of the sun hung low in the sky behind Nordenham and the Weser sparkled quietly as it made its way towards the North Sea. Paul Scheibe had never set foot in Nordenham before, which was an irony when he considered how this small provincial town had cast a giant shadow over his life.

For a moment, Scheibe became again purely the architect as he gazed at Nordenham railway station. Architecturally, it was not really his kind of thing: but it was, nevertheless, a striking building, albeit in the solid, sometimes austere, traditional North German style. He remembered reading that it was over one hundred years old and was now an officially protected building.

Here.

It had happened here. On this platform. This was the stage on which the most important drama in his life had been played out and he had not even been here. Nor had the others. Six people, a hundred and fifty kilometres away, had made a decision to sacrifice a human being on this platform. One life brought to an end, six lives free to begin again. But it had not just been one life that had been lost in this place. Piet had also died here. As had Michaela and a policeman. But Paul Scheibe had never found he could feel guilty about those lost lives – everything else had been eclipsed by the intense feeling of relief, of liberation, that had come from knowing it was all over. But it was not over. Something – some*one* – had returned from that dark time.

Work it out, he kept telling himself. Work it out. Who was killing the members of the group? It had to have something to do with this place and what had happened here. But who was behind it? Could it be one of the remaining four members of the group? Scheibe found that almost impossible to imagine: there was simply nothing to gain, and there were no grudges, no old scores to be settled. Just a desire to have nothing to do with each other.

Scheibe felt something chill grip him: what if Franz had not died here? They had loved Franz, they had followed him; but more than anything, they had feared him. What if his death had been a sham, a conspiracy, some kind of deal with the authorities? What if, somehow, he had survived?

It didn't make sense, but these killings *had* to have something to do with what had happened here, on this provincial railway platform, twenty years before. Scheibe already regretted having left that message for

211

Cornelius. He was not going to make it easier for the killer, and he was not going to risk his career by renewing associations that were best forgotten. He had worked too hard for all that he had achieved since the last time they had met; he was not going to give any of it up.

Scheibe looked at his watch: it was nearly eight. He felt tired and unclean. He hadn't eaten since the lunch in the Rathaus and he felt empty inside. Scheibe sat on a bench on the platform and gazed blankly out across the tracks, across the flat landscape beyond, across the Weser towards the Luneplatte on the far side.

He could think this through. That was what they had always relied on him for back then: his ability to plan a strategy in the same way he could plan a building. More than a structure, but every detail integrated. He had been the architect of what had happened here: he had freed himself and the others. Now he needed to do it again. Scheibe reached into the pocket of his crumpled black linen jacket and pulled out his cellphone. No, his number could be traced: he had, after all, only recently been lectured about the insecurity of using a mobile telephone. Scheibe knew he had to play this carefully. He would phone the police. Anonymously. He would do a deal that kept him out of it. Like the last time.

A payphone. He needed to find a payphone. Paul turned and scanned the landscape around him.

It was then that the young man with the dark hair stepped out onto the platform. There was no vague sense of recognition. Paul did not struggle with where or when or how he had seen the face before. Maybe because he was seeing it in this context.

The young man strode across to Paul purposefully.

'I know who you are,' said Paul. 'I know exactly
who you are.'

The young man smiled and took his hand briefly
out of his jacket pocket to reveal the Makarov automatic.

'Let's go somewhere more private to talk. My car
is parked outside,' he said, indicating the platform's
exit with a nod of his head.

### 8.00 p.m.: St Pauli, Hamburg

'Just let me know if I'm cramping your style.' Anna
Wolff grinned at Henk Hermann as they approached
the bar.

The Firehouse was a large, square-set building in
the St Pauli Kiez. Externally it was one of those
unremarkable 1950s brick-built buildings that had
erupted across Hamburg like weeds on the gap sites
created by Second World War bombs. Internally, it
was just as unremarkable, but in a totally different
way. The decor was the kind of variation on the
same theme of generic designer cool that could be
found in bars and clubs around the world: an unsur-
prising, uninspiring, vaguely retro sophistication.
Even the music in the background was the predictable
chill-out soundtrack. The Firehouse left Anna, who
preferred clubs and bars that had more of an edge,
totally cold. But there again, it was not aimed at
Anna. Or anyone of her gender.

'Very funny.' Henk muttered and nodded towards
the shaven-headed black barman who came over to
their end of the bar.

'What can I get you?' The black barman spoke

German that was spun through with something between an African and an English accent.

In reply, Henk held up his oval Criminal Police shield. 'We'd like to ask you about one of your customers.'

'Oh?'

'It's in connection with a murder inquiry,' said Anna. 'We believe the victim was a regular here.' She laid a photograph of Hauser on the bar. 'Know him?'

The barman looked briefly at the photograph and nodded.

'That is Herr Hauser. Yes, I know him. Or knew him. I read about his death in the newspapers. Terrible. Yes, he was a regular here.'

'With anyone in particular?'

'No one special that I know of. Lots of guys in general . . .'

The other two barkeepers were occupied and a customer called over to the black barman from the other side of the bar.

'Excuse me a moment . . .' While he went over to serve the customer, Anna surveyed the club. Considering it was so early in the evening, and so early in the working week, there was a substantial number of customers. As she expected, it was populated by an exclusively male clientele, but other than that there was nothing to distinguish it from any other bar or club. Some of the men had the business-suited look of having come straight from their offices. Anna found it difficult to imagine Hauser in the club: it all seemed too 'corporate', too mainstream. The black barman came back and apologised for the interruption.

'Herr Hauser came in here a lot, but he tended

to hang around with younger guys. *Much* younger guys. I just asked the other barmen about him. Martin says he used to come in a lot with a guy with dark hair.'

'Sebastian Lang?' Anna placed a photograph of Lang on the counter next to the one of Hauser.

'I wouldn't know him . . . Martin?' The barman called over to his colleague who came over and examined the photograph.

'That's him,' the second barman confirmed. 'They came in here together for a while, but then the younger guy stopped coming. But before him, Herr Hauser used to drink with a man more his own age. I don't think they were an item, or anything. I just think they were friends.'

'Do you have a name for this friend?'

'Sorry.'

'Does he still come in here?'

The barman shook his head. 'I couldn't say when he might turn up. I think he only came in to meet Herr Hauser.'

'Thanks,' said Henk and handed the barman his Polizei Hamburg contact card. 'If you do see him again, you can contact me on this number.'

The barman took the card. 'Sure.' He frowned. 'You don't think this guy had anything to do with Herr Hauser's murder, do you?'

'At the moment we're just trying to build a picture of the victim's last days,' said Anna. 'And the kind of people he used to hang out with. That's all.'

But, as she and Henk left The Firehouse, Anna could not help thinking that they had built no picture at all.

# 9.

# Twelve Days After the First Murder:
# Tuesday, 30 August 2005.

### 10.30 a.m.: Police Presidium, Hamburg

Fabel phoned Markus Ullrich, the BKA officer, from his office in the Murder Commission. Ullrich sounded surprised to hear from Fabel, but there was no sense of the BKA man being guarded in his response.

'What can I do for you, Chief Commissar? Is this about Frau Klee?'

'No, Herr Ullrich, it isn't.' The truth was that Fabel did want to pursue the issue with Ullrich, but now was not the time. Fabel was looking for a favour. 'You will remember that Criminal Director van Heiden asked about the case I'm working on? The so-called "Hamburg Hairdresser"?'

'Yes, I do.'

'Someone has suggested that I should be looking more closely into the history of the victims. Specifically that there may be some skeletons in the closet dating back to their days as student activists – or later, during the years of unrest. Both were politically active to varying degrees. And I thought that if there were any suspicions about them . . .'

'. . . That we at the BKA would have them on file – is that it?'

'It's just a thought . . .' Fabel went on to outline what they knew to date about both victims.

'Okay,' said Ullrich. 'I'll see what I can do.'

After Fabel hung up he went through to the main Murder Commission office and spoke to Anna Wolff. He gave her the details from the Second World War identity card of the HafenCity mummy.

'Could you get on to the state archives and see if we can dig anything up? I'd like to find out if there is any surviving next of kin we should notify.'

Anna looked at the information Fabel handed her and shrugged. 'Okay, *Chef*.'

Fabel did the rounds of his officers to get updates on progress. The two scalping murders had eclipsed everything else and Fabel was glad that the Kiez brawl killing was the only other continuing case, because it was a comparatively easy one to tie up. Fabel often caught himself thinking like that: grateful that the violent ending of another human's life was conveniently straightforward and therefore less demanding on his team's resources. He hated the forced callousness of being an investigator of the deaths of others.

'Still nothing on the phone accounts of either victim,' Henk Hermann anticipated Fabel's question. 'We've found no numbers that cannot be accounted for.'

Fabel thanked Henk and made his way back to his office. It still nagged at Fabel. He had a gut instinct that the victims had known their killer.

### 11.45 a.m.: Schanzenviertel, Hamburg

The room was filled with the rich, sweet smell of incense. The blinds were drawn and the room was illuminated by the soft, dancing light of two dozen candles.

Beate Brandt sat with her eyes closed, one hand resting on the forehead and the other on the chest of her client. Her hair was long, cascading over her shoulders, just as it had when she was eighteen. But the glossy, sensual lustre with which it had once ensnared men's hearts had faded over a decade ago. Now it was more grey than black and its sheen had been replaced by a dry coarseness. Similarly, Beate's dark beauty, which she had inherited from her Italian mother, had faded. The strong bone structure and the fineness of her features remained, but the skin in which they were wreathed had become creased and wrinkled, as if someone had stored a fine painting carelessly.

'Breathe deeply . . .' she said to the client, who she reckoned was about the same age as her own son and who lay on his back, his eyes closed tight. 'We are travelling back. Back to a time beyond life but before death. Only once we confront the life that has gone before can we experience rebirth.'

She pressed down on her client's forehead. Her fingers were covered with large rings, some of which bore astrological symbols. Her client had pale, flawless skin and she compared the smooth perfection of his brow with the wrinkles on the back of her hand and the thickening of her once-slender fingers. Why, she thought, do our bodies age, yet inside we feel exactly the same as we did half a lifetime ago?

'Go back . . .' Her voice was just above a whisper. 'Go back to your childhood. Do you remember? Then back further. Further back . . .'

Beate had always struggled to make ends meet. Or, more correctly, she had struggled to make ends meet while maintaining a low profile. She had hated the idea of becoming a small-time capitalist but hated the idea of working for someone else even more. Beate also had to think of her son. She had done her best to make sure that he never wanted for anything. As a single mother, it had been difficult for her. And, of course, there had always been the added difficulty of how deeply someone would look into her history when she applied for a job. She had started off with a small fashion business in the Viertel, but, as time went on, it became clear that Beate's idea of Schanzenviertel chic was out of step – a decade out of step – with what customers were looking for. After the shop had closed, she had struggled to find something that she could do to earn money. Then she came up with the Rebirthing concept. Beate knew it was all nonsense. Some part of her, deep down inside, found the idea of re-incarnation attractive – plausible, even – but the whole 'Rebirth Induction' thing was a pile of crap. She ought to know: after all, it had been Beate who had invented it.

She looked down at the client lying on the floor. He was a regular and had been coming for three months. Since Hans-Joachim and Gunter's murders she had taken the decision to see no new clients. No strangers. The deaths had shocked her. Frightened her. After all, although their paths had not crossed in twenty years, Hans-Joachim had lived only a couple of streets away.

Now Beate would admit only those clients whom she had dealt with for some time. She had even tried spinning a new thread of 'group therapy' so that she would see more than one client at a time. But because of the intimately personal nature of her 'treatment', her clients were reluctant to participate in group sessions. Beate's most inspired idea had been to set up a website through which she could conduct on-line consultations. She had even bought some software which let people type in their dates and places of birth and receive an outline of a likely past life. And all paid for through a secure on-line credit card system. No risk, no outlay, all profit.

At the heart of Beate's business was an essentially simple idea: that everyone had lived before, several times, and that there had to be a key to unlocking those past lives. Of course, with an exponentially growing global population, for everyone to have had a past life was a statistical impossibility. Beate, who had studied applied mathematics at the Universität Hamburg, knew that only too well. But there had been a time, long ago, when she had been prepared to suspend her disbelief in the name of something bigger. Furthermore, the world today was full of people seeking something to make sense of their existence; or wanting to seek refuge in some other truth, some other life: anything that offered them something less banal than their everyday existences. So Beate, the atheist, the rationalist, the mathematician, had established herself as a New Age guru who helped people rediscover their past lives. She had learned the basic principles of hypnotism, although she doubted that she had ever successfully hypnotised a client. It was more likely that they deluded themselves that they were in a hypnotic state so that they could believe the nonsense they spouted about a past life; could believe that it came from somewhere deeper than simply a mixture of imagination, wish-fulfilment and something they had probably read somewhere once. But to cover herself she had talked about 'guided meditation', placing the onus on the client for their own hypnosis.

But the original concept had been flawed: Beate had learned very quickly that once she had helped a client to uncover one 'past life' the client went away happy – and a source of income walked out of the door. She had realised that she needed to add another dimension to her 'therapy': something that would prolong the course of treatment. It was then that she came up with both the idea for the website and the concept of 'Whole Person Rebirth'. The principle was that to be 'complete' one had to uncover *all* one's past lives, combine them with one's current existence and to then undergo a 'rebirthing' where one became whole and put behind everything in the past and began anew. A true new life.

The irony was not wasted on Beate. Here, in this room within her apartment, she spouted a home-grown mixture of New Age claptrap and psychobabble about reincarnation and rebirth. Like the others in the group, she had reinvented herself, putting distance between herself and her past life. Unlike some of the others, however, Beate had chosen to keep as low a profile as possible. Whereas some of the group had clearly felt immune to discovery, she had sought anonymity. But it seemed that keeping a low profile offered no protection. Hans-Joachim Hauser had always been a self-promoting, self-important egotist; but she had guessed that Gunter Griebel, like her, had chosen to live his life as unnoticed as possible. Yet someone *had* noticed.

She cast a glance at the wall clock. This session seemed to be taking for ever. The young patient was convinced that he had multiple past lives to uncover, yet claimed there was some obstacle in the way, something he could not navigate around. Beate sighed patiently and tried to ease him through the years, through the centuries, to discover who and when he had been before.

Sometimes she felt like screaming in the faces of her clients that it was all a sham, a fraud; that there was nothing to uncover other than their own inadequacies and failure to come to terms with the fact that this world, here and now, was all there was to life. It always amused Beate that, in uncovering their past lives, most of her clientele displayed the same lack of chronological and technical accuracy as the average historical-romance novelist. Many clients were middle-aged women who fulfilled some fantasy by remembering a past life as a beautiful courtesan, a voluptuous village maid or a fairy-tale princess. Few 'past lives' involved the plagues, diseases, famines and extreme poverty that had been commonplace throughout history.

But this young man was different. He had approached the whole process with earnestness. From the very beginning he had spoken with conviction about his need to visit a previous life. It was as if he were seeking some form of truth. A real past. A real life.

The one thing that Beate could not deliver.

'Can you see anything yet?' she asked.

The young man furrowed his broad, pale brow in concentration. Beate had noticed how attractive he was from their first meeting. And she had had the strangest feeling that she had known him from somewhere. At one time, she could have had him. At one time, she could have had any man. Any*thing*.

The world had rolled itself out before her, wide and fresh and clean, waiting for Beate's footfall. Then it had all turned to dust.

'I see something,' he said hesitantly. 'Yes, I see something. A place. I am standing in front of a large building and I am waiting for something or someone.'

'Is this in this lifetime, or a time before?'

'Before. It was before.'

'Describe the building.'

'It is large. Three storeys high. It has a wide front with several doors. I am standing outside it.' The young man kept his eyes closed, but suddenly there was a great urgency in his voice. 'I see it. I see it all so clearly.'

'What do you see?' Beate glanced again at the wall clock. If he had seen into a previous life, then it had better be a short one or he would be paying for an extra hour.

'Two lives. Three lives, counting this one. It is all so clear to me and I see each one as if I were remembering yesterday.'

'Three lives, you say?'

'Three lives, but one life. A continuum. Death was not the end: it was merely a brief interruption. A pause.'

That, thought Beate, I have got to remember. 'A continuum with death as a brief interruption.' Brilliant. I can use that. 'Go on,' she urged her young client. 'Tell me about your first life. Is that when you stood outside this large building?'

'No . . . no, that was the second time. That was the time before.'

'Tell me about your first life. Where are you? Who are you?' Beate struggled to keep the impatience from her voice.

'It's not important. My first life was simply preparation . . . I was being readied.'

'When was this?'

'A millennium ago. Longer. I was sacrificed and laid in the bog. Under the muddy water. Then they laid hazel and birch branches over me and weighted them with stones. It was so cold. So dark. Ten hundred years in the dark and cold. Then I was reborn.'

'As whom were you reborn?'

'Someone . . .' The client's frown deepened. 'Someone . . . you *knew*.'

'*I* knew you?' Beate looked down on her client and studied the face. His eyes remained closed. For some reason his claim had disturbed her. It was all nonsense, of course, but she thought back again to their first session. To begin with she had thought she recognised him, that she knew him from somewhere. But then she realised that he merely reminded her of someone else, someone whom, at that time, she could not quite identify.

'I am there now. The building. I can see it clearly . . .' The young man ignored her question. He opened his eyes and looked up towards the ceiling, but his gaze was fixed on somewhere, sometime else. 'It's a railway station. I can see that now. I am standing at a railway station. It is a small station but the building behind me is large and old. In front of me, beyond the opposite platform, the land is empty and flat. There is a wide river . . .'

He fell silent for a moment and an expression of intense concentration spread across his features. Then he shook his head.

'Sorry . . .' He looked at her directly for the first time since the session began. He smiled apologetically. 'It's gone.'

'You said you knew me in this previous life.'

Her client spun his legs around and sat up on the edge of the therapy bench. 'I dunno . . . it was just a feeling I got. I can't explain it or anything.'

Beate considered his words for a moment. Then she looked at her watch. The hour was up.

'Well, maybe we can pick up where we left off with our next session.' She checked her diary and confirmed the date and time. Her client rose and put on his jacket. 'I think the session has done you good this week,' she said. 'You look more relaxed than you have since you first started to come here.'

'I *am* more relaxed.' He smiled as he walked to the door. 'I feel as if I'm approaching a very special, very peaceful state of mind. The Japanese have a name for it . . .'

'Oh?' Beate held open the door for him. Her noon appointment would be there at any moment.

'Yes,' he said as he left. 'They call it *zanshin*.'

### 12.40 p.m.: Winterhuder Fährhaus, Hamburg

The café at the Winterhude ferry point was reasonably close to the Police Presidium. Fabel often used it as somewhere he could gather his team to discuss a case less formally: a change of scene, away from the Murder Commission. When Markus Ullrich had called Fabel that morning, Fabel had suggested that they should meet at the Fährhaus café.

Fabel arrived early and ordered a coffee from the waiter who knew him as a regular customer but had no idea that he was a murder detective. Fabel liked the fact that most people would never think of him as a policeman, and he never volunteered the information freely. It was as if he had two identities. Two separate lives occupying two separate Hamburgs: the city he lived in and loved, and the city he policed. He often wondered if, even after all this time, he belonged in the profession. He was good at his job, he knew that, but each new case, each new cruelty inflicted on one human being by another, chipped away at him. Not for the first time, Fabel was lost in thought about what might have been, who he might have been, had he not taken the decision to join the Polizei Hamburg. And all the time he was aware of Roland Bartz's business card in his wallet: a ticket back to a normal life.

He snapped out of his reverie when he spotted the squat form of Ullrich coming down the steps to the café. The BKA man was dressed in a dark business suit with a dark shirt and tie and carried a small executive attaché case. He could have been coming to sell Fabel insurance. Fabel thought back to his meeting with Professor van Halen, the business-suited geneticist: it seemed as though the whole world was becoming 'corporate'.

'Thanks for doing this,' he said as he shook Ullrich's hand. 'I just thought there was an off chance that you might have something on file about either or both of the murder victims, given their backgrounds.'

The two men sat down and further conversation was suspended while the waiter came over and took their orders.

'I've some interesting stuff for you, Herr Fabel.' Ullrich held the attaché case across his lap and patted it, as if hinting at treasures hidden within. Then, very deliberately, he set the case down on the floor beside him in a clear 'for later' gesture. 'We have quite a bit to discuss, but before we do I just wanted to clear the air about the situation with Maria Klee . . . I hope you didn't think that I was being too hard on her. But she did compromise a major operation.'

'I would have much preferred it if you had discussed the matter with me first, instead of going directly to Criminal Director van Heiden.'

Ullrich shrugged. 'I didn't really have the opportunity to deal with it that way. The operation's commanders – especially, I have to say, those from the Polizei Hamburg's LKA Six – were incensed that Frau Klee was trampling all over their case. It has been a highly sensitive operation.'

'But for God's sake, Ullrich, you know how *intimately* my team were involved with the Vitrenko investigation.'

'That was a previous case. I'm sorry, Fabel, but life moves on. We are dealing with the threat Vitrenko presents *now*. And it's much bigger than the Polizei Hamburg can handle alone. We had officers from the BKA, from LKA Six, from the Federal Border Police, from the Cologne Police organised-crime squad . . . a hell of a lot of man-hours went into the operation. I'm sorry I couldn't talk to you about it personally, but there was a lot of politics involved too. I just wanted you to know that I wasn't deliberately going over your head . . .'

'Fair enough,' said Fabel.

'Anyway . . .' Ullrich lifted his briefcase. 'I did what you asked and did a bit of checking into your two murder victims.'

'And?'

'And, although the connections are vague, there are too many coincidences – in my opinion, anyway – to suggest that your so-called Hamburg Hairdresser is making random selections. As you suspected, there were Hamburg LKA and Federal BKA intelligence files on Hans-Joachim Hauser. He was very active all the way through to the nineteen eighties. I thought it would be of interest to you. Just as background. I had a copy made of the file . . .' Ullrich reached into his briefcase and pulled out a thick file which he laid on the white-painted surface of the metal café table. There was nothing on the buff-coloured cover to hint at what lay within. Fabel was about to pick up the file when Ullrich laid his hand flat on it. 'Please don't *mislay* it. Even if it is a copy, it would be most embarrassing. There's not a lot in there that would surprise you, Herr Fabel. But this is where it gets interesting . . .' He laid a second file on top of the first. 'Your second victim also had a BKA file back then.'

Fabel leaned forward. 'Griebel was under surveillance?'

'I thought that would intrigue you.' Ullrich smiled. 'On the surface there's no direct connection that I can see between Hauser and Griebel, other than, as you said, that they were at the Universität Hamburg at roughly the same time and they were both politically active, if to different degrees. But the thing that's most interesting is that both men later fell under general suspicion of being figures in the so-called RAF-Umfeld.'

'Griebel too?' Fabel was familiar with the term: 'RAF-Umfeld' referred to the vague general network of supporters who had provided assistance, often financial or logistical, for the Red Army Faction/Baader-Meinhof gang and other terrorist organisations.

'Griebel too,' confirmed Ullrich. 'As you know, all

through the nineteen seventies and nineteen eighties, anarchist terror groups in Germany were sustained by these networks. To begin with there was the "Schili" or the "chic left" who were mainly middle-class liberals who funded the activities of the anarchists. The Schili were mainly left-wing lawyers, journalists, university lecturers and the like who coughed up money to support the "direct-action" activities of the anarchists . . . until that "direct action" moved on from "walk-ins" on posh restaurants, daubing slogans on government buildings and posing naked for the press, to kidnap, murder and bombings. The activists became terrorists and it all became too much for the trendy left. It really sorted the wheat from the chaff, and the terrorist groups ended up with a hard core of helpers who were deployed in roles where they did not actually break the law.'

'I know,' said Fabel. 'The so-called "legals".'

'Exactly. But as well as the "legals" there was a nationwide network of sleepers. These people could be called on to break the law to finance or support the activities of the main terror group, maybe even to carry out a high-profile assassination . . . but, on the surface, they led normal lives and did not draw attention to themselves. The terrorist groups often picked people who had never been connected officially with the protest movement or with any type of political activity.' Ullrich gave the files a nudge towards Fabel. 'In there, you'll see that Hans-Joachim Hauser was suspected of being a "legal": he was openly in support of the "cause", but did not break the law. Herr Dr Griebel, on the other hand, was considered a possible sleeping agent . . .'

'And they were suspected of being tied in with the Red Army Faction?'

'That's the thing. As you know, there was a fair amount of cross-fertilisation between groups – the Socialist Patients' Collective, the Revolutionary Cells, Rote Zora and the Baader-Meinhof gang – and there was also a fair amount of *freelance* activity, for want of a better word. And I know that you yourself encountered one of these splinter groups early in your police career.'

Fabel nodded curtly. Ullrich was clearly referring to the 1983 Commerzbank shootings carried out by Hendrik Svensson's Radical Action Group – in the course of which Franz Webern had been killed and Fabel had been wounded and forced to take a life to save his own. Fabel did not like the idea that the BKA man probably had, sometime, run a check on him. But there again, he told himself, that was the business Markus Ullrich was in.

'You will remember,' continued Ullrich, 'after the Stammheim prison suicides of Meinhof, Baader, Ensslin and Raspe in nineteen seventy-six and nineteen seventy-seven, German domestic terrorism lost its focus and became very fragmented – which actually made our job more difficult. It also resulted in a steeply increased level and intensity of violence. The truth is that Hauser and Griebel were both low-priority subjects . . . and there was never any suggestion of a connection between them. They did share common acquaintances – but, there again, so would anyone involved even marginally with that scene. There is something else about Griebel.'

'Oh?'

'I noticed that his file was recently updated. He was looked at again only a couple of years ago, in fact. I get the feeling it had to do with his field of research. Why his particular speciality was of interest

I couldn't tell you, but our counter-terrorism people felt the need to run another check on him. But again, low-priority stuff. Anyway . . . happy reading.'

'I really do appreciate you doing this for me,' Fabel said as their lunches arrived.

'You're welcome. All I would ask is that if the political backgrounds of your murder victims turn out to be a positive lead, please do let me know. It may be that there is a *dimension* to this case that may interest us. And Herr Fabel . . .' Ullrich looked uncertain, as if weighing up whether to say what he had to say or not.

'Yes?'

'Be careful. As you'll see from the files, some of the figures who were subject to our scrutiny in the past have become important people today. All you need to do is look at Gerhard Schröder's government cabinet. A Foreign Minister who has admitted to street violence and an Interior Minister who was a defence attorney for the Baader-Meinhof gang.' Ullrich was referring to Joschka Fischer who had been 'outed' when Bettina Röhl, the daughter of Ulrike Meinhof, had released to the press photographs of Fischer assaulting a police officer, and to Otto Schily, who had represented the terrorists early in his legal career. 'And there are others with big ambitions much closer to home . . .'

'Like Müller-Voigt?'

'Exactly. If you find yourself going down this line of inquiry, watch your back.'

Fabel gave a grim laugh. 'I'm not worried about political flak,' he said. 'I'm well used to that by now.'

'Political flak isn't all you have to worry about . . .' Ullrich said. 'I can't believe that the so-called sleepers who were put in place back then believe in any of that crap now, but they have been living their *normal* lives for two decades. I'm sure some of them are quite prepared to go to any lengths to protect themselves. Like I said: be careful.'

## 7.30 p.m.: Pöseldorf, Hamburg

Fabel spent the afternoon reading the BKA files. Everything was as Ullrich had described it: Hauser and Griebel had inhabited the same landscape, had followed similar paths, had known the same people, but there was no evidence to suggest that those paths had ever crossed. Still, logic suggested that it was not impossible that at least they knew *of* each other. And just because no contact had been established by the security services it did not mean that they had in fact never met.

Susanne was working late at the Institute for Legal Medicine, so Fabel returned home alone. His lunch with Ullrich meant that he still had no appetite to speak of, so he took a sandwich and a bottle of Jever through to the living room and set them on the coffee table next to his laptop and the files. He sat for a moment sipping his beer and looking through his picture windows out over the Alsterpark and the wide expanse of Alster, whose water glittered gently in the early evening light. It was a scene that should have put him at peace, but something he could not quite identify nagged at him. Fabel was an orderly man: he needed balance in his universe; logic in the mechanics of his life. And, as with most orderly men, this necessity came from his fear of the chaos that often raged within him. It had scared him to see the same paranoia displayed at its most extreme in Kristina Dreyer. The tenuous connections and the broad coincidences that surrounded the two murder victims offended his need for order. When he looked at them from a distance, he could perceive a network of interconnecting threads, but when he drew close it all fell apart like a spider's web in the wind.

Fabel heard the sound of the door of his flat being opened and Susanne's voice announcing her arrival. She came in and in a gesture of exaggerated exhaustion flopped down into the sofa next to Fabel, dumping her keys, bag and cellphone next to her. She kissed Fabel.

'Tough day?' he asked.

Susanne nodded wearily. 'You too?'

'More confusing than anything. Let me get you a glass of wine . . .' When Fabel came back from the kitchen he went on to explain about his meeting with Ullrich and the information in the files. 'Do you think I'm barking up the wrong tree with this? The personal histories of the victims, I mean?'

'Frankly . . . yes.' Susanne's voice was tinged with tired irritation. Fabel was breaking their unspoken rule against talking about work during their free time together. 'You're overcomplicating this. Think it through. Look at the disfigurement of the bodies. The killer's small rituals, including pinning up the scalps as a display. It's the work of a psychopath. You see a significance in the background of the victims, but they share a similar background because they're roughly the same age. It could be as simple as your killer having a psychotic hostility to middle-aged men. And the mutilation of the bodies has psychosis written all over it. Think about politically motivated murder . . . nine times out of ten we're talking about assassination: a bomb planted in a street, a bullet through the head.'

Fabel sipped his beer. 'I suppose you're right,' he said and rose from his chair. 'Anyway, I'll go and fix you something to eat.'

### 7.40 p.m.: Schanzenviertel, Hamburg

Stefan Schreiner loved the Schanzenviertel. It was, for him, the most energetic, most varied, most vibrant part of Hamburg. His apartment was here. As was his beat.

Schreiner had been a Commissar in the uniformed branch of the Polizei Hamburg for seven years and he had been patrolling the Schanzenviertel for the last four of those years. Schreiner prided himself on being *in tune* with the Schanzenviertel: he was known by shopkeepers, by residents, even by those who peddled the occasional bit of dope, as a laid-back and easygoing street cop. But it was also known that, while he was willing to turn the odd blind eye where it did no harm, Stefan Schreiner was an honest, dedicated and efficient police officer.

The same could not be said of the officer with whom he had been teamed for the back shift: Peter Reinhard had the blue shoulder pips of a Polizei-meister, and was therefore Schreiner's subordinate. Schreiner reckoned that Polizeimeister was as far as Reinhard would ever get in the Polizei Hamburg. He watched his junior officer walk back to the car from the snack stand, a plastic-lidded paper coffee cup in each hand. Reinhard was a huge man who spent a disproportionate amount of time lifting weights in the gym and there was more than an element of swagger in the way he moved. It wasn't a good idea to swagger in the Schanzenviertel if you were a cop, thought Schreiner. He had spent so much time building bridges here and Reinhard was not the kind of partner he liked to be seen with.

Reinhard squeezed into the passenger seat of the silver and blue Mercedes patrol car and handed Schreiner one of the coffees. As he did so, he smoothed down his blue tie and shirt front, making sure he had not spilled anything on them.

'These new uniforms are cool, aren't they?' he said.

''Spose so.' It was not an issue that had occupied Schreiner much. The Polizei Hamburg uniforms had changed over the previous year from the traditional green and mustard to a dark blue.

'They remind me of American uniforms . . .' Reinhard paused. 'N – Y – P – D . . .' He pronounced the initials the English way. 'The old ones were crap – they made you look like you were a forestry warden.'

'Mmmm . . .' Schreiner was only half listening. He sipped his coffee and watched a cyclist approach down the narrow street. Schreiner suddenly thought how much better it would be to patrol the quarter on a bike. It was done in other parts of the city. He would ask about it. The cyclist drew closer. The other advantage would be that there would not be room for Reinhard on a bike.

'I just think that these are more like *police* uniforms . . .' Reinhard seemed content to carry on the discussion with himself. 'I mean, blue is the international colour for police . . .'

The bicycle passed the patrol car and Schreiner nodded to the cyclist, who ignored him. It was not uncommon in the Schanzenviertel for locals to be wary of the police, even hostile towards them. There was still a hangover from more radical days when the police were seen as fascists by the average Viertel dweller.

'Shit!' Suddenly Schreiner was galvanised into action. He thrust his coffee towards Reinhard to hold, splashing some on his junior officer's precious blue uniform shirt. Schreiner threw open the car door and stepped out.

'Just a minute! Stop!' he called after the cyclist, who looked over his shoulder at the policeman and responded by peddling hard away from him. Schreiner jumped back into the patrol car, slammed the door and gunned the engine. He took off from his standing start so violently that more coffee slopped over Reinhard's shirt.

### 7.40 p.m.: Pöseldorf, Hamburg

'What I don't get,' said Fabel as he placed a plate of pasta in front of Susanne, 'is why did the BKA reinvestigate Griebel recently? Surely there is no significant national interest to be protected in Griebel's research?'

'You said he was an epigeneticist?' Susanne took a mouthful of too-hot pasta and made a fanning movement in front of her mouth with her hand before continuing. 'What kind of work was he involved in?'

Fabel gave her a breakdown of all he knew, and the little that he understood, about Griebel's work. 'Some of the other stuff he was involved in – you know, all this inherited-memory stuff – sounds a bit, well, unscientific to me.'

'Not really,' said Susanne. 'An amazing amount of the DNA that is passed from one generation to the next has no known use: while the human genome was being mapped it revealed that more than ninety-eight per cent of our DNA is so-called "junk DNA" . . . or, to give it its proper name, "non-coding".'

'What do you think this DNA is for?'

'God knows. Some scientists believe that it's the accumulated defences against retroviruses. You know, all the bugs that we've fought off throughout our history as a species. Others believe that some of it has specific functions that we simply don't understand. One theory is that we inherit instinctive behaviours through it, even that it contains genetic memories. That actual experiences from an ancestor can be passed on to his or her descendants.'

'It all sounds a bit unlikely to me.'

'It's not really my field, of course.' Susanne shrugged. 'But I have come across it. There's a theory that some irrational fears or phobias owe their origins to genetic memory stored in this so-called junk DNA. A fear of height, for example, becoming encoded because some ancestor was traumatised by either falling or witnessing the death of someone else falling. Just as we can develop a fear of fire, claustrophobia, et cetera, because of some trauma in our own direct experience, it could be that those phobias that seem to have no direct source may have been inherited.'

Fabel thought of Maria and her fear of being touched because of the trauma she had experienced. It chilled him to think that such fears could be passed on from one generation to the next.

'But surely this is all speculation?' he said.

'There are a lot of things that cannot be explained by normal chromosomal inheritance. Lactose toler-ance, for example. We shouldn't be able to drink the milk of other species. Yet in all those cultures in which the herding and farming of cattle, goats, yaks and the like was common, we developed a tolerance for drinking the milk of livestock. But each generation did not need to redevelop that tolerance – it simply passed on once it was gained. And that cannot be explained by natural selection or the passing on of congenital DNA. There must be some other mechanism for genetic transference.'

Fabel's expression was one of a man contemplating things he did not fully understand. 'What about memories? Do you think it's possible for them to pass down from one generation to the next?'

'Honestly . . . I don't know. For me, the main problem is the totally different and separate processes at work. Memories are neurological phenomena. They're all to do with synapses, brain cells, the nervous system. DNA inheritance is a genetic process. I don't understand what biomolecular mechanism could be at work to imprint one on the other.'

'But . . . ?'

'But instinctive behaviour is a difficult thing to explain, particularly the more abstract forms of instinct that have nothing to do with our origins as a species. Of course, psychology has been through the whole thing with Jungian psychology, which simply took these theories far too far, but there are simple common experiences that I find intriguing.'

'Such as?'

'When we were on Sylt you told me how the first time you visited the island you felt you'd known it all your life. It is a relatively common psychological . . . *experience*, I suppose you would call it. For example, a farmer who has never been out of Bavaria, far less Germany, finally takes a foreign holiday –

in Spain, say. But when our reluctant virgin-tourist who has never expressed any interest in Spain arrives in some remote mountain town, he experiences an unaccountable feeling of familiarity. He *instinctively* knows where to go to find a castle, the old part of town, a river, et cetera. And once he is home in Oberbayern, he suffers from this strange form of homesickness.'

'This is common?'

'Reasonably. There are several studies under way at the moment into the phenomenon. We're not talking about some kind of extended déjà vu, mind you. These people have specific knowledge of a place they have never visited before in their life.'

'So what does it mean? Some kind of evidence of reincarnation?'

'A lot of people have taken it as such. Which is, of course, nonsense, but you can understand the logic . . . or lack of it, if you know what I mean. But some serious psychologists and geneticists believe that it may be evidence of some kind of inherited or genetic memory. But, like I said, I cannot see how the neuro-logical or psychological phenomenon of memory can become transferred and imprinted on the physical biomolecular structure of DNA. I tend to think that these experiences come from information that has perhaps been picked up in pieces over a lifetime of reading, watching television documentaries, and so on. All scattered throughout the subconscious but brought together by some single point of recognition. For example, our Bavarian farmer sees the church steeple when he dismounts from the bus. He has this weird déjà vu-type feeling of familiarity because his subconscious is putting that image together with a scattered jigsaw of bits of information.'

'But some other scientists, like Gunter Griebel, believe it's something to do with this DNA soup that we all carry around with us.'

'Yep. For example, maybe our Bavarian farmer had a distant forefather who lived in that area of Spain and he has inherited ancestral memories of it. And, of course, there is another phenomenon that we all experience. That feeling that you've met someone somewhere before even though you're meeting them for the first time. It's not just their appearance that seems familiar, but their personality too. Or the way we take an instant like or dislike to someone, with absolutely no basis for our prejudice. It's a favourite notion cited by re-incarnationists, that a group of individuals are bound together through all their incarnations. And that we recognise them as soon as we meet them again in a new life.'

Fabel went to the fridge and took out another bottle of Jever. 'And what's the scientific theory behind this phenomenon?'

'God, Jan . . . that depends on your perspective. As a psychologist I could point to dozens of psychological factors that stimulate a false sense of recognition, but I know that there are some wild theories about it. The fact is that every person on this planet is related: no matter how far-flung we are, we all share a common genetic ancestor. The world today has a population of about six and a half billion. But if we go back only three thousand years, to roughly the time of those mummies in western China that you told me about, there would only be, what . . . less than two hundred million people worldwide. We are all just variations on the same themes, over and over again. So it is more than conceivable that the same configuration of features is repeated with the same personality type. We all tend to associate certain features with certain personalities and prejudge people by their looks. We say someone looks intelligent, or friendly or arrogant, based on their features and on our experience of people with a similar appearance. And sometimes when we meet people for the first time we feel we've met them before because we're putting together a composite picture of a number of people who looked similar and who had similar personalities.' Susanne took a sip of her wine and shrugged. 'It's not reincarnation. It's coincidence.'

### 7.42 p.m.: Schanzenviertel, Hamburg

It should have been an unequal contest: a Mercedes patrol car against an ageing bicycle. But the Schanzenviertel was a warren of narrow streets, lined by parked cars, and Stefan Schreiner was forced to accelerate and brake in short, ineffective bursts. As he negotiated the obstacles and the corners in pursuit of the cyclist, his partner Peter Reinhard struggled to replace the plastic lids on the coffee containers and put them into the car's cup-holders.

'Would you mind telling me what the *hell* is going on?' Reinhard had found a paper towel and was dabbing at his coffee-soaked shirt front.

'That bike . . .' Schreiner stayed focused on his quarry. 'It's stolen.'

They were now in a one-way street, again lined with parked cars, allowing no opportunity to turn. The cyclist clearly realised that he had the police at a disadvantage and stopped suddenly, forcing Schreiner to brake hard. But before the policemen had time to get out of the car, the cyclist had squeezed between two parked vehicles, mounted the pavement and was heading back the way they had come. Schreiner slammed the patrol car into reverse and, twisting round in his seat, drove back up the street as fast as its width and congestion would allow.

'What?' Reinhard said incredulously. 'I get soaked in coffee for the sake of a stolen bike?'

'Not just any stolen bike.' Schreiner paused as he swung the Mercedes, tail first, out into Lipmannsstrasse. He took off after the cyclist again with a screech of tyres. 'The person it was stolen from was Hans-Joachim Hauser. This could be his killer.'

The cyclist had lost the advantage of parked cars restricting the speed of the police car and again he mounted the pavement. Reinhard leaned forward in his seat, forgetting all about the coffee spilled on his uniform shirt. 'Then let's get the bastard.'

Schreiner could tell that the cyclist knew the Viertel well. He made a sudden left turn, swinging into Eifflerstrasse, heading against the flow of traffic on the one-way street and forcing Schreiner to slam on the brakes to avoid hitting an oncoming Volkswagen. Schreiner leaped from the car and raced along the pavement after the cyclist, Reinhard hard on his heels and the curses of the VW driver in his ears. The cyclist was getting away; he looked back over his shoulder at the policemen, grinning and raising a fist in a gesture of defiance. It was short-lived: oblivious to the chase on the pavement, the driver of a parked car swung open his door and its edge caught the passing bike, sending it crashing into the wall of one of the buildings. By the time the cyclist had rolled over onto his back, clutching his bruised knee, the two policemen had caught up with him and towered over him, their handguns trained on his head.

'Stay on the ground!' Reinhard shouted at the stunned bicycle thief. 'Stretch your hands out above your head.' The cyclist did exactly as he was told.

'Okay . . . okay . . .' he said as he gazed at the firearms pointed at him. 'I admit it, for Christ's sake . . . I stole the fucking bike!'

## 9.10 p.m.: Police Presidium, Hamburg

It was clear to Fabel that the pale-faced, blond-haired young man sitting in the Murder Commission interview room had nothing to do with Hans-Joachim Hauser's murder. Leonard Schüler had the look of an animal caught in headlights. And from what Fabel had read of Schüler's record as a petty criminal, he simply did not fit as Hauser's killer.

Fabel hung back, leaning against the wall by the door. He let Anna and Henk lead the interview.

'I don't know anything about any murder,' Schüler declared, his stare darting from one police officer to the other as if seeking confirmation that they believed him. 'I mean, I *heard* about that guy Hauser getting killed, but until I was arrested I didn't even know it was his place that I took the bike from.'

'Well.' Anna smiled. 'The bad news for you is that you're all we've got at the moment. Herr Hauser chained his bike up when he got home about ten p.m., then his cleaner finds him missing his hair at nine a.m. the following morning. There's only one person we can place anywhere near him between those times. You.'

'But I *wasn't* anywhere near him,' protested Schüler. 'I didn't set foot inside the apartment. I just saw his bike and I stole it.'

'When was this?' asked Henk.

'I reckon about eleven. Eleven-thirty. I'd been drinking with friends and I suppose I'd had a bit too much. I was walking along the street and I saw the bike. And I thought, well, why walk when you can ride? It was just a prank. A joke. It was chained up, but I was able to prise the lock open.'

'With what? From what we can gather, Herr Hauser was pretty fond of that bike and I would guess he had a reasonably sturdy security chain on it.'

'I had a screwdriver with me . . .' Schüler paused. 'And a pair of pliers.'

'Do you normally go out for a drink with your pockets full of tools?' Henk threw a plastic evidence bag onto the table with a clatter. 'This is what was found on you when you were arrested tonight . . . Screwdriver, pliers, hacksaw blade and – this is really interesting – a couple of pairs of disposable latex medical gloves. I can't work out whether you're a twenty-four-hour joiner or a moonlighting surgeon.'

Schüler once more looked from Henk to Anna and back, as if hoping that they would give him an idea what to say.

'Listen, Leonard,' Henk continued. 'You have three convictions for breaking into private dwellings and one for car theft. That's why you did a runner when the patrol car tried to stop you. Not because you were worried about being caught on a stolen bike – you could have claimed that you'd found it dumped. You were out looking for an apartment to do over. Just the same as you were the night you stole the bike. I find it difficult to believe that you didn't think it worthwhile to have a little look-see to find out if there was anything else worth nicking.'

'I keep telling you . . . I didn't go anywhere near Hauser's apartment. I was a bit pissed so I nicked the bike. For Christ's sake, do you think I would have held on to it if I had topped the owner?'

'Good point . . .' Fabel moved over from the door. He pulled up a chair next to Schüler and leaned his face close in to the young man. When he spoke it was with a quiet, deliberate menace. 'I want you to listen to me, Leonard. I want you to understand something very clearly. I hunt people. In this case I am hunting a very particular man . . . like me, he is a hunter of other men. The difference is that he stalks them, he finds them, and then he does this to them . . .' Fabel looked across to Anna and snapped his fingers impatiently. She handed him the file with the scenes-of-crime photographs. Fabel took one from the file and held it so close to Schüler's face that the young thief had to pull back from it. When Schüler focused on the image, his expression contorted with disgust. Fabel snapped the photograph away and replaced it with another. 'Do you see what my guy does? *This* is the person who interests me, Leonard. *This* is who I am after. You, on the other hand, are a worth-less piece of shit that I am only taking the time to wipe off my shoe.' Fabel leaned back in the chair. 'I believe that it is important to establish a sense of perspective in these things. I just want you to understand that. You *do* understand that, don't you, Leonard?'

Schüler nodded his head silently. There was a heartbeat's pause.

'I also want you to understand this.' Fabel laid the photographs of both victims face up on the table's surface. As with all scenes-of-crime photographs the colours were camera-flash stark and vivid. The dead-stare eyes of Hans-Joachim Hauser and Gunter Griebel gazed out towards the ceiling from beneath their ravaged heads. 'If you do not convince me, within the next two minutes, that you are telling me the absolute truth . . . do you know what I'm going to do?'

'No . . .' Schüler tried to sound as though Fabel had not rattled him. He failed. 'No . . . what will you do?'

Fabel stood up. 'I will let you go.'

Schüler gave a confused laugh and looked across at Anna and Henk, both of whom remained expressionless.

'I will let you walk out of here,' continued Fabel. 'And I will make sure that it is public knowledge that you are our principal witness to this murder. I might even allow one of the less scrupulous local newspapers to feel that they have tricked your name and address out of me. Then . . .' Fabel gave a small, cruel laugh. 'Oh, then, Leonard my boy, then you won't ever have to worry about us again. Like I said, I don't hunt small fry like you. But I can use you as bait.' Fabel leaned close to Schüler once more. 'You don't understand this man. You could never even begin to think in the same way. But *I* can. I have hunted so many killers like him. Too many. Let me tell you, they don't see or feel the world in the same way we do. Some of them don't feel fear. Honestly. Some – most of them, actually – kill just to watch what it is like for another human being to die. And quite a few of them savour each death in the same way the rest of us would enjoy a fine wine or a good meal. And that means they like to make the experience last. To relish every last second. And trust me, Leonard . . . if my friend here believes that you might lead us to him, that you maybe saw him without him seeing you, it won't cost him a thought to hunt you down and kill you. But he doesn't just kill. Just imagine what it must feel like to be tied to a chair while he slices you up and tears your scalp from your head. And all that pain, all that horror, would be the very last thing on earth that you would experience. An eternal moment. Oh no, Leonard, he won't just kill you. He'll take you with him into hell first.' Fabel stood up and extended an arm towards the door. 'So, Leonard, do you want me to release you . . . ?'

Schüler shook his head determinedly. 'I'll tell you everything. Everything I know. Just make sure my name doesn't get out.'

Fabel smiled. 'That's a good boy.' He turned to Anna and Henk as he made his way to the door. 'I'll leave this to you . . .'

Fabel poured himself a coffee when he got back to his office. He sat down at his desk, hung his jacket over the back of his chair and checked his watch. It was now nine-thirty. Sometimes Fabel felt that there was no refuge from his work: that it had the ability to reach out to him no matter where he was or what time of day it was. Fabel was annoyed with himself that he had discussed the case with Susanne during their time off together, even if it had only been about Griebel's work. He even regretted taking home the files that Ullrich had given him. But something nagged relentlessly at Fabel about the second victim and he could not put his finger on it. It was like not being able to locate a tiny stone in your shoe, yet feeling it with every step.

Fabel reached into his desk and took out a large sketch pad from the drawer. He flipped it open at the page on which he had begun to map out the Hamburger Hairdresser case. It was a process that Fabel had repeated so many times before, with so many cases: a perversion of the creative function for which the sketch pads were intended. Fabel mapped out the profiles of sick and twisted minds, of death and pain. He thought back to what he had said to Schüler: all bluff, of course, but it bothered Fabel how true it was when he said that he was a hunter of men; someone who found it increasingly easy to enter the mindset of the men he hunted.

Again Fabel found himself wondering how it had come to pass that he had ended up here, up to his elbows in the blood and filth of others. This life had crept up on him. There had been definite, discreet steps along the way. The first had been the murder of Hanna Dorn, his girlfriend at university. He had not really known her that long or that well, but she had been a significant figure in his landscape. And she had been taken from it, suddenly and violently, by a killer who had chosen her as a victim, completely at random. Fabel had been as much confused as grief-stricken, and as soon as he had graduated he had joined the Polizei Hamburg. Then there had been the Commerzbank shoot-out. Fabel – the pacifist Fabel who had for his national service elected for Civilian Duty, driving ambulances in his native Norden rather than opting for a shorter conscription period in the armed forces – had been forced to do that which he had always promised himself he would never do. He had taken a human life. Then, during his time at the Murder Commission, each new case had chipped away at him, reshaping him into someone he had never thought he would become.

Sometimes Fabel felt that he was wearing someone else's life, as if he had picked up the wrong coat from a restaurant cloakroom. This was not what he had planned for himself at all.

He gazed down at the sketch pad, not seeing it for the moment but trying to look into another life. Not, this time, into the mind of a killer or into the life of a murder victim, but into a life that should, that could, have been his. Maybe that was what Fabel had become: a victim of murder himself.

He reached into his jacket and pulled out his wallet. He took out the slip of paper with her telephone number on it that Sonja Brun had given him, and Roland Bartz's card, and laid them on the desk. A new life. He could pick up the phone, make two phone calls and change everything. What would it be like, he wondered, to have small worries? Not to have to make life-or-death decisions? He looked at the phone on his desk for a moment, imagining it as a portal to a new life. Then he sighed and put the scrap of paper and the business card back into his wallet before turning his attention again to the sketch pad.

Two victims in a single day. No solid leads and little to connect them. One a flagrant attention-seeker, the other practically a recluse. The only common theme that Fabel could discern, other than the suggestion of political radicalism in their youth, was the way they seemed to exist only in reflection. Hauser had sought to establish himself as an environmental guru and significant figure on the Left, only to become a footnote in the biographies of others. Griebel had seemed to exist only through and for his work, even when his wife had been alive.

Earlier, Fabel had written Kristina Dreyer's name on the page, looped it with a highlighter pen and linked it to Hauser's. He crossed it out. He had also linked Sebastian Lang's name to Hauser's. Fabel had not interviewed Lang personally, but Anna had assured him that Lang's alibi was solid. A question mark indicated the older man who Anna had said had been seen with Hauser in The Firehouse. Could that have been Griebel? There were so few clear pictures of the camera-shy scientist in life, and the mortuary photograph of him with the top of his head sliced off did not help with identification. Fabel made a note to have Anna take an artist's impression of Griebel down to The Firehouse to see if any of the staff recognised him.

There was a knock on the door and Anna Wolff walked in, as usual without being invited. Henk Hermann followed her.

'Thanks for softening up Schüler,' said Anna, in a tone that left Fabel unsure of whether she meant it or not, as she sat down opposite him. 'It was difficult to get him to shut up, he's so scared of the bogeyman you threatened to unleash on him.'

'Anything useful?' asked Fabel.

'Yes, *Chef*,' said Henk. 'Schüler admitted he was cruising the area on foot, checking out likely apartments and houses. According to him it was only a half-hearted reconnaissance . . . apparently he does his best work in the wee small hours when the occupiers are asleep, but the Schanzenviertel is a clubby and pubby type of area so he thought he might find a few empty flats at that time of evening. Anyway, he hadn't had any luck and had nearly been caught once by a householder, so he had decided to call it a night. It was on his way home that he noticed the bike chained up outside Hauser's apartment and he thought "Why not?" The interesting thing is he said he wanted to check the apartment out, just in case, so he went around to the back where there's a small courtyard with access to the lounge, bedroom and bathroom windows. He says he didn't take it any further because he could see that the occupier was at home.'

'He saw Hauser?'

'Yep,' said Anna. 'Alive. He was sitting in the lounge drinking, so Schüler decided to settle for the bike.'

'But the main thing is that Hauser was not alone,' said Henk. 'He had a guest.'

'Oh?' Fabel leaned forward. 'Do we have a description?'

'Schüler says that Hauser's guest was sitting with his back to the window,' said Anna. 'Schüler was keen to get out of the courtyard in case he was spotted, so he didn't pay much attention to either of the men. But, from what he said, one of them was definitely Hauser. Schüler described the other man as younger, maybe early thirties, dark hair and slim.'

'Doesn't that description fit with the guy who discovered Kristina Dreyer cleaning up after the murder?' said Fabel.

'Sebastian Lang . . . It does, doesn't it?' Anna grinned. 'I have a photograph of Lang that I've been using when I've been asking around about Hauser.'

'Lang gave you a photograph voluntarily?' asked Fabel.

'Not exactly.' Anna exchanged a look with Henk. 'I *borrowed* it from the crime scene. Technically, it was the property of the deceased. Not Lang's.'

Fabel let it go. 'Did you show the photograph to Schüler?'

'Yep,' said Anna. 'Inconclusive, I would say. Schüler says that it could be the same guy – the colouring is the same and, roughly, so is the build. But he didn't get a close enough look at Hauser's guest to make a positive identification. Nevertheless, I think we should pay Herr Lang another visit. I'd like to have another look at that alibi.'

'This time,' said Fabel, 'I think I'll come along too.'


10.35 p.m.: Eimsbüttel, Hamburg

It was after ten-thirty by the time Fabel, Anna and Henk knocked on the door of Sebastian Lang's apartment. Lang lived on the second storey of an impressive building in Ottersbekallee, only a few minutes from Hans-Joachim Hauser's Schanzenviertel apartment. Fabel had never met Lang before: he was a tall man in his early thirties, very slim, with a pale complexion, pale blue eyes and dark hair. His appearance certainly fitted the rough description of the man Schüler had seen in Hauser's apartment. Lang's face was perfectly proportioned, yet instead of making him handsome the perfection of his features seemed to feminise him. A 'pretty' boy was how Maria had described him. The other thing that was remarkable about Lang's face was its lack of expression, and when he stood to one side with a sigh to allow the officers to enter there was nothing in the mask of his face to reveal the extent of his annoyance.

He directed Fabel, Anna and Henk into the lounge. Like its occupier, the flat was immaculately presented, with not a thing out of place. It was as if Lang made the minimum possible impact on his living environment. He had clearly been reading when Fabel and the others arrived and he had set the book down, neatly, on the coffee table. Fabel picked it up. It was some kind of political history of post-war Germany, open at a chapter on German domestic terrorism in the 1970s and 1980s.

'You a student of history, Herr Lang?' asked Fabel.

Lang took the book from Fabel's hands and closed it, placing it back into the space it had left in Lang's tidily arranged bookshelf.

'It's late, Herr Chief Commissar, and I don't really appreciate being pestered at home,' Lang said. 'Would you please tell me what this is all about?'

'Certainly, Herr Lang. And I do apologise for disturbing you in the evening, but I assumed you'd be only too willing to answer any questions that might take us closer to understanding what happened to Herr Hauser.'

Another sigh. 'You're trying my patience, Herr Fabel. Of course I want to help catch Hans-Joachim's killer. But when the police turn up mob-handed at my door after ten in the evening, I assume that there is more to their visit than just checking a few facts.'

'True . . .' said Fabel. 'A witness has come

forward. He saw someone in Herr Hauser's apartment on the night of his murder. Someone who fits your description.'

'But that's impossible.' Still the protesting tone in Lang's voice did not translate into any animation of his features. 'Or, at least, it is possible that someone *like* me was there. But it was not me.'

'Well,' said Anna, 'that is something we have yet to establish.'

'For God's sake, I gave you full details of where I was that night . . .' Lang walked over to a bureau by the door and opened a drawer. He turned back to the officers with something in each hand. 'Here is my ticket stub for the exhibition I attended. See, it's dated for that Thursday. And here . . .' He gave the stub to Fabel. In his other hand was a pen and notebook. 'Here are the names and telephone numbers *again* of the people who can and will confirm that they were with me that night.'

'You came home about one, one-fifteen in the morning, you say?' Fabel passed the stub to Anna.

'Yes.' Lang folded his arms defiantly, 'We – I mean my friends and I – went for a meal afterwards. I've already given her' – he nodded in Anna's direction – 'the name of the restaurant and the waiter who served us. We left the restaurant about a quarter to one.'

'And you came home alone?'

'Yes. Alone, Herr Fabel. So I can't provide an alibi after that.'

'That may be immaterial, Herr Lang,' said Fabel. 'All the indications are that Herr Hauser died between ten and midnight.'

Fabel thought he detected something disturb

Lang's impassive expression, as if pinning a time to Hauser's ordeal and death had made it more real.

'Your relationship with Herr Hauser was not exclusive?' asked Anna.

'No. Not on Hans-Joachim's side, anyway.'

'Do you know of anyone else he might have been involved with?'

For a moment Lang looked confused. 'What do you mean involved? Oh . . . oh, I see. No. Hans-Joachim had countless flings, but there was no one . . . well, I was his only *companion*.'

'What did you think we meant when we asked you if he was *involved* with anyone else?' asked Fabel.

'Nothing, really. I just wasn't sure if you meant privately or professionally. Or politically in Hans-Joachim's case. It's just that he was very, well, *strange* about his associations. He got a bit drunk one night and lectured me about not getting involved with the wrong group of people. About making the wrong choices.'

Fabel looked across to where Lang had replaced the book on the shelf. 'Did Herr Hauser ever discuss the past with you? I mean his days as an activist, that kind of thing?'

'Endlessly,' Lang said wearily. 'He would rant on about how his generation had saved Germany. How their actions back then shaped the society we live in now. He seemed to think that my generation, as he would put it, was screwing the whole thing up.'

'But did he ever say anything about his activities? Or his associates?'

'Oddly enough, no. The only person he tended to go on about was Bertholdt Müller-Voigt. You know, the Environment Senator. Hans-Joachim hated him with a vengeance. He used to say that

Müller-Voigt believed that he could be Chancellor one day, and that was what all this "Lady Macbeth" crap with First Mayor Schreiber's wife was all about. Hans-Joachim said that Müller-Voigt and Hans Schreiber were cut from the same cloth. Shameless opportunists. He had known them both at university and had despised them even then – particularly Müller-Voigt.'

'Did he ever discuss the allegations made against Müller-Voigt in the press by Ingrid Fischmann – all that stuff about the Wiedler kidnapping?'

'No. Not with me, anyway.'

'Did Herr Hauser have any contact with Müller-Voigt? Recently, I mean.'

Lang shrugged. 'Not that I know of. I would have thought that Hans-Joachim would have gone out of his way to avoid him.'

Fabel nodded. He took a moment to process what Lang had told him. It did not add up to much. 'You are probably aware that another man was killed in the same way, within twenty-four hours of Herr Hauser's death. The man's name was Dr Gunter Griebel. Does that name mean anything to you? Did Herr Hauser ever discuss a Dr Griebel?'

Lang shook his delicately sculpted head. 'No. I can't say that I ever heard him mention him.'

'We spoke to the staff at The Firehouse,' said Anna. 'They told us that Herr Hauser was sometimes seen drinking and talking with an older man, about the same age as him. Would you have any idea who it might have been?'

'Sorry. I wouldn't,' said Lang. 'Listen, I'm not being obstructive or awkward or anything. It's just that Hans-Joachim only included me in his life when it suited him. There's practically nothing you could

256

tell me about him that would surprise me. He was a very, very secretive man . . . despite all his publicity-seeking. Sometimes I think that Hans-Joachim was hiding in plain sight – concealing himself behind his public persona. It was like there was something deep down inside that he didn't want anyone to see.'

Fabel considered Lang's words. What he had said about Hauser was true of Griebel, but in a different way.

'We're all like that,' said Fabel. 'To one degree or another.'

In the car on the way back to the Presidium, Fabel discussed Lang with his two junior officers.

'I'll double-check these details,' said Anna. 'But, to be honest, his alibi doesn't put him entirely in the clear for Hauser's death. If he had gone straight from the restaurant to Hauser's apartment, and if we allow a margin of error in the estimated time of death, then he could just about have done it.'

'It would be stretching the timeline pretty far,' said Fabel. 'Although I have to admit there's something about Lang that bothers me. But the main thing that puts him out of the picture is the fact that your sequence of events just doesn't fit with Schüler's statement. He saw Hauser sitting with a guest who broadly fits Lang's description somewhere between eleven and eleven-thirty; Lang's alibi is solid for that time.'

Fabel dropped Henk and Anna back at the Presidium and drove home to Pöseldorf. Hamburg glowed in the dark warmth of the summer night. Something sat heavy in the back of Fabel's mind, obscuring what this case was all about, but his tired brain could not shift it out of the way. As he drove, he knew that he was dealing with a case that was growing cold on him. A lead-less case. And that meant he might not get a break in it until the killer struck again. Considering he had killed twice within a twenty-four-hour period, and had not struck since, it was entirely possible that the killer's work was over.

And that he had got away with it.

### Midnight: Grindelviertel, Hamburg

As Fabel was driving home from the Police Presidium, Leonard Schüler was sitting in his one-bedroomed Grindelviertel apartment, counting his blessings. He had not been charged with anything. He had admitted to stealing the bike, to going out equipped to break into houses that night but, just as the older cop had said, they had not been interested in any of that. The older cop had really rattled Schüler with his talk of hanging him out as bait for the nutter who was scalping these guys. But even if Leonard had been scared, he had stayed smart: he knew not to give them any more than the absolute minimum. The reason the older cop's threat had scared him so much was because Leonard had got a much better look at the guy in the apartment than he had admitted. And the guy in the apartment had got a good long look at Schüler.

It had been Schüler's intention to break into the flat if there had been no one at home. He had planned his getaway with slightly more foresight than usual. Having prised open the lock on the bike, he had left it propped against the wall of the alley before slipping around to the courtyard. It had not been too dark that night, but when Leonard had sneaked around to the back of the apartment the height of the buildings surrounding the yard had cast it into dark shadow. It had been a gift to a burglar, thought Schüler, but one of the occupiers had obviously been security conscious and a motion-sensitive security light had suddenly flooded the small courtyard with blazing light. Schüler had been temporarily dazzled and had taken a blind step forward. The recycling bins must have been too full because he had knocked over some bottles that had been set beside the bins, causing them to clatter loudly on the cobbles of the courtyard.

Schüler had taken a moment to allow his eyes to adjust to the sudden bright light. It was then that he had seen the two men. They had clearly been disturbed from their conversation by Schüler's clumsiness and had come to the window and looked out directly at him – he was only a metre and a half away. There had been an older guy, whom he now knew to have been Hauser, and a younger one. It had been the expression, or lack of it, on the face of the younger man that had really spooked Schüler. Even more so now, knowing as he did what this individual had gone on to commit.

He had looked into the dead, expressionless face of a killer.

Now, when Schüler thought back to that stare, to that dreadful calm on the face of a man who must have known what horrors he was about to perpetrate, it chilled him to the core.

The older cop, Fabel, had been right. He had described a monster who took people into hell before they died. Schüler wanted no part of it. Whoever – whatever – this killer was, the police would never catch him.

Schüler was out of it now.

# 10.

# Thirteen Days After the First Murder:
# Wednesday, 31 August 2005.

### 9.10 a.m.: Police Presidium, Hamburg

Fabel had been at his desk since seven-thirty. He had again gone through the BKA files that Ullrich had lent him and had taken out the sketch pad from his desk and plotted out as much as he could from the information at his disposal.

He phoned Bertholdt Müller-Voigt's office. After he explained who he was, Fabel was told that the Environment Senator was working from home, which he often did, as yet another visible commitment to reducing his travel kilometres and therefore his impact on the environment. His secretary said she could, however, get right back to Fabel with an appointment for that day.

Fabel made another call. Henk Hermann had got Fabel the number for Ingrid Fischmann, the journalist.

'Hello, Frau Fischmann? This is Principal Chief Commissar Jan Fabel of the Polizei Hamburg. I work for the Murder Commission, and I am currently investigating the murder of Hans-Joachim Hauser. I wondered if it would be possible to meet. I think you could help me with some background information . . .'

'Oh . . . I see . . .' The woman's voice at the other end sounded a lot younger and lacked the authority that Fabel had somehow expected. 'Okay . . . how about three p.m. at my office?'

'That's fine. Thank you, Frau Fischmann. I have the address.'

Within a few minutes of hanging up from Ingrid Fischmann, Bertholdt Müller-Voigt's secretary phoned back saying that the Senator could fit Fabel in if he could make his way directly to Herr Müller-Voigt's house. She gave Fabel an address near Stade in the Altes Land, outside Hamburg and on the south side of the Elbe. He doesn't mind *me* clocking up the kilometres, thought Fabel as he hung up.

Müller-Voigt's house was a huge modern home that had 'expensive architect' written in every angle and detail, and Fabel reflected on how the former left-wing environmentalist firebrand seemed to have embraced conspicuous consumption with great enthusiasm. As he approached the front door, however, Fabel noticed that what had appeared to be blue marble tiling along the whole front elevation was, in fact, a façade made up entirely of solar panels.

Müller-Voigt answered the door. As Fabel remembered him from Lex's restaurant, he was a smallish but fit-looking man with broad shoulders and a tanned face broken by a broad, white-toothed smile.

'Herr Chief Commissar, please . . . do come in.'

Fabel had heard of Müller-Voigt's charm: his primary weapon, apparently, with women and political opponents alike. It was well known that he could turn it off whenever necessary. He could be an aggressive and highly outspoken opponent. The politician showed Fabel into a vast living room with a pine-lined double-height vaulted ceiling. He offered Fabel a drink, which the detective declined.

'What can I do for you, Herr Fabel?' asked Müller-Voigt, sitting down on a large corner sofa and indicating that Fabel should do likewise.

'I'm sure you've heard of the deaths of Hans-Joachim Hauser and Gunter Griebel?' asked Fabel.

'God, yes. Terrible, terrible business.'

'You knew Herr Hauser rather well, I believe.'

'Yes, I did. But not socially for years. Not so much at all recently, in fact. I would bump into Hans-Joachim at the occasional conference or action meeting. And, of course, I knew Gunter, too. Not so well, and I hadn't seen him for an even longer time than Hans-Joachim, but I did know him.'

Fabel looked startled. 'I'm sorry, Herr Müller-Voigt – did you say you knew *both* victims?'

'Yes, of course I did. Is that strange?'

'Well . . .' said Fabel. 'My entire purpose in coming here was to see if you could cast light on any possible connection between the two victims. A connection, I have to add, that so far we have been unable to establish. Now it looks like you are that link.'

'I'm flattered that I seem so important to your investigation,' said Müller-Voigt, smiling. 'But I can assure you that I was not the only connection. They knew each other.'

'Are you sure about that?'

'Absolutely. Gunter was a strange fellow. Tall and lanky and not much of a talker, but he was active in the student movement. It doesn't surprise me that the connection didn't appear on your radar, though. He dropped out of sight after a while. It was as if he lost interest in the movement. But he and Hans-Joachim were both members of the Gaia Collective for a while. As was I.'

'Oh?'

'The Gaia Collective was a very short-lived phenomenon, I have to admit. A talking shop more than anything. I gave up on it when it became too . . . *esoteric*, I suppose you would say. The political objectivity got muddied with wacky philosophies – Paganism, that kind of thing. The Collective just sort of evaporated. That happened a lot back then.'

'How well did Hauser and Griebel know each other?' asked Fabel.

'Oh, I don't know. They weren't friends or anything. Just through the Gaia Collective. They might have met outside, but I wouldn't know about that. I know that Griebel was highly regarded for his intellect, but I have to say I always found him a very dull fellow. Very earnest and rather one-dimensional . . . like a lot of the people involved in the movement. And not particularly communicative.'

'And you've had no contact with Griebel since the Gaia Collective days?'

'None,' said Müller-Voigt.

'Who else was involved?'

'It was a long time ago, Herr Fabel. A lifetime away.'

'There are bound to be *some* people you recall.'

Fabel watched Müller-Voigt as he rubbed at his trimmed, greying beard thoughtfully. Fabel found it impossible to get the measure of the man or of how much, if anything, he was holding back.

'I remember there was a woman I was involved with for a while,' said Müller-Voigt. 'Her name was Beate Brandt. I don't know what happened to her.

264

And Paul Scheibe . . . he was a Gaia Collective member too.'

'The architect?'

'Yes. He has just won a major architectural project in the HafenCity. He is the only person from the group that I still have regular contact with, if you exclude the odd times when I would run into Hans-Joachim. Paul Scheibe was and still is a very talented architect . . . very innovative in designing minimum-environmental-impact buildings. This latest concept for the Überseequartier of the HafenCity is inspired.'

Fabel made a note of the names Beate Brandt and Paul Scheibe. 'Do you remember anyone else?'

'Not really . . . not names, anyway. I never really did get *into* the Gaia Collective, if you know what I mean.'

'Do you remember if Franz Mühlhaus was involved with the Collective?'

Müller-Voigt looked taken aback by the mention of the name, then his expression became clouded with suspicion. 'Oh . . . I see. It's not my possible connection to the victims that interests you at all, is it? If you've come here to question me about Red Franz Mühlhaus because of the false allegations that Ingrid Fischmann has been circulating, then you can get the hell out of my house.'

Fabel held up a hand. 'Firstly, I am here exclusively because I am trying to establish a connection between the victims. Secondly – and I do assure you of this, Herr Senator – this is a murder inquiry and you *will* answer all the questions I have for you. I don't care what your position is: there is a maniac out there mutilating and murdering people who were connected to your circle in the nineteen seventies and nineteen eighties. We can either do this here or at the Presidium, but we're going to do it.'

Müller-Voigt's stare was locked on Fabel. Fabel realised that the intensity of the politician's gaze came not from fury but from the fact that he was appraising Fabel, trying to decide if he was bluffing or not. It was clear that Müller-Voigt had been in too many political tussles to become easily rattled. Fabel found his cool, emotion-free detachment disturbing.

'I don't know what you think of me and my type, Herr Chief Commissar.' Müller-Voigt let the tension ease from his posture and leaned back into the sofa. 'I mean those of us who were active in the protest movement. But we changed Germany. Many of the liberties, many of the fundamental values and freedoms that everyone takes for granted about our society, are directly attributable to us taking a stand back then. We are nearing a time, if in fact we have not already reached it, when we can again be proud of what it is to be German. A liberal, pacifist nation. We did that, Fabel. My generation. Our protests blew the last dark cobwebs out of the corners of our society. We were the first generation without a direct memory of the war, of the Holocaust, and we made it clear that *our* Germany was going to have nothing to do with *that* Germany.

'I admit I was on the streets. I admit that things got heated. But at the heart of my beliefs lies my pacifism: I don't believe in doing violence to the Earth and I don't believe in doing violence to my fellow man. Like I said, in the heat of the moment there were things I did back then that I regret now, but I could never – not then, not now – take a human life for the sake of a political conviction, no matter

how strongly held. For me, that is what differenti-
ates me from what went before.'

Müller-Voigt paused, keeping Fabel fixed with his
gaze. 'If there is a question lurking there that you
maybe don't want to ask, then let me answer it for
you. Despite Ingrid Fischmann's insinuations, and
despite the political capital that the First Mayor's
wife has sought to make of them, I was not, in any
way, involved with the kidnap and murder of
Thorsten Wiedler. I had nothing whatsoever to do
with it or the group behind it.'

'Well, like I said, my sole interest is in the connection between the two victims,' said Fabel. 'I merely
wanted to know if Mühlhaus had been a member
of the Gaia Collective.'

'Good God, no. I think I would remember that.'
Müller-Voigt looked thoughtful for a moment.
'Although I do understand why you ask. Mühlhaus
had a pretty odd perspective on the movement and
there were certain similarities between his ideas and
those of the Collective. But no . . . Red Franz Mühlhaus
had absolutely no involvement.'

'Who was the Collective's leader?'

For a moment Müller-Voigt looked confused by
Fabel's question. 'There was no leader. It was a
collective. Therefore it had a collective leadership.'

They talked for another fifteen minutes before Fabel
rose and thanked Müller-Voigt for his time and for
being cooperative. In return, Müller-Voigt wished Fabel
the best of luck in tracking down the killer.

As Fabel turned out of the sweeping drive and
onto the road back to the city, he considered the
fact that he now had a point of direct contact
between Hans-Joachim Hauser and Gunter Griebel,
and he thought back on how open Müller-Voigt had

seemed. So why was it, thought Fabel, that he felt as if Müller-Voigt had told him exactly nothing?

As he headed back to Hamburg along the B73, Fabel phoned Werner. He told him about the link between the victims and went through the highlights of what else Müller-Voigt had said to him.

'I need to talk to this architect, Paul Scheibe,' he said. 'Could you get a contact number and arrange something? If you try his practice number, that would probably be best.'

'Sure, Jan. I'll get back to you.'

Fabel had just turned onto the A7 and was heading towards the Elbtunnel when his car phone buzzed.

'Hi, Jan,' said Werner. 'I have just had the strangest conversation with the people at Scheibe's architectural practice. I spoke to his deputy, a guy called Paulsen. He got really quite wound up when I said I was phoning from the Murder Commission . . . He thought I was phoning because we'd found Scheibe's body or something. According to Paulsen, Scheibe attended a lunch reception at the Rathaus on Monday and hasn't been seen since. Apparently the formal launch of this big HafenCity project is being held tonight and they're worried that he isn't going to show. Looks like we've got a missing person.'

'Or a murder suspect on the run,' said Fabel. 'Send someone over there to get details. I think we should turn up at the launch party this evening ourselves. I'll be back in before five. I'm heading up to the University right now and then I'm meeting the journalist Fischmann at three. Anything else?'

'Only that Anna has turned up a lead on your World War Two mummy. The family no longer lives in that street. They were bombed out during the war, but Anna's tracked down someone who was a friend of the dead guy. Do you want her to follow it up?'

'No, it's okay. I want to do it. It was my call-out. Tell Anna to leave the details on my desk.'

Fabel had just hung up when his car phone buzzed again.

'Fabel . . .' he said impatiently.

There was a sound of electronic static. Then a voice that was not human.

'You are going to get a warning . . .' The voice was distorted, as if through an electronic voice-changer. Fabel checked the caller display but no number had registered.

'Who the hell is this?' Fabel asked.

'You will get a warning. Only one.' The line went dead.

Fabel stared ahead at the traffic heading towards the Elbtunnel. A crank call. Maybe even someone who did not realise they had reached a police officer's number. But somewhere, at the back of his head, an alarm was sounding.

## 10.00 a.m.: Archaeology Department, Universität Hamburg

'Have you found the relatives of our HafenCity dweller?' Dr Severts smiled and offered Fabel a chair.

'No. Not yet, unfortunately. I'm afraid I've had much more pressing things on my mind.'

'This so-called Hamburg Hairdresser?'

'Yes. It's proving to be a . . .' Fabel sought the right word. '. . . *Challenging* case for us. And, to be honest, I am clutching at any straws I can think of.'

'Why do I get the feeling that I'm one of those straws?'

'I'm sorry, but I am trying to approach this from every angle. I need to establish the significance of this maniac taking the scalp of his victims. I just thought you might be able to give me a historical perspective on it.'

'I have to say that the significance is not difficult to read, as far as I can see,' said Severts. 'Taking the head or the scalp of a vanquished enemy is one of the oldest and most widely practised forms of trophy-taking. When you kill an enemy, you take his scalp. By doing so you haven't just killed your enemy, you have belittled or humiliated him, and you have a trophy to prove your success as a warrior. Every continent has experienced at least one culture where taking the head or the scalp of enemies has been a major feature.'

'I don't know . . .' Fabel frowned as he conjured up the image of Griebel's study, his thinning scalp dyed an unnatural red and pinned to his bookshelves. 'This killer doesn't remove the scalp from the murder scene. He makes an exhibition of it, displaying it prominently in the home of his victim.'

'Maybe that's his way of showing off his prowess. Scythian warriors used to wear the scalps of their enemies on the bridles of their horses, simply so that everyone could see them there. Your "Hairdresser" maybe feels that exhibiting them where he has killed the victim is the most effective way of displaying them.'

'You say that scalping was a common practice. Here too? In this part of Europe?' asked Fabel.

'Certainly. There have been many examples discovered in Germany. Particularly in your neck of the woods – Ostfriesland, I mean. That's not necessarily to say that your Frisian ancestors took more scalps than other cultures, it's merely that the environmental conditions in Ostfriesland have ensured the preservation of so many bog bodies and artefacts. We talked about Red Franz the last time we spoke. Well, in Bentheim, near the Dutch border and not far from where Red Franz was found, they discovered scalped skulls, and some of the scalps themselves, at a Bronze Age site.' Severts walked over to his bookshelves and selected a couple of textbooks, bringing them back to his desk. He searched in one of them for a moment. 'Yes . . . here's an example that's really close to your home town. In the eighteen sixties five bog bodies were recovered from Tannenhausener Moor.'

Fabel knew exactly where Severts was talking about. Tannenhausen was a village that lay in the northern suburbs of Aurich, Ostfriesland's biggest town. It was a few kilometres south of Norden and Norddeich, where Fabel had grown up. It was an area of rich green moor, dark bogs, ponds and lakes. Tannenhausen sat between three heaths: Tannenhausener Moor, Kreihüttenmoor and Meerhusener Moor. As a boy, Fabel had cycled to the area often. It was a mystical place. And at the heart of the moor was a vast, ancient lake – the Ewiges Meer, the Eternal Sea. The name itself spoke of time immemorial; added to which was the fact that the moor around the lake had been found to be interlaced with wooden walkways that had been constructed four to five thousand years before.

'All five Tannenhausen bodies had been scalped,' Severts continued. 'And similar examples have been found all over Europe, even as far away as Siberia. It seems that it was a very common custom in Bronze

Age Europe, from the Urals to the Atlantic. In fact, the Scythians did it so much that the ancient Greek word for scalping was *aposkythizein*.'

Fabel thought for a moment of the Scottish part of his ancestry. The Scots claimed that their original homeland had been Scythia, on the Steppes, and that they had passed through North Africa, pausing for generations in Spain and Ireland before conquering Scotland. He pictured someone maybe not unlike him and not too many generations before, who might have routinely committed the same act as the killer he was hunting.

'And the significance of scalping was always triumphal?' he asked. 'Just to prove how many enemies a warrior had killed?'

'Mainly, but perhaps not exclusively. There is evidence of scalps being taken from people, including children, who had died natural rather than violent deaths. It would seem to indicate that taking the scalp might have been a way of commemorating or remembering the dead. Of honouring ancestors.'

'I don't think that's what is motivating this guy,' said Fabel.

Severts leaned back in his chair, the huge poster of the Beauty of Loulan as his backdrop. 'If you want my opinion – personal rather than professional – then I would say that scalp-taking has been so common across all cultures that it is almost an *instinct*. I don't know that much about psychology or about your line of work, but I do know that serial killers and psychos like to take trophies from their victims. I think that taking a scalp is the archetypal form of trophy-taking. Your killer could be doing it just because he feels it's the thing to do, rather than making any clever cultural or historical reference.'

Fabel stood up and smiled. 'Maybe you're right.' He shook hands with Severts. 'Many thanks for your time, Herr Doctor.'

'Not at all,' said Severts. 'May I ask one favour in return?'

'Of course . . .'

'Please let me know if you manage to track down the family of the mummified body down by HafenCity. It's not often that I can put a real name and a real life to the human remains I find through my work.'

'I'm afraid the reverse is true in my line of work,' said Fabel. 'But of course I shall.'

## Noon: Harvestehude, Hamburg

Fabel had phoned in to the Presidium and asked Werner to tell Paul Scheibe's deputy to expect him. The architectural practice was housed in a very modern-looking building, between the NDR radio studios and Innocentia-Park in Harvestehude. The clean lines and sweeping angles of Scheibe's offices reminded Fabel of Bertholdt Müller-Voigt's house in the Altes Land. Fabel wondered if Scheibe had been Müller-Voigt's architect and was annoyed that he had not asked the politician such an obvious question.

The midday sun had drawn a thin veil of cloud over her face, and Fabel took off his sunglasses and sat quietly in the car for a moment before going in. When he had phoned Werner he had also asked him to find out if there was anything that Technical Section could do to track down who had made the hoax call on his car phone. Fabel knew it was unlikely, but the call had disturbed him. The voice-changing electronics seemed very elaborate for a phone hoaxer and Fabel had the uneasy feeling that he might just have spoken to the so-called Hamburg Hairdresser. He watched as a pretty girl walked past the car, laughing as she chatted to someone on her cellphone: someone leading a normal life and having normal conversations.

When Fabel entered through the vast glass doors of the Architekturbüro Scheibe, he was greeted by a tall, thin man of about thirty-five with a shaven head. He introduced himself as Thomas Paulsen, the Deputy Director of the practice. His smile had something of an apology in it.

'Thank you for coming, Herr Chief Commissar, but I am glad to say that our concerns about Herr Scheibe have been allayed. We heard from him just ten minutes ago.'

'I'm not here to follow up a missing person,' said Fabel. 'I need to talk to Herr Scheibe about a case that I am investigating. Where is he?'

'Oh . . . he didn't say. He apologised for dropping out of sight, but said that a family emergency had come up and he had had to attend to it at very short notice. He had to go out of town immediately after the Rathaus luncheon on Monday, and that's why we have not been able to get in touch with him since,' Paulsen explained. 'I can tell you, we're all very relieved. The main public and press launch is to take place tonight down at the Speicherstadt. Herr Scheibe has assured us that he will be there to make the presentation.'

'You spoke to him yourself?'

'Well, no . . . not spoke. He sent an e-mail. But he has guaranteed that he'll be there.'

'Then so shall I,' said Fabel. 'If you hear from

Herr Scheibe again, please tell him that he will have to make time to speak to me.'

'Very well . . . but I know that he will be extremely busy. There will be—'

'Trust me, Herr Paulsen: what I have to talk to Herr Scheibe about is much, much more important. I'll see you – and him – this evening.'

Fabel decided to have lunch at Dirk Stellamanns's stand down by the harbour. The veil of cloud had shifted from the sun and the brightness became more vivid and sharp-edged, highlighting the bright tables and parasols ranged around Dirk's cabin. It was busy when Fabel arrived but Dirk beamed over the heads of his customers when he saw his friend.

Fabel felt hot and sticky and ordered a Jever beer and a mineral water, along with a cheese-and-sausage roll, and took them over to one of the few free chest-high tables. Once the rush died down, Dirk came over to him.

'How's your Apache hunt?'

Fabel made a puzzled face.

'The scalper – any closer to nailing him?'

'Doesn't feel like it.' Fabel shrugged despondently. 'I seem to have got bogged down in all kinds of crap. Genetic memories . . . terrorists . . . and I could write a book on scalping through the ages . . .'

'You'll get him, Jannick,' said Dirk. 'You always do.'

'Not always . . .' Fabel thought of how Roland Bartz had called him Jannick. 'I'm thinking of chucking it in, Dirk.'

'The job? You'd never do that. It's your life.'

'I don't know that it is,' said Fabel. 'Or if it ever

should have been. I've been offered something else. A chance to become a civilian again.'

'I can't see it, Jan . . .'

'*I* can. I'm fed up with death. I see it around me all the time. I dunno. Maybe you're right. This case is getting to me.'

'What did you mean about genetic memory? What's that got to do with these killings?'

Fabel outlined as briefly and coherently as he could the work that the victim Gunter Griebel had been involved in.

'You know something, Jan . . . I believe it. I think there's something in it.'

'You?' Fabel grinned sceptically. 'You're joking . . .'

'No . . .' Dirk's face was serious. 'I really do. I remember, I'd only been in the force for a couple of years and we were called to a break-in. It was winter and it had been snowing. This guy had gone out through the back window in the middle of the night and had left his footprints in the snow. The only ones around. So all we had to do was to follow the footprints. We tracked him through the snow, moving fast to catch up with him. And we did, eventually.'

'What's your point?' asked Fabel suspiciously, as if he was expecting a punchline.

'It's just that when we were doing it, when we were moving fast and at night, tracking down another human being, I got this really weird feeling. Not a nice feeling. I really felt that I had done it before. I felt it, but I couldn't remember it.'

'Don't tell me you believe in reincarnation?' asked Fabel.

'No. No, it's not that at all. But it was like a memory that wasn't mine but had been passed down to me.' Dirk laughed, suddenly self-conscious. 'You know me . . . always had a mystical side. It was odd – that's all.'

### 3.00 p.m.: Schanzenviertel, Hamburg

The building sat discreetly on a corner in the Schanzenviertel. Its architecture was *Jugendstil* and Fabel could see that behind the ugly graffiti the elegant stonework had been gracefully styled with Art Deco features. There was no door plate or any other notice on the wall to indicate the function of the offices within and, after he had shouted his name and the nature of his business through the entry system's speakerphone, Fabel had to wait a few seconds before the buzz and clunk of the door indicated that he could enter.

Ingrid Fischmann was waiting for him at the top of the short flight of stairs. She was in her mid-thirties and had long straight light brown hair. Her face could have been pretty, were it not for the heaviness of her features that made them almost masculine. The shoulder-length hair and the long and loose-fitting skirt and top she wore combined in a vaguely hippie look that seemed out of sync with her age.

She smiled politely and extended her hand in greeting. 'Herr Fabel, please come in.'

There were two main rooms off the tiny reception hall. One was clearly used exclusively for file storage and reference materials, the other was Frau Fischmann's office. Despite the clutter of filing cabinets and bookshelves, and the wall planner and noticeboard on the walls, it still had the feel of a converted living room.

'My apartment is two streets away,' explained Frau Fischmann as she sat down behind her desk. Fabel noticed a copy of the 1971 'wanted' poster of the Baader-Meinhof gang on the wall over by the office's only window. Nineteen black-and-white faces were ranged under the title *Anarchistische Gewalttäter – Baader/Meinhof-Bande*. The poster had taken on an almost iconic status, symbolising a particular moment and mood in German history. 'I rent these offices. I don't know why, but I've always felt it necessary to separate my living and working environments. The other thing is I use this as an address for all my business correspondence. Given the sensitivity of some of the people I write about, it's a good idea not to advertise where I live. Please, Herr Fabel, sit down.'

'May I ask why you write what you write? I mean, most of it happened before your time, really.'

Fischmann smiled, exposing slightly too-big teeth. 'Do you know why I agreed to meet with you, Herr Fabel?'

'To help me catch a psychotic killer, hopefully.'

'Of course, there's that. But I am a journalist, first and foremost. I smell a story in this, and I expect a little quid pro quo.'

'I'm afraid I am not interested in horse-trading, Frau Fischmann. My only concern is to catch this murderer before more lives are lost. Lives are more important to me than newspaper stories.'

'Please, Herr Fabel. I agreed to meet you because I have spent many years exposing the hypocrisy of those who dabbled or actively participated in domestic terrorism in the nineteen seventies and nineteen eighties, and who now seek public office or commercial success. In all my studies I have yet to come across a single solid intelligent reason for these spoilt middle-class brats to have been playing at revolutionaries. What offends me more than anything is the way some figures on the left sought to intellectualise the murder and mutilation of innocent citizens.' Fischmann paused. 'As a Hamburg policeman, you will be aware that the Polizei Hamburg experienced its fair share of suffering at the hands of the Red Army Faction and its supporters. You know that the first German policeman to be murdered by the Faction was a Polizei Hamburg officer.'

'Of course: Norbert Schmid, in nineteen seventy-one. He was only thirty-three.'

'Followed by the May nineteen seventy-two gun battle between the Polizei Hamburg and the Red Army Faction in which Chief Commissar Hans Eckhardt was wounded and later died.'

'Yes, I know about that, too.'

'And then, of course, there was the shoot-out between Hamburg police officers and members of the breakaway gang, the Radical Action Group, following a botched bank raid in nineteen eighty-six. One policeman was killed and another very seriously wounded. The wounded officer was lucky to survive. He shot and killed Gisela Frohm, one of the terrorists. As soon as you said your name, I knew who you were, Herr Fabel. Your name came up in my research into Hendrik Svensson and the Radical Action Group. It was you who shot and killed Gisela Frohm, wasn't it?'

'Unfortunately it was. I had no choice.'

'I know that, Herr Fabel. When I heard it was you who was investigating Hauser's murder, I felt

279

there was a story in it for me, as I have already admitted.'

'These killings may have nothing to do with your research. It's just that the two victims, Hauser and Griebel, were contemporaries and formerly involved, to differing degrees, with radical politics. I've looked into their backgrounds and can find no direct link between them. But their histories tend to be populated by the same figures. One of those figures is Bertholdt Müller-Voigt, Hamburg's Environment Senator. I understand you have been researching Müller-Voigt's history as an activist.'

'His history as a *terrorist*.' There was a bitterness in Fischmann's voice. 'Müller-Voigt has political ambitions that extend far beyond the Hamburg Senate. Big ambitions. He has already declared war on the person who was his closest political ally, First Mayor Hans Schreiber, simply because he sees Schreiber as a potential rival further down the road – a road that Müller-Voigt hopes will lead to Berlin. His ambition offends me because I have absolutely no doubt that he was the driver of the vehicle in which the industrialist Thorsten Wiedler was kidnapped and later murdered.'

'I know of your claims about Senator Müller-Voigt. I also know that Hans Schreiber's wife has been quoting you. But do you have proof?'

'As for Frau Schreiber . . . I find her husband's political ambitions only slightly less nauseating than Müller-Voigt's. She is using me for her own ends, but she is generating a level of public awareness that I could not have achieved alone. But to answer your question . . . No, I have no proof that will stand up in court. But I'm working on it. I'm sure you'll know how difficult it is to work on an old case where the trail has long been cold.'

'That I do.' Fabel smiled bitterly. He thought of the many cold cases he had reopened during his career. He also thought about his neglected quest to find the family of the teenager who had lain in the dry sand of the harbour for sixty years.

'Everything else I have done in my career up until now, all of those whose political past I have exposed . . . it's all been a preparation for destroying Müller-Voigt's career and hopefully getting him before a court for his crimes. Something we can perhaps work together to achieve, Herr Chief Commissar.'

'But why Müller-Voigt? Why have you singled him out?'

There was a cold, bitter determination in Ingrid Fischmann's expression. She opened a desk drawer, took two photographs from it and handed them to Fabel. The first was of a large black Mercedes limousine of a model that dated back to the 1970s. It was parked outside a large office building and a black-uniformed chauffeur was holding the rear door open for a middle-aged man with thick black-rimmed spectacles.

'Thorsten Wiedler?' asked Fabel.

Fischmann nodded. 'And his chauffeur.'

The second photograph was of the same car, but closer up and parked on a gravel drive. Fabel saw the same chauffeur, but this time without his cap or jacket. The Mercedes gleamed in the sunlight and a bucket and cloth sat next to the front wheel arch. Fabel looked at the photograph and understood everything. The chauffeur was taking a break from cleaning the car and had squatted down on his heels next to a small girl of about six or seven. His daughter.

'And again,' said Ingrid Fischmann, 'Herr Wiedler's chauffeur. Ralf Fischmann.'

'I see,' said Fabel. He handed the photographs back. 'I'm so sorry.'

'Thorsten Wiedler's death made the headlines. My father was left paralysed by the attack and was worth nothing more than a passing mention. He died from his injuries, Herr Fabel, but it took more than five years. It was an experience that also destroyed my mother. I grew up in a home that knew no joy. All because a bunch of middle-class kids with half-baked borrowed ideas felt justified to destroy any life that happened to be on the fringes when they carried out one of their so-called missions.'

'I understand. And I really am sorry. You are totally convinced that Müller-Voigt was involved?'

'Yes. The group that carried out the attack was not the Red Army Faction. It was one of the many splinter gangs that cropped up at that time. The one thing that differentiated them from the rest was their more poetic choice of name. Everyone else was obsessed by initials – by the way, did you know that one of the reasons why the Red Army Faction chose that name was because it shared the initials RAF with the Royal Air Force? A sick joke, you see. The Royal Air Force bombed Nazism out of Germany. The new RAF saw it as their role to bomb and murder fascism and capitalism out of the West German state. And of course you had direct contact with the RAG gang set up by Svensson. But this bunch had a much more esoteric turn of mind. They called themselves "The Risen". Their leader was Franz Mühlhaus, also known as Red Franz.'

Fabel felt a jolt of recognition. The other Red Franz. The object of a very special terror. Red Franz

Mühlhaus and his group had been seen as on the extreme fringe of the extreme Left. Fabel thought back to the image he had seen in Severts's office of the original Red Franz, the mummified bog body that had slept for centuries in the cold, dark peat bog near Neu Versen.

'Mühlhaus and his group were difficult to classify,' Ingrid Fischmann continued. 'They were even viewed with mistrust by the other groups on the extreme anarchistic Left. One could argue that they were in fact not on the Left at all. They were a manifestation of environmental radicalism which very often went hand in hand with leftist groups. But Red Franz and his Risen were not considered to be making a serious contribution to the movement.'

'Why?'

Ingrid Fischmann pursed her lips. 'Many reasons. They didn't have a clearly Marxist agenda. Of course, there were other groups who were not clearly Marxist who were more clearly allied or aligned with Baader-Meinhof, like the West Berlin-based Second of June Movement, which was more anarchist in philosophy. The Risen was not expressly associated with Baader-Meinhof and their focus was environmental. There were, at that time, two areas of common ground for Marxists, anarchists and eco-militants . . . the anti-nuclear protests of the nineteen sixties onwards. And, of course, Vietnam.'

'But there still was some doubt about how much common ground was shared with The Risen?' asked Fabel.

'Exactly. Like the other groups, they targeted industrialists. But not specifically because they were capitalists – more because of the perceived damage their businesses did to the environment. Same targets, different rationale . . . in a way, The Risen did not travel the same path as the RAF and other leftist groups, more a coincidentally parallel path. A good example is the kidnap and subsequent murder by Baader-Meinhof-RAF of Hanns-Martin Schleyer in October of nineteen seventy-seven and that of Thorsten Wiedler by The Risen in early November. Both part of the so-called German Autumn of nineteen seventy-seven. The difference is that Schleyer was picked out as a target because first, he had been a former Nazi and an SS Hauptsturmbannführer in Czechoslovakia during the war and second, he was a wealthy industrialist, board member of Daimler-Benz and leader of the West German employers' federation, with strong political connections with the ruling CDU party. And, of course, the background to Schleyer's six-week-long kidnap and eventual murder was the whole Mogadishu hijack and the suicides of Raspe, Baader and Ensslin in Stammheim prison.

'On the other hand, while Thorsten Wiedler was also a successful industrialist, he was not in the same league as Schleyer. He came from a Social Democrat, working-class background, had been too young to see military service during the war and had no particular political leanings or significance. The reason he was targeted by The Risen was, apparently, that his factories were major polluters. Of course there was a lot of rhetoric about so-called "solidarity" with the RAF during the German Autumn, and Wiedler also represented, in a more modest way, West German capitalism. But his abduction was seen as counter-productive to the "revolution" and served to isolate The Risen even further. I think that was why there was never any full statement issued by the group about Wiedler's fate. It became an embarrassment to them. The body was never found and the Wiedler family were denied the right to bury and mourn him. But added to all of this was the very "hippie" twist that Red Franz and The Risen gave to their politics. There was a lot of what we would consider New Age claptrap involved.'

'What kind of claptrap?' asked Fabel.

'Well, The Risen is one of the more difficult groups to research, because they were relatively isolated, but one of their group, Benni Hildesheim, became disaffected and defected to the RAF. When Hildesheim was arrested in the nineteen eighties he claimed The Risen had been too wacky for him. He said that they took their name from the belief that Gaia, the spirit of the Earth, would protect itself by generating a band of warriors, of true believers, to defend her when she was in danger. These warriors would rise again and again, across time, whenever needed. Hence, The Risen. Red Franz Mühlhaus used to claim, apparently, that they were drawn together as a group because they had all lived and fought together before, at other times in history when the Earth needed them for protection. It was not something that fitted with the uncompromisingly rational and inflexible Marxist ideology of Baader-Meinhof.'

'And where do Müller-Voigt and Hans-Joachim Hauser fit in with Red Franz Mühlhaus?' asked Fabel.

'Hauser? I don't know. Hauser was a self-promoter and a hanger-on to others. I don't know of any direct link to The Risen or Mühlhaus other than that he was a vocal supporter of Red Franz's earlier "interventions" – disrupting Hamburg Senate sessions, sit-ins at corporate or industrial premises, that kind of thing. But after things started to heat up and banks began to be robbed, bombs planted and people killed, Hauser, like so many others on the trendy Left, suddenly became less vocal in his support. That doesn't mean to say that he did not become directly involved. In fact, his comparative silence could be easily be taken as him keeping a low profile. As for Müller-Voigt, he and Red Franz got together in the late nineteen seventies. After Mühlhaus was put on the wanted list for the murder of the boss of a Hanover pharmaceutical company, and then, of course, for the Thorsten Wiedler affair, I suspect that Müller-Voigt was operating as a "legal" for The Risen.'

'But you think his involvement went deeper?'

'I'll tell you something very personal, Herr Fabel. My father made a tape. He asked for a cassette recorder while he was still in hospital. He had been a very energetic and fit man and faced with a future in a wheelchair he became deeply depressed. But he became angry, too. He was determined to do anything he could to help find Herr Wiedler and catch his abductors. A long time after my father died, when I was at an age when I was deciding what I should study at university, I listened to the tape. My father described the events of that day in great detail. It was as if he wanted the truth to be known. It was after I listened to that tape that I decided to become a journalist. To tell the truth.'

'And what did he say?'

Ingrid Fischmann looked undecided for a moment. Then she said, 'I tell you what, I'll send you a copy of it. And I'll dig out some photographs and general information and mail them to you. But, in short, my father said he estimated that there were six terrorists involved. He only got a good look at the face of one of them in particular. The others were wearing ski masks. He was able to give a very detailed description to the police and they produced an artist's impression of the terrorist. Not that it did any good. As you know, no one was caught for the Wiedler kidnap. Except if you count Red Franz Mühlhaus's demise as justice.'

'And how do you know for sure that Bertholdt Müller-Voigt was involved?' asked Fabel.

'You remember Benni Hildesheim, whom I mentioned earlier? The defector from The Risen to the Baader-Meinhof group? Well, I interviewed him after his release from prison and he claimed that there were a number of individuals who are influential today who had been either directly involved in the actions of The Risen or who had supplied logistical and strategic support. Safe houses, weapons and explosives, that kind of thing. Hildesheim told me that there were six people involved in the Wiedler kidnapping, which fits with my father's account. He claimed to know the identity of all six, as well as the identities of everyone in the support network.'

'He didn't tell you?'

Ingrid Fischmann gave a small laugh laden with cynicism. 'Hildesheim displayed a remarkably capitalist streak for a former Marxist terrorist. He wanted money for the information. Of course, he did not know that I was the daughter of one of the group's victims, but I did tell him he could go to hell. I wanted the truth about who shot my father. But not at any price. Hildesheim seemed convinced that some tabloid would meet his price. He insisted that some of the names would shake the Establishment to its foundations, that kind of crap. You have to remember that this was about the time when Bettina Röhl, Ulrike Meinhof's daughter, sent a sixty-page letter to the State Prosecutor demanding that Foreign Minister Joschka Fischer be charged and brought to trial for the attempted murder of a policeman in the nineteen eighties. It is not inconceivable that there are others in the government and other high office who have the odd skeleton in the cupboard.'

'But Hildesheim didn't get his deal?' asked Fabel.

'No. He died before any deal was concluded.'

'How did he die? Was there anything suspicious about it?'

'No. No grand conspiracy. Merely a middle-aged man who smoked too much and exercised too little. Heart attack. But he did give me something on account. He told me that he knew for an absolute fact who the driver was that day – and that they had gone on to become a prominent public figure. But getting a firm statement and proof to back it up was part of the deal he struck. Unfortunately he didn't live to share it with me.'

'Hildesheim never mentioned Hauser?'

Fischmann shook her head.

'Nor Gunter Griebel?'

''Fraid not . . . I don't think I've even come across the name in my research.'

They talked for another fifteen minutes. Ingrid Fischmann outlined the history of the militant movement in Germany and its transition from protest to direct action to terrorism. They discussed the aims of the various groups, the support they got from the former communist East Germany, the networks of supporters and sympathisers who made it possible for so many terrorists to evade capture for so long. They also discussed the fact that out there, unknown to others, perhaps even unknown to their closest friends and families, there were people hiding a violent past behind a normal life. Eventually, they had said all there was to be said and Fabel stood up.

'Thanks for taking so much time to talk to me,' said Fabel. He shook hands with Fischmann. 'It really has been most useful.'

'I'm glad. I will send you that information when I can find it. It might be a day or two,' she said, smiling. 'Wait a minute and I'll come down with you. I have to get into town.'

'Can I give you a lift?'

'No, thanks,' she said. 'I have a few stops to make on the way.' She perched a pair of glasses on the tip of her nose and searched through her large shoulder bag, eventually pulling out a small black notebook. 'Sorry . . . I have this new security alarm. I have to put the code in when I leave and I'm damned if I can ever remember it.'

They paused at the door while Fischmann slowly typed the code into the alarm control panel, checking each number in the black notebook.

Out on the street, Fabel said goodbye to Ingrid Fischmann and watched her receding back as she headed down the street. A young German woman who spent her life investigating the generation before her. A seeker after Truth. Fabel remembered young Frank Grueber's reason for becoming a forensic specialist: *Truth is the debt we owe to the dead.*

It could, thought Fabel, almost be Germany's national motto.

## 7.30 p.m.: Speicherstadt, Hamburg

Fabel had got back to the Presidium before five. He had hastily called together a meeting in the Murder Commission and had briefed his team on what he had found out over the course of the day. It was beginning to look like these killings were not random serial murders but that the motive lay in the political histories of the victims.

Anna and Henk had gone over what they had found out, or not found out, at The Firehouse. It looked less and less likely that the killings were linked to Hauser's sexuality, and Anna had the feeling that the older guy whom Hauser had met at The Firehouse perhaps had more to do with his political past than with his sexual preferences.

'Maybe it was Paul Scheibe,' Werner suggested.

'Then we'll find out tonight,' Fabel said. 'I want you – Anna, Henk, Werner and Maria – to come with me to this launch event. I want us to have a good look around the guests, and I need to have a long chat with Scheibe.'

Fabel had gone home and had eaten, showered and changed before meeting up with the team down at the Speicherstadt. Anna and Henk had arrived first and had spoken to Scheibe's team.

'The shit's hitting the fan,' Anna told Fabel. 'It looks like we've got a no-show. No one has seen Scheibe. And this is his big night. His staff are getting very agitated because Scheibe has been very insistent that he should be the only one to reveal the concept model. Apparently he has been finishing it off himself and although the Senate have seen the concept, this is the big unveiling for everyone else . . . he's supposed to have added a few touches that no one knows about until tonight.'

'So what are Scheibe's team going to do?'

'At the moment they're going up the wall. They've got all Hamburg's great and good assembled in there, and no star to launch the show.'

'Has he done this kind of thing before?'

'Not with something as important as this . . . But Paulsen has been increasingly worried about him recently. It's like Scheibe's been stressed out about something, which apparently is rare for him. Drinking, yes, arrogance and inflated self-belief, yes . . . but Scheibe is definitely not someone who is prone to stress.'

'Which would suggest that something new has been added to the mix recently,' said Werner.

'Or something old . . .' said Fabel. 'Okay – let's go mingle.'

Fabel led his team into the hall, showing their oval *Kriminalpolizei* shields to the disgruntled door staff. The hall was filled with well-heeled, well-groomed people who gathered in small scattered groups, chatting and laughing while uniformed waiting staff kept their Pinot Grigio topped up.

Fabel, Maria and Werner headed over to the far side of the hall; Fabel told Anna and Henk to stay by the door and keep an eye out for any sign of Scheibe arriving. As he made his way through the crowd, Fabel noticed Müller-Voigt holding court with a particularly large cluster. Fabel caught the Environment Senator's eye and nodded, but Müller-Voigt merely frowned as if confused by Fabel's presence.

The house lights dimmed, and Fabel watched as there was a flurry of activity over by the illuminated platform, where a white canopy concealed Paul Scheibe's vision of the future from the expectant and increasingly agitated audience. Paulsen, Scheibe's deputy, was in animated discussion with two other members of the architect's team.

After a pause, Paulsen awkwardly took centre stage at the podium in front of the display. For a moment he looked apprehensively at the microphone.

'Ladies and gentlemen, thank you very much for your patience. Unfortunately, Herr Scheibe has been unexpectedly and unavoidably detained by a family emergency. Obviously, he is doing his best to get here as soon as he possibly can. However, the power and innovation of Paul Scheibe's work speaks for itself. Herr Scheibe's vision for the future of HafenCity and for the state of Hamburg itself is a bold and striking concept that reflects the ambition of our great city.'

Paulsen paused. He looked across to the side of the hall, where a woman whom Fabel took to be another member of the Scheibe team had just entered. The woman gave an almost imperceptible shake of her head and Paulsen turned back to the audience with a weak and resigned smile.

'Okay . . . I think that . . . em . . . it would be best if we were simply to proceed with the presentation . . . Ladies and gentlemen, it is my great pleasure, on behalf of the Architekturbüro Scheibe, to unveil Herr Scheibe's creatively unique and daring new aesthetic for the HafenCity's Überseequartier. I give you *KulturZentrumEins* . . .'

Paulsen stood to one side and the pristine white

canvas canopy began to rise. The audience began to applaud, but with muted enthusiasm, as the vast architectural model was revealed.

The applause died.

As the canvas covering disappeared up and out of the spotlight, a silence fell across the hall. A silence that seemed to freeze the moment. Fabel knew what he was seeing, yet his brain refused to process the information. The rest of the audience were similarly trapped in that fossilised moment as they too sought to grasp the impossibility of what they were looking at.

The spotlights, one red, one blue and the main white light, had been carefully sited to pick out every edge, every angle of the vast white architectural model: to dramatise, to emphasise. But the creativity they illuminated with such stark drama and emphasis was not Paul Scheibe's.

The screaming began.

It spread from person to person like a white-hot flame. Shrill and penetrating. Through it, Fabel could hear Anna Wolff cursing. Several people, particularly those nearest the display, vomited.

The landscape in miniature lay under the lights. But the centrepiece, *KulturZentrumEins,* was itself not visible. Paul Scheibe's naked body had crushed it beneath its weight. It was as if some vast, hideous god had been cast out from the heavens and had smashed into the Earth in the HafenCity. Scheibe sat, semi-recumbent, among the shattered elements of his vision. His naked flesh gleamed blue-white in the spotlights and his blood glistened bright red on the model. Whoever had placed the corpse here had used part of the display to prop it up, and Scheibe gazed out at his audience.

His scalp had been removed. It lay at his feet, spread out and dyed, like those of the other victims, unnaturally red. The gore-streaked dome of his skull glistened under the lights. His throat had been slashed.

Fabel was suddenly aware that he was running. He pushed members of the stunned audience out of his way as he rushed forward and they gave way unprotestingly, as if he were charging through a storeroom of shop-window mannequins. He sensed Anna, Henk and Werner in his wake.

One of the press photographers lifted his camera and it flashed in the auditorium. Anna shouldered her way through to the photographer, grabbed his camera with one hand and shoved him backwards with the other. The photographer started to protest and demanded his camera back.

'It's not your camera any more. It's police evidence.' She scanned the rest of the press photographers with her laser gaze. 'And that goes for the rest of you. This is a murder scene and I'll seize any camera used here.'

By now Fabel had reached the front and grabbed hold of Paulsen, who still stood gazing blankly at the display.

'Get your people out into the corridor! Now!' he shouted into Paulsen's face. He turned to his officers. 'Anna, Henk . . . get the audience out into the corridor too. Werner . . . secure the main door and make sure that no one leaves the building.' He snapped open his cellphone and hit the pre-set button for the Murder Commission. He gave orders that the forensics team were to be dispatched and that he needed uniformed units to secure the scene immediately. He also arranged for extra plain-clothes officers to attend to take statements from every member of the audience. As soon as he hung up from talking to the Murder Commission he hit another button.

Van Heiden made no protest at being disturbed at home: he knew that for Fabel to call it must be urgent. Fabel heard himself describing the scene to van Heiden in a dead, toneless voice. Van Heiden seemed to react more to the very public context in which the body had been found than to the fact that someone else had lost their life.

After he ended his call to van Heiden, Fabel found himself alone in the auditorium. Alone except for that which had once been Paul Scheibe. Scheibe had had something to tell Fabel. Something valuable, maybe something that would not be told willingly. Now Scheibe sat elevated on his throne of smashed balsa and card, scalped, naked and dead: a crownless, silent king looking out over his empty kingdom.

### 11.45 p.m.: Grindelviertel, Hamburg

Leonard Schüler had had too much to drink. It was not uncommon for him to do so. And, after all, it had been a hard week. He was still haunted by that face – that cold, pale, emotionless face at the window of Hauser's apartment – but it came to his mind less and less as the days went by. More than ever, he was convinced that he had done the right thing in not giving a complete description of the killer to the police. Leonard Schüler, who did not believe in any thing much any more and was not one for deep thought, had found himself thinking back to that night, to the man in the window, and

295

wondering if there really was such a thing as the devil.

But it was time to forget about it. To put it where it belonged, in the past.

Schüler had felt like celebrating and had met up with friends in the bar on the corner two blocks away from his flat. It was a raucous, smoky place, buzzing with crude exuberance and over-loud rock music. It was exactly the kind of place he needed to be.

It was one in the morning when he left. He did not stagger as he walked, but he was aware that the normally unconscious act of taking a step now required a degree of concentration. It had been a good night, and a lot of steam had been let off: a bit too much for Willi, the land-lord. But as he walked home, Schüler was aware of a hollow feeling inside. This was his life. This was all he had amounted to. He had not come from the best background, true, but others from similar circumstances had done more, made more of themselves. He was honest enough to blame himself for the failures in his life, although, in darker moments, he allowed himself to share some of the responsibility with his mother. Schüler's mother was still a young woman, in her forties, having given birth to Leonard when she was eighteen. Leonard had never known his father, and doubted if his mother even knew for sure who he was. It was a subject his mother had always avoided, claiming that Leonard's father had been a boyfriend who had died from an undisclosed disease before they could marry. But, by putting together the tiny and disparate scraps that he had been able to garner about his mother's past life, and by a lot of reading between the lines, Leonard had come to suspect that she had worked as a prostitute at one time in her life, and he often speculated that his anonymous male parent might have been a client.

But all that had been before Leonard's first memories of the world. His mother, as a single parent, had brought him up on her own and had displayed an anachronistic sense of shame about it. At some time in Leonard's infancy, his mother had become a 'born-again' Christian. She was now the model of prissy probity and abstemiousness, and his childhood had been overshadowed by the omnipresence of religion. He had hated his mother's righteousness for as long as he could remember. It had embarrassed him. Irritated him. He would have been less ashamed of his mother if she had still sold blow jobs to strangers. Leonard often thought that that was why he had become a thief: to witness his mother's shame.

'Thou shalt not steal . . .' she had repeated over and over, shaking her head when the police had brought him home the first time. 'Thou shalt not steal . . . Do you know what will become of you, Leonard?' she had said. 'The devil will come for you. The devil will come for you and take you straight to hell.'

It had been those words that had echoed in Leonard's head when the senior detective had talked to him; when he had described what that psycho would do to him if he knew about him. If he found him.

Schüler knew that he was not stupid. He had no illusions about the act that had conceived him. A quick, grubby fuck for a few Deutschmarks. But he always imagined that his biological father would perhaps have been a wealthy, successful businessman or professional of some kind who, probably drunk at the time, had been a one-off customer of his mother's. Someone with a bit going on up top. A better class of person. How else could Leonard explain his own intelligence? He had gone to a comprehensive *Gesamtschule* school and there was no doubt that, with just a little effort on his part, he could have passed his *Abitur* leaving exam, which would have guaranteed him a place at university. But Schüler had not made that effort. He had worked out that there were two ways to get the things you wanted in life: you could earn them, or you could steal them. And earning them required too much effort.

And this was how he had ended up. Jobless, twenty-six years old, a thief. Was it too late to change things? To start afresh? To build a new life?

He swung open the main door of his apartment building. Each step up the stairwell seemed to take a monumental effort. He unlocked the door of his apartment and threw the keys onto the second-hand dresser by the door. Leaning against the door frame for a moment, he stood on the threshold between the stark light of the stairwell and the dark of his flat. There was a click as the hall light, on an economy timer, went out, plunging Schüler into total darkness. He breathed it in for a moment, the hoppy taste of beer thick in his mouth and his head suddenly light without a visual anchor.

The light in his living room snapped on. Schüler stood blinking, trying to work out how he had acci-dentally hit the light switch, when he saw him sitting in the chair by the television. The same man. The same face that had gazed out at him through the window of Hauser's flat. The killer.

The devil had come to take him to hell.

# 11.

## Fourteen Days After the First Murder:
## Thursday, 1 September 2005.

### 12.02 a.m.: Grindelviertel, Hamburg

Leonard knew, the instant he saw the man with the gun sitting in the corner by the television, that he was going to die. One way or another.

The first thing that struck Leonard was how dark the young man's hair was – too dark against his pale complexion. He was holding a black automatic and Leonard noticed that he was wearing white surgical gloves. The man with the gun stood up. He was tall and slim. Leonard reckoned that he could have taken him on, easily, if it had not been for the gun in his hand. Rush him, thought Leonard. Even if he squeezes off a round, at least you will die quickly. He might even miss. Leonard thought of the two pictures the police had shown him; of what this tall, dark young man with a pale, impassive face had done. Leonard thought hard, so hard that his head hurt. Why don't you just rush him? What have you got to lose? A bullet is better than what he'll do to you if you let him.

'Relax, Leonard.' It was as if the dark-haired man had read his thoughts. 'Take it easy and there's no reason for you to get hurt. I just want to talk to you. That's all.'

Leonard knew he was lying. Just rush him. But he wanted to believe the lie.

'Please, Leonard . . . please sit down so we can talk.' The man indicated the chair that he had just vacated.

Do it now . . . grab the gun. Leonard sat down. The other man watched him impassively. The same lack of emotion, of expression.

'I didn't tell them. I didn't tell them anything,' Leonard said earnestly.

'Now, Leonard,' the dark-haired man said, as if reproaching a child, 'we both know that's not true. You didn't tell them *everything*. But you did tell them enough. And it would be most inconvenient if you were to tell them anything more than you have.'

'Listen, I don't want any part of this. You must know that. You can see that I'm not going to tell them any more than I already have. I'll go away . . . I promise . . . I'll never come back to Hamburg.'

'Take it easy, Leonard. I'm not going to hurt you. Unless you try anything silly. I just want to discuss our . . . *situation* with you.' The dark-haired man leaned against the wall and placed the gun on the table next to Leonard's keys. *Do it! Do it now!* Leonard's instincts were screaming at him, yet he sat as if his body had fused with the chair. The dark-haired man reached into his jacket pocket and took out a pair of handcuffs. He tossed them to Leonard before picking up the gun again. 'Now don't panic, Leonard. This is merely for my protection, you understand. Please . . . put them on.'

Now. Do it now. If you put these on, he will have total control of you. He will be able to do anything he wants. Do it! Leonard snapped the handcuffs on one wrist, then the other.

'Okay,' the dark-haired man said. 'Now we can relax.' But as he spoke he walked into Leonard's bedroom and returned with a large black leather holdall. 'Now don't be alarmed, Leonard. I just need to secure you.' He produced a roll of thick black insulating tape from the holdall and started to wrap it across Leonard's chest and upper arms and around the chair back. Tight. Then he took a strip and stretched it across Leonard's mouth. Leonard's protests were reduced to loud muffles. The combination of the gag and the over-tight tape made it difficult for him to breathe, and the hammering of his heart was exaggerated in his confined chest. Satisfied that Leonard no longer represented a threat, the other man again laid the gun on the table. He pulled over the only other chair in the apartment and drew it opposite and close to Leonard's. He leaned forward, elbows on knees, and rested his chin on a cradle of interlaced fingers. He seemed to study Leonard for a long time. Then he spoke.

'Do you believe in reincarnation, Leonard?' The bound man stared uncomprehendingly at the killer.

'Do you believe in reincarnation? It's not a complicated question.'

Leonard shook his head vigorously. His eyes were wide, wild. Scared. They searched the face of his assailant for any sign of sympathy or compassion, for anything approaching a human emotion.

'You don't? Well, you're in the minority, Leonard. The vast majority of the population of this world include reincarnation in their belief systems. Hinduism, Buddhism, Taoism . . . many cultures find it natural and logical to have a belief in some kind of return of the soul. In villages in Nigeria you'll often come across an *ogbanje* . . . a child who is the reincarnation of someone who died in childhood themselves. Sorry . . . you don't mind if I talk while I'm getting everything ready, do you?' The dark-haired man stood up and removed a large square sheet of black polyurethane from the holdall; he then took out a black plastic bag. Behind his gag, Leonard made an incomprehensible noise that the killer seemed to take as assent and he continued with his lecture.

'Anyway, even Plato believed that we existed as higher beings and were reincarnated in this life as a punishment for falling from grace – something that was part of early Christian belief, actually, until it was excised and branded as heresy. If you think about it, reincarnation is easy to accept because we have all had experiences that cannot be explained any other way.' The killer spread out the square plastic sheet on the floor and stepped onto it. He removed his jacket and his shirt, folded them carefully and put them into the black bag. 'It happens to us all . . . we meet someone that we have never met before in our lifetime, yet we experience that strange sense of recognition or we feel that we have known them for years and years.' He took off his shoes. 'Or we will go somewhere new, somewhere we have never been before, yet we feel an unaccountable familiarity with the place.' He unbuckled his belt, then removed his trousers, which he placed with his shoes in the bag. He now stood on the black square in only his socks and underwear. His body was pale, thin and angular. Almost boyish. Fragile. From the holdall he took out a white one-piece coverall suit, like those used by forensic experts at the scene of a crime, except this one seemed to be coated with a plastic sheen. Leonard suddenly felt sick as he realised that it was the kind of protective clothing used by abattoir workers. 'You see, Leonard, we've all been here before. In one form or another. And sometimes we come back, or are sent back, to resolve some outstanding issue or another from a previous life. I have been sent back.'

The man took a hairnet from the holdall, tucked his thick dark hair in it and then pulled the hood of his coverall up and over it, pulling the drawstring closed until it formed a circle tight around his face. He covered his feet with blue plastic overshoes before starting to clear a space in the centre of the room, moving furniture and Leonard's few personal belongings into the corners with great care, as if afraid of breaking anything. 'Don't worry, Leonard, I'll put everything back the way it was . . .' He smiled a cold, empty smile. 'When we're finished.'

He paused, looking around the room as if inspecting its readiness for whatever he had planned next. He carefully refolded the square of black plastic and replaced it in the holdall.

Leonard felt the sting of tears in his eyes. He thought of his mother. About how disappointed she had been in him. About how he had stolen to hurt her.

The killer unfolded a second heavy-duty sheet of black plastic, much larger than the first, and laid it on the space he had cleared. He then came around behind Leonard, grabbed the back of his chair, tilted it backwards and started to 'walk' it across the floor on its two rear legs onto the black plastic. Leonard could now feel and hear his own pulse, the blood rushing in his ears, his lips throbbing against the insulating tape gag.

'Anyway,' continued the killer. 'It's not simply that I believe in reincarnation. I know it to be a fact. A law of nature, as sound and incontrovertible as gravity.' He took a velvet roll-pouch from his holdall and placed it on the black plastic next to the chair. 'You see, Leonard, I have been given a gift. The gift of memory – memory beyond birth, beyond death. Memory of my past lives. I have a mission to fulfil. And that mission is to avenge an act of betrayal in my last life. That was why I was there that night when you saw me, when you were skulking around behind Hauser's apartment. That was the very beginning of my quest. Then, the next night, I killed Griebel. But there is more that I have to do, Leonard. Much more. I can't let you interfere with that.'

The dark-haired man took a couple of steps back and examined his victim, bound tightly to his chair. He adjusted the black plastic sheeting, smoothing it flat. Then he scanned the walls of the room, seeming to assess them. He moved across to one wall and ripped down a poster of an American rock group, revealing the stain that Leonard, in an uncharacteristically house-proud moment, had sought to conceal. Again the killer stepped back and surveyed the wall.

'This will do nicely.' He turned back to Leonard and smiled broadly, revealing his perfect white teeth. 'Do you know, Leonard, that scalping was part of the European cultural tradition since its very beginnings?'

Leonard screamed, but his cries were reduced to frantic high-pitched mumbling behind the gag of insulation tape.

'All of those who have contributed their blood to our lineage did it: the Celts, the Franks, the Saxons, the Goths and, of course, the ancient Scythians on the lonely, empty Steppes that were the cradle of Europe. To take the scalps of those who had succumbed to us in battle, or simply to take the scalp of a personal enemy whom we had killed in single combat to settle a disagreement or grudge, is at the very heart of our cultural identity. We were scalp-takers and we did so with pride. Have you heard of an ancient Greek historian called Herodotus?'

There was no answer from Leonard other than the desperate, body-racking sobs of a man facing a terrible death protesting against his bonds and gag. The killer took no notice and continued to talk in his relaxed, chatty manner, as if he were at a dinner party. It was his calm, his nonchalance, that Leonard feared most: it would have been easier to understand, to deal with, if the man who was about to take his life had been enraged, or afraid, or in any form of heightened emotion.

'Herodotus is considered the father of history. He travelled the then-known civilised world and wrote about the peoples he encountered. But Herodotus also wandered into the unknown lands, the wild lands, beyond the cultured world. He visited the Ukraine, which was the heart of the Scythian kingdom, and documented the lives of those he found there.'

The killer examined the wall again where he had torn down the poster. He paused for a moment to remove the tacks and fragments of poster left there, brushing the stained surface with his latex-gloved hand. 'According to Herodotus, Scythian warriors would scrape away all the flesh from the inside of the scalps they had taken and would then continuously rub them between their hands until they became soft and supple. Once they had done this, they would use the scalps at feasts as napkins, hanging them on the bridles of their horses between uses. The more scalp-napkins a warrior had, the greater his status among the others. According to Herodotus, many of the most successful warriors would even sew their collected scalps together to make cloaks.'

Something like awe fleeted across the killer's otherwise empty face. 'And we are not talking about some remote land and distant people. This was *our* culture. This was where we all have roots.' He paused and seemed to be deep in thought for a moment. 'Think of this . . . think of a hall filled with ninety, maybe a hundred people. It is not a lot. And each person in this room is as closely related as it is possible to be: father and son, mother and daughter. Imagine that, Leonard, but imagine that they are all the same age, ninety generations brought together at the same time of life. Across this room you can see the family similarities. Maybe six, seven, eight generations back you see a face just like yours. That is all that separates you and me from those Scythian warriors, Leonard. Ninety closely related individuals. And the truth is, the truth that I have come to learn, is that it is not just our features, our gestures, our aptitude for certain skills or the propensity for particular talents that are repeated across the generations. We repeat ourselves, Leonard. We are eternal. We come back, time and again. Sometimes our lifetimes even overlap. As mine have. I have been my own father, Leonard. I have seen the same time from two perspectives. And I can remember them both . . .'

The dark-haired man took the dark blue velvet roll-pouch and unrolled it on the black plastic sheeting. He stood back for a moment, examining his preparations. Leonard looked down at the laid-flat roll-pouch. On it lay a large knife, its handle and blade forged from a continuous piece of glittering stainless steel. Leonard's sobbing grew in intensity. He started to struggle wildly but impotently against his bonds. The killer laid his hand gently on Leonard's shoulder, as if to comfort him.

'Settle yourself, Leonard. You chose this. Remember you wondered about trying to wrestle the gun from me? Oh yes, Leonard, I could read you like a book. But you decided not to. You chose to hang on to every last second of life, no matter how terrible. Do you want a laugh, Leonard?' He picked up the gun and held it out towards his captive. 'It's not even real. It's a replica. You consigned yourself to me, to this death, based on the *idea* of a gun. On a lump of functionless metal.'

Behind his gag Leonard wailed. His face was streaked wet with tears.

'Now, Leonard,' said the killer without malice. 'I know that you are not very happy with this life. So now I am going to send you on to your next. But first, do you see the space I cleared on the wall over there? That's where I'm going to pin up your scalp.' He paused, ignoring the desperate muffled screaming of his victim, as if he was thinking something through. Then a smile broke across his face: a cold, callous smile of a terrible intensity that did not belong on the hitherto expressionless mask. 'No . . . not there . . . now that I think about it, I have a much, much better place for it . . .'

### 10.00 p.m.: Pöseldorf, Hamburg

Fabel had been awake for twenty-four hours.

All hell had broken loose with the media and with

anyone who had a say in anything in Hamburg. Fabel found himself, once again, having to plan out the course of the investigation while navigating around the twin whirlpools of media attention and political pressure. It was another feature of his work that wore him down: there must have been a time when policing had been much easier, when the only pressure on an investigator had been to detect and apprehend the perpetrator.

Having spent almost all day at the scene, Fabel had come back to the Presidium for a major strategy meeting. All of a sudden, resources ceased to be an issue and Fabel found himself with detectives from across Hamburg allocated to him. He set up a major incident room in the main conference hall, having the incident boards and files moved there from the Murder Commission. A weary Fabel had found himself addressing a fifty-strong audience of detectives, uniform branch commanders and top brass. He had also noticed that Markus Ullrich and a couple of his BKA buddies had come along for the show: Fabel could not now deny that there was a political dimension, and possibly some kind of terrorist element, to the case.

Susanne had driven them home in Fabel's car. She said that he was too tired to drive and that he needed some sleep. Fabel said that what he needed was a drink. Anna, Henk and Werner had all said they would come along too. It was clear that they needed to take time out and catch their breaths after the events of the last twenty-four hours. Maria, too, agreed to meet at Fabel's usual pub in Pöseldorf, but she was going to wait for Frank Grueber and they would both take a taxi.

It was nearly ten p.m. by the time they arrived. Bruno, the head barman, greeted Fabel enthusiastically. Fabel shook his hand and smiled a weary 'it's been a tough day' smile. Fabel, Susanne and the team sat at the bar and ordered their drinks. A CD was playing the football song '*Hamburg, meine Perle*' and a group of young people at the far end of the bar were singing along to Hamburg's unofficial anthem with immense gusto. Their passion seemed to intensify as they delivered the verse that informed Berliners that 'we shit on you and your song'. It was loud, it was raucous, it was cheerful. Fabel soaked it up. It was the vulgar, ebullient sound of life, of vigour; it was a million miles away from the death realm where he and his officers had spent the last thirty-odd hours. It was what he needed to hear.

Fabel wanted to get drunk. After his sixth beer, he could feel its effects; he was aware of the leaden deliberateness in his speech and movements that always came with having drunk that little bit too much. He always came to this point. And never beyond it. Tonight, he thought, tonight just get drunk. The truth was that Fabel never felt comfortable when he had had too much alcohol. He had never in his life got really, seriously drunk, even when he had been a student. There had always been a point when he was drinking that his fear of losing control would kick in. When he would become afraid of making a fool of himself.

Maria and Grueber joined them and they all moved away from the bar and its raucous choir and found a table together at the back of the pub. For some reason, Fabel got onto the subject of Gunter Griebel's field of work and what Dirk had said to him about his experience.

'Maybe we all come back,' said Anna – her gloomy expression did not suggest that she relished the concept. 'Maybe we are all just variations on the same theme and we experience each consciousness as if it were unique.'

'There's this wonderful, tragic Italian short story called "The Other Son" by Luigi Pirandello,' said Susanne. 'It is all about this Sicilian mother who gives letters to everyone she hears is emigrating to America, so that they can pass them on to her two sons who emigrated years before but from whom she has never heard. The pain of separation that she feels is enormous. But these sons really had not given her a second thought, while she has a third son who has stayed with her and is as loving and devoted as a son can be. Yet she cannot bear to set eyes on him, far less show him any form of affection or love. It emerges that, years before, while the mother was a young woman, a notorious bandit had raided the village with his gang. While there, he had brutally raped her and, as a result, she had become pregnant. As the child grew, despite being a sensitive and caring boy, he developed a massive build and had become the image of his natural father, the bandit. And every time the mother looked at her devoted, loving son, she felt loathing and contempt. He was not his father. But all she saw was the reincarnation of the bandit who had raped her. It is a tragic and beautifully written story. But it is also one that resonates with us, because it's something we all do. We see continuity in people.'

'But that story is about appearance. About a physical similarity between father and son. The son's personality was totally different,' said Fabel.

'Yes,' replied Susanne. 'But the mother suspected

that beneath the surface similarity the person was somehow the same. A variation on a theme.'

'I remember,' said Henk Hermann, looking thoughtful, 'when I was a child, I used to get so fed up with my mother and my grandmother always going on about how like my grandfather I was. Looks, mannerisms, personality – the whole package. I used to get so fed up with hearing, "Oh, that's just his grandad . . ." or, "Isn't he the spit of his grandad . . ." To me he was someone buried, literally, in history. He had died in the war, you see. There were photographs of him around the place and I couldn't see what they were on about. Then, when my grandmother died and I was an adult, I found all those photographs of him again. And it *was* me. There was even one of him in his *Wehrmacht* uniform. I tell you, that was a spooky experience, seeing my face in that uniform. It really makes you think. I mean, someone just like me living through those times . . .'

They moved on to a new topic. But Fabel had noticed that Henk seemed more subdued than normal for the rest of the evening and found himself regretting having brought up the subject.

The pub was just around the corner from Fabel's flat and he and Susanne walked home. When they arrived, Fabel opened the door to the apartment and made an exaggeratedly gentlemanly sweep of his arm to indicate that Susanne should precede him into the flat.

'Are you okay?' asked Susanne. 'You must be exhausted.'

'I'll survive . . .' he said and kissed her. 'Thanks for caring.' He switched on the light.

They both saw it at the same time.

Fabel heard Susanne's shrill scream and was surprised to feel any hint of drunkenness swept suddenly from him by the tidal wave of horror that washed over them both.

Fabel ran across the room. He unholstered his service automatic and snapped the carriage back to put a round in the chamber. He turned to Susanne. She stood frozen, both hands clamped to her mouth and her eyes wide with shock. Fabel held up his hand, indicating that she was to stay where she was. He moved over to the bedroom, threw the door wide and stepped inside, sweeping the room with the gun. Nothing. He switched on the bedroom light to check again and then moved on to the bathroom.

The apartment was clear.

Fabel moved back towards Susanne, putting his gun down on the coffee table as he crossed the room. He put his arm around her and steered her towards the bedroom, placing his body between her and the apartment's picture window.

'Stay in there, Susanne. I'll phone for help.'

'Christ, Jan – in your *home* . . .' Her face was drained of colour and her tear-streaked make-up stood out harshly against the pallor.

He closed the bedroom door behind her and crossed the living room again, deliberately not looking at the picture window that had given him so much pleasure, with its ever-changing vista across the Alster. He snapped up the phone and hit the pre-set dial button for the Presidium. He spoke to the duty Commissar in the Murder Commission and told him that Anna Wolff, Henk Hermann, Maria Klee and Werner Meyer would be on their way to their respective homes and that he was to call them

313

on their cellphones and tell them to make their way to his apartment.

'But first of all,' he said, hearing his own voice dull and dead in the quiet of his apartment, 'send a full forensic team. I have a secondary murder locus here.'

He hung up, resting his hand on the phone for a moment and deliberately keeping his back to the window. Then he turned.

In the centre of the window, pressed flat against it and adhering to the glass by means of its own stickiness and strips of insulating tape, was a human scalp. Viscous rivulets of blood and red dye streaked the pane. Fabel felt sick and turned his face from it, but found that he could not banish the image from his brain. He made his way over to the bedroom and to the sound of Susanne sobbing. In the distance, he heard the growing clamour of police sirens as they made their way towards him along Mittelweg.

## 1.45 a.m.: Pöseldorf, Hamburg

Fabel had arranged for a female officer to take Susanne home to her own flat and stay with her there. Susanne had recovered significantly from the shock and had sought to apply her professional detachment as a practising forensic psychologist. But the truth was that this killer had reached out and touched their personal lives. Something that no one had done before. Fabel tried to contain the fury that raged within him. His home. The bastard had been here, in his private space. And that meant that he knew more about Fabel than Fabel knew about him. It also meant that Susanne had to be watched. Protected.

The whole team turned up. The shock and anger they felt was apparent on all their faces, even on Maria Klee's. It was her boyfriend, Frank Grueber, who led the forensic team on site, but, realising that his own boss had a close professional and personal relationship with Fabel, Grueber had phoned Holger Brauner at home. Brauner had turned up within minutes of the others and, although he allowed Grueber to process the scene, he scrutinised every sample, every area personally.

Fabel felt nauseated. The shock and horror of what he and Susanne had been faced with, the drink he had consumed earlier, the cumulative exhaustion of not having slept for two days and the violation of his personal space all combined in a sickening churning in his gut. His apartment was too small to hold everyone and the team stood outside on the landing. Fabel had already had to deal with his neighbours, who were displaying that excited, alarmed curiosity that Fabel had seen at countless crime scenes before. But these were *his* neighbours. This crime scene was *his* home.

Fabel was aware that the team had been engaged in some kind of debate out on the landing. Then Maria broke off and came across to him, collecting Grueber on her way.

'Listen, *Chef*,' said Maria. 'I've been talking with the others. You can't stay here and I think Dr Eckhardt needs some time to recover from all this. You'll have to stay with one of us for a couple of nights at least. It's going to take hours to process the scene and afterwards . . . well, you're not going to want to stay here. Werner said you can stay with him and his wife, but it would be a bit of a squeeze. Then I talked to Frank about it.'

'I have a big place over in Osdorf,' said Grueber. 'Tons of room. Why don't you pack a few things? Then you can crash there for as long as you need.'

'Thanks. Thanks a lot. But I'll check into a hotel . . .'

'I think you should take up Herr Grueber's offer.' The voice came from behind Fabel. Criminal Director Horst van Heiden stood at the top of the stairs. Fabel looked startled for a moment. He was pleased that his boss had taken the time to come down in person, and in the middle of the night. Then the significance of it hit him.

'Are you worried about my expense account?' Fabel smiled weakly at his own joke.

'I just think that Herr Grueber's apartment would be more secure than a hotel. Until we get this maniac, you are under personal protection, Fabel. We'll put a couple of officers outside Herr Grueber's place.' Van Heiden glanced across at Grueber, seeking the formality of his approval. Grueber nodded his assent.

'Okay,' said Fabel. 'Thanks. I'll get some stuff together later.'

'That's decided, then,' said van Heiden. Grueber took Fabel's car keys and said that Maria would take him over to his place and he would drive Fabel's car over once he had finished processing the scene.

'Thanks, Frank,' said Fabel. 'But I'll have to go into the Presidium first. We need to get a handle on what this all means.'

Van Heiden took Fabel's elbow and guided him into a corner. Despite the fog of tiredness that seemed to cloud his every thought, Fabel could not help wondering how van Heiden managed to look so well pressed at two in the morning. 'This is bad, Fabel.

I don't like the way this man is targeting you. Do we know how he got in?'

'So far forensics have been unable to find any hint of a forced entry. And, as usual with this guy, he's left practically no trace evidence of his presence at the scene.' Fabel felt another churn in his gut as he referred to his own home as 'the scene'.

'So we don't know how he got in,' said van Heiden. 'And God only knows how he found out where you live.'

'We've got a much more pressing question than that to answer . . .' Fabel nodded over to where the bright red dyed hair and skin was still plastered to the glass of the window. 'And that question is: to whom does that scalp belong?'

## 2.00 a.m.: Police Presidium, Hamburg

The entire Murder Commission team had turned out. It unnerved Fabel that van Heiden had felt his continued presence was somehow necessary. Everyone wore the unnatural expressions of people who should be exhausted, yet are agitated with an electric nervousness. Fabel himself found it difficult to focus, but was aware that it was up to him to pull the team, and himself, together.

'Forensics are still processing the scene,' he said. 'But we all know that we're only going to get whatever this guy decides he wants us to get. This scene differs from the others in two respects. Firstly, we have a scalp but no body. And there has to be a body somewhere. Secondly, we now know for sure that this killer is using these scalps to send a message. In this case directed at me. Some kind of warning or threat. So, if we follow the logic, the scalps displayed at the other scenes were intended to send out a message. But to whom?'

'To us?' Anna Wolff sat slumped in a chair. Her face was naked of its usual lipstick and make-up and looked pale and tired under her shock of black hair. 'Maybe he feels he's taunting the police with them. After all, we've been in similar territory before. And the fact that he's used one of our homes as a showplace would seem to support that.'

'I don't know,' said Fabel. 'If it were just the scalps, maybe. But this thing with dying the hair red . . . if he is talking to us, then he is using a vocabulary that we don't understand. Maybe, instead of talking to us, this guy is talking *through* us. I get the feeling that his main audience is someone else.'

'That's as may be, but who is this third victim?' Van Heiden stood up and walked over to the inquiry board. He examined the images of both victims. 'If this has got something to do with their histories, then we have to assume that we have another victim in their fifties or early sixties lying somewhere.'

'Unless . . .' Anna stood up suddenly as if stung.

'Unless what?' asked Fabel.

'The guy you had in. The potential witness. You don't think—'

'Witness?' Van Heiden looked surprised.

'Schüler? I doubt it.' Fabel paused for a moment. He thought about how he had threatened the small-time crook with the spectre of the scalp-taker. It couldn't be: there was no way the killer could have found out about him. 'Anna – you and Henk go and check him out, just in case.'

'What's this about a witness, Fabel?' said van

Heiden. 'You didn't tell me anything about having a witness.'

'He's not. It was the guy who stole the bike from Hauser's place. He saw someone in the apartment, but could only give a partial and pretty vague description.'

After Anna and Henk had left, Fabel took the rest of the team through the case again. There was nothing. No new leads to follow. This killer was so skilled at eliminating his forensic presence from a scene that they were totally dependent upon what they could deduce from the selection of the victims. Which left them nothing other than the suspicion that it was connected to their political pasts.

'Let's take a break,' said Fabel. 'I think we could all do with a coffee.'

The Presidium canteen was all but deserted. A couple of uniformed-branch officers sat in the corner, chatting quietly. Fabel, van Heiden, Werner and Maria collected their coffees and made their way across to a table at the opposite end of the canteen from the two uniformed officers. There was an awkward silence.

'Why did he target you, Fabel?' asked van Heiden at last.

'Maybe it's just to prove that he can,' said Werner. 'To show us how clever and resourceful he is. And how dangerous.'

'Does he seriously think he can frighten off the police? That we'll drop the case?'

'Of course not,' said Fabel. 'But I do think that Werner has a point. I got this *odd* phone call in the car the other day. At the time I thought it was a hoax. But I'm pretty sure it was our guy. Maybe he feels he can compromise my effectiveness. Shake me up a bit, as it were. He's bloody well succeeded. Maybe he even hopes that I'll be taken off the case if he makes my involvement more personal.'

Another silence. Fabel suddenly wished that he was alone. He needed time to think. He needed to sleep first, then think. A pressure seemed to build in his head. He found that van Heiden's presence, no matter how well meant, stifled his thought processes. Fabel sipped at his coffee and it tasted bitter and gritty in his mouth. The pressure in his head grew and he felt hot and sweaty. Dirty.

'Excuse me a moment,' he said and headed across to the male toilets. He splashed water on his face, but still did not feel any cooler or cleaner. The nausea hit him so fast that he only just made it into the cubicle before he vomited. His stomach emptied and he continued to retch, his gut clenching in spasms. The nausea passed and he returned to the basin and rinsed his mouth out with cold water. He splashed his face again; this time it made him feel a little fresher. He was aware of Werner's massive bulk behind him.

'You okay, Jan?'

Fabel took some paper towels and dried his face, examining himself in the mirror. He looked tired. Old. A little scared.

'I'm fine.' He straightened himself up and threw the towels into the wastebasket. 'Honestly. It's been a pretty full day. And night.'

'We'll get him, Jan. Don't worry. He's not going to get away with—'

The ringing of Fabel's cellphone cut Werner off.

'Hello, *Chef* . . .' Fabel could tell from the tone, from the faint tremulousness in Anna Wolff's voice, what she was about to say. 'I was right, *Chef*, it was him. The bastard's killed Schüler.'

### 3.00 p.m.: Osdorf, Hamburg

Fabel woke up and felt the panic of the lost.

There was a hint of daylight at the edges of the heavy dark curtains that hung over a window that should not have been where it was. He lay on a bed that was smaller than it should have been and in the wrong position in the wrong room. For a moment that seemed to stretch into infinity he could not work out where he was or why he was there. His disorientation was total and his heart hammered in his chest.

When he remembered, it was in stages. Each part of his recent history colliding with him like a steam train. He remembered the horror in his flat, the nauseating violation of his home; Susanne's scream; van Heiden's concerned presence; vomiting in the canteen toilets. The memory of relaxing with Susanne and the team seemed a lifetime away.

He was at Frank Grueber's. He remembered. They had agreed. He had packed a suitcase and a holdall and Maria Klee had driven him across town to Osdorf. Van Heiden had arranged for there to be a silver and blue patrol car outside.

But immediately before they had come here. Fabel remembered that, too. More horror. This time it had been a sad, pathetic horror: Leonard Schüler, whom Fabel had sought so hard to frighten, sitting strapped to a chair in his squalid little flat, his scalp missing and his throat sliced open, his dead face streaked with blood, with red dye. With tears.

As they had stood gathered around Schüler's sitting

body, they had all thought the same terrible thought that had burned in Fabel's mind but to which no one had dared give voice: that what Fabel had threatened Schüler with, that terrible fiction he had used to frighten the small-time crook, had really happened to him. Fabel had grasped Frank Grueber, who had led the forensic team at the scene, by the arm and had said pleadingly, 'Find me something to go on. Anything. Please . . .'

Fabel swung his legs around and sat up on the edge of the bed. He rested his elbows on his knees and cradled his head, which still pounded nauseatingly. He felt listless and weary. It was as if a dense damp fog had gathered around him, insinuating itself into his brain, clouding his thought processes and making his limbs heavy and aching. He tried to remember what it was that the sickening feeling that sat in the centre of his chest reminded him of. Then it came to him. It reminded him of bereavement: it was an attenuated form of the grief he had felt when he had lost his father. And when his marriage had died.

Fabel sat on the edge of a strange bed and thought about what it was that he was mourning. Something precious, something special that he had kept separate from his world of work had been violated. Fabel was anything but a superstitious man, but he thought back to how he had broken the unspoken rule of not talking shop with Susanne; of how he had done so in his apartment. It was almost as if he had opened a door and the darkness that he had sought so hard to keep out of his personal world had come rushing in. After nearly twenty years, his two lives had collided.

Fabel found the bedside light and switched it on, blinking in the sudden painful brightness. He checked his watch: it was three p.m. He had only slept for three hours. Fabel had been amazed at the size and comfort of Grueber's apartment. 'Parents with money – *lots* of money . . .' Maria had said in a mock-conspiratorial tone, her attempt at unaccustomed humour clumsy and inappropriate. Grueber had shown him to a vast spare bedroom that was about the size of the living room in Fabel's apartment. Fabel dragged himself up from the bed and made his way into the en-suite bathroom; he shaved before stepping into a cool shower that did little to ease his feeling of pollution. He had seen it so many times before, with victims of or witnesses to a violent act. But he had never felt it. So this was what it was like.

Fabel reckoned that Maria and Grueber were still in bed and he did not want to disturb the rest that they both needed after such a gruelling night. He had watched them together when they came home. Fabel had always liked Grueber and found it sad that, although he was clearly very fond of Maria, they did not jell as a couple. Now, of course, Fabel knew the basis for Maria's lack of intimacy with Grueber, and he could understand the caution with which Grueber displayed any kind of physical affection. But it made him sad to see two young people who obviously had strong feelings for each other unable to function fully as a couple because of an invisible wall between them.

The apartment was on two levels and, after he had showered and dressed, Fabel went downstairs to the kitchen. After a brief search he found some tea and made himself a cup, sitting down at the large oak kitchen table. He heard the sound of someone coming down the stairs and Grueber entered the room. He looked remarkably fresh and Fabel felt a little resentful of his youthful energy.

'How are you feeling?' Grueber asked.

'Rough. Where's Maria?'

'She's grabbing a couple of hours' sleep. Do you want me to wake her?'

'No . . . no, let her sleep. But I've got to get back to the Presidium. This is one trail we can't let go cold.'

'I'm afraid it's cooling as we speak,' said Grueber apologetically. 'I did my best, I really did. But we got nothing from either scene that is going to help us identify this madman. He did leave his trademark single red hair – this time in your apartment rather than at the primary locus. I called Holger Brauner while you were asleep: he said that the hair matched the other two and is of the same antiquity, about twenty to thirty years old.'

'Nothing else?' There was a tone of bleak disbelief in Fabel's voice. Just one break, that was all he wanted. Just for this killer to slip up once.

'I'm afraid not.'

'*Shit*.' Fabel used the English word. 'I can't believe that this bastard can walk into my apartment and plaster a human scalp to a window without leaving a trace.'

'I'm sorry,' said Grueber, a little defensively this time. 'But he did. Both Herr Brauner and I checked and double-checked both scenes. If there was anything to find we would have found it.'

'I know – sorry, I didn't mean to imply that you didn't process them properly. It's just . . .' Fabel let the sentence die with a gesture of impotent frustration. Fabel's own team had questioned his neighbours over and over again: no one had seen anyone come in or leave his apartment. It was as if they were dealing with a ghost.

'Whoever this killer is,' said Grueber, 'I get this weird feeling every time . . . almost as if he *deprocesses* a scene before he leaves it. As if he knows forensic techniques.'

'What, by the way he cleans up after himself?'

'More than that.' Grueber frowned as if trying to focus on something out of his range. 'I sense three stages to it. Firstly, he must come heavily prepared and sets up something to protect the scene. Sheeting, maybe, and perhaps even some kind of protective clothing that prevents him leaving traces at the scene. Secondly, he must clean up after each murder. We blamed that woman, the cleaner, for destroying forensic evidence at the first murder. She didn't. There would be none to destroy. Then he leaves his signature – the single ancient red hair – and he does so in a way that he knows we will find. Again, it's as if he understands how we process a scene.'

'But you nearly didn't find it the first time,' said Fabel.

'And that *was* the cleaning woman's fault. She had partially bleached it and it had been pushed well into the seam at the base of the bath. My guess is that the killer left it somewhere more obvious.'

'You can't seriously be suggesting that we are dealing with a forensic technician?'

Grueber shrugged. 'Or maybe he has read extensively about forensic techniques.'

Fabel stood up. 'I'm going in to the Presidium . . .'

'If you want my opinion,' said Grueber, pouring Fabel a second cup of tea, 'you should rest up for the remainder of the day. Whoever this killer is, whether or not he has experience of forensics, he's smart, and he likes to prove it. But, as we both know, these people are never as smart as their egos tell them they are. He'll slip up soon. Then we'll get him.'

'You reckon?' said Fabel dismally. 'After last night I can't be so sure.'

'Well, I really do think you should stay here and rest. The fresher you are, the more likely you are to think straight.' Fabel gave Grueber a sharp look and the younger man held up his hands defensively. 'You know what I mean . . . Anyway, like I said before, make yourself at home. In fact . . . follow me . . .'

Grueber led Fabel out of the kitchen, along the corridor to a large bright room which Grueber had converted into a study. The walls were lined with bookcases and there were two desks: one was clearly a general working desk with a computer, notepads and files on it; the other was used as some kind of workbench. What caught Fabel's attention was a clay model head, punctuated at regular intervals, like points on a grid, with small white pegs.

'I thought this room would interest you – this is where I do my moonlighting. And most of my research.'

Fabel walked over and examined the clay head. 'I heard about this,' he said. 'From Holger Brauner. You're quite an expert on reconstruction, I believe.'

'I'm happy to say that I'm kept reasonably busy with it in my spare time. Most of what I get is archaeological, but I'm hoping to use it more in a forensic context. When a body is discovered and is too decomposed for the usual means of identification.'

'Yes – we would find that very useful. Is there a skull under this?' asked Fabel. Despite his tiredness he could not help but be intrigued. He could see how Grueber had been building up the layers of soft tissue onto the bone. First the main muscles, then the smaller tendons. It was a perfect representation of a human face stripped of its outer layer of fat and skin. There seemed to Fabel to be an anatomical precision about it. And, in a strange way, it was beautiful. Science becoming art.

'Yes,' said Grueber. 'Well, no, not the original. The university sent me a cast. They make a mould in alginate and the cast they create is an absolutely perfect reproduction of the real skull. That's what I base my reconstructions on.'

'Who is it?' Fabel examined the detail of Grueber's work. It was like looking at one of Da Vinci's anatomical drawings.

'She's from Schleswig-Holstein. But from a time when there was no concept of Schleswig-Holstein or Germany and the language she spoke would not have been related to German. She would have been a Proto-Celtic speaker. She most likely belonged to the Ambroni or Cimbri. That would mean that her native tongue would be closer to modern Welsh than anything else today.'

'It – she – is beautiful,' said Fabel.

'She is, isn't she? I reckon I'll have her finished in a couple of weeks. The only thing I have left to do is to add the soft tissue over the muscle layer. That's what gives living form to the model.'

'How do you judge the thickness of the tissue?' asked Fabel. 'Surely it's pure guesswork.'

'Actually, it isn't. There are guidelines for the thickness of facial tissue for each ethnic group. Obviously, she might have been fat, or particularly thin. But she comes from a time when there was not a surplus of food, and everyday life was much more

327

strenuous than it is today. I think I will manage to get pretty close to what she looked like two thousand, two hundred years ago.'

Fabel shook his head in wonder. As with the image of Cherchen Man that Severts had shown him, he was being offered a window on a life that had burned and been extinguished two millennia before he had been born.

'Is it mainly bog bodies you work on?' he asked.

'No. I've reconstructed soldiers killed in the Napoleonic Wars, plague victims from the late Middle Ages, and I get a great deal of work to do on Egyptian mummies. I enjoy them the most – because of their antiquity, I suppose. And the exoticism of their culture. It's funny, I often feel a bond with the surgeon-priests who prepared the bodies of their kings, queens and Pharaohs for mummification. They were preparing their masters for reincarnation, for rebirth. I often feel that I am fulfilling their task . . . giving life again to the mummies they prepared.'

Fabel remembered the archaeologist Severts saying something almost identical.

'The most important thing for me,' said Grueber, 'is that what I create should be accurate. Truthful. I do this for the same reason I studied archaeology in the first place, why I chose to become a forensics specialist. The same reason you and Maria chose to become murder detectives. We all believe the same thing: that truth is the debt we owe to the dead.'

'After last night, I don't know why I do it any more, if I'm honest.' Fabel said. He looked at Grueber's earnest, concerned face. Fabel had been so concerned about Maria, but he could not imagine her being with anyone who would be better for her.

'Take a look at this.' Grueber pointed to the side

of the reconstructed head, above the temple. 'This muscle is the first we apply, it's the temporalis. And this . . .' He pointed to a wide sheet of muscle on the forehead. 'Is the occipitofrontalis. These are the largest muscles in the human head and face. When this killer takes a scalp he cuts around the full circumference of the cranium.' He picked up a pencil and, without touching the surface of the clay, indicated a sweep across the muscles that he had described. 'It is comparatively easy to remove a scalp. By cutting through the full dermis all the way around, it can be pulled free with little effort. The scalp basically sits on top of the muscle layer and is anchored by connective tissue. The last two scalps have been taken that way, but he cut much deeper with Hauser, the first victim. Remember he looked almost as if he was frowning? That was because the occipitofrontalis was severed, causing his brow to droop.' Grueber threw the pencil down on the table. 'He's getting more proficient. Our scalp-taker is perfecting his craft.'

For a moment, Fabel was again transported back to the night before, to his apartment. To the example of his 'craft' that the killer had left for him.

'Like I said,' said Grueber. 'This guy is not as clever as he thinks he is. I know it's not much, but at least it proves he doesn't always do everything perfectly.' Grueber sighed. 'Anyway, I thought you might be interested in my library. Maria told me that you studied history. As you know, I'm an archaeologist by training – please help yourself to anything you want to read while you're here. I'll have to head in to work . . . there are a few things I need to tie up and I haven't had as stressful a night as you.'

After Grueber had gone, Fabel sat and studied

the partially reconstructed head. It was as if he were willing it to speak, to flex its fleshless muscles and move the mouth to whisper the name of the monster he was hunting. Grueber himself must have been loaded to afford a place like this. The furnishings were mainly antique and contrasted starkly with the computer and other equipment in the room, which were clearly expensive and state-of-the-art.

The curious mixture of professional and personal items in the study reminded Fabel of the room in which they had found Gunter Griebel's body, although a great deal more cash had been spent on this environment. Fabel was disturbed by the similarity and for a second his imagination took him to a place he did not want to be: what if the maniac they were hunting was turning his attention on Fabel and his team? In an unbidden and sudden image that formed in his mind, Fabel saw young Frank Grueber bound to his antique leather chair, the top of his head disfigured. He thought of Maria, who had already survived the horror of a knife attack, sleeping upstairs, and of how her experience had caused her to develop a phobia of physical contact. He thought back to how, during the same previous inquiry, Anna had been drugged and abducted. And now there had been the atrocity in his own home.

Fabel felt the urge to grab his keys and rush off to the Presidium, but Grueber had been right: he was too exhausted and too muddled to be of any use to anyone. He would rest up for a couple of hours, maybe even sleep, before going in.

He wandered over to the walnut bookshelves. Fabel had always felt comforted when he was surrounded by books and Grueber's collection was extensive but not wide-ranging in subject matter.

Archaeology formed the core of his library: the rest of the books covered history from various periods, geology, forensic technologies and methodologies and anatomy. Everything that was not archaeology was a related subject.

Taking a couple of volumes from the shelves, Fabel slumped onto the antique leather chesterfield. The first book that had caught his interest dealt with mummies. It was a large-format book with big glossy colour plates and in it Fabel discovered exactly the same photograph of Cherchen Man that Severts had shown him. Again Fabel felt awe as he looked on the perfectly preserved face of a fifty-five-year-old man who had died three thousand years before Fabel had been born. He read for a minute and then flicked through the book again until he came across the equally striking image of Neu Versen Man: Red Franz. He felt a lurch in his gut when he looked at the skeletonised skull with its shock of thick red hair. It reminded him of the scalps that the killer had been leaving behind at each scene. The book detailed Red Franz's discovery on Bourtanger Moor, near the small town of Neu Versen, in November 1900. It also offered a hypothesis on the nature of Red Franz's life and death. How he had, during his lifetime, been wounded in battle. Of how his life had been ended by having his throat cut, perhaps ceremonially, before he was interred in the dark peaty bog of Bourtanger Moor.

Fabel flicked through some more pages. Each colour plate showed a face from the past, preserved in dank bogs or in arid deserts or prepared for the afterlife by the surgeon-priests of whom Grueber had spoken. Fabel tried to read, to focus his attention on something that would take his mind from

331

everything that had happened over the last twenty-four hours, but his eyelids felt leaden.

He fell asleep.

It had been a while since Fabel had had one of his dreams. And it had been even longer since he had admitted having one to Susanne, who he knew was concerned about the way the stresses and horrors of his working days manifested themselves in the vivid nightmares that haunted his sleep.

He dreamed that he stood on a vast plain. Fabel, who had grown up on the baize-green flatlands of Ostfriesland, knew that this was somewhere else. Somewhere that was as alien as it was possible to be. The grass he stood in came halfway up his calf, but was dry and brittle: bone-coloured. The horizon in the distance was so uncompromisingly flat and sharp that it made his eyes hurt to look at it. Above it a vast sky that sat colourless and leaden was broken only by sickly streaks of rust-coloured clouds.

Fabel turned a slow three hundred and sixty degrees. Everything looked the same: an unbroken, sanity-shredding sameness. He stood and wondered what to do. There was no point in walking, for there was nowhere to walk to and there was no landmark to guide his walking. This was a world without direction, without destination.

Suddenly there were figures in the landscape, moving towards him. They were not together, walking several hundred metres apart like a strung-out camel train crossing a featureless desert.

The first figure drew near. A tall, lean man, dressed in brightly coloured clothes. He had a neatly trimmed beard and longish light brown hair that fingered the air with tangled wisps as he walked. Fabel held out his hand, but the figure did not seem to notice and instead walked straight past him as if he wasn't there. As he did so, Fabel noticed that the man's face was unnaturally thin, his eyelids unevenly pulled down. His bottom lip was twisted, revealing the teeth on one side of his face. Fabel recognised him. He held out his hand to Cherchen Man, who walked on by, blind to Fabel's presence. The next figure who passed him was a very tall, graceful woman whom Fabel recognized as the Beauty of Loulan.

But as the third figure approached there was a terrible sound. Like thunder but louder than any thunder Fabel had ever heard before. He felt the dry earth shake and crack beneath him, bristling the dry grass, and suddenly, all around him, broken black buildings, like jagged blackened teeth, thrust up out of the ground. The third figure was smaller than the others and was dressed in modern clothes. He drew near: a youth with fine wispy fair hair, wearing a blue serge suit that was too big for him. By the time he had reached Fabel, an ugly black city of angular buildings, as empty as death, had grown all around them. Like the other mummies who had walked past Fabel, the youth's cheeks were hollow and his eyes were sunken and shadowed. As he walked he held one arm stiffly out before him in the same death-frozen gesture as when Fabel had first seen him, half-buried in the sand of the Elbe waterfront. As he reached Fabel he did not, as the others had done, simply pass by. Instead he tilted his head and looked, with his hollow eyes, up at the vast bleak sky.

Fabel looked up too. The sky darkened as if filled with birds, but he recognised the dull, menacing drone of ancient warplanes. The drone grew louder, deafening, as the planes came overhead. Fabel stood, mute and motionless, watching the bombs cascade from the sky. A great storm began to rage, the excoriatingly hot air swirled and screamed, and the black buildings now glowed like coals. Yet Fabel and the youth remained untouched by the firestorm raging around them.

For a moment the youth looked blankly at Fabel, with his expressionless, ageless face. Then he turned away and walked the few paces to where the nearest building raged with fire, greedily sucking on the air to feed the great flame that lived within. The youth lay down before the building, which Fabel thought may have been the Nikolaikirche, pulled a red blanket of molten asphalt and embers over himself, and went to sleep, his outstretched arm reaching out to the burning building.

Fabel sat upright, still halfway in his dream, for a few moments straining his ears for the sound of bombers overhead. He looked around and recognised Grueber's study with its expensive antiques, its walnut bookshelves and the half-finished bust of a long-dead girl from Schleswig-Holstein.

Fabel looked at his watch: it was now six-thirty. He had slept for another two hours. He still felt the lead of exhaustion in his limbs but, hearing movement in the kitchen, he went through to find Maria Klee drinking a coffee.

'You fit enough to come in with me?' His question sounded more like a statement than he would have liked. Maria nodded, stood up and took a final sip of her coffee. 'Good,' he said. 'Let's get the team together. We're going to go over everything we've got. Again. There's got to be something we're missing here.'

As he made his way out of Grueber's apartment,

Fabel used his cellphone to call Susanne to check how she was. She told him she was fine, but there was a tone of uncertainty that Fabel had never heard before in her voice. He grabbed his jacket and keys and made his way out to the waiting silver and blue marked police car outside.

Part Three

# Part Two

# 12.

## Twenty-Four Days After the First Murder: Sunday, 11 September 2005.

### Midnight: Altona, Hamburg

The audiences were getting smaller.

It was during the 1980s and 1990s that he had seen the greatest reduction in audience size, when a new generation of performer had come along. *Schlager*, the bland, schmaltzy form of German pop music, had always been there, its inane presence actually helpful to singers like Cornelius Tamm; its complete lack of substance counterpointing their music, underlining its intellectualism. But then came punk, then rap which gave voice to the disaffection of a new, apolitical generation. And, of course, there had been the irresistible wave of Anglo-American imports. Each had, in its own way, marginalised Cornelius and others like him, pushing them out of the limelight. And off the radio.

But there had always been his concert audiences: the constant faithful followers who had grown older, had matured with him. But the Wall had come down and Germany had become reunited. Protest became redundant. Political lyrics seemed irrelevant.

Now Cornelius performed in cellars and town halls for audiences of fifty or so. There were other performers of his vintage who had simply given up touring and sold their own back catalogue, as Cornelius also did, from their websites.

But Cornelius needed an audience. No matter how small. And he always gave the best performance he could, even when his fans would sicken him with the way they'd make up for their lack of numbers with an excess of enthusiasm. He would look out over a small mass of balding or greying heads and corpulent or haggard faces and go through the motions of reviving the dully depressing memories of their youth.

The audience tonight was no different. Cornelius laughed and joked and sang, playing the same tunes on the same guitar he had played for nearly forty years. Tonight he played in the cellar of an old brewery that sat between two of the canals that wove through Hamburg like the thread that held the city's fabric together. The audience all sat on benches at the side of long, low tables, drinking beer and grinning inanely as he sang. He did not even have the power to bring an audience to its feet any more.

He did notice one younger face. It was a man in his early thirties, standing over by the bar. He was pale with very dark hair. Cornelius was not sure, but he thought he recognised the young man from somewhere.

Cornelius always finished his performance with the same number. It was his signature piece. Reinhard Mey had '*Über den Wolken*', Cornelius Tamm had '*Ewigkeit*'. Eternity. At last the audience dragged themselves to their feet, singing along to the song that promised that members of their generation were eternal. That they would triumph. Except they were not, and they had not. They had all surrendered to the banal; the mediocre. Cornelius too.

340

After he finished his set Cornelius went through the usual routine. It was, of course, humiliating to sit at a table with a case full of CDs for sale, but he engaged in the task with the same practised enthusiasm as he had learned to invest in his performances. More often than not he sold no more than a handful. He was, after all, preaching to the converted who, in most cases, already had all his songs. He had, as the capitalists would say, saturated his market.

Still, he smiled and chatted politely with those who lingered after the performance, talking to strangers as if they were old friends because of their vaguely common chronologies. But, inside, Cornelius Tamm's soul screamed. He had been the voice of a generation. He had given expression to a special moment in time. He had spoken to and for millions who had raged against the sins of their fathers, against the sins of their own time. And now he sold CDs of his songs from a suitcase in a Hamburg *Bierkeller*.

It was nearly two in the morning by the time he reversed his van up to the back door and loaded his amplifier and other equipment into the back. As he did so, Cornelius felt every one of his sixty-two years weigh down the equipment. It had been raining while he had been performing and the cobbles in the yard behind the old brewery glistened in the moonlight. One of the bar staff helped him out with the amp, said goodnight and closed the delivery doors, leaving Cornelius in the courtyard alone. He looked up at the moon and the silver-etched edges of the roofs around the courtyard. Somewhere over on Ost-West Strasse a siren whined past. Cornelius thought about Julia lying warm and fresh and young in their bed. About how he did not belong beside her. About how he did not belong anywhere, any more. Cornelius Tamm looked up at the moon from the empty courtyard of an old brewery pub and felt so terribly lonely. He sighed and slammed shut the rear doors of the van.

He gave a jump when he saw the young man with the pale face and dark hair standing there.

'Hello, Cornelius,' said the stranger. His arm arced round and Cornelius caught the black blur of something long and heavy-looking. It slammed into his cheek and there was the sound of something cracking and Cornelius felt a white-hot pain explode in the side of his face and down his neck. He hit the ground so fast that his brain did not have time to register his falling. He felt the glossy, rounded top of a cobble against his uninjured cheek and realised that it was sleek not with rain but with his blood.

'I'm sorry about your face . . .' His assailant was now bending over him. 'But I couldn't hit you on the head.' Cornelius felt the sting of a hypodermic needle in his neck and the moonlight faded from the night. 'That would have damaged your scalp . . .'

## 11 a.m.: HafenCity, Hamburg

The very first thing that struck Fabel about the view was that he could see the site where they had found the mummified body. It made him think of the nightmare he had had while staying at Grueber's. The procession of mummies; the firestorm dream. Maybe inherited memories had nothing to do with genetics.

The apartment was, undoubtedly, the best they had seen so far. But somehow Fabel found he could not muster sufficient enthusiasm for it. The estate agent, Frau Haarmeyer, was a tall middle-aged woman with an expensive haircut dyed the same pale sand-coloured blonde that so many middle-aged, middle-class northern German women seemed to favour when their fair hair started to turn grey. Throughout the showing, Frau Haarmeyer managed to convey two sentiments wordlessly: that she clearly believed the apartment was really very much above Fabel and Susanne's reach, and that this kind of work was really very much beneath her. Although she enthused about the flat and its neighbours in the HafenCity development, there was an undertone that suggested she was simply going through the motions.

Susanne was obviously taken with the apartment and followed the estate agent, listening intently and holding her head angled in her distinctive pose of concentration. Accordingly, Frau Haarmeyer focused her attention on her, largely ignoring Fabel until he wandered off to some corner or other to inspect a particular detail, at which point Frau Haarmeyer would tilt her head to see past Susanne and frown in Fabel's direction.

At one point he noticed the same kind of frown on Susanne's brow. Fabel knew that somehow he had to project more interest than he felt. After all, it had been his idea that they should move in together. Susanne had at first been reluctant and it had been his enthusiasm for the notion that had won her round. Yet every apartment they had seen had left him cold when he compared it to the view from and location of his Pöseldorf home. But Fabel knew that, since the violation of his private space, he would never feel the same about the view again. It reminded him of how he had felt when his marriage had failed: that he was being forced into a new life, when all he wanted was to have his old one back. To turn back the clock and repair that which had been shattered.

Susanne did not seem to understand his reluctance; she had even hinted that it was his fear of change, his inability to break away from routines that was holding them back. But it was more than that. Exactly what it was he had yet to define, but something twisted in his gut whenever he thought about giving up his apartment. He had, after all, been lucky to buy where and when he did. But what was more important to Fabel was that it had been in that apartment that he had rebuilt himself after the break-up of his marriage. It was there that he had redefined who Jan Fabel was. He had found his new life.

Frau Haarmeyer led them through to the kitchen. As in the other rooms, the outer wall was all window. The kitchen shone with glass and brushed steel and was filled with a faint, pleasant odour of coffee. Fabel idly wondered if the developers had a special spray to infuse the kitchen with its appealing fragrance, or if it was the phantom aroma of the coffee roasters in the nearby Speicherstadt.

'Isn't this wonderful?' asked Frau Haarmeyer with an enthusiasm that was as fake as her hair colour.

'Very impressive . . .' Susanne shot Fabel a meaningful look.

'Great,' he responded with the same degree of conviction as Frau Haarmeyer. He again looked down to the site where they had found the mummified corpse. The archaeological dig had been completed weeks ago and now the developers had moved in. Bright yellow earth-movers and tractors, small and scarab-like from Fabel's elevated position, moved across the site; the next phase of Hamburg's vision for the future was being superimposed on a past where a young man had been suffocated and baked to death by the hellish heat of a man-made firestorm.

Fabel felt the dull anxiety of unfinished business. He had promised himself that he would find the family of the mummified man, and he still had to achieve that.

As the estate agent explained, yet again, that they would have a view of the *Kaispeicher A* with its amazing new opera house and concert hall, and how this was going to be among the most desirable addresses in Hamburg, Fabel's gaze remained on the building site in the distance and below them. He wondered how an estate agent would market a memento mori as a sales feature of a property.

It was cool outside, but the sun was shining and the sky was a silky pale blue.

'I really liked that place,' Susanne said as they walked back to the car. Buried somewhere in the softness of her faint Bavarian accent was a sharp edge. 'You didn't say much.'

Fabel explained about the view.

'Would it really bother you that much?' asked Susanne in a tone that suggested it should not. 'It's better than the memory of . . . well, *that* . . .'

'The other thing,' Fabel sought a less subjective reason for rejecting the apartment, 'is it just seemed so . . . I don't know, cold. Soulless. Like living in an office block.'

Susanne sighed. 'Well, I liked it.'

'I'm sorry, Susanne. It's just that with this case still going on, my mind's not up to dealing with moving.'

'Listen, Jan, this case has given us one of the main reasons for getting you out of that apartment. We can afford this place. It would mean a new start for us. Together.'

'I'll think about it.' Fabel smiled. 'I promise.'

## 11 a.m.

Cornelius Tamm woke up in stages.

His first sensation was pain: a great blooming of it in the side of his face and a pounding in his head. Next he became aware of sounds: indistinct and as if in the far distance. A metallic whirring and the sound of air being moved mechanically. Then came a growing awareness that he was not free to move, but the drug that had been administered by his assailant confused his sense of his own body and he could not work out for the moment why his movements were restricted. As the sense of the geography of his body returned, he realised that he was bound to a chair, his hands tied behind him and some kind of gag taped over his mouth. Finally, as his consciousness was at last restored to him in its full pain and horror, Cornelius's eyes opened and slowly focused on his new environment.

To start with he thought he was sitting in a cave that had glistening grey walls. Then he realised that he was surrounded by curtains of thick, almost opaque plastic sheeting. The chair to which he was bound also rested on a sheet of heavy-duty black polyurethane. He felt a churning between his gut and his chest: it was clear that the sheeting was intended to contain a mess. And that mess would be his blood and flesh as his life was brought to an end. He struggled violently against his bonds. The effort turned up the volume of the pain and a rivulet of blood escaped from the nostril on the side of his face that had been hit. The chair to which he was tied was obviously robustly built, because it hardly moved on its carpet of polyurethane.

Cornelius got the impression that he was in some kind of cellar. Whoever had brought him here had been painstaking in their preparation of the chamber: even the ceiling had been covered with plastic, stretched tight and held in place with strips of black tape. But a single bulb hung from it and Cornelius could see grey plaster around the light fitting. The ceiling was low: too low for it to belong in a room used for normal living or working, and he continued to hear the metallic whirring sound, like an air-conditioning system in a factory.

The curtains of dense plastic parted and a figure entered the small space. Cornelius recognised the young man who had been sitting by the bar during his gig; who had been waiting for him with an iron bar in the courtyard of the brewery pub. He was wearing a pale blue coverall suit with blue plastic overshoes. His black hair was hidden beneath an elasticated plastic shower cap. As he entered, he pulled a surgical mask over his nose and mouth, and when he spoke his voice was slightly muffled.

'Hello, Cornelius. It has been more than twenty years since I last saw you. You look, if you don't mind me saying, like crap. I have never understood why men of your age wear their hair in a ponytail. The world has moved on since you were a student, Cornelius. Why haven't you moved on with it?' He leaned close, placing his face a few centimetres from his captive's. 'Do you recognise me, Cornelius? Yes . . . it's me. It's Franz. I'm back.'

Cornelius felt as if he was going as mad as his tormentor. For a moment he considered the similarity in appearance between the young man and the person he claimed to be. But it was impossible. Franz had been dead twenty years, and the resemblance was only superficial. Still, it had been enough to trigger that feeling of recognition when Cornelius had first noticed him at the gig.

'You are a nobody, Cornelius. No one cares about your stupid lyrics any more. You even succeeded in making a mess of your marriage. You are the most comprehensive of failures – you have failed as a father, as a husband, as a musician. You betrayed me so that you could turn your back on one life and start another. Is this it? Is this what you have done with the time, the life, that you bought by betraying me?'

Cornelius stared at his tormentor, his eyes wide with terror and awe at the monumentality of the man's madness. He clearly believed he was who he claimed to be. Then, through the fear and the pain, Cornelius realised that he *had* seen this person before.

'At least Gunter tried to do something with his life. At least he used the time he obtained through his treachery in trying to do something positive. But you, Cornelius. You gave me up for nothing . . . to waste your future on trying to recapture the past. You betrayed me. You and the others.'

The young man squatted down and opened out the velvet roll-pouch on the carpet of black sheeting. He exposed three blades, all forged in the same way from single pieces of glittering steel, but each one a slightly different shape and size.

'The others were afraid when they died. I ended their lives in fear and pain. But they were not special to me. You were more than a comrade. I called you friend. Your betrayal was the greatest.'

I know who you are! The thought blazed across Cornelius's brain and he sought to give it voice, but it was stifled into incoherence by the gag taped across his mouth.

'We are eternal,' said the young dark-haired man. But Cornelius knew now that his hair was not really dark. 'The Buddhists believe that each life, each consciousness, is like a single candle flame, but that there is a continuity between each flame. Imagine lighting one candle with the flame of another, then using that flame to light the next, and that to light the next, and on and on for ever. A thousand flames, all passed from one to another across the generations. Each is a different light, each burns in a totally different way. But it is, nevertheless, the same flame.

'Now, I'm afraid, it is time for me to extinguish your flame. But don't worry – the pain I give you will mean that you will burn brightest at the end.'

He paused and took the smallest blade from the roll-pouch.

'I have something very special planned for you, Cornelius. I am going to devote more time and effort to you than I did to all of the others put together. The ancient Aztecs also believed in reincarnation. I don't know if you are aware of that. They saw the growth of a new crop every year as parallel to the renewal of the soul. The eternal cycle.' Cornelius could see the madness burning like a black sun in the younger man's eyes. 'Each spring they would make a sacrifice, a human sacrifice, to the gods of fertility. They would see serpents shed their skins, crops shed their flowers, and they sought to mirror this in the ritual. You see, they would take the human sacrifice and flay him alive. Cut away all of his skin.

'Your death is not enough. Your pain is important to me. I'm going to hurt you, Cornelius. I am going to hurt you so terribly . . .'

# 13.

## Twenty-Five Days After the First Murder: Monday, 12 September 2005.

### 3.00 p.m.: Police Presidium, Hamburg

Fabel spent the greater part of the day collating and analysing the information that the team had gathered, disseminating it, redirecting investigative routes and reallocating resources.

Anna Wolff had taken a photograph of Paul Scheibe into The Firehouse and the black barman had said that Scheibe could have been the older man with whom Hauser had met. But he could not be sure. Fabel was alone in his office when Markus Ullrich, the BKA man, knocked on his door. He was not wearing his trade-mark smile.

'Herr Fabel . . . I wonder if I could have a word with you and Frau Klee – in private . . .'

'I'm going to Cologne,' said Maria after Ullrich had finished. 'This was no bloody accident.'

'Like hell you are,' said Fabel. Only he, Ullrich and Maria were in the conference room. 'It's up to the Cologne police to investigate this. And it may have escaped your notice, but we are in the middle of our own investigation.'

'The Cologne police don't know Vitrenko.' Maria's expression had hardened. 'They clearly believe that this was an accident. An accident and one hell of a coincidence.'

Ullrich held up his hand. 'They're not stupid, Frau Senior Commissar. What I said is that the evidence suggests it was an accident. A high-speed blow-out on the autobahn. Believe me, I have left the Cologne police in absolutely no doubt about the significance of Herr Turchenko's death. And, as I told you, they are already involved in the Vitrenko investigation.'

Fabel remembered sitting in the Presidium canteen, only two weeks before, chatting to Turchenko about Ukraine's renaissance. Now Turchenko was dead and his GSG9 bodyguard, who had been travelling with him, was lying in a coma in a Cologne hospital.

'Okay,' said Maria. 'I will see this case out. But as soon as we nail this bastard I am going to Cologne to follow up this Turchenko thing.'

'With the greatest respect,' said Ullrich, 'your *involvement* with our investigation has already led to the disappearance of one witness. You would be well advised to stay out of this.'

Maria ignored the BKA man. 'As I said, *Chef*, I am going to Cologne to follow this up as soon as this case is over. I have leave due and I will take it. If you order me not to go I will resign and go anyway. Whatever you say, I am going.'

Fabel sighed. 'We'll talk about this later, Maria. But right now I need you focused one hundred per cent on the business at hand.'

Maria nodded curtly.

'In the meantime,' said Fabel. 'I have to see someone about a different matter.'

Beate held the door ajar, anchored to its frame by the security chain. She had seen who it was through the fish-eye lens peephole, but she still did not want to let her guard down until she knew what he was doing there, without an appointment, in the evening. Both the chain and the door lens were new security measures that she had installed since she had heard of Hauser's and Griebel's murders. She would not even have answered the door had it not been for the fact that she had read of another murder that had taken place yesterday: a third victim who had absolutely nothing to do with the group. Maybe it had all just been coincidence.

'I'm sorry,' the young dark-haired man said earnestly. 'I didn't mean to disturb you. It's just that I had to see you. I don't know how to describe what's happening to me . . . I think it must be my rebirth . . . you know, the way you said it has to happen . . . I have been having all these dreams.'

'It is too late. Phone me tomorrow and I will make you a new appointment.'

'Please,' said the young man. 'I think our last session must have stimulated them. I know I am on the verge of a breakthrough, and it's driving me nuts. I really need your help. I don't mind paying extra for it being after normal hours . . .'

Beate examined the earnest young man and sighed. Pushing the door closed, she slid the security chain free of its housing and reopened it to let him in.

'Thanks, I'm really sorry about the inconvenience. And please excuse this . . .' he said as he entered Beate's apartment, indicating the large holdall he carried in his right hand. 'I was on my way to the gym . . .'

Heinz Dorfmann was lean and fit-looking, but each of his seventy-nine years had left its mark on him, Fabel found on examining the older man more closely. He had seen the photograph of him together with Karl Heymann: two youths smiling out of a monochrome past. Yet Fabel had seen the corpse of Heymann only a few weeks before: the body of a sixteen-year-old boy; a face bound to an eternal, desiccated youth. Herr Dorfmann excused himself while he went into the small kitchen of his apartment.

'My wife died seven years ago,' he said, as if to explain why he had to perform the duty of fetching the coffee himself.

'I'm sorry to hear that, Herr Dorfmann' said Fabel. As the older man poured the coffee, Fabel took in the room. It was clean and tidy, and to start with Fabel had thought it had not been decorated since the 1970s or early 1980s. But then he realised that it was simply that it had been redecorated in the same style, the same tonal beiges and off-whites over the decades. It always fascinated Fabel, the way older people often became stuck in a particular period: as if that one time defined who they were, or marked when it was that they stopped noticing the world changing around them.

The shelves were filled with books about Hamburg: street plans, photographic studies of the city, history books, reference books of *Hamburger Platt*, the form of Low German unique to the city, as well as English dictionaries and other language reference books. An embossed copper plaque depicting the Hammaburg fortress, used on the city's coat of arms, sat on one of the shelves, mounted on a teak shield.

'You were a tour guide, I believe, Herr Dorfmann?'

'I was a teacher for twenty years. English. Then I became a tour guide. To begin with I worked for the city and then as a freelancer. Because I speak English so well, most of the time I looked after groups from Canada, America and Great Britain, as well as tours from within Germany. It wasn't like a job for me. I love my city and I enjoyed helping people discover it. I retired over ten years ago, but I still do part-time work at the Rathaus . . . taking tourists around the city chambers. You wanted to ask me about Karl Heymann?' Herr Dorfmann poured the coffee. 'I tell you, that's a name I haven't heard in a long, long time.'

'You knew him well?' Fabel showed him the photograph of the two teenage boys, smiling uncertainly at the camera.

'My goodness.' Dorfmann smiled. 'Where on earth did you get that? Karl's sister took it. I remember posing for that photograph as though it were only yesterday. It was a bright sunny day. Summer of forty-three. One of the hottest I can remember.' He looked up. 'Yes, I knew Karl Heymann. He was my friend. We were neighbours and he was in my class at school. Karl was a bright lad. He used to think about things too much at a time when it didn't pay to think. I also knew his sister Margot – she was a few years older than Karl and always clucked around him like a mother hen. She was a beautiful girl and all the boys were in love with her. Margot absolutely doted on Karl . . . after he disappeared, she always claimed that he had got away from Germany. That he had taken a job on a freighter to avoid being conscripted. I met her after the war and she told me that Karl had gone to America and was doing very well. She said that Karl had always talked about doing that before the war.'

'Did you believe her?'

Herr Dorfmann shrugged. 'That's what she told me. I wanted to believe it. But we all knew that Karl had gone missing after the night of the firestorm. So many people had. And it was on that night that I saw him for the last time. That night belonged to the dead, Herr Fabel, not to the living. Afterwards, I always just assumed he was one of the dead. Another name on a note pinned to a wall. There were thousands of them, you know. Thousands and thousands – countless pieces of paper with names on them, sometimes with a photograph, asking if anyone had seen them, stuck to the ruins of a house or apartment block, telling them where to find their families. Do you remember they did the same thing when those terrorists attacked the towers in New York? Walls covered with notes and pictures? It was like that, but ten times as many.'

'You say you saw Karl that night? The night of the twenty-seventh of July?'

'We lived on the same street. It was just around the corner from here. We were close friends. Not best friends, but close. Karl was a quiet lad. Sensitive. Anyway, we had arranged to head over to the other side of the Alster and were about to take a tram into town together. But we didn't go.'

'Why?'

'We were about to get on the tram when Karl suddenly grabbed my sleeve. He said he thought he should stay close to home. I asked why and he didn't have a reason. More of a gut feeling, I suppose.

Anyway, we didn't go. We went home and got our bicycles. He was right. It was a night to be close to home.'

'Were you with Karl when the bombing started?'

Heinz Dorfmann smiled a sad, uncertain smile and for the first time Fabel could detect the ghost of the youth in the photograph with Heymann. 'As I said, it was a wonderful summer. I remember how tanned we were.' He tilted his head up, as if towards the phantom of a long-extinguished sun. 'So bright, so hot. So dry. The British knew that. They knew it and used it to their advantage. They knew they were setting light to a tinderbox.

'We had become used to the raids. The British had been bombing Bremen and Hamburg during nineteen forty-one but they weren't able to launch significant raids. The planes had to turn back after only a minute or so over the city. What was more, Hamburg had been well prepared: we had been encouraged to convert and fortify our cellars into bomb shelters. And then there were the huge public shelters. They were massive and could take up to four hundred people easily. The shelters had been built with two-metre-thick concrete and were probably the most bombproof shelters in any European city. They may have protected us from the blasts, but they didn't protect us from the heat.

'By nineteen forty-three the British bombers were able to bring much bigger payloads and to stay over the city longer. We were spending more and more time in the shelters. Then, at the end of July nineteen forty-three, the British came over in force. Two nights before they had bombed the city centre . . . that's when they hit the Nikolaikirche and the Zoo. The night after that there had been a tiny raid, just to unnerve

357

everyone. But on the night of the twenty-seventh and the morning of the twenty-eighth they turned Hamburg into hell. They made their intention clear in the name they gave their operation – there was no way they could claim that what happened was an accident. "Operation Gomorrah", they called it. You know what happened to the city of Gomorrah in the Bible, don't you?'

Fabel nodded.

'It was just before midnight. For some reason the sirens didn't give as much warning as usual. We didn't have a cellar in our building so we all spilled out onto the streets. It was a beautiful clear warm night and the sky was suddenly filled with "Christmas trees" as we had all come to call them. They were beautiful – really beautiful. Huge clusters of sparkling red and green lights, great clouds of them, drifting gracefully down onto the city. I actually stopped to watch them. Of course, what they were were marker flares for the next wave of bombers. I heard it approach. You can't imagine what it sounded like: the engines of nearly eight hundred warplanes combined into a single deafening, reverberating drone. It is amazing the terror that a sound can stimulate. It was then that we heard another sound. An even more terrible sound. Like thunder, but a thousand times louder, rolling across the city. People started to panic. Running. Screaming. It all became crazy and I lost sight of my family in the crowds. And Karl. I couldn't see him either. Then he just appeared from nowhere and grabbed my arm. He was mad with worry – he had lost his family too. We decided to head for the main public shelter, assuming our families would do the same.

'We made it to the public shelter but the blast

doors were closed and I had to hammer on them before an old man in a *Luftschutz* warden's helmet let us in. We searched but couldn't find our families and we demanded to be let out again but they wouldn't open the blast doors. I remember thinking that it didn't matter. That we were all going to die anyway. I had never heard so many bombs hit us before. It sounded as if some giant was hammering the city flat. Then it eased off. The next wave was not so loud. Quieter explosions, as if they were using a much lighter bomb. But, of course, that wasn't it. The bastards were dropping phosphorus on us. They had it all planned out: first the high explosives to shatter the buildings and then the phosphorus to start the fires. I had to sit there and think of my mother and my two sisters somewhere out there. I could only hope that they had found a shelter. Karl was the same, but he was almost hysterical about it. He wanted to get out to find his sister and his mother. Everyone had been calm in the shelter to start with, but soon our nerves were as shattered as the buildings outside. Then it started to get hotter. A heat that I can't begin to describe. That public shelter began to turn into an oven. Like all the shelters, it was airtight apart from the pumps to bring air in from the outside. We were using a manual bellows pump but we had to give up because we were filling the shelter with smoke and scorching hot air. Eventually, we started to suffocate. What we didn't know was that it was happening in cellars and shelters all over Hamburg. The firestorm, you see. It was like a hungry beast that fed on oxygen. It sucked it out of the air. All over the city, first the children and the old people, then the others, either suffocated or baked to death in the airless shelters.

Some of us insisted that the doors were opened so that we could see what was happening outside, but the others said no. Eventually, once the sound of the bombing had ceased, everyone was so desperate for air that it was decided to risk it.

'I cannot begin to describe what we saw, Herr Fabel. When we opened those doors, it was like opening the gates of Hell itself. The first thing we noticed was the way the air was sucked out of the shelter, dragging people with it. Everything was burning. But not the way you imagine buildings burning. It was like a huge blast-furnace. The British had calculated that by smashing the buildings, then dropping the phosphorus, they could create updraughts that would raise the temperature high enough to cause the spontaneous combustion of buildings, of people, that hadn't been directly hit. In some parts of the city the temperature hit a thousand degrees. I staggered out of the shelter and I started to pant and gasp as if I'd been running a race. I simply couldn't get enough air into my lungs. I couldn't believe what I was seeing. People glowing, like torches. There was a child . . . I don't know if it was a boy or a girl, but from its size I guessed it was about eight or nine, lying face down, half sunken into the road. The tar had melted, you see. It was then that I saw this figure walking down the street. It was the most horrific, yet most mesmerising thing I have ever seen. It was a woman, holding something close to her chest. I think it was a baby. She was walking in a straight line down the street. Not staggering. Not rushing. But she and the baby in her arms were . . . the only way I can describe it is *incandescent*. It was as if they were moulded from a single bright flame. It was like looking at some fire angel. I remember thinking at that moment that it did not matter if I lived or died. That to see such a thing was more than anyone should endure in their lifetime. And then she was gone. As you know, the firestorm created ground draughts of hurricane force. Winds of two hundred and fifty kilometres per hour scooping people up and sucking them into the flames. She and the baby were picked up and swept into a burning building as if the fire had reached out its hand to snap up a morsel.'

Fabel watched the older man. His voice stayed steady, calm; but his eyes were now glossy with unshed tears.

'I remember cursing God for having given me life. For allowing me to be born at that time of all times; in that place of all places. And I thought that perhaps this was the last of all times. I found it easy to imagine that the whole world would end with this war. It was then that I realised that Karl was not with me any more. I looked around for him, but it was like seeking a single soul in the chaos and horror of Hell.

'I remember my instinct telling me to get to water. I reckoned that if I got to the Alster or the Elbe – the Alster was nearer – then I would have a better chance of survival.'

Dorfmann looked lost in thought for a moment.

'I wonder if that's what Karl was trying to do. You said on the phone that you found him down by the harbour. Maybe he had the idea to get down to the Elbe. By the time I got to the Alster it was already full of people. Dead or dying. More human candles. They had thrown themselves in to try to put the flames out, but they'd been splashed with phosphorus and were still burning as they floated on the water.'

Fabel placed the Nazi identity card and the photograph of the mummified body on the coffee table. Heinz Dorfmann put on his reading glasses again. 'That's Karl . . .' He frowned when he examined the photograph of the body. 'This is what he looks like now?' He shook his head in wonder. 'It's amazing. Obviously he is all thin . . . dried out. But I would have recognised Karl straight away.'

'Do you know what happened to his sister Margot? Do you have any idea where she lives – if, indeed, she's still alive? I'm trying to locate any next of kin.'

'Not that much, I'm afraid. She married an older man after the war was over. His name was Pohle. Gerhard Pohle.'

### 8.30 p.m.: Hammerbrook, Hamburg

Fabel walked back to his car. It had been raining while he had been in Herr Dorfmann's apartment and the rain after such a warm day had lent the evening air a freshly washed scent. Fabel looked down at the pavement as he walked, at the damp-darkened asphalt, and he thought back to the description that Herr Dorfmann had given of that hot, dry night when Hamburg had become a burning hell on earth. He could not imagine it. His Hamburg.

He reached his car, unlocked it with the key-fob remote, climbed in and closed the door. He rested his hands on the steering wheel for a moment. History. He had studied it; he had wanted to teach it. The irony was that in investigating these cases, he was becoming smothered by it.

He put the key in the ignition and turned it. Nothing.

362

'*Shit!*' Fabel said in English. Fabel was a man of broad wisdom: his knowledge extended over a variety of subjects and he always enjoyed learning something new, stretching the boundaries of his understanding of the world. But that knowledge did not and never had extended to car mechanics. He bad-temperedly fumbled in his pocket to find his cellphone. He had just retrieved it when it pre-empted him by ringing. He snapped it open.

'Hello . . .' He failed to keep the irritation from his voice.

'Hello, Herr Fabel . . .'

Fabel knew it was the killer. The caller had again used some kind of electronic filter that altered his or her voice. It came across the connection as unnaturally deep and slow, distorted, artificial. Inhuman. 'I am so glad you did not remove your key from the ignition; otherwise we would not be having this conversation.'

'What do you mean?' Fabel's mouth suddenly went dry. He knew what the caller meant. A bomb. He leaned forward and searched the car's floor at his feet; checked under the steering column for wires. 'Who is this?'

'We can talk about that in a minute, Herr Fabel. But, for now, I need you to know that I have planted an unnecessarily large explosive device in your car. If you open the door for a second time, the device will detonate; if you remove the key from the ignition, the device will detonate; or if you take your weight off the driver's seat . . . well, I think you get the picture. I'm afraid the consequence of any of these actions would be a disproportionately large explosion. It would result not just in your demise, Herr Fabel, but in the deaths of several residents of

Hammerbrook, as well as widespread damage to property throughout the area. Oh, I should also tell you that I can, at any time of my choosing, also detonate the device remotely.'

'Okay,' said Fabel. 'You've got my attention.' He could feel his heart pound in his chest. He looked out through his windshield at a pleasant summer's evening, at the rain-washed street and the red that the low sun had splashed on the west-facing walls of the buildings. At people going about their business. Fabel felt so alone in the centre of his own universe, the only one aware that death and destruction were only a breath away. Suddenly, the images that Herr Dorfmann had conjured in Fabel's mind earlier returned with a renewed clarity. A young couple with a toddler in a pushchair strolled past Fabel's BMW, walking with no apparent purpose other than to enjoy the summer evening. Fabel wanted to wind down his window and scream at them to run and take cover but, for all he knew, the windows too were booby-trapped. He watched them take what seemed like an eternity to pass the car.

'I'm sure I do have your attention, Herr Fabel.' The electronically distorted voice had been stripped of any subtlety of intonation. 'And I expect to have the attention of a great many other Polizei Hamburg officers, including the bomb squad, for a few hours to come. You see, it suits me better to leave you alive, because it will take an age for your people to extricate you from this situation. Added to which is the time your forensics people will have to spend on site. But don't be in any doubt that if you try anything inadvisable, I will detonate the device. The effect will still be the same.'

Fabel's mind raced. For all he knew, the person

on the phone could be watching him from a safe distance. He scanned both sides of the street and checked the rear-view mirror, doing his best to keep his backside firmly planted on the seat.

'So all of a sudden you're an explosives expert?' Fabel's voice was thick with contempt. 'You expect me to believe that you have the capability to plant a bomb in my car, in a public street, while I was away from it for forty-five minutes? I thought taking scalps was the name of your game, *Winnetou*.'

'Very amusing.' The low, distorted voice laughed and it sounded like something from a nightmare. '*Winnetou* . . . But don't pretend you don't understand my cultural references, Herr Fabel. I am no Red Indian, no character out of a Karl May novel. You know that the tradition I revive is very ancient and very European in its origin. And, in any case, please feel free to test my skills as a bomb designer . . . or hoaxer. All you have to do is step out of your car. If I'm lying, nothing will happen. On the other hand . . . As for the device . . . it has been attached to your vehicle for some time. I have merely activated it remotely. Oh, by the way, did you like the little gift I left you in your apartment?'

'You sick bastard . . .' Fabel hissed into the phone. 'I'm going to get you. I swear to you that I will find you, no matter how long it takes.'

'You know, Herr Fabel, you are remarkably aggressive for a man who is currently sitting on a large quantity of high explosives. If I were to hit the right button, you would be incapable of *getting* anyone. Ever. So why don't you simply shut up and listen to what I have to say?'

Fabel said nothing. He felt a film of sweat between his ear and his cellphone. His heart still pounded and he felt sick. He believed the inhuman voice in his ear. He believed in the bomb beneath him.

'Good,' said the voice. 'Now we can talk. First of all, you may be wondering why I have gone to such lengths to place you in peril. And, for that matter, why I have not detonated the bomb before now. Well, it's simple. As I said, extricating you from this particular predicament will take time. And while it is all going on I shall be taking another scalp. It's an interesting predicament for you, Herr Fabel. You will have to decide how many resources are devoted to rescuing you and how many to stopping me ending another life.'

'We have more resources than you can tie up,' said Fabel in a flat, dead voice.

'That's as may be, but I have to tell you that you are sitting on only one of a pair of bombs. The other is at a location which I shall not disclose at the moment. But I have printed a note with the address and all the details.'

'Where?'

'That's the thing. I have attached the address to the explosive in the bomb in your car. So, even if the bomb squad find a way of disabling the pressure switch under your seat or in the door, they cannot carry out a controlled explosion. If they do, they destroy the only clue to the location of the second bomb. And the second bomb *will* be detonated, trust me, Herr Fabel.'

'When? What time is the second bomb set to go off?'

'I said nothing about it being on a timer, Herr Fabel.'

'So now you're a terrorist? What is this all about?'

'You are not a stupid man, Herr Fabel. This has

always been about *terrorism*, as you call it. It's also about betrayal. Which brings me to my main point. I want you to resign from this case. Take a holiday. A break. I have given you an excuse. The stress of this current ordeal. You see, Herr Fabel, I am now going to volunteer more information about this case than you have been able to gather yourself. The people I am killing deserve to die. They are murderers themselves. And when I have finished I shall never kill again. There are not many left, Fabel. Only another two. After they are dead, I shall disappear and never kill again. And, as I said, all of my victims are guilty. In fact, you yourself would consider them guilty of crimes against the state.'

'Hauser? Griebel? Scheibe? Are you telling me they were terrorists?'

'You heard what I said.' The electronically dead-ened voice spoke without passion. 'But mark this well, Herr Fabel, it is your decision. You can choose to withdraw from the case and allow me to finish what I have started, or I will add other victims to my list. Very specific victims. No one need know about this aspect of our conversation. You can choose to walk away and live your life, and to allow others to live theirs. At the end of the day, the people I have to execute are nothing to you. But others, Fabel . . . Other people who do not deserve to die may die, depending on the choice you make. I am going to hang up now. I suggest you contact your colleagues in the bomb squad without delay. But, before I go, I'm going to send you a few photo-graphs on your cellphone. By the way . . . such beau-tiful hair. A wonderful shade of auburn. Almost red.'

The line went dead. The phone trilled and the screen told Fabel that he had received a message with images. He opened the message and his gut gave a sudden, intense lurch.

'You bastard . . .' Fabel felt tears sting his eyes as he scrolled through the images.

He looked through them again. Photographs of a girl with long auburn hair. Photographs of her on her way home from school; of her with her friends; of her shopping in the stores on Neuer Wall with her father.

### 9.15 p.m.: Hammerbrook, Hamburg

The entire street had been turned into a stage set. Fabel sat squinting against the dazzle of the arc lights, mounted on high stands, that had been set up around his car. The area had been completely evacuated and Fabel found himself worrying about what they had said to Herr Dorfmann as they ushered him from his home: anything but that there was a bomb in his street.

The first person to talk to Fabel was the commander from the LKA7 bomb squad, who approached the car alone. The commander spoke in an even tone, but loudly so that Fabel could hear him through the glass of the still-closed side window, and asked him to remember absolutely everything the caller had told him about the device, as well as anything he had said that might give them a clue as to where the second bomb was hidden. Fabel's mouth was dry and he had felt sick, but he tried to stay composed and focused as he went through every detail.

The bomb-squad commander listened, nodded, took notes and all the time spoke in a steady voice of practised calm, which only served to make Fabel more anxious about his situation. Nor did the appearance of the bomb-squad boss do much to put Fabel's mind at ease: he had appeared beside Fabel's car wearing a wide apron of thick Kevlar, divided into articulated segments, over his black overalls, his head encased in a heavy helmet and his face shielded by a thick perspex visor. The specialist eased himself down and lay on his side beside the car, extending a telescopic black pole with a mirror at its end and slowly and carefully sliding it beneath the car.

After a moment, he re-emerged at Fabel's window, grunting with the effort of straightening himself. 'Okay . . .' He smiled grimly. 'I'm afraid it's no hoax – or not as far as I can see. Unless it's a very convincing-looking dummy, we would appear to have a very substantial amount of high explosive strapped to the underside of your car. We will get you out of this, Herr Chief Commissar. I can promise you that. But you're going to have to sit tight for a while.'

Fabel smiled weakly, leaned his head back against the headrest and closed his eyes. He felt impotent and helpless. Fabel knew that he was almost obsessive about being in control and minimising the random element. But now he was in a situation over which he had absolutely no control. He tried not to think about the explosives beneath him, about the fact that his life lay as much in the hands of the specialists who would defuse the bomb as it would if they were surgeons and he lay on an operating table. All he could do was sit there, without moving, and wait to be liberated.

At least it bought him time to think.

He knew that his team would be somewhere on

the perimeter of the evacuated area, waiting. When he had phoned in to the Presidium, he had spoken first to the bomb squad and then had asked for the Murder Commission. But the bomb squad had told Fabel not to make any more calls on his cellphone and to switch it off as soon as he hung up. Fabel could have left some kind of message, but he had decided not to. He still didn't know what he was going to tell his colleagues. Seeing the photographs of Gabi had spooked him badly.

This guy had obviously been tailing Fabel. Stalking him. That would explain, perhaps, how he had found out about Leonard Schüler: the arrogant son of a bitch must have somehow been tracking every move that the Murder Commission team made. Maybe he had even followed Schüler home from the Presidium. No. That did not fit. How could he have known about Schüler? The young thief had been brought in by a uniform unit. Schüler had only ever been seen by the murder team while inside the Presidium building. An idea started to form in Fabel's brain: Leonard Schüler had not been fully honest about what he saw; about all he knew about the killer. Why had Schüler held back? Had he been involved in the killings after all? Had he been in this together with the voice on the phone? Maybe Fabel's radar had been faulty on this one.

Three LKA7 bomb-disposal officers joined their commander. They brought with them four large black canvas holdalls which they placed a few metres from the car and took equipment from them, laying it out on the ground. Fabel took comfort from the clearly well-practised methodology and the reassuringly purposeful movements of the squad members. Two officers took something that looked like an oversized chunky laptop computer along with some cables and disappeared from Fabel's view and under the car.

Fabel sat in the BMW convertible that he had owned for six years and waited. As he did so, he did his best to think his way though this mess.

Gabi. Fabel had fought back the instinct to panic, to get the bomb squad to tell his team to arrange protection for her. If he had, he would have shown his cards to the killer, who would know that Fabel had divulged all their conversation to his superiors. For now, Gabi was safe: whatever business the Hamburg Hairdresser had that evening, it involved one of the people on his list. Gabi was his trump card held back for the moment. Fabel knew that while the killer had seemed to tell him more than would be advisable, he had told him only those things that he wanted Fabel to know. At least now Fabel knew for sure that this was all about the victims' past.

There was a tapping sound from under the car as the bomb-disposal specialists worked. Delicate work, but to Fabel's fear-heightened senses every tap reverberated through the car and his body like a hammer striking a bell.

He could do it. He could just drop the case. In fact, if he told Criminal Director van Heiden exactly what the killer had said to him his boss would probably insist that he pass the case on. Fabel reflected bitterly on the truth of the killer's logic: these people meant nothing to him; his daughter meant everything. Give up the case. Let someone else take it on.

More tapping. Fabel's mouth felt even dryer. He looked at his watch: 11.45 p.m. For three hours he had not been able to open a door or window and consequently had not had access to water. Maybe it would end here. A slip of a pair of pliers, the wrong connection severed, and it would all be over. This could be the end of the path he had taken all those years ago, after Hanna Dorn had been murdered. The wrong path.

Sitting in the stifling heat of his car, aware of every sound made and every move taken by the bomb-disposal specialists beneath him, Fabel was conscious of the fact that the person he had spoken to on his cellphone nearly three hours ago had probably already murdered and mutilated another victim. Ideas and images bustled around in a brain that was too tired to think; that had been too afraid for too long to see beyond this single experience. The pictures of his daughter, taken covertly by a maniac, flashed repeatedly through his head.

As Jan Fabel sat there, waiting for rescue or for death, he made a decision about his future.

It happened so fast that it was all over before Fabel knew what was happening. Suddenly the car door was thrown open by one of the bomb-squad team and he was being pulled out by another. The two men rushed Fabel clear of the car, out of the glare of the arc lights and across to the secured perimeter. Van Heiden, Anna Wolff, Werner Meyer, Henk Hermann, Maria Klee, Frank Grueber and Holger Brauner were all gathered by the cordon. Grueber and Brauner were already kitted out in their forensic oversuits, as were the five-strong forensics team with them. Fabel was handed a bottle of water which he gulped at greedily.

The LKA7 commander came over to Fabel. 'We've made safe the device. We're taking it apart to find the location for the second bomb. So far, nothing.

What's the deal with this guy, Herr Fabel? Is he a terrorist or an extortionist, or just a maniac?'

'All of the above,' said Fabel wearily.

'Whatever his motive, this guy knows what he's doing.' The bomb-squad chief made to head off to his armoured vehicle. Fabel stopped him by placing a hand on his arm.

'He's not the only one who knows what they're doing,' he said. 'Thanks.'

'You're welcome.' The bomb-squad commander smiled.

'You okay, Jan?' asked Werner.

Fabel took another slug from the water bottle. He wiped his mouth with the back of his hand. 'No, Werner. Far from it.' He turned to van Heiden. 'We need to talk, Herr Criminal Director.'

# 14.

## Twenty-Six Days After the First Murder: Tuesday, 13 September 2005.

### 9.45 a.m.: Police Presidium, Hamburg

It was Police President Hugo Steinbach, Hamburg's chief of police, with Criminal Director van Heiden by his side, who made the statement to the assembled press, radio and television journalists who formed a jostling throng on the steps of the Police Presidium.

'I can confirm that a senior police officer serving with the Polizei Hamburg was the victim of an unsuccessful attempt on his life yesterday evening. As a result of this, for his own safety and to allow him to recuperate fully from the ordeal, he has been removed from duty.'

'Can you confirm that this officer was Principal Chief Commissar Fabel of the Murder Commission?' A short, fat, dark-haired reporter in a too-small black leather jacket had pushed his way to the front. Jens Tiedemann was well known to his fellow journalists.

'We are not prepared, at this stage in the investigation, to give details of the identity of the officer involved,' answered van Heiden. 'But I will confirm that it was a member of the Murder Commission who was on duty at the time.'

'Last night an area of Hammerbrook was evacuated and cordoned off,' Tiedemann was insistent and raised his voice above the others. 'It was reported that an explosive device was found and it was assumed that it was a piece of British ordnance from the Second World War and that a team from the bomb squad was defusing it. Can you now confirm that this was in fact a terrorist bomb planted in the vehicle of this officer?'

Tiedemann's question seemed to fall like a spark that ignited a barrage of other questions from the rest of the journalists. When Police President Steinbach answered he directed his response at the small reporter.

'We can confirm that members of the bomb-disposal team were deployed to make safe an explosive device at the scene,' said Steinbach. 'There is no suggestion of any terrorist involvement.'

'But this was no World War Two bomb, was it?' Tiedemann clung on with the persistence of a terrier. 'Someone was trying to blow up one of your officers, weren't they?'

'As we have already stated,' said van Heiden, 'an attempt was made on the life of a Murder Commission officer. We cannot say any more at the moment, as our investigation is continuing.'

Several of the other journalists took over from where Tiedemann had led them. But without the information that he clearly had, their questions were shots in the dark. The small newspaperman stood silent, allowing the others to harass the senior officers for a while; then he delivered his *coup de grâce*.

'Criminal Director van Heiden . . .' He could not be heard above the others. 'Criminal Director van Heiden . . .' He repeated the name more loudly, and his peers fell silent, ready to follow his lead again. 'Is it true that the bomb under Chief Commissar Fabel's car was placed there by the Hamburg Hairdresser – the serial killer who is currently murdering former members of the radical movements of the nineteen seventies and nineteen eighties? And is it also true that, as a result of this attempt on Herr Fabel's life, he has withdrawn from the case?'

Van Heiden's expression darkened and he glowered at Tiedemann. 'The Murder Commission officer in question is withdrawing from all his current caseload and handing it over to other officers. The sole reason for this is that he is taking a leave of absence to recover from his experience. There is nothing more to it than that. I assure you that Polizei Hamburg officers cannot be so easily frightened off a case . . .'

The small reporter said nothing more. But he smiled and allowed the clamour of his colleagues to wash over him. Van Heiden and Police President Steinbach turned their backs on them and made their way back up the steps and into the Presidium while the Polizei Hamburg's press officer fended off the journalists.

As the clot of journalists on the Presidium steps dissolved, one of them turned to Tiedemann.

'How did you know all that about what happened?'

The newspaperman indicated the Presidium building with a jerk of his head. 'I've got an inside source. A really good inside source . . .'

## 10.15 a.m.: Schanzenviertel, Hamburg

Maybe she should not have set the alarm system for such a short absence from her office: Ingrid

Fischmann had returned from the post office a block away, where she had mailed the package of photographs and information she had prepared for the policeman, Fabel.

She cursed as she dropped the black notebook with the alarm number on the floor. She bent down to pick it up, causing some of the contents to tumble from her open shoulder-bag, and she heard the clatter of her keys on the tiled floor of the hallway. It was always such a fuss just to get in and out of her office, mainly because the key code refused to take up residence in her memory. But Ingrid Fischmann knew that it was a necessary evil: she had to be careful.

The Red Army Faction had officially disbanded in 1998 and the fall of the Berlin Wall had rendered the foundations of the belief system behind such groups redundant. The RAF, the IRA – even, it seemed, ETA – were consigning themselves to the history books. European domestic terrorism seemed an ever more remote concept, compared to that which came from outside. Terrorism in the twenty-first century had taken on a totally different hue and the ideology was religious rather than socio-political. Nevertheless, the people Fischmann exposed through her journalism were very much of the here and now. And many had a history of violence.

'Okay, okay . . .' she said to the alarm control panel in response to its imperative of rapid, urgent electronic beeps. She retrieved the notebook and, not having time to find her glasses, peered at it from a distance to transfer the numbers to the control keypad, stamping the last number with her finger in decisive conclusion. The beeping stopped. Except it did not.

It was like an echo of the alarm sound, but a different pitch. And it wasn't coming from the keypad.

It took Fischmann a moment, standing stock-still and frowning in concentration, to work out the direction of the sound. From her office.

She followed the beeping sound into the office. It was coming from her desk. She unlocked and opened the top drawer.

'Oh . . .' was all she said.

It was all she had the chance to say. Her brain had only just enough time to process what her eyes were telling it; to take in the cables, the batteries, the blinking LED display, the large sand-coloured packet.

Ingrid Fischmann was dead the instant after her brain had put together the elements to form a single word.

Bomb.

## 10.15 a.m.: Police Presidium, Hamburg

'I hope this pays off,' said van Heiden. 'A great deal of our work depends on the cooperation of the media. When they get wind of this they will not be happy.'

'It's a risk we've got to take,' said Fabel. He sat at the conference table with Maria, Werner, Anna, Henk and the two forensic specialists, Holger Brauner and Frank Grueber. There was another man at the table: a short, fat man with glasses and a black leather jacket.

'They'll get over it,' said Jens Tiedemann. 'But, for the sake of my paper, I would rather everyone thought I was duped into the story, rather than being a co-conspirator, as it were.'

Fabel nodded. 'I owe you, Jens. Big time. This killer knows how to communicate with me, but it's a one-way street. The only way I can get him to believe that I have dropped the case is for it to be announced publicly.'

'You're welcome, Jan.' Tiedemann stood up to leave. 'I just hope he buys it.'

'So do I,' said Fabel. 'But at least we've got my daughter Gabi out of the city and under protection. I've got a twenty-four-hour watch on Susanne as well. As for me, I will have to spend most of my time in here, out of sight but running the show through my core team. Officially, Herr van Heiden has taken over the case.' He stood up and shook Tiedemann's hand. 'You put on a convincing show. It's bought us some time. Like I said, I owe you.'

'Yes – I rather think you do.' Tiedemann's fleshy face was split by a broad smile. 'And you can be certain that I'll call it in one day.'

'I'm sure you will.'

After the reporter left, the smile faded from Fabel's lips. 'We've got to move fast on this. The Hamburg Hairdresser seems to have an ability to second-guess everything we do. And he seems to have enormous resources, both intellectual and material, to call on. For all I know, he was expecting exactly the kind of announcement that was "forced" out of us by Jens at the press conference. In which case we're screwed. But if he has gone for it, then he may feel less under pressure because he believes that I'm no longer leading the inquiry. What I don't understand is why it is so important for him that I am out of the picture.'

'You are our best murder detective. And with a particularly high conviction rate,' said van Heiden.

\* \* \*

After the meeting Fabel asked to speak to van Heiden in private.

'Certainly, Fabel. What is it?'

'It's this . . .' Fabel handed him a sealed envelope. 'My resignation. I wanted you to have it now so that you are aware of my intentions. Obviously, I am not going to leave until this case is over. But as soon as it is I am quitting the Polizei Hamburg.'

'You can't mean this, Fabel.' Van Heiden looked shocked. A reaction that Fabel hadn't expected from van Heiden, a man he had always assumed had been indifferent to him; particularly because of Fabel's apparent disregard for van Heiden's authority. 'I meant what I said earlier – we can't afford to lose you, Fabel . . .'

'I appreciate the sentiments, Herr Criminal Director. But I'm afraid my mind is set on it. I had already decided, but when I saw those photographs of Gabi on my cellphone . . . Anyway, I'm sure you will find a replacement. Maria Klee and Werner Meyer are both excellent officers.'

'Do they know?'

'Not yet,' said Fabel. 'And, if you don't mind, I'd like to keep it under wraps until the case is over. They have enough to think about for now.'

Van Heiden tapped the envelope against his open palm, as if assessing the weight of its contents. 'Don't worry, Fabel. I am telling no one about this unless I have to. In the meantime, I just hope that you change your mind.'

There was a knock on the conference room door and Maria came in.

'I don't know how low a profile you want to keep, *Chef*. But we know where he planted the second bomb . . .'

There was a hierarchy emerging at the site of the explosion, and Fabel felt he was struggling to remain at its top.

In an attempt to sustain the pretence that he had been removed from the case, they had found a traffic Commissar's uniform to fit Fabel and he had been driven to the scene in the back of one of the riot police's bottle-green Mercedes-Benz transporters with blacked-out windows. A Polizei Hamburg's *Libele* helicopter hung in the sky over the scene.

The uniformed branch had secured the site and evacuated the surrounding buildings.

Fabel stepped from the transporter and surveyed the devastation. All the windows of Ingrid Fischmann's offices had been blasted out and gazed from the blackened shell onto the street like empty eye sockets. The narrow pavement, the roadway and the roofs of the parked cars, the alarms of which still whined in shocked protest at the blast, glittered with gem-sized fragments of glass. From one of the windows hung the frayed and scorched ribbons of Fischmann's vertical blinds. The perimeter had been secured by the Polizei Hamburg MEK special-weapons unit that Fabel had requested, but there were also a large number of heavily armed officers wearing jerkins bearing the large initials BKA on the back, indicating that they were from the Federal Crime Office. And Fabel was not surprised to see Markus Ullrich. This had all become very political, very suddenly.

Holger Brauner and his deputy Frank Grueber had both turned out with an expanded team to process the site, but an even larger forensics unit had been ordered in by the federal BKA.

Everyone, however, was left standing outside while the fire service and the bomb disposal unit made sure that the site was safe to enter. Fabel took the opportunity to tackle Markus Ullrich who was standing outside the building by the door that, because it had been slightly lower than the main office level, had survived the blast. Ullrich was talking to a BKA officer but broke off when he saw Fabel approach. He smiled grimly.

'Very fetching,' he said, nodding at Fabel's borrowed uniform. 'I'm guessing this is not a gas explosion.'

'I very much doubt it,' said Fabel. 'Listen, I need to get one thing straight. This is a Polizei Hamburg inquiry. The woman who rents these offices has been helping me with the background to the Hauser and Griebel murders. It is more than a coincidence that her offices have been attacked.'

'Yes, I understand that. But she was also someone who dabbled in a very dangerous area of German public life. There is a chance that she got too close to someone who maybe decided to revive some old skills they learned two decades ago – including how to use a detonator and Semtex. You have to understand that there is a sound basis for BKA interest.' There was nothing confrontational about Ullrich's tone, but Fabel did not feel reassured. 'Listen, Herr Fabel, I don't want to compete; I want to cooperate. We have a common interest in this case. I simply arranged for these extra resources to be made available to you. Same goes for the forensics team: they'll work under your chief's direction. Do we know if she was inside?'

Fabel sighed and some of the tension eased from his posture. He knew that Ullrich was on the level.

'We don't know yet,' said Fabel. 'We checked out

her home and she's not there, and we've tried her cellphone. Nothing.' He looked up at the building. 'I'm guessing that the bomber hit his target. Anyway, Herr Ullrich. This is my case, first and foremost, and I want you to understand that.'

'I do. But we are going to have to work together on this, Herr Fabel. Whether you like it or not, we may be dealing with something here that has implications that go beyond Hamburg. You may find it useful to have a federal agency on your team. You'll need all the help you can get if you have to run this inquiry by remote control – and in disguise. I am happy to let you call the shots. For the meantime.'

'Okay . . .' Fabel nodded. 'Let's deal with what you said about it maybe being some former terrorist sleeper protecting himself, rather than my so-called Hamburg Hairdresser case. I'm afraid the two things might not be mutually exclusive.' Fabel gave Ullrich a summary of what Ingrid Fischmann had told him of her connection to the Wiedler kidnapping and of Benni Hildesheim's claim that he knew the identity of several of The Risen, including hinting that he had positive proof that Bertholdt Müller-Voigt was the driver of the van in which Thorsten Wiedler had been kidnapped.

'That's been around for a long time, Fabel,' said Ullrich. 'We've looked into it long and hard. There's no evidence to link him to the abduction, or even to membership of the group. After Hildesheim died we got a warrant to go through all his stuff to see if we could find the proof he claimed to have. Nothing. That doesn't mean to say that I don't believe it. It's just that I don't think that, if Müller-Voigt really took part in Wiedler's kidnap and murder, we'll ever be able to prove it.'

Fabel nodded towards the broken building with its graffiti and *Jugendstil* architectural details. 'Maybe she was too close to doing just that . . .'

His phone rang.

'Don't bother trying to set up a trace,' the electronically altered voice rasped. 'I'm talking to you on my latest victim's cellphone. By the time you get a location I'll be gone and the phone will have been destroyed. As you can see, I have been busy. That bitch Fischmann had it coming to her. I just regret that she died so quickly. But I had more fun last night. I won't tell you where to find the next body. By my reckoning, her son will discover it very shortly.'

'Give it up—' Fabel said.

'You disappoint me, Fabel.' The voice cut across Fabel. 'You tried to deceive me with that little public charade this morning. Playing dress-up and skulking around in vans. I'm afraid I will have to punish you for that. For the rest of your life you will curse yourself, every day, and blame yourself for the horror your daughter had to endure before she died.'

The phone went dead.

'Gabi!' Fabel strode across to Maria. 'Give me your car keys, Maria . . . He's going after Gabi! I've got to get to her.'

Maria grabbed his arm. 'Wait!' She placed herself in front of Fabel and stared hard into his face. 'What did he say?'

Fabel told her. By this time Werner, van Heiden and Ullrich had rushed over to them.

'How did he know? How could he work it out so fast?' Fabel looked down at his borrowed uniform, frowning. 'And how the hell did he know about the disguise? I've got to get to Gabi.'

'Hold on a moment,' said Maria. 'You said yourself there was a good chance that he wouldn't fall for it. There's a world of difference between that and him knowing where we've stashed Gabi. For all we know he's watching us right now and you would lead him straight to her. But I don't think he's interested in going after Gabi at all, just like he wasn't really interested in killing you with that bomb. It's just the same as that night with Vitrenko, Jan. A diversion. A delaying tactic.' There was an earnestness in Maria's eyes. All the defences, all the shields, had fallen away. 'He's playing you, Jan. He wants to divert your attention. The bomb was to tie you up while he worked. This is exactly the same. He wants you to go to Gabi so that he can finish what he's started.'

'It makes sense, Fabel,' said Ullrich.

A uniformed officer ran over to Fabel. 'There's a call on the radio for you, Herr Chief Commissar. Someone has just reported a scalped body. A few blocks from here.'

Maria let go of Fabel's arm. 'It's your call, *Chef*.'

## 11.00 p.m.: Schanzenviertel, Hamburg

A uniformed unit had already arrived at the scene and the first thing they had done was to get Franz Brandt out of the room where he had found his mother's body. When Fabel got there, Brandt was still in deep shock. He was in his early thirties but looked younger; the most conspicuous thing about his appearance was the shock of long, thick auburn-red hair above his pale freckled face. The room that he had been moved into was large and combined a bedroom and a study. The books that filled the shelves reminded Fabel of Frank Grueber's study:

almost all were university textbooks devoted to archaeology, palaeontology and history.

The books were not the only thing that Fabel recognised: there was a large poster of the Neu Versen bog body on the wall. Red Franz.

'I am very sorry for your loss,' he said. Fabel invariably felt awkward in these situations, despite years of experience of them. He always did feel genuinely sorry for the families of victims, and he was always aware that he was stepping into shattered lives. But he was also there to do a job.

'I take it this is your room?' he asked. 'You live here permanently with your mother?'

'If you can call it permanent. I'm often away abroad on digs. I travel a lot, generally.'

'Your mother ran a business from home?' asked Fabel. 'What was it she did?'

Franz Brandt gave a bitter laugh. 'New Age therapies, mainly. It was crap, to be honest. I don't think she believed any of it herself. Mostly to do with reincarnation.'

'Reincarnation?' Fabel thought of Gunter Griebel and his researches into genetic memory. Could there be some kind of link? Then he remembered. Müller-Voigt had mentioned a woman who had been involved with the Gaia Collective. He took his notebook out and searched through his notes. It was there. Beate Brandt. He looked at the pale young man before him. He was near to breaking down. Fabel looked around the bedroom-cum-study and his gaze again fell on the poster.

'I know this gentleman . . .' said Fabel, smiling. 'He comes from Ostfriesland, like me. It's funny, but recently he seems to keep on cropping up in my life. Synchronicity or something.'

Brandt smiled weakly. 'Red Franz . . . It was my nickname at university. Because of my hair. And because everyone knew that he was my favourite bog body, if you know what I mean. It was Red Franz that inspired me to become an archaeologist. I first read about him at school and became fascinated with finding out about the lives of our ancestors. Discovering the truth about how they lived. And died.' He went quiet and turned his head towards the door that led to the living room where his mother lay. Fabel rested a hand on his shoulder.

'Listen, Franz . . .' Fabel spoke in a quiet, soothing tone. 'I know how difficult this is for you. And I know that you are shocked and afraid right now. But I need to ask you some questions about your mother. I need to get to this maniac before he gets to anyone else. Are you up to this?'

Brandt stared at Fabel for a moment, his eyes wild. 'Why? Why did he do . . . *that* . . . to my mother? What does it all mean?'

'I don't know, Franz.'

Brandt took a sip of water and Fabel noticed how his hand trembled.

'Does your mother have any connection with the town of Nordenham?'

Brandt shook his head.

'Was she politically active in her youth, as far as you know?'

'What's that got to do with anything?'

'I just need to know – it may have something to do with the killer's motives.'

'Yes . . . yes, she was. Environmentalism. And the student movement. Mostly in the nineteen seventies and early nineteen eighties. She remained involved in environmental issues.'

'Did she know Hans-Joachim Hauser or Gunter Griebel? Do these names mean anything to you?'

'Hauser, yes. My mother knew him well. Earlier, I mean. They were both involved in anti-nuclear protests and later with the Greens. I don't think she had much contact with Hauser over recent years.'

'And what about Gunter Griebel?'

Brandt shrugged. 'It's not a name I can say I've heard of. She certainly never discussed him. But I can't say for certain that she didn't know him.'

'Listen, Franz, I have to be totally honest with you,' said Fabel. 'I don't know if this maniac is acting out of a desire for revenge or just has something against people of your mother's generation and political leanings. But there has to be something linking all the victims, including your mother. If I'm right, she may have made the link between the deaths of Hauser and Griebel. Have you noticed anything strange in your mother's behaviour over recent weeks? Specifically since the press announced the first killing, Hans-Joachim Hauser?'

'Of course she reacted to that. Like I said, she had worked with Hauser in the past. She was shocked when she read about what had been done to him.' Brandt's eyes filled with pain as he realised that he was talking about the same horrific disfigurement that had been performed on his own mother.

'What about the other murders?' Fabel sought to keep Brandt focused on his questions. 'Did she talk about them at all? Or did they seem to trouble her particularly?'

'I can't say. I was away on another dig for the university for about three weeks. But, now that you mention it, she did seem very withdrawn and quiet over the last couple of days.'

Fabel watched the young man closely. 'You found your mother this morning when you came down for breakfast?'

'Yes. I was late in last night and I went straight to bed. I assumed that my mother was already asleep.'

'How late?'

'About eleven-thirty.'

'And you didn't go into the living room?'

'Obviously not. If I had, I would have seen my mother like . . . like *that*. I would have phoned you right away.'

'And where were you last night until eleven?'

'At the university, writing up some notes.'

'Anyone see you there? I'm sorry, Franz, but I have to ask.'

Brandt sighed. 'I saw Dr Severts, briefly. Apart from that, I don't think so.'

It was at the mention of Severts's name that it fell into place for Fabel.

'That's where we met before. It's been bothering me. It was you who discovered the mummified body down at the HafenCity site.'

'That's right,' said Brandt bleakly. His mind was on things other than where he had previously met the detective investigating his mother's brutal murder.

'You're not aware of your mother expecting any visitors last night?'

'No. She told me that she was going to have an early night.'

Fabel caught sight of Frank Grueber, who had entered the room and nodded now to indicate that the scene was clear for Fabel to enter.

'Is there anywhere you can spend the night?' Fabel asked Brandt. 'If not, I can arrange for a car to take you to a hotel.' Fabel thought about his own recent situation; about how he had been torn from his own home by an act of violence.

Brandt shook his shock of red hair. 'That's not necessary. I have a friend, a girl, who I can stay with. I'll phone her.'

'Okay. Leave the address and number where we can reach you. I really am so terribly sorry for your loss, Franz.'

# 15.

# Twenty-Seven Days After the First Murder: Wednesday, 14 September 2005.

### 1.00 p.m.: Police Presidium, Hamburg

The days were losing their definition: running into each another with a seamless lethargy. Fabel had grabbed a couple of hours of fractured sleep at the Presidium. But the fact that two murders, executed in totally different ways by the same killer, had co-incided meant that, even with all the resources at his disposal, he was working himself and his team harder and longer than he should. They were all tired. When you were tired, you did not work at maximum efficiency. And they were hunting a maximum-efficiency killer.

It had been the morning before Fabel had found the time to head home for a few hours' sleep and a shower that would, hopefully, refresh his senses and his ability to think.

Fabel found himself, frustratingly, driving home through the start of the early-morning rush-hour flow and it was eight o'clock by the time he turned the key in the door of his apartment. As he did so, the images from Brandt's home haunted him. He half expected to find another scalp in his apartment. This had been his refuge. His secure place away from the madness and violence of others. No more.

The windows had been thoroughly cleaned, as had the rest of the apartment, but he could have sworn he smelled the subtlest hint of blood hanging in the air. The morning sun burned bright in the sky above the Alster and flooded into Fabel's east-facing windows. Yet, to Fabel's weary eyes, somehow the light seemed sterile and cold. Like in a mortuary.

The alarm woke him up just before noon. He had found it difficult to sleep with the sound of the city around him and when he rose he was disappointed to find that the dragging weight of his tiredness clung to him. He took a shower and decided to have something to eat before heading back into the Presidium.

'There's a package on your desk, *Chef*,' said Anna as Fabel passed through the Murder Commission on the way to his office. 'It arrived this morning while you were out. Given what's been happening it was held up downstairs by security and run through the scanner twice. It's clean.'

'Thanks.' Fabel entered his office and hung his jacket on the back of his chair. The package was large and thick and when he opened it he found a heavy file in a blue cover, held together by two thick rubber bands. Tucked under one of the bands was a tape cassette; there was a 'with compliments' card under the other. He took out the card and stared at it for a long time, almost as if, although the handwriting was neat and clear, he could not comprehend the meaning of it.

*As promised. Hope this helps. With friendly greetings, I. Fischmann.*

He stared at a note written by the woman to whom he had spoken only two weeks before. It seemed impossible that, in that small space of time, the intelligence, the being behind the handwriting had been extinguished.

Fabel removed the cassette and the bands from the file. Ingrid Fischmann had painstakingly put together a dossier of all the information she had on The Risen, as well as background information on Baader-Meinhof and other militant and terrorist groups. She had photocopied and scanned articles, photographs, files. Nothing was in its original form: she had made the effort to make copies for Fabel of all the most important files. Except now he held in his hands all that survived of Ingrid Fischmann's work: the ghosts of the originals she had been so keen to keep safe, but which had been destroyed in the explosion and the fire that followed.

It took him a while to locate a cassette player in the building and it was a full fifteen minutes before it was delivered to his office. While he waited he flicked through the other material in the file; it was certainly comprehensive and it would take Fabel a long time to go through it in detail, but he knew he would have to. In that information could be the smallest detail, the finest thread that would provide the coherence he desperately sought for this case.

After the uniformed officer delivered the cassette player, Fabel closed his office door, something that everyone who worked with him knew to be a signal that he did not want to be disturbed, and he switched his phone to voicemail. The cassette that Ingrid Fischmann had sent Fabel was not of the same vintage as the original recording, and it was clear from the static hiss as soon as he pressed the Play button that it was probably a copy of a copy. He turned the volume up slightly to compensate. There were a few clunks and the muffled sound of a microphone being moved. Then a man's voice.

'My name is Ralf Fischmann. I am thirty-nine years old and I was the chauffeur for Herr Thorsten Wiedler of the Wiedler Industries Group. For performing this duty, I was shot three times, once in the side and twice in the back by the terrorists who kidnapped Herr Wiedler. I cannot understand what my sin was that I deserved to be shot. But, for that matter, I cannot understand what great sin Herr Wiedler has committed to deserve being torn from his family.

'It has been more than two months since I was shot. The doctors started off by being cheerily optimistic and telling me that it was like allowing a bruise to heal. That, when the swelling in my spinal chord went down, who knows? Well, the swelling has gone down now and they don't sound so optimistic any more. I am a cripple. I will never walk again. I know that already, just as the doctors know it but won't yet admit it. I am a simple man. I am not stupid, but I was never one for great ambition. All I wanted to do was work hard, provide for my family and be as good a person as I could. Somehow, the way I have lived my life, honestly and modestly, was offensive to someone. So offensive that they deemed it necessary to put bullets in my spine.

'I have been working for Herr Wiedler for three years. He was a good man. I use the past tense because I think it highly unlikely that he is still alive. A good man and a good employer. He came from Cologne and was typically friendly and down-to-earth . . . he treated all his employees as equals. If you did something wrong, something he was not happy about, he would tell you. By the same token, he would buy you a drink in the pub and talk to you about your family. He was always asking about how my daughter Ingrid and my son Horst were getting along. He knew that Ingrid was a bright little thing and promised me that she would go far.

'The work I did for Herr Wiedler was general driving. I drove him between his home and office every day, and to meetings in Hamburg and all across the Federal Republic. Herr Wiedler hated flying, you see. If we were travelling the length of the country, to Stuttgart or Munich, for example, he would take my mind off the boredom of so much autobahn driving by chatting with me. Sometimes he would do some paperwork in the back of the car, but generally he would sit up front with me and talk. Herr Wiedler really liked to talk. I liked him very much and found him to be the kind of man that, were he not my employer, I would gladly call a friend. I like to think he thought the same way about me.

'On the morning of the fourteenth of November nineteen seventy-seven we were both in the car. I had collected Herr Wiedler, as usual, from his family home in Blankenese. Unlike most other mornings, when I would take Herr Wiedler directly to his office, I had picked him up later in the morning and we were heading directly to Bremen, where Herr Wiedler had a meeting with a client company. This is something that I have puzzled about ever since the kidnapping. I would have understood it better if the ambush had taken place on our normal route to the Wiedler main offices, which were to the north, but they were waiting for us on our way into the city centre where we would join the A1 towards Bremen. I can only conclude from this that the terrorists had someone on the inside of the Wiedler company, or that some of the gang followed us from the Wiedler residence and were in touch with the others via walkie-talkie.

'It was about ten thirty a.m. We were just about to join the autobahn when I saw a black Volkswagen van, stationary but sitting at an angle that suggested it had swerved suddenly. A man in a business suit was waving his arms frantically around his head and there was what looked like a body lying in the middle of the road. It looked to me as if the person on the road had been hit by the van. I pulled over to the side of the road. There was another car behind us and it stopped too. Herr Wiedler and I ran over to the injured person on the road. A young couple got out of the car behind us and followed us. When we got near to the body we saw that it was wearing blue overalls and we could not tell if it was a man or a woman. Then, suddenly, the person on the ground leaped to their feet and we saw that they were wearing a ski mask over their face. I think it was a man, but not a particularly tall man. He had a sub-machine gun. The man in the business suit and smart coat produced a handgun and pointed it at us. We all froze. Herr Wiedler, me and the young couple. Suddenly two more people in blue boiler suits and ski masks leaped out from the VW van. They had sub-machine guns too. I remember thinking that the terrorist who had pretended to be a businessman was the only one who was not wearing a ski mask and I made sure I got a good look at him. He saw this and got very angry and shouted at me and the others to stop looking at him.

'The two masked men from the VW van ran over and grabbed Herr Wiedler and started to rush him over to the van while the other two kept their guns aimed at us. I stepped forward and the man in the overalls raised his gun, so I stopped and kept my hands up. That was all I did. I made no other move and the time for action was past. That is why I do not understand why he shot me. The man in the business suit said I was looking at him again and the next thing I remember was the sound of his gun. I remember thinking then that they must have been using blanks, because there was no way he could have missed me at that range, but I felt no pain, no impact. Nothing. Then I was aware of something wet at my side and running down my leg. I looked down and saw that I was bleeding from a wound just above my hip. I turned away and started to walk back to the car. I wasn't thinking straight: it must have been the shock. I just remember thinking that I had to get to the car and sit down. Then I heard two more shots and I knew I had been hit in the back. My legs just stopped working and I fell flat on my face. I could hear the woman from the young couple screaming, then a screech of tyres as the van drove off with Herr Wiedler in it. I didn't see this, because I was face down, but I know that's what it was.

'The young couple ran over to me and then the woman ran off down the road to get help while the young man stayed with me. It was the strangest sensation. I lay there with my cheek pressed against the road surface and I remember thinking that it felt warmer than I did. I also remember thinking that I had let Herr Wiedler down. That I should have done more. I was going to die anyway, so I should have made it count. Then I started to think about my wife Helga and little Ingrid and Horst and how they were going to have to manage without me. It was then that I got really angry and decided that I was not going to die. As I lay waiting for the ambulance to come, I concentrated hard on staying conscious and the way I did that was by trying to remember every detail of the face of the man who had not been able to hide his face. If he could be caught, I thought, they would get the rest of them.

'It is those details that I was able to give to the police artist. I made him rework the picture over and over again. When he asked me if we had captured a good general likeness of the terrorist, I said he had, but that his job was not over. I told him that we could get it to an exact likeness of the man who shot me. So we did the drawing over and over again. What we finished up with was no artist's impression. It was a portrait.

'I will be confined to this wheelchair for the rest of my life. Over the last two months I have tried to understand what it is that these people think they can achieve with violence. They say this is a revolution, a rebellion. But a rebellion against what? The time will come when I shall have my reckoning. I may die first, but this tape, and the likeness I helped create of the terrorist who shot me, is my statement.'

Fabel pressed the Stop button. Now he understood why Ingrid Fischmann had been so motivated to uncover the truth. The voice on the tape had made Fabel feel obligated to find the people who had kidnapped and murdered Thorsten Wiedler and consigned Ralf Fischmann to a short and unhappy butt-end of a life spent in a wheelchair; he could not imagine the pressure that Ingrid, as Fischmann's daughter, must have felt.

He opened the file and searched through it for the artist's impression that Ralf Fischmann had described in the tape. He found it. An electric current coursed through his skin and ruffled the hairs at the nape of his neck. Ralf Fischmann had been right: he had pushed the police artist to a level of detail far beyond the usual bounds of the pictures of suspects that they normally circulated. It was, indeed, a proper portrait.

Fabel looked hard at a very real face of a very real person. And it was a face he recognised.

'Now I understand, you bastard,' Fabel said out loud to the face before him. 'Now I know why you never wanted anyone to take your photograph. The others all had their faces hidden – you were the only one that anyone saw.'

Fabel laid the image of a young Gunter Griebel down on his desk, rose from his chair and flung the door of his office open.

## 1.20 p.m.: Police Presidium, Hamburg

Werner had assembled the entire team in the main meeting room. Fabel had asked Werner to arrange the meeting so that he could share his discovery about Gunter Griebel. It was now clear that all the victims had been members of Red Franz Mühlhaus's terror group, The Risen. It was also more than likely that they were all involved in the Thorsten Wiedler kidnap and murder. Fabel was convinced that the motive for these killings lay in that event: but the person most motivated to carry out the murders, Ingrid Fischmann, was herself dead. She had mentioned a brother, as had her father on the tape recording. Fabel had decided to get someone on to tracing her brother and establishing his whereabouts at the times of each murder.

All of Fabel's thinking, however, was to be over-taken.

Most of the Murder Commission team, like Fabel, had been seriously deprived of sleep over the last couple of days, but he could tell that something had blown away all weariness from them. They sat, expectantly, around the cherrywood conference table, while a row of dead, scalpless faces – Hauser, Griebel, Schüler and Scheibe – looked down at them from the inquiry board. They had not had time to obtain an image of the latest victim, Beate Brandt, but Werner had written her name next to the other images: a space prepared for her among the dead, like a freshly dug but still empty grave. Centred above the row of victims, the intense gaze of Red Franz Mühlhaus radiated across the room from the old police photograph.

'What have you got?' Fabel sat down at the end of the table nearest the door and rubbed at his eyes with the heels of his hands, as if trying to banish the tiredness from them.

Anna Wolff stood up.

'Well, to start with, we've been alerted about a missing-person report. A Cornelius Tamm has been reported missing.'

'The singer?' asked Fabel.

'That's the one. A bit before my time, I'm afraid. It's shown up on our radar because Tamm is a contemporary of the other victims. He went missing three days ago after a gig in Altona. His van hasn't been found, either.'

'Who's following it up?' asked Fabel.

'I've got a team on it,' said Maria Klee. She looked as tired as Fabel felt. 'Some of the extra officers we've had allocated. I've told them that they're probably looking for the next victim.'

'Are you okay?' asked Fabel. 'You look shattered.'

'I'm fine . . . just a headache.'

'What else have we got?' Fabel turned back to Anna.

'We've been trying to work out what this has all been about.' Anna Wolff smiled. 'Has Red Franz Mühlhaus, supposedly dead for twenty years, returned from the grave? Well, maybe he has. I checked through all the records we've got on Mühlhaus, as well as media stuff from the time.' Anna paused and flicked through the file that sat before her on the table. 'Maybe Red Franz has come back to avenge himself. In the form of his son. Mühlhaus was not alone on that railway platform in Nordenham. He had his long-term girlfriend Michaela Schwenn and their ten-year-old son with him. The boy saw it all. Watched his father and mother die.'

Fabel felt a tingle in the nape of his neck, but said, 'That doesn't mean that this son is out for revenge.'

'According to the GSG Nine officers on the scene, Mühlhaus's dying word was "traitors". These killings aren't motiveless psychotic attacks, *Chef*. This is all about vengeance. A blood feud.' Anna paused again. There was the hint of a smile playing around the corners of her full red lips.

'Okay . . .' Fabel sighed. 'Let's hear it. You've obviously got a killer blow to deliver . . .'

Her smile broadened. She pointed towards the black-and-white photograph of Mühlhaus on the inquiry board.

'It's funny, isn't it, how some images become icons. How we automatically associate an image with a person and the person with a time and a place, with an idea . . .'

Fabel made an impatient face and Anna continued.

'I remember being shocked to see a photograph of Ulrike Meinhof before she became a shaggy-haired, jeans-wearing terrorist. It was of her and her husband at a racecourse. She was dressed as a typical demure nineteen sixties *Hausfrau*. Before her radicalisation. It got me thinking and I searched for other photographs of Mühlhaus. As you know, they are notoriously thin on the ground. This image we have here is the one that we are familiar with, the one that was used on the wanted posters in the nineteen eighties. It's black and white but, as you can see, Mühlhaus's hair is very, very dark. Black. But then I remembered the photographs of Andreas Baader when he was arrested in nineteen seventy-two. With his dark hair dyed ash-blond.'

Anna took a large glossy print and taped it next to the police photograph. This time the photograph was in full colour. It was of a younger Franz Mühlhaus, without his trade-mark goatee beard. But there was one feature that stood out above all others. His hair. In the police wanted poster Mühlhaus's hair had been combed severely back from his broad pale brow, but in this photograph it frothed across his forehead and framed his face in thick, tangled ringlets. And it was red. A luxuriant red flecked with golden highlights.

'The nickname "Red Franz" didn't come from his politics. It was his hair.' Anna stabbed a finger onto the black-and-white photograph and looked directly at Fabel. 'Do you see? All the time he was on the run, he hid his distinctive red hair by dying it dark. The BKA got intelligence that Mühlhaus had darkened his hair and they changed the image accordingly. But there's more . . . apparently Mühlhaus's son had the same distinctively coloured hair. And when they were on the run together Mühlhaus dyed his son's hair too.'

There was a small silence after Anna stopped speaking. Then Werner gave voice to what they were all thinking.

'Shit. The thing with the scalps and the hair dye.' He turned to Fabel. 'Now you've got your symbolism.'

'What do we know about what happened to the son?' Fabel asked Anna.

'Social services won't release the file until we get a warrant to access the information. I'm already onto it.'

Fabel stared at the photograph of the young Mühlhaus. He would have been in his late teens or early twenties. It was clearly an amateur photograph, taken outdoors in the sunshine of a long-distant summer. Mühlhaus smiled broadly at the camera, narrowing his pale eyes against the sunlight. A care-free, happy youth. There was nothing written in that face to suggest a future tied to murder and violence. Just as Anna had described the photograph of Ulrike Meinhof. Fabel had always found images such as this fascinating: everyone had a past. Everyone had been someone else once.

Fabel's attention focused on the hair that shone red and gold in the summer sun. He had seen hair like that before. He had seen it only hours before.

'Anna . . .' He turned round from the inquiry board.

'*Chef?*'

'Check out Beate Brandt's background as a priority. I need to know what relationship, if any, she had with Franz Mühlhaus.' Fabel turned to Werner. 'And I need you to check out that address that Franz Brandt gave us. I think we need to have another chat with him.'

Fabel's cellphone rang at that moment. It was Frank Grueber, who had been heading up the forensics team at Beate Brandt's home.

'I take it you've found another hair?' said Fabel.

'We have,' said Grueber. 'Our guy is getting poetic. He left it arranged on the pillow next to her body. But that's not all. We've been checking the entire house to see if the killer slipped up when entering the house.'

'And?'

'And we've found traces of something in a desk drawer. In her son's bedroom-cum-study. It looks as if a quantity of explosives has been stored there.'

## 2.10 p.m.: Eimsbüttel, Hamburg

It had all fallen into place for Fabel as they had sped across Hamburg to the address in Eimsbüttel that Franz Brandt had given Werner.

Brandt had been cool. Very cool. While Fabel had been questioning him, Brandt had asked Fabel why the killer dyed the hair red. He had already known the reason but had used his mock grief to camouflage his intent as he interrogated the interrogator: trying to find out how much the police knew about his motives. He had even sat with a poster of the other Red Franz, the bog body, on the wall above them and had talked about how 'Red Franz' had been his nickname at university.

It all fitted: the same hair, the same choice of profession, even the same forename. Brandt's age also fitted. It was Fabel's guess that Beate Brandt had taken in the ten-year-old Franz after he had witnessed his father and his natural mother die in the gun battle on the platform at Nordenham. Maybe Beate had been motivated by guilt. Whatever the treachery that had been committed, she had been part of it and, despite being brought up as her son, Franz had administered the same ritual justice to her as he had to his other victims.

They pulled up at the cordon that the MEK unit had set up at the end of the street. The first thing Fabel had arranged was for an MEK weapons support unit to be deployed. Fabel had often wondered if there was ever really a distinction between a terrorist and a serial killer: both killed in volume, both worked to an abstract agenda that was often impossible for others to understand. Brandt, however, had blurred the distinction between them like no other. His crimes of vengeance were carried out with the ritualistic symbolism of a florid psychosis, yet he coolly planted sophisticated bombs to dispose of anyone who presented a threat. And when Brandt had called Fabel on his cellphone to tell him he was sitting on a bomb, he had used voice-altering technology, just in case Fabel recognised his voice from their previous brief encounter down at the HafenCity site.

The address that Franz Brandt had given was a four-storey apartment block with an entrance directly onto the street, limiting the opportunity to storm the apartment with complete surprise.

'Get your men to cover the back,' Fabel told the MEK commander. 'This guy doesn't think we suspect him yet and I've got a legitimate reason for questioning him again about his mother's death. That's if she *was* his natural mother. I'll take two of my team up with me to his door.'

'Given what you've told me about this guy, I don't think that's advisable,' said the MEK commander. 'Especially if he is as skilled as he appears to be with explosives. I've contacted the bomb squad and they've got a unit on the way. I say we wait until they get here, then my guys go in with bomb-squad support.'

Fabel was about to protest when the MEK commander cut him short. 'You and your team can follow us in but, if you insist on going it alone, you could end up with dead officers.'

The MEK man's statement stung Fabel. He had been there before, facing down a dangerous opponent in a confined environment. And it had cost lives.

'Okay,' he sighed. 'But I need this guy alive.'

The MEK commander's expression darkened. 'That's what we always aim to achieve, Herr Chief Commissar. But this person is obviously a professional terrorist. It's not always that easy.'

Fabel, Maria, Werner, Anna and Henk were all given bulletproof body armour and followed on as the MEK team of four officers and a bomb-disposal specialist made their way along the front of the building, moving in their practised crouching run, keeping their profiles low and their bodies pressed close to the apartment block wall. After they entered the building, the MEK commander indicated with a hand gesture that Fabel and his officers were to stay in the lobby, while the special-weapons team went up the stairs. Fabel found it remarkable that a team of heavily built, heavily armed men, bulked up with body armour, could move with such stealth.

The quiet weighed heavily on the Murder Commission team in the lobby, then it shattered simultaneously with the door above as the team burst it in. From the hallway Fabel and the others could hear the shouting of the MEK team. Then silence. Fabel indicated to his team to follow him up the stairs, pausing on the landing below. The MEK commander re-emerged from the apartment.

'It's clean. But wait there until the bomb squad check it out.'

At that, a second blue-overalled bomb technician rushed past them and up the stairs.

'The hell with this,' said Fabel. 'Brandt has no idea we're onto him. And this is his girlfriend's apartment. He won't have planted a bomb here. I'm going up.' He took the stairs two at a time, following the bomb technician into the apartment, brushing aside the protests of the MEK commander. Werner gave a shrug and went after his boss, followed by Maria, Anna and Henk.

The apartment was small and everything about the decor and the furnishings suggested a feminine environment. Fabel guessed that Brandt did not spend a lot of time here. It had also been clear that the young archaeologist did not use the room at his mother's house that much, and the thought crossed Fabel's mind that Brandt perhaps had another place, a bolt-hole that they did not know about. There was not a lot of point in hanging around: the small flat was overfull with officers and Fabel knew at first glance that there was nothing to be gained by searching the place, although he would have to go through the motions of getting a forensics team in as soon as the flat was given the all-clear.

Maria's cellphone rang. She struggled to hear the caller over the bustle in the apartment and stepped out into the hall.

It was one of those moments in which a thousand thoughts, a thousand outcomes, flash through one's mind in a time too small to be measured. It started with one of the bomb technicians suddenly holding a hand up, his back to the rest of the police officers, and shouting a single word: 'Quiet!'

It was then that Fabel heard it. A beeping noise. The second bomb specialist moved over to the first and removed his helmet, turning his ear to the sound. Everyone turned at the same moment, following the gaze of the bomb-squad men.

It sat on top of the CD player. At first glance it looked like simply another piece of audio equipment: a small grey metal box with a red light that flashed in time with the beeping sound.

As Fabel stared at the device, hypnotised by the red light flashing in rhythm with the beeps, he wondered why he was standing stock-still and not running for his life.

It was then that the beeping changed to a constant tone, and the red light on the bomb's detonator stopped flashing and remained on.

## 2.20 p.m.: Eimsbüttel, Hamburg

When Maria Klee stepped back into the apartment, her cellphone still in her hand, the faces that turned towards her seemed drained of both their colour and expression.

'I miss something?' she asked.

'Not exactly,' said Fabel. 'I think that something just missed us.'

The bomb-disposal technician stood with the grey metal detonator box clutched in his black-gloved hand, its wires trailing. When the light had turned to a constant red he had lunged forward and simply yanked the detonator and its wires free. 'Nothing to lose,' he explained afterwards. His colleague was now carefully taking the CD player and amplifier from the shelves.

'Got it,' he said, easing a small plastic-wrapped grey package from behind the unit. 'It's safe.'

'Well done,' said Fabel to the first technician. 'If you hadn't moved so quickly . . .'

The bomb-squad man shook his head. 'I'm afraid I can't take credit for that. I acted more from a reflex than anything else. It would have been impossible for me to move fast enough to disconnect the detonator in time. It was the device itself that failed. Misfired for some reason or other. My guess is that there was a fault in the detonator. I think it's unlikely that the wires worked loose – from what I gather about the bomb under your car, this guy is pretty meticulous.'

The other technician carefully lowered the package of explosives into a thick-walled container. 'The mass of the device was enough to kill everyone inside the flat, but it would not have compromised the integrity of the structure, other than blowing the windows halfway to Buxtehude.'

'I guess I really did miss something,' said Maria.

'Who was that on the phone?' asked Fabel.

'Oh . . . it was Frank. I mean Frank Grueber. He's back from the murder scene at Brandt's mother's house. He took some hair from Brandt's bedroom. From a hairbrush. He managed to rush a DNA analysis to see if there is a familial link between his hair and the ancient hair.'

'And?'

'Enough common markers to suggest a very close

relationship. Probably father and son. It looks like we've found Red Franz junior.'

There is a weariness that comes after being in a situation of great danger and threat. The adrenalin that has coursed through the body lingers and sucks up every last bit of energy. Muscles that have done nothing but have been drawn as taut as violin strings begin to ache and a jittery, nauseating exhaustion settles into the brain and body. As Fabel made his way back to his car, he felt totally spent.

Werner placed his reassuring bulk into the passenger seat of Fabel's BMW. The two men sat for a moment, not speaking.

'I'm getting too old for this crap,' he said. 'I really thought we'd had it in there. I've never been so scared in my life.'

Fabel sighed. 'Unfortunately, Werner, I have been. That's the third time I've been at the business end of a bomb and I've had enough. All I have ever wanted to do was to protect people. That's what being a policeman has always meant to me – putting ourselves between the ordinary man, woman or child and danger. Years ago, when Renate and I were still together and Gabi was a kid, we went over to the United States for a holiday. New York. I remember seeing an NYPD police car go by. It said, in English, *"To Protect and Serve"* on the side. I remember thinking then that we should put that on all Polizei Hamburg cars. I thought: that's what I do, what I am.'

'Jan,' said Werner, 'it's been a hell of a long day. Let me drive. I'll take you home.'

'What are we doing here, Werner? Some lunatic is wreaking revenge on people who conspired to kill

410

others twenty years ago. A murderer killing murderers. You have to admit it, there is some kind of natural justice at work here. Our country was almost ripped apart by these wankers. I still have bullet fragments in me from an eighteen-year-old girl's gun. And for what? What was achieved by Franz Weber's death? By me blowing the face off a young girl who should have had her head filled by nothing more than boys and what she should wear to the disco? She would have been thirty-eight now, Werner. If I hadn't killed her. If Svensson hadn't got his claws into her, she would have been running her kids to school. She would have been going to the gym three times a week to try to reduce her waist. And maybe, now and again, she would have thought to herself, wasn't I mad when I was young? What was I thinking about? She would have had kids, Werner. An entire generation has been wiped out because I squeezed a trigger.'

'It's what we do, Jan,' said Werner. 'If you hadn't been there during that bank raid, someone else would have died. Maybe many more people.'

'I want a new life, Werner. A life away from all of this. I have told van Heiden that this case will be my last. It is over – I am resigning from the Polizei Hamburg as soon as this bastard is behind bars. An old schoolfriend has offered me a job. I am going to take it.'

'You can't be serious, Jan. I don't care what you say, we would never have had the number of convictions we have had if you had not been in charge. And, for all your talk about death, every time you've put a killer away you have saved God knows how many lives.'

'Maybe that's true, Werner. But it's time for

someone else to do it.' Fabel smiled a weary, sad smile at his friend. 'My mind's made up. Anyway, let's get back to the Presidium. I've got a job to finish first.'

Fabel had just turned the ignition key when he felt the weight of Werner's hand on his arm. When Fabel turned to him, Werner was looking directly ahead through the windscreen, as if hypnotised by something.

'Tell me I'm not seeing things,' said Werner, nodding towards the police cordon.

Fabel followed his gaze. A young couple was remonstrating with a uniformed officer and the man was pointing towards the apartment building.

Fabel and Werner threw open the car doors at the same time and started sprinting across to where Franz Brandt stood arguing with the policeman.

### 9.30 p.m.: Police Presidium, Hamburg

Fabel had led the questioning of Franz Brandt. Anna and Henk had taken his girlfriend, Lisa Schubert, into another interview room. Franz Brandt had responded to Fabel's questions with confused disbelief, then distress and, eventually, raw and bitter anger. He claimed to know nothing about the bomb in Schubert's apartment and became increasingly incensed by the suggestion that he was in any way involved in his mother's death. After Fabel suspended the interview and Brandt was removed to a cell, he spoke with Anna and Henk, who confirmed that Lisa Schubert had responded similarly. She had even shown signs of mild shock.

Fabel did not like it. Brandt had been so clever and so careful throughout his campaign. He had seemed always to be a step ahead. It just did not fit for him to adopt such a thoughtless strategy of transparent denial. But, there again, he was clearly mad to have committed the crimes that he had.

Fabel went back to his office. He had sent Maria home earlier: she had started to look really unwell and her headache had not lifted. Anna and Henk had stayed on. The warrant had come through and Anna had secured the codes and passwords with which to access the social-services records; they were now focused on establishing as a legal fact that Franz Brandt was the ten-year-old boy who had watched Red Franz Mühlhaus die on Nordenham railway station. The boy who had heard his father with his dying words call for revenge on those who had betrayed him. After they came out of the interview, Fabel told Werner he could go home and get some rest, but he had said that he had 'stuff to do' in the office first.

Fabel took the Ingrid Fischmann file out of the drawer and laid it on his desk. As he did so, he sighed the sigh of a man going over old ground again in search of answers.

### 9.30 p.m.: Osdorf, Hamburg

Grueber had given Maria two codeine before he had gone to take a shower. She went into the vast kitchen for a glass of water to take them with.

What had started as a vague general headache had found its focus and become a sharp migraine that pressed mercilessly behind Maria's retinas. She had always had a thing about taking headache pills: a hint of the austere Lutheran within telling her it was better to let nature take its course. But water and North German Puritanism alone were not going to fix this one. She took a tumbler from a kitchen cabinet and filled it with water. As she turned the glass slipped from her hand and shattered on the tiled kitchen floor. Maria cursed and looked around for where she might find a pan and brush. She found them in the under-sink cupboard, where Grueber obviously kept cleaning materials.

There was something about the container, shoved to the back of the cupboard and facing away from the door, that drew Maria's attention. She had the feeling that it had been deliberately put out of sight, out of reach. And that was why she knelt down on the hard kitchen tiles and stretched into the cupboard to pull the container out.

Hair dye.

It was the craziest conclusion to draw, and it burned in her mind only for a split second: her brain ran a slide show of the murder scenes, with the severed scalps soaked in red dye. And Grueber standing there, in his forensic overalls, holding the hair dye in his hand. Then it was gone. It was a mad thought: what possible connection could Frank have to the victims? She looked again at the plastic bottle. It was dark brunette; not red. She sighed and started to put it back but paused, bringing it out to re-examine it. It was Grueber's hair colour. Very dark brunette. Almost black. Frank dyed his hair?

Maria replaced the container at the back of the cupboard, the label facing away as she had found it, and she put back the other items that had originally obscured it from view. She allowed herself a smile at her boyfriend's vanity. Why did he dye his hair? Was it that he had gone prematurely grey? Maria had seen the photographs of his parents who both had the same dark hair as Grueber but had not gone white before their time as far as she could see. Unless, of course, they too dyed their hair. She stared in at the hair dye under the sink for a moment. Maria could not understand why such a small mystery was causing a fluttering of unease deep within. It had been hidden. Maybe it belonged to a former girlfriend. But why had he placed it where he had, rather than throwing it out?

Maria stood up and her heel crunched on a fragment of broken glass. He was there when she turned around. Standing close. Too close. He was standing where Vitrenko stood in her dreams. His eyes were totally different in colour and in shape, but for the first time ever Maria could see they held the same emotionless, callous cruelty.

She knew. She smiled at Grueber and said light-heartedly, 'I didn't see you there. You gave me a fright.' But she knew.

Frank Grueber offered a cold, sterile reflection of Maria's smile. He reached out his hand and stroked back a short strand of blonde hair from Maria's brow.

'Do you remember the first time we met?' he said.

Maria nodded. 'You were processing that body in Sternschanzen Park. Fabel was away and I was leading the investigation . . .' Maria smiled again. She tried to look relaxed. Her gun was out in the hall where she had left it on the antique hallstand. So many antiques in this house. Everything was to do with the past.

'That's right.' Grueber continued to stroke her hair, her cheek, his gaze empty and focused somewhere and sometime else. 'I remember the very first time I saw you. After a single second everything was locked into my head, every feature, every gesture. It was as though I recognised you. As though we had known each other before but couldn't remember where and when. Did you feel like that?'

Maria thought about lying, but shrugged instead. She tried to work out the distance to the kitchen door, then to the hallstand, then the time to unholster her gun and take the safety off. If she hit him hard enough . . .

Grueber smiled. He took his other hand from behind his back and raised Maria's gun, pressing it gently into the soft flesh under her jaw.

'I love you, Maria. I don't want to hurt you, but if I must, I must. It means that we will have to wait until our next lives to see each other again.'

Maria tilted her head back, but Grueber maintained the gun barrel's pressure, placing his other hand on the nape of her neck, cradling the back of her head. 'Don't do anything stupid, Maria. I'm quite capable of killing us both. Please don't force me. We've died together once before. On a railway platform a long, long time ago. But this is not our time. Not yet.'

'Why, Frank? Why did you kill all those people?'

Grueber smiled. 'Come, Maria. You still haven't seen everything there is to the house.'

## 9.45 p.m.: Police Presidium, Hamburg

Anna Wolff arched her back and rubbed her eyes. She needed a break from the computer screen. She had spent the last hour going through the social-services records to find where and when Beate Brandt had adopted Franz. There was nothing. She went out into the hall and got herself a coffee from the machine. A couple of other Murder Commission officers came along and she chatted to them for a while, deliberately putting off going back to the computer screen and the endless names in the archive.

She had just headed back into the office when Henk came in.

'How's it going?' he asked. Anna grimaced.

'It's not. I can't find any record of Brandt going into care or of his adoption by Beate Brandt.'

'That's because I think we've been looking at the whole thing the wrong way round.' Henk sat on the edge of Anna's desk. There was a hint of triumph in his smile. 'I think we'd better go and see Fabel.'

### 9.55 p.m.: Osdorf, Hamburg

Maria's brain processed all the available data at the highest possible speed. She tried to draw a curtain across the panic that hammered to get in and assessed her situation. Grueber had told her that she had to put her hands behind her back, presumably to allow him to bind her. Then she would be powerless. But she had good reason to believe that, despite his insanity and despite the extreme violence and ritualistic mutilation of his victims, he didn't intend to kill her. She was not part of his string. Not a victim on his list. But there had been others who had got in the way: Ingrid Fischmann and Leonard Schüler. Grueber had killed them despite them not being on his list. He had even scalped Schüler to make a point by sticking his scalp to Fabel's window.

Maria remembered the call that Grueber had made to her cellphone when she had been at the apartment of Franz Brandt's girlfriend. He had set it up so that she would step out of the apartment while he remotely detonated the bomb inside. He had wanted her to live.

She did what Grueber asked and placed her hands behind her back. He bound her wrists with rope and she knew that he must have put the gun down, on the kitchen counter. For a split second she measured her chances of knocking him off balance and seizing the gun. But then she felt the rough bite of the rope as it tightened against her skin.

Grueber took Maria by the arm, not roughly, and led her out of the kitchen, along the hall to where the stairway rose up from the entrance vestibule. There was a low-arched doorway beneath the stairway which Grueber had previously told Maria led to a cellar crammed with storage boxes. He indicated with a wave of Maria's gun that she should step back from him while he recovered the key from his pocket. He opened the door, reached in and switched on a light before beckoning for Maria to precede him into the cellar.

As she did so, she began bitterly to regret not having taken her chances before he had tied her hands.

## 10.00 p.m.: Police Presidium, Hamburg

Fabel was sitting at his desk, staring at a photograph and trying to wrest its true meaning from it, when his phone rang. It was Susanne phoning from her flat and Fabel was, for a moment, a little fazed.

'Are you okay?' she asked. 'You sound strange.'

'I'm fine,' he said, still looking at the picture on his desk. 'Just tired.'

'When will you be home?'

'I don't know,' said Fabel, 'I'm completely bogged down with stuff here. I reckon I won't be through until pretty late on. There's no point in waiting up for me. In fact, it's probably better if I stay at my place tonight. It'll save me disturbing you when I get in.'

'Okay,' she said and there was a hint of uncertainty in her voice. 'I'll see you tomorrow, then. You sure you're all right?'

'I'm fine. Don't worry about me. I just need to get some sleep. Listen, I'd better get on . . . I'll see you tomorrow.'

Fabel hung up and left his hand resting on the phone. He remembered having had so many similar telephone conversations with his wife, Renate. Late-night calls from the Murder Commission, or a murder scene, or a morgue. He had made too many such calls and his marriage and his wife's fidelity had been steadily eroded by them.

But this time he had been less than honest with Susanne about his reasons for not coming over. Tonight he needed to be alone, he needed his own time and space to think about things. He felt buried under an unbearable weight that could not be shifted with a single huge effort. It was like rubble that he had to dig himself out from under, piece by piece.

And one of the pieces lay on the desk before him.

Everyone has a past. Everyone has been someone else once. It was the thought that had occurred to him as he had looked at the family photograph of the young, pre-terrorist Franz Mühlhaus; when Anna had described the photograph of the newly married Ulrike Meinhof. A life before the life we know.

Fabel had spent the last two hours going through

419

the file that Ingrid Fischmann had sent him immediately before her death. He had spread the contents out over his desk: press cuttings, interviews, a chronology charting the evolution and diversification of protest, activist and terrorist groups, photocopies from books of German domestic terrorism.

And photographs.

The picture itself had nothing to do with the case he was investigating. And it had nothing to do with what had happened to him twenty years ago. It had to do with something, and someone, totally different.

Fabel had found the photograph, with a sticker note attached to the back, at the end of Fischmann's file. It dated from 1990, a time when the will and the *raison d'être* of Left-wing activism was waning fast. The Wall had just come down and two former Germanys were still embracing each other with enthusiasm and hope. It was a time when the world watched millions across Eastern Europe rise in true protest against communist dictatorships. The old slogans of Left-wing activism had begun to ring hollow; even to sound embarrassing.

The caption attached to the photograph read: 'Christian Wohlmut, Munich-based anarchist, wanted on suspicion of attacks on US governmental and commercial interests within the Federal Republic. Photographed with unknown female.'

Unknown female. The photograph was blurry and looked as if it had been taken from some distance. The girl, about the right age to be a student, was to the left and slightly to the rear of Wohlmut. She was tall and slim and had long dark hair, but her features were out of focus. But recognisable. To someone who knew her.

Fabel read the file associated with Wohlmut. It

had been the last twitching of a dying movement. He had formed a group that had eventually fizzled out, but not before they had planted a couple of crude devices in American targets. A letter bomb had taken the fingers off the right hand of a nine-teen-year-old secretarial worker in the offices of an American oil company. Wohlmut had been caught and had spent three years in prison.

Fabel looked again at the tall girl with the long dark hair. Wohlmut was talking to someone off camera, and the girl beside him was listening intently. As she did so, she held her head at a distinctive angle. A pose of concentration.

Everyone has a past. Everyone was someone else once. There was a knock at the door and he slipped the photograph back to the bottom of the file.

Anna and Henk came in.

## 10.00 p.m.: Osdorf, Hamburg

There were no storage boxes in Grueber's cellar. There was no disorder.

The cellar was vast: out of proportion with the small understairs door that served it. Maria scanned the walls to see if she could locate a window or door that opened out directly onto the outside world. But she knew they were too deep. She thought of how the dying evening sun would be dappling the lawn through the bushes and plants of Grueber's garden. Suddenly Maria became aware of the mass of the house above her; the dark soil that lay, cold and pressing, beyond the cellar walls that surrounded her.

The cellar had a surprising amount of headroom, she guessed somewhere just under two metres, and it had been kitted out as a working environment by Grueber. There were benches and equipment along the walls, bookshelves and metal tool cabinets. She heard a continuous metallic whirring and noticed a large brushed-steel housing bolted to one wall with a fan spinning behind a mesh protector. Maria guessed that Grueber had installed some kind of temperature- and humidity-control system. The space of the cellar was broken up by a series of heavy square pillars that clearly supported the walls above. In the centre of the cellar, four pillars served as the corners of an area that was shielded off in what looked like an improvised clean room, with semi-opaque heavy-duty plastic sheeting providing the walls. Maria felt her fear ratchet up several notches: it was clear that this area had a special purpose and she had a sickening feeling that that purpose might have something to do with her immediate future.

Grueber seemed to sense her fear. He frowned and there was both anger and sadness in his expression. He reached out and stroked her cheek.

'I'm not going to hurt you, Maria,' he said. 'I would never, *ever* hurt you. I am not a psychopath. I don't kill without reason. You should realise that by now. I have been given the gift to see through the veils that separate each life, each existence. And because of that I value life more – not less. The ones who died . . . they deserved it. But not you. And not Fabel. That's why I didn't detonate the bomb I planted in his car. You see, we are all bound together. In each life, we all come together again to resolve that which has been left over from our last incarnation. You, me, Fabel – we have all been here before and we shall be here again. Don't worry, Maria. I won't hurt you. It's just that I can't let you disturb what must happen tonight. Tonight my vengeance shall be complete.'

'Frank,' said Maria. 'No more killing. Let it end here. I'll look after you. I'll help you.'

Grueber smiled at her again. 'Sweet Maria, you don't understand, do you? All that I have learned in this lifetime, all the skills I have gained, have been acquired so that I can finish what I must finish tonight.' He took her by the arm and led her over to the thick semi-opaque sheets.

'I'll give you an example of what I'm talking about. You have seen my reconstruction work. Where I rebuild the dead, applying layer on layer, giving flesh and substance and skin to them. Restoring their identity. Well, I can do the same in reverse – removing the layers from the living. Destroying their identity . . .'

Grueber pulled back the thick plastic curtain. Maria heard a shrill sound fill the cellar and realised it was her own scream.

### 10.03 p.m.: Police Presidium, Hamburg

'Henk's found something out,' said Anna.

'Okay,' said Fabel, leaning back in his chair. 'Let's have it . . .'

'Like you asked, we've been going over Brandt's history and that of his mother, Beate. Frank Grueber over at forensics has, as you already know, confirmed Franz Brandt's paternity. He is definitely the son of Franz Mühlhaus.'

'Tell me something I don't know,' said Fabel wearily.

'Franz Mühlhaus may have been his father, but he was not adopted by Beate Brandt.' Henk dropped a photocopy onto Fabel's desk. 'Birth certificate for Franz Karl Brandt. Father unknown. Mother Beate Maria Brandt, at that time resident at twenty-two Hubertusstrasse, Niendorf, Hamburg. She didn't adopt him. He told us the truth: she is his natural mother. He maybe doesn't even know that Red Franz Mühlhaus is his natural father. There is absolutely nothing to link Beate Brandt to Red Franz Mühlhaus or to suggest that she was a radical of any kind in the nineteen seventies or nineteen eighties. But the DNA proves that she had a child with him.

'Where that leaves us is with Franz Brandt being Mühlhaus's son. But *not* Michaela Schwenn's son. And that, in turn, means he wasn't the small boy on the platform in Nordenham with his hair dyed black.'

'A brother?'

'We know that Mühlhaus had sexual relationships with many of his female followers, as well as with other women who may not have been connected to his movement. It could be that our killer is a half-brother who Brandt probably doesn't even know exists,' said Anna.

'But wait a minute,' said Fabel. 'You're forgetting that Brandt left a bomb in his girlfriend's apartment to blow us all to pieces.'

'And then he and his girlfriend walk straight into our hands,' said Henk. 'You said yourself that it seemed strange. My guess is that he didn't know anything about the bomb.'

'*Shit*,' said Fabel, in English. 'That means the killer is still out there. We have to find out what happened to that kid on the platform.'

'That's what I meant when I said we were coming at it from the wrong direction,' said Henk. 'We were trying to prove that Brandt was the son we were looking for. Working the connection backwards. We'll have to check the adoption files again. This time searching for the surname Schwenn.'

'I have the access codes here.' Anna waved her notebook. 'May I use your computer?'

Pushing Ingrid Fischmann's information file to one side, Fabel stood up and let Anna take his seat. She logged onto the database and entered her search criteria: the name 'Schwenn' and the time-frame of 1985 to 1988.

'Got it!' she said. 'I've got four names here. Two are nineteen eighty-six adoptions. It'll be one of these . . .' Anna clicked on the first file. 'Nope – this is a four-year-old girl.' She clicked on the next. 'This is a possible . . . no . . . the age is wrong.' She hit the third file.

It was Anna's expression that shook Fabel. He had expected her usual grin of insolent satisfaction at having nailed a crucial piece of evidence. But she stood up suddenly and Fabel noticed that her face had drained of colour.

'What is it, Anna?' asked Fabel.

'Maria . . .' It was as if every muscle in Anna's face had pulled itself taut. 'Where is Maria?'

'I sent her home. She had a migraine,' said Fabel. 'She'll be back tomorrow morning.'

'We've got to find her, *Chef*. We've got to find her *now*.'

### 10.05 p.m.: Osdorf, Hamburg

'Fascinating, is it not?'

Maria did not hear Grueber's question. Her ears seemed to ring, every nerve seemed to burn as she

425

looked down at the male body lying on the metal trestle table. It was naked. Naked not only of clothes, but also of skin. It was sculpted from raw, red sinew. Small round droplets of blood dotted the aluminium surface of the table that supported it.

'I have invested heavily in making this working environment perfect.' Grueber did not rant nor rave. Maria gauged the scale of his madness from his measured, conversational tone. 'I spent a fortune on soundproofing this cellar. The contractors were told that I would be operating noisy equipment down here. That is why I have had to install the air pump and temperature control. When the door is closed, this is totally airtight and soundproof. Which is just as well, because he' – Grueber indicated the figure on the table, stripped of its skin, of its humanity – 'screamed like a girl.'

Maria's head pounded and she felt sick.

'Oh, sorry – this is Cornelius Tamm.' Grueber apologised as if he had forgotten to introduce someone at a cocktail party. 'You know, the singer.'

'Why?' Maria found the word from somewhere.

'Why? Why did I do this? Because he betrayed me. They all did. They did a deal with the fascist authorities and sold me. My life. Piet van Hoogstraat was the only other person the police knew about, so they sent him to identify me. But it was Paul Scheibe who negotiated it all, from a safe distance. The others went along with it. Even Cornelius. My friend.' He turned to Maria. There was the hint of tears in his eyes. 'I died, Maria. I died.' He rested a hand on his chest. 'I can still feel where the bullets hit me. I saw you die, and then I died, kneeling on that railway platform.'

'What are you talking about? What do you mean, you died? Who do you think you are, Frank?'

Grueber straightened his back. 'I am Red Franz. I am eternal. I have lived for nearly two thousand years. And probably before that, but I cannot yet remember. I was a warrior who gave up his life as a sacrifice for his people, for the Earth to renew. Twice. Once over a millennium and a half ago, the second time as Red Franz Mühlhaus.'

'Red Franz Mühlhaus?' said Maria incredulously. 'Without even getting into the whole reincarnation thing, your arithmetic is all wrong. You were born long before Mühlhaus died.'

'You don't understand.' He smiled patronisingly. 'I was the father *and* the son. My lifetimes overlapped. I saw my own death from two perspectives. I am my own father.'

'Oh. I see. I'm sorry, Frank.' Maria understood it all now. 'Red Franz Mühlhaus was your father?'

'We were always on the run. Always. We had to dye our hair. Black.' Grueber ran a hand through his thick, too-dark hair. 'Everyone would notice our red hair otherwise. And then we were betrayed. My mother and father were both murdered by GSG Nine troops. A sacrifice organised by those traitors. I watched my father die. I heard him say "traitors". I was taken away after that. The Gruebers adopted me. They had no children. They couldn't have them. But they brought me up as if the first ten years of my life hadn't happened. As if I was their own and always had been. After a while, even I started to feel like all that had happened before had just been a bad dream. I found I couldn't remember things. It was like all that life was being wiped out. Erased.'

'What happened, Frank? What happened to change you?'

'I was at university, studying archaeology. I visited

the Landesmuseum in Hanover. It was there that I saw him. Red Franz. He was lying in a display case, his face rotted almost to nothing, but with that glorious mane of red hair still intact. I just knew, in that instant, that I was looking at the remains of a body that I had once occupied. I realised that we can look upon ourselves as we once were. As we lived before. It was then that it all came back to me. I remembered my father telling me that he had hidden a box in an old archaeological site. He had told me that if anything ever happened to him, I was to find the box and I would know the truth.'

Grueber let the thick plastic sheeting fall to veil the horror of Cornelius Tamm's flayed body. He walked over to one of the cabinets ranged along the cellar wall. When he turned his back, Maria struggled furiously to free her hands from the rope bonds. But they were too well tied. Grueber took a rusted metal box from the cabinet.

'My father's secret diary and details of his group. I remembered where he'd said it was hidden. Exactly. I went and dug it up and it told me the whole story. And it gave me the names of all the traitors.' Grueber paused. 'But it was more than my memory of my childhood that returned that day as I looked down on Red Franz. It was my *whole* memory. My memory of all that went before this life. I knew that the body I looked at had once been mine. That I had inhabited it more than one and a half thousand years ago. I also knew that I had inhabited my father's body. That the father and the son were one. The same.'

'Frank . . .' Maria looked at the pale, boyish face. She remembered how she had christened him 'Harry Potter' when they had first met. How she had always seen him as a good man. A kind man. 'You're ill.

You are suffering from delusions. We only live once, Frank. You have got things all ... *muddled* in your head. I understand. I really do. Seeing your parents killed like that. Listen, Frank, I want to help you. I *can* help you. Just untie me.'

Grueber smiled. He eased Maria over to a chair and made her sit.

'I know you mean well,' he said. 'And I know that when you say you want to help me it's the truth, not some kind of ploy. But tonight, Maria, the biggest traitor of them all is going to die. He was my closest friend, my deputy in The Risen. He planned the Wiedler kidnap. It was he who pulled the trigger that killed Wiedler. An event he has tried to bury, along with me. He saw me as a hindrance to his political ambitions. Ambitions he continues to follow. But tonight those ambitions, and his life, will come to an end. I can't let you interfere with what I have to do tonight. Maria. I'm sorry, but I can't ...'

Grueber took a roll of heavy-duty packing tape and wrapped it around Maria's torso and the back of the chair. Binding her tight. 'I really can't allow you to stop me ...' he said, reaching for the velvet roll-pouch.

### 10.30 p.m.: Osdorf, Hamburg

Fabel and Werner pulled up outside Grueber's house. The two silver and blue Polizei Hamburg cars behind them had killed their flashing lights at the corner and parked behind Fabel. Four uniformed officers got out.

Werner's cellphone rang as they all gathered on the pavement. After a brief series of one-word answers, Werner hung up and turned to Fabel.

'That was Anna. She and Henk weren't able to get Maria on her cellphone or on her home number. They've checked out her apartment. Nobody home. They're on their way over here.' Werner looked up at the substantial bulk of Grueber's villa. 'If Maria's anywhere, she's in there . . .'

'Okay.' Fabel turned to the uniformed officers. 'Two of you take the back. You two, come with us.'

The main entrance to Grueber's house was made of oak and had the shape and substance of a church door. It was clear that it would not yield easily to a ram, so Fabel ordered the uniforms to smash one of the huge rectangular windows. He roughly recalled the layout from his brief stay as Grueber's guest and guided them round to Grueber's study.

'When we smash the window, we need to get in and find Maria as fast as we can.'

At Fabel's signal, the two uniformed policeman swung the door-ram hard and fast into the centre of the window, shattering the glass and the wooden ribs that held the panes in place. The space it cleared was not enough to allow a man to enter and they swung the ram twice more. Fabel unholstered his service automatic and climbed through the shattered window, clambering over Grueber's desk and sending the reconstructed head of the girl who was two and a half thousand years old tumbling to the floor. Werner and the two uniforms followed him.

Ten minutes later they stood in the main hallway, at the foot of the stairs. They had checked every room, every cupboard. Nothing. Fabel even called out Maria's name into the void of a house that he knew to be empty.

There was a knock on the front door and Fabel opened it, letting the other two uniformed officers in.

'We've checked the gardens and garage. There's no one there, Herr Chief Commissar.'

A car pulled up outside and Anna and Henk came running into the hallway.

'Nothing . . .' Fabel said grimly. 'He's obviously taken her with him.'

'Herr Chief Commissar!' one of the uniformed officers called from behind the ornate stairway. 'There's some kind of door here. It could be a cellar . . .'

### 10.40 p.m.

Frank Grueber had thrived on knowledge all his life. He had formally studied archaeology and history, but had spent so much of his spare time learning a multitude of disparate skills. His wealthy step-parents had provided him with the means to turn his entire life into one continuous training programme; an endless preparation for his life's mission. Now, as he stood outside the home of his ultimate target, the sense of convergence was at its strongest. Overwhelming.

Grueber stood on the driveway to the house, the roll-pouch in one hand, Maria's service pistol in the other, closing his eyes and taking a long, slow, deep breath. He let every emotion drain from his body. He allowed the great calm to descend on him: the calm that would allow him to act with perfect precision and deadly efficiency.

*Zanshin.*

### 10.40 p.m.: Osdorf, Hamburg

The small locked door was made of the same heavy oak as the entrance and would not yield to the kicks of the police officers. It was only after several hard slams with the door-ram that it eventually gave way.

'Maria!' Fabel called as he struggled through the door and into the cellar.

'Over here!'

Fabel followed her voice, running through the vast cellar. He found her bound to the chair, close to the plastic-curtained area.

'Grueber . . .' she said. 'It's Frank. He's mad. He thinks he's Red Franz Mühlhaus reincarnated – I think he really may be Mühlhaus's son.'

'He is,' said Fabel, untying Maria's hands and struggling with the parcel tape. He jerked his head questioningly towards the enclosed plastic-screened area.

'Cornelius Tamm,' she said. Fabel used a penknife to cut the tape. Maria stood up. 'Trust me, Jan. It's not pleasant. But you have to leave that for now . . . He's going after his last victim.'

'Who?'

'Bertholdt Müller-Voigt. Frank said he was going after the most senior member of the group after Mühlhaus. He also said that he was a politician. Look over there. That box. Mühlhaus buried it and told Frank where to find it after his death. It has all the names.'

Fabel opened the box. There were several note-books, a diary, a small plastic bag, a photograph and a ledger. They were all bound in brown leather that had tarnished with being buried in the damp earth. Fabel examined the photograph. A family snap: Mühlhaus, a woman with long, bone-coloured hair whom Fabel assumed was Michaela Schwenn, and a boy of about nine, clearly Grueber. But it was the woman who captured Fabel's attention.

'Shit, Maria,' said Fabel, handing the photograph to her. 'Michaela Schwenn – she could be you . . . the similarity is amazing . . .'

Maria stared at the image. Fabel went through the rest of the box's contents. He lifted out the plastic bag and saw that it contained a thick lock of hair. Red hair. Grueber had placed one hair at each scene, and when the forensic team had missed the hair in Hauser's bathroom the first time round, Grueber had moved it to where it could be found. Fabel flicked through each of the notebooks, scanning the information as quickly as he could to try to find the information he needed. Then he found it.

'Let's go!' He started towards the cellar door, ordering two uniformed officers to stay and preserve the scene. 'You've got the wrong politician, Maria – and I think I know where he's taking him.'

For a moment, Maria continued to stare at the image of a woman who looked just like her. Then she dropped the photograph back into the box and followed Fabel out of the cellar.

# 16.

## Twenty-Eight Days After the First Murder: Thursday, 15 September 2005.

### 12.15 a.m.: Nordenham Railway Station, 145 Kilometres West of Hamburg

Fabel had left his car abandoned, skewed at an angle and with the headlights still full on. He and Werner had come round the south end of the station building. Following Fabel's orders, Anna, Maria and Henk drove round to the north end. To Fabel's intense annoyance, the Nordenham uniformed units had announced their arrival from kilometres away, with lights and sirens blazing in the cool night. Three units came around the back and sides of the building, while three more skidded to a halt on the far side of the railway tracks, their headlights trained on the platform and station building.

After the sirens, after the running, after the shouted orders, it suddenly became very quiet. Fabel now stood on the station platform and became very aware of his rapid breathing: he could hear it in the sudden silence; he could see it bloom as grey clouds in the still, thin, chill air. Fabel was filled with a deep sense of unease. There seemed an inevitability, a surreal familiarity in the fact that this group of people should come together in this place at this time. A feeling of destiny fulfilled.

But it was another group of people who had cast the mould for this destiny. It had all been so cleverly organised. No one would look too closely for deeper meaning in the death of a murderer and terrorist. With the demise of Franz Mühlhaus, it would be seen that the head, the brain and the heart of The Risen had been excised. His death meant the death of the organisation. The deal that Paul Scheibe had brokered anonymously with the security services had been that no further inquiries would be made about The Risen. And, of course, there had been a guarantee that The Risen would simply disappear.

The lights of the Nordenham police cars, ranged along the far side of the tracks, illuminated the figures on the platform like players on a stage, their exaggerated shadows cast giant on the façade of the railway station.

Fabel drew his service automatic as he ran towards them.

'I would stop there, if I were you.' Frank Grueber called across to Fabel. The blade in his hand glittered cold and keen in the night. Grueber had forced the man before him to his knees. 'Do you think that I care if I die here, Fabel? I am eternal. There is no such thing as death. There is only forgetting . . . forgetting who you were before.'

Fabel's mind raced through the thousand possible ways this could all end. Whatever his next words were, whatever action he now took, would have consequences; would set in train a sequence of events. And an all too conceivable consequence would be the death of more than one person.

His head ached with the weight of it. The night air that made grey ghosts of his breath felt meagre and sterile in his mouth, as if in coming together to this moment they had reached a great altitude. It seemed as if the air was too thin to carry any sound other than the desperate half-sobbed breathing of the kneeling man. Fabel glanced across at his officers who stood, white-faced in the harsh light, taking aim in the hard, locked-muscle stance of those who stand on the edge of the decision to kill. It was Maria he noticed most: her face bloodless, her eyes glittering ice-blue, the bone and sinew of her hands straining against the taut skin as she gripped her SIG-Sauer automatic.

Fabel made a movement of his head, hoping that his team would interpret it as a signal to hold back.

He stared hard at the man who stood in the centre of the harsh cast light. Fabel and his team had struggled for months to put a name, an identity, to the killer they had hunted. He had turned out to be a man of many names: the name he had given himself in his perverted sense of crusade was 'Red Franz', while the media, in their enthusiastic determination to spread fear and anxiety as far as possible, had christened him the 'Hamburg Hairdresser'. But now Fabel knew his real name. Frank Grueber.

Grueber stood staring back at the headlights with eyes that seemed to shine with an even brighter, even starker, even colder gleam. He held the kneeling man by his hair, angling his head back so that the throat lay exposed and white. Above the throat, above the terror-contorted face, the flesh of the kneeling man's forehead had been sliced across in a straight line the full width of his brow, just below the hairline, and the wound gaped slightly as Grueber yanked the man's head back by the hair. A pulse of blood cascaded

436

down the kneeling man's face and he let out a high, animal yelp.

'For Christ's sake, Fabel.' The kneeling man's voice was tight and shrill with terror. 'Help me . . . Please . . . Help me, Fabel . . .'

Fabel ignored the pleading and kept his gaze locked like a searchlight on Grueber. He held his hand out into empty air, as if halting traffic. 'Easy . . . take it easy. I'm not playing along with any of this. No one here is. We're not going to act out the parts you want us to play. Tonight, history is not going to repeat itself.'

Grueber gave a bitter laugh. The hand that held the knife twitched and again the blade flashed bright and stark.

'Do you honestly think that I am going to walk away? This bastard . . .' He yanked again on the hair and the kneeling man yelped again through a curtain of his own blood. 'This bastard betrayed me and all that we stood for. He thought that my death would buy him a new life. Just like the others did.'

'This is pure fantasy . . .' said Fabel. 'That was not your death.'

'Oh no? Then how is it that you started to doubt what you believe while you searched for me? There is no such thing as death; there's only remembrance. The only difference between me and anyone else is that I have been allowed to remember, like looking through a hall of windows. I remember *everything*.' He paused, the brief silence broken only by the distant sound of a late-night car passing through the town of Nordenham, behind the station and a universe away. 'Of course history will repeat itself. That's what history does. It repeated *me* . . . You're so proud that you studied history in your youth.

But did you ever truly understand it? We're all just variations on the same theme – all of us. What was before will be again. He who was before shall be again. Over and over. History is all about beginnings. History is made, not unmade.'

'Then make it your own history,' said Fabel. 'Change things. Give it up, man. Tonight history *won't* repeat itself. Tonight no one dies.'

Grueber smiled. A smile that was as scalpel-bright and hard and cold as the knife in his hand. 'Really? Then we must see, Herr Chief Commissar.' The blade flashed upwards to the kneeling man's throat.

There was a scream. And the sound of gunfire.

Fabel turned in the direction of the shot in time to see Maria fire again. Her first shot had hit Grueber in the thigh and he had buckled. Her second caught his shoulder and he lost his grip on the kneeling man. Werner rushed forward, grabbed Grueber's captive and pulled him clear.

Maria moved forward, keeping her gun trained on Grueber, who had now sunk to his knees. Her face was streaked with tears.

'No, Frank,' she said. 'Tonight no one dies. I'm not going to let you do that. Drop the knife. There's no one left to hurt.'

Grueber looked at the retreating figures of Werner and the man Grueber had intended to kill. The final sacrifice. He looked up at Maria and smiled. A sad little-boy smile. Then he took a long, deep breath. There was a flashing bright arc as he swung the blade up with both hands and brought it back down with all his strength into his own chest.

'Frank!' Maria screamed and ran forward.

Grueber's head sank slowly forward and down. As he died, he spoke a single word into the night.

'Traitors . . .'

## 1.40 a.m.: Wesermarsch-Klinik Hospital, Nordenham

When Fabel and Werner entered the hospital room on the third floor of the Wesermarsch-Klinik, Criminal Director Horst van Heiden was already there, standing at the bedside of Hamburg's head of government, First Mayor Hans Schreiber. The nurse at the desk had informed Fabel that Schreiber had been given a mild sedative but was otherwise alert.

Schreiber's forehead was covered by a heavy surgical dressing, but Fabel could see that the ridge of his browline had swollen and discoloured in protest at the violence done to his scalp. The rest of his face had a puffed-up appearance and Fabel would hardly have recognised him. Schreiber turned in Fabel's direction but clearly did not have the strength to ease himself up into a sitting position. He smiled weakly.

'I'm glad you're here, Fabel,' said the First Mayor. 'I owe you my thanks.' He paused and corrected himself. 'I owe you my life. If you hadn't got there when you did. If Frau Klee had not fired when she did . . .' He left the thought hanging, to emphasise the unspeakable alternative.

Fabel nodded. 'I was just doing my job.'

Schreiber indicated his bandaged head. 'I'm told that I will need plastic surgery. There's quite a bit of nerve damage, too.' Two uniformed officers entered. Fabel ordered them to take their position outside the room.

'No one is to enter other than the medical professionals directly involved in Herr Schreiber's care,' Fabel said to the two officers as they left.

'My wife will be here later,' said Schreiber.

'No one,' repeated Fabel.

'Surely that isn't necessary, Herr Fabel,' protested Schreiber. 'The danger is past. Grueber is dead and he was clearly acting alone under his own insane agenda.'

'So why did he pick you?' asked Fabel. 'Every other victim was directly connected to Red Franz Mühlhaus and The Risen. Why did he single you out?'

'God knows.' Schreiber's swollen face was incapable of expression but his tone was one of irritation. Fabel half-expected van Heiden to protest at his questioning of the First Mayor, but the Criminal Director remained silent. 'Listen, Fabel,' continued Schreiber. 'I am in too much pain and too exhausted and distressed to psychoanalyse a lunatic who just tried to kill me or to speculate about his motives. He was mad. He also styled himself as a terrorist. I am the head of the Hamburg city and state government. Go and work it out for yourself. After all, that's what I pay you to do.'

'Oh, I have, Herr First Mayor.' Fabel turned to Werner and held out his hand. Werner handed him a clear plastic evidence wallet. Inside was a thick notebook, its leather binding stained with damp and age. 'Red Franz Mühlhaus knew that his time was over. He knew that the authorities would track him down. He was, however, determined that he would not be taken alive. He also had very grave doubts about the loyalty of his followers. Particularly his deputy, whom the journalist Ingrid Fischmann identified as Bertholdt Müller-Voigt. It was also Mühlhaus's deputy who had been the driver of the van that abducted the industrialist, Wiedler, eight years previously. Whereas the rest of the group had disappeared into the undergrowth after the Wiedler kidnapping, Red Franz and the Dutchman, Piet van Hoogstraat, were the only members identifiable by the authorities and were forced to continue to live fugitive lives, funded by their fellow former gang members.'

'Fabel . . .' Schreiber sighed and turned his head painfully in the direction of van Heiden. 'Can we talk about this some other time?'

'That's what happened that day in nineteen eighty-five on the platform in Nordenham,' Fabel continued as if Schreiber had not spoken. 'The Dutchman, van Hoogstraat, did not share Mühlhaus's revolutionary zeal. He was exhausted after nearly a decade of living on the run. He wanted a way out without having to spend the greater part of the remainder of his life behind bars. So a deal was done. A deal to get van Hoogstraat a reduced sentence. A deal conceived by the remaining gang members who wanted to close that chapter in their lives. A deal conceived by Mühlhaus's deputy and brokered anonymously by the group's head of planning, Paul Scheibe. They knew that Mühlhaus would not be taken alive, and that his death would finally close the door on the threat of exposure and arrest. They had already bought the Dutchman's silence with the deal they had done with the authorities, but it was a bonus for them that van Hoogstraat also died on that platform. The silence was total. The Risen would rise no more.'

Fabel paused and looked at the bagged notebook in his hand.

'It's funny,' Fabel said, with a sad half-smile. 'It was Frank Grueber who said to me once that "truth is the debt we owe to the dead."' Fabel moved closer to Schreiber's bed. 'The puzzle is, how did Grueber find out the identities of the former members of The Risen? The only people who knew were the members themselves. If Brandt had been the killer, then it would have made sense – his mother, a former member herself, might have confided in her son. But the secret was so great, so closely guarded, that she didn't even tell Franz Brandt that Mühlhaus was his father. So, how did Frank Grueber discover their identities? After all, he had been adopted when he was eleven and brought up in a different universe with wealthy adoptive parents in Blankenese. His early childhood, constantly on the move, being deprived of any education apart from political brainwashing by his parents, must have seemed like a distant nightmare. But there was one thing he remembered. Like I said, Mühlhaus had not trusted any of his former associates, but there'd been one person he did trust. His son. Franz Mühlhaus was an archaeologist and he must have told the young Frank how the earth protects the truth about the past for future generations. Mühlhaus told his son how he had buried the truth in the earth, carefully wrapped and protected and hidden from the world. He must have made the young Frank memorise the location so that, if Mühlhaus was betrayed, then the others would not be free to live their lives with impunity.'

Hans Schreiber lay still and said nothing, gazing up at the ceiling from beneath his distended brow and swollen eyelids.

'Red Franz Mühlhaus buried this notebook, along with a number of other documents giving detailed accounts of everything that happened during the active life of The Risen. It also meticulously details each member of the group and their special responsibilities. There is a diary, too. I've got someone going through that as we speak. I'm sure we shall uncover a great deal.

'The funny thing is . . . the one name I expected to see on the list isn't there. Bertholdt Müller-Voigt. He wasn't Mühlhaus's deputy. He wasn't even a member of the group. I don't even think he was an active or secret supporter. You see, terrorist organisations like The Risen are like black holes in space. They are small but their mass, their influence on everything around them, is huge. The gravity they generate sucks in everything within reach. Take, for example, a young lawyer and radical journalist who starts out as a broad supporter, then becomes a member. Then the second-in-command. Not Müller-Voigt. His sole connection with The Risen was that, like Mühlhaus, he had a relationship with Beate Brandt. Something that you and Paul Scheibe could not forgive, because you had both been besotted with her. That was why you couldn't resist, twenty years on, conspiring to place evidence in Ingrid Fischmann's hands that would seem to incriminate him. But not enough fully to reignite interest in The Risen. It was a dangerous game to play, particularly when your own wife began to turn up the heat. But the fact is that Müller-Voigt never did cross the line. He cared passionately about the environment and about social justice, but his principles also extended to not taking human life. Ingrid Fischmann got the wrong politician, didn't she, Herr First Mayor?'

'My God, Fabel,' said van Heiden. 'Are you sure about this?'

'There's no doubt. It's all in here.' Fabel held up the notebook. 'And Mühlhaus buried other corroborative evidence with it. We recovered it all from Grueber's cellar. That was how I knew he was going after Schreiber. He had saved the best until the last.'

Werner stepped forward.

'Hans Schreiber, I am arresting you for the kidnap and murder of Thorsten Wiedler, on or sometime after the fourteenth of November nineteen seventy-seven. I'm sure that, as a qualified lawyer, you understand your rights under the Basic Law of the Federal Republic of Germany.'

# Epilogue

# February 2006:
## Six Months After the First Murder.

### Barmbek, Hamburg

Hamburg looked unreal, like some romantic painter's fantasy of a city. The sheer volume of snow had taken the authorities by surprise and it took them some time to clear the main roads and pavements. Then the snow had stopped and the clouds had cleared, but now the temperature had plummeted and the blankets of snow that bedecked the roofs, the parks and the edges of the streets were frozen fast and sparkling under a brilliant blue sky.

The care home in which Frau Pohle lived was in Barmbek, on the far side of the city. Fabel had phoned the home's director, Frau Amberg, to arrange the meeting.

'Frau Pohle is a little confused, Herr Fabel. She finds it difficult to remember things from yesterday, but she has excellent recall of things that happened decades ago. I'm afraid it's typical for the type of incipient dementia that Frau Pohle suffers from. And she can become easily distressed. I am concerned that she may be disturbed by your visit.'

Fabel had then explained that he had uncovered property belonging to Frau Pohle's long-time-missing brother. Frau Amberg had then seemed less reluctant and had arranged a time for him to visit.

Fabel took the bus to Barmbek; partly because of the weather but also because lately he seemed to find excuses for not using his car. He had had his BMW convertible for six years and it had served him well. But since the night when he had spent three hours sitting anchored to his seat while the bomb squad defused the device that Grueber had placed beneath it, he had yet to feel comfortable in it.

As Fabel sat in the bus and watched picture-postcard Hamburg drift by, he considered his mission. He did not know why it had become so important to him to find Karl Heymann's sister and to inform her that her brother's body had been found. He always imagined that she had suffered from the lack of a funeral for her brother and that she could maybe take some solace or comfort from having a place to visit and mourn her sixty-year-old loss. Frank Grueber had got one thing right: truth is the debt we owe to the dead.

Frau Amberg met Fabel on his arrival and led him into a bright day-room that had picture windows that looked out over a large garden with a fountain at its centre. The garden and the fountain were only hinted outlines under the thick, crisp snow.

Frau Pohle sat in a high-backed chair near the window. It saddened Fabel to see how youthful she was for her eighty-eight years: it seemed to him that she had been cheated by the deterioration within, of her mind. She was very smartly dressed and again it pained Fabel to think that she might have deliberately worn her best outfit because she seldom had visitors. As Fabel approached, she smiled at him eagerly. Expectantly.

'Good day, Frau Pohle. My name is Jan Fabel. I've come to talk to you about your brother, Karl.' Fabel extended his hand to shake Frau Pohle's. She grasped it with both of hers.

'Oh, thank you for coming, Herr . . .' Fabel's name had already escaped her. 'I am so glad you came. You must be tired, coming all that way. I have been waiting so long for news of Karl. How is he?' She laughed. 'I'll bet he has an awful American accent by now. You tell him when you see him that I am so angry. I can't remember the last time I heard from him. Please – you sit down and tell me all about Karl's life over there.'

A care assistant arrived with some tea and biscuits and Frau Pohle went on to explain how Karl had always talked about getting away from Germany and going to America before the Nazis could conscript him into the army. She had always known that he had used the confusion of the bombing raid to disappear, to escape. Was Fabel from America and was Karl well?

Despite the profound sadness that filled him, Fabel smiled as he listened to an old woman's fantasy about her brother's survival and his prospering in a far-off land. A fantasy that had sustained Frau Pohle for sixty years; and now, in her fading mind, that fantasy had become a concrete truth.

For fifteen minutes Fabel sat and lied to an old woman. He invented a life and a family that should have been but never was. As he got up to go, Fabel saw the tears in Frau Pohle's eyes and knew that they came from a bitter joy.

'*Goodbye, Mrs Pohle*,' he said in English as he left her sitting by the window that looked out over the snow-covered garden.

Sometimes truth is not the debt we owe the dead.

# *Flesh and Blood*

## John Harvey

Fifteen years ago Susan Blacklock disappeared. Although Detective Inspector Frank Elder has taken early retirement, the case still plagues his mind. Prime suspects, Shane Donald and Alan McKeirnan, were convicted a year later of the brutal rape and murder of a young girl, and now that Shane has been granted parole, Elder feels compelled to revisit the past.

Then Shane disappears and another young girl is murdered. Elder's involvement is now crucial. Taunted by postcards from the killer, an increasingly desperate Elder battles to keep his estranged family from being drawn into the very heart of the crime.

'John Harvey is lights out one of the best and with this book the word is going to spread far and wide'
Michael Connelly

arrow books

ALSO AVAILABLE IN ARROW

# The Skin Gods

### Richard Montanari

Philadelphia is blistering in the summer heat and detectives
Kevin Byrne and Jessica Balzano prowl the streets with growing
unease. Suddenly, a series of crimes shatters the restless city.
A beautiful secretary is slashed to death in a grimy motel
shower; a street hustler brutally murdered with a chainsaw.
Piece by piece, a sickening puzzle presents itself: someone
is recreating famous Hollywood murder scenes and inserting
the clips into videos – for an unsuspecting public to find.

Investigations reveal a violent world of underground film, porno-
graphy and seedy nightclubs, hidden to all but the initiated. None
of The Actor's victims are as innocent as they appear, though,
and Kevin and Jessica soon discover they're not just chasing
a homicide suspect. They are stalking evil itself . . .

arrow books

ALSO AVAILABLE IN ARROW

# Triptych

## Karin Slaughter

When Atlanta police detective Michael Ormewood is called out to
a murder scene at the notorious Grady Homes, he finds himself
faced with one of the most brutal killings of his career: Aleesha
Monroe is found in the stairwell in a pool of her own blood, her
body horribly mutilated.

As a one-off killing it's shocking, but when it becomes clear that
it's just the latest in a series of similar attacks, the Georgia
Bureau of Investigation are called in, and Ormewood is forced
into working with Special Agent Will Trent of the Criminal
Apprehension Team – a man he instinctively dislikes.

But then, only twenty-four hours later, the violence Michael sees
around him every day explodes in his own back yard. And it
seems the mystery behind Monroe's death is inextricably
entangled with a past that refuses to stay buried . . .

arrow books

# *Disturbed Earth*

## Reggie Nadelson

**'Reggie Nadelson's Cohen books get better and better.
*Disturbed Earth* is the best yet.' Salman Rushdie**

Winter 2003: war is looming and New York is paralysed by the
worst blizzard in years. Artie Cohen is called in to investigate a
case: a pile of blood soaked children's clothes have been found
on the beach in Brooklyn. Almost against his will, Artie finds himself drawn into a case that involves the death of a child and the
unaccountable disappearance of another, all against the background of a city already stricken by fear.

In his increasingly obsessive search for the missing child, Artie
finds himself in the remote coastal suburbs of Brooklyn, among
the Russian community he thought he had left behind him – and
way out of his depth. Along the way he falls in love with one
woman and is seduced by another, but little can calm his mind
as his past comes back to haunt him . . .

'Artie Cohen is one of crime fiction's most deeply
and sensitively drawn cops.'
*The Times*

'A brilliant, unexpected final twist resolves the suspense . . .
The denouement is stunning.'
*Daily Telegraph*

arrow books